HISTORICAL

Your romantic escape to the past.

Penniless Until The Earl's Proposal
Helen Dickson

The Truth Behind The Governess
Carol Arens

MILLS & BOON

PENNILESS UNTIL THE EARL'S PROPOSAL
© 2024 by Helen Dickson
Philippine Copyright 2024
Australian Copyright 2024
New Zealand Copyright 2024

First Published 2024
First Australian Paperback Edition 2024
ISBN 978 1 038 92179 6

THE TRUTH BEHIND THE GOVERNESS
© 2024 by Carol Arens
Philippine Copyright 2024
Australian Copyright 2024
New Zealand Copyright 2024

First Published 2024
First Australian Paperback Edition 2024
ISBN 978 1 038 92179 6

MIX
Paper | Supporting
responsible forestry
FSC® C001695

Published by
Harlequin Mills & Boon
An imprint of Harlequin Enterprises (Australia) Pty Limited
(ABN 47 001 180 918), a subsidiary of HarperCollins
Publishers Australia Pty Limited
(ABN 36 009 913 517)
Level 19, 201 Elizabeth Street
SYDNEY NSW 2000 AUSTRALIA

Cover art used by arrangement with Harlequin Books S.A.. All rights reserved.

Printed and bound in Australia by McPherson's Printing Group

Penniless Until The Earl's Proposal

Helen Dickson

MILLS & BOON

Helen Dickson was born and still lives in South Yorkshire, UK, with her retired farm-manager husband. Having moved out of the busy farmhouse where she raised their two sons, she now has more time to indulge in her favourite pastimes. She enjoys being outdoors, travelling, reading and listening to music. An incurable romantic, she writes for pleasure. It was a love of history that drove her to writing historical fiction.

Visit the Author Profile page
at millsandboon.com.au for more titles.

Author Note

I always enjoy both reading and writing stories that blend history and romance, featuring enigmatic heroes and audacious heroines.

Penniless Until the Earl's Proposal is a Regency romance, featuring Lady Juliet Sinclair and Marcus Cardell, the Earl of Ashleigh.

Juliet's life is in turmoil and her future far from secure. Due to her brother's persistent gambling that has resulted in debts they are unable to pay, she has to deal with challenges no lady should. On the brink of losing the family estate, she agrees to wed the Earl of Ashleigh—an answer to their prayers. Juliet needs what he has to offer; he needs a wife and mother for his daughter. There is attraction between them from the start—until the past reappears and threatens their future happiness.

Chapter One

It was a glorious May day. The sun had risen out of a broad expanse of opal mist, and scraps of cloud floated like spun gauze in the sky. Oak, ash, sycamore, cherry and lilac trees were bursting into full flower, and trumpet-headed daffodils and clusters of primroses were scattered throughout the park that belonged to the Sinclair family of Endcliffe House.

This was the day Lady Juliet Sinclair first set eyes on Marcus Cardell, the younger brother of the Earl of Cranswick. Seated in the trap, she slowed her pony to a more sedate trot. The park stretched out in shades of green and brown and grey. Stabs of sunlight between the clouds edged the colours in bright gilding. For those few short minutes as she travelled along, there was just her and her pony—no duties, no expectations, just a wonderful forgetfulness of all the trials and duties that awaited her back at Endcliffe House.

Juliet had set out to take Mrs Ruskin some freshly baked bread. With three children to feed and her husband unable to find employment, Rose Ruskin struggled daily to give them sustenance. A movement to her right caught her attention. She glimpsed a rider and horse galloping with exhilaration some distance away. Halting the pony, she paused to watch with interest the sheer might of the large bay horse and the energy of the claret-jacketed rider, seemingly at one with his mount. Directing her pony beneath some sheltering trees, she continued to watch until he had disappeared from sight.

With a flick of the reins, Juliet continued on her way, having a strong inkling as to the identity of the rider. He belonged to the gentry, that was for sure. She had heard that Marcus Cardell had taken up residence at Mulberry Hall, a property passed on to him by his mother, the dowager Countess of Cranswick. The house had been occupied by the Countess's widowed brother, Lord John Sutherland, the Earl of Ashleigh, who had died when he had taken a tumble from his horse during a hunt two years back. Without offspring, the property had passed to his sister, whose eldest son was to inherit the Cardell ancestral estate in Sussex. The dowager countess handed over Mulberry Hall to her second son, Marcus Cardell, a military man. The title went with it, and Marcus Cardell had become Lord Cardell, the Earl of Ashleigh. Juliet assumed the gentleman she had seen must be him.

Rose Ruskin, a small brown-haired woman in her thirties, welcomed her warmly and invited her inside her spotlessly clean cottage. Juliet placed the basket of bread with the addition of some cold meats on the table, which was immediately scrutinised and exclaimed over by her three young daughters with great excitement.

'Thank you, Lady Juliet,' Rose said, gently shoving her daughters aside. 'I am pleased to see you, and I am always grateful for the food you bring. Things are—difficult just now, with Joe unable to find work.'

'I know that, Rose, and I like to think what I bring alleviates the difficulties you face. When my brother decides to come home, I will try and persuade him to find your husband some kind of employment on the estate.'

'I can't pretend that I won't be pleased if you could do that. Joe's at his wit's end not knowing where to turn next—and now he's been accused of poaching on the Mulberry Hall estate. I fear he is to be arrested at any time.'

'And has he, Rose? Is there any truth in what he is accused of?'

Rose lifted her chin, and her voice when she spoke was adamant. 'No, there is not. My Joe knows the punishment for poaching. He's a proud man and knows it's more than his life is worth to steal from another man's property.'

'That's just as I thought.' Juliet knew Joe Ruskin as a fine, upstanding and honest man, and she could not imagine him doing anything that was against the law. 'Try not to worry, Rose. I will do what I can. I promise.' Stepping outside, she was stopped in her tracks when she came face to face with the gentleman she had seen riding through the park striding across the yard, having tethered his horse to the gatepost. He presented a dark, forbidding figure, his grey breeches moulding to his muscular legs and thighs, his claret coat fitting his physique without a crease. His white shirt was open at his tanned throat, and his hair was as black as a panther's pelt.

'Can I be of help, sir?'

He looked at Juliet with cool disdain, his eyes, as they passed over her, condescending. 'I am here to speak with Mrs Ruskin. It concerns her husband.'

Juliet was unsure whether to take this as information or an instruction to move out of the way. There was an authority and assuredness of his own infallibility in his look and his manner that she did not like. She thought she had never seen such a dark and dangerous face in her life. His eyes were light blue to be almost silver, glittering beneath scowling dark brows. His nose was straight and haughty, and those hooded eyes with their thick lashes were mesmerising. They seemed to glow, seemed to promise future delights. He exuded sensuality and animal magnetism, and she could well imagine that women would vie for his attention.

'Mrs Ruskin is inside. I do so hope you don't bring bad news, sir.'

He glanced at her and looked away again, as if she were a person of no consequence. 'And you are?'

'Juliet Sinclair,' she answered amiably, though it almost choked her to be polite in the face of so much rudeness.

'Well, Miss Sinclair—'

'*Lady* Juliet Sinclair.'

This caught his attention and he looked at her again, one dark brow cocked.'

'My, my,' he remarked with an underlying sarcasm. 'This just gets better and better. You are a relation of Richard Sinclair?'

'He is my brother.'

'Yes, of course he is. I remember meeting him in the long and distant past when I visited my aunt at Mulberry Hall. On the demise of your father, he is now Earl of Endcliffe, I believe.'

'Yes, he is.'

'Of Endcliffe House—although I hear he spends most of his time in London, squandering his time at the card tables, while the running of his estate is left to his steward. His tenants feel at liberty to poach game on my estate—while, it would appear, his sister plays lady bountiful,' he said, eyeing the basket on the table, visible through the open doorway.'

Juliet's face was a mask of indignation, her hands clenched, but when she spoke, she kept her anger in check, knowing she had to placate this insufferably arrogant lord if she was to plead Joe's case and keep him out of the lock-up to await the magistrate's pleasure.

'If that is how you see me, then, yes, that is what I am. I do what I can, Lord Cardell.'

'I do not recall introducing myself, yet you know who I am.'

'You accused Mr Ruskin of poaching game on your estate, sir, so I assume you must be Lord Cardell.'

'How perceptive you are, Lady Juliet.' He looked at her hard for a moment longer before turning his attention to Mrs Ruskin, his gaze resting briefly on the three children standing as stiff as little soldiers in a row, their eyes wide and their mouths agape with fear in the face of this new threat in the shape of the all-powerful Lord Cardell to their young lives.

Juliet felt anger rising inside her on seeing the confusion and fear on the children's young faces. Lord Cardell approached Mrs Ruskin.

'May I speak with you, Mrs Ruskin?'

Rose bobbed an awkward curtsy. 'You may, sir. Please step inside—but if it's Joe you want to speak to, he isn't here just now.'

'That's unfortunate,' he said, stepping over the threshold into the kitchen. 'Have you any idea as to his whereabouts? Apparently, he was seen by one of my keepers running off, having bagged a couple of hares.'

'That would not be possible,' Juliet said, quick to contradict him.

'Oh?' he said, turning his head to look at her once more. 'And you would know that? Why not, pray? You are accusing my keeper of lying, are you, Lady Juliet?'

'I'm afraid I am, Lord Cardell ,' she replied, facing him squarely. 'You see, Mr Ruskin lost a leg in the Peninsular War. I imagine it is rather difficult trying to run on a wooden leg, wouldn't you agree? So, either you have a very slow-moving keeper, sir, or he is lying. Which is it to be?'

Lord Cardell's gaze remained fixed on her while he digested this piece of information and then looked back at Mrs Ruskin, clutching her youngest child to her skirts. 'Lost a leg, you say?'

'No, I say,' Juliet countered firmly. 'Mr Ruskin has been unable to find work due to his disability.'

'He is your tenant, Lady Juliet. If, as you say, Mr Ruskin's disability has prevented him finding work—'

'Not prevented, Lord Cardell. He has tried. No one will employ him.'

'Then as an act of generosity, could you not find some employment on your estate to suit his disability?'

Furiously, Juliet found her cheeks turning red. How she would like to tell this arrogant lord to go to the devil and mind his own business, but it would do Joe no good in the long run if she were to lose her temper. One of the girls had picked up on the mood inside the room and started to cry and shrank into the girl next to her.

'Don't cry, Mary,' Juliet said gently. 'Everything will be all right. I'm sure Lord Cardell doesn't mean any harm to come to your father, and that it's all one big misunderstanding.'

'It most certainly is not,' Lord Cardell stated coldly.

Juliet glared at him. 'Do you have to do this in front of the children?' she remarked haughtily. 'Can you not see that your very tone and accusation against their father frightens them?' She saw his shoulders stiffen and his eyes sliced over her. She could almost feel the effort he was exerting to keep his anger under control. The man had a ramrod posture and an aura of exacting discipline as he irritatingly slapped his boots with the crop in his gloved hand. She glanced at it as it tapped out a rhythm. 'And do you have to do that? You act as if you are about to set about us all with your crop for some misdemeanour reported to you by your incompetent keeper without knowing the true facts.'

'Might I remind you that neither do you, Lady Juliet.'

'No, I do not, but unlike you—who was so quick to jump to conclusions and think the worst of Mr Ruskin, I am willing to give both men the benefit of the doubt until I have been made aware of them.'

Lord Cardell returned her gaze steadily, studying her as though she were some strange creature he had just uncovered. At least six feet four inches tall and with amazingly arresting light blue eyes he was a strikingly handsome man. Rugged strength was carved into every feature of his bronzed face, from his straight dark brows and nose to his firm and sensually moulded lips to the square, arrogant jut of his chin. To Juliet at that moment, he was also formidable, every line of his face set with disapproval.

Turning her back on him, Juliet settled her attention on the quietly weeping child. 'Hush now, Mary. Lord Cardell will do you no harm—is that not so, Lord Cardell?' she said, hoping for confirmation without looking at him.

'Of course not. Don't be ridiculous.' Looking at Mrs Ruskin, his expression softened slightly. 'I apologise if my coming here has upset your daughters. That was not my intention. They are children—I have a daughter of my own, and I would not dream of harming her or frightening her in any way.'

'Of course not, Lord Cardell, but they are sensitive souls. Anything that is said against Joe distresses them,' said Rose.

'Precisely,' Juliet said, 'and for that reason alone you should have more control over your temper.'

'Then I will be on my way before I cause more upset.' With a nod to Rose he went outside.

Juliet looked at the weeping child. 'Come, Mary,' she said as Lord Cardell strolled across the yard with a loose, confident stride, looking as though he owned the place. 'Dry your tears. Lord Cardell did not mean to frighten you.'

Her words seemed to calm the child, not because she was able to believe them but because of the unselfish confidence of the lady uttering them. Raising her head, she smiled at Juliet, but her shoulders remained drooped in dejection. Juliet fished a handkerchief out of her pocket and went to the unhappy girl. 'Here, let me wipe your face.' Gently she dabbed at the cheeks of the child, who was looking up at her with solemn brown eyes that reminded Juliet of a wounded puppy.

Rose stepped forward and put her arm about her distressed daughter. 'Don't worry about Mary, Lady Juliet. She cries all the time since Joe came home without a leg. She'll get over it given time.'

Juliet looked at Rose and smiled, wishing she could dispel the unhappiness and the fear she felt for her husband from her eyes. 'I'm sure she will—as sure as I am that everything will work out, Rose. Tell Joe to come and see me when he comes home and we'll see what is to be done about this poaching business. I don't believe it of him for one minute—and I think Lord Cardell will realise his mistake of listening to his keeper without proof of Joe's guilt.'

Without looking in Lord Cardell's direction, where he was trying to calm his restless mount that was pawing at the ground, eager to be on its way, she walked to where she had left her pony and trap, surprised when he followed her, feeling his penetrating eyes on her all the time. She turned to face him.

'Have you had an edifying look at me, Lord Cardell?'

'Not quite. It is to my advantage that I get to know who my neighbours are. I hope this minor issue with your tenant is not going to affect neighbourly relations between us.'

'As to that, we shall have to wait and see,' Juliet replied tightly, finding it difficult to show leniency towards him in light of what had just occurred. 'Where Mrs Ruskin is concerned, having her husband accused of poaching is far from being a minor issue. What are you? Some kind of monster? The Ruskins are gentle people, living their lives and troubling no one. And suddenly you come along and threaten to have Mrs Ruskin's husband and the father of those children arrested, thrown into jail and transported to goodness knows where.'

'Come now, that's a bit extreme, don't you think?'

'No, it is not. That's what happens to anyone caught poaching. How could you do that?'

'I can and I will. I cannot have anyone poaching my game. If he is indeed guilty of the offence and is seen to get away with it, it will send out the wrong message, and I will have all and sundry doing the same. I will not have it.'

'I can see that,' she retorted scathingly. 'You really are the most ill-mannered, inconsiderate man I have ever encountered, Lord Cardell,' Juliet upbraided him coldly. 'My mother always told me that such an outward display of temperamental frustration as you have just shown is regarded as a sign of bad breeding.'

His eyes narrowed and his lips tightened. 'Your mother was probably right, and I daresay I am what you accuse me of being. It goes with the title.'

Juliet was in no mood to be mocked, and she could see by the gleam in his eyes that he was doing exactly that. 'Then with you as an example, I can only hope that you are the last titled Englishman I shall ever meet.'

'As the sister of an earl, I would very much doubt that. And since we are bandying words, Lady Juliet, you really are the most infuriatingly outspoken woman I have ever met.'

Raising her head, she fixed him with a level gaze. 'I agree, I am outspoken—be it a failing or a blessing, I care not one whit. I dare say a lot of things to a man who scares children half to death,' she said, and with good reason, for the terror she had felt as a child locked in a dark cupboard for hours on end by this particular gentleman she had not forgotten—although in his arrogance he would have no recollection of the fact, and she would not humiliate herself by reminding him of the incident. She would not forgive him that act of cruelty. 'I imagine you also terrify each and every one of your servants so they creep about in fear of you, and that your whole house vibrates with tension that springs from you, Lord Cardell. By the look on your face, I would wager I have hit a sore spot. Please don't disappoint me by holding your temper. I would hate to see you explode with the effort.'

'Believe me, Lady Juliet, you would not want to see me explode. I have a temper, I admit it, when I am driven to it. And how I run my household and treat my servants concerns only myself.'

'Be that as it may,' she said with a defiant upward tilt to her chin, her voice edged with high indignation, 'you still have no proof of Joe Ruskin's guilt. Besides, innocent or guilty, you have no standing here. While my brother is absent, I have the authority on this estate.'

Lord Cardell cocked an arrogant brow. 'And you are sure of that are you, Lady Juliet?' Her expression told him that she wasn't. 'We will have to wait and see what the law has to say about that. Now I must be away. I have an appointment to keep and I am already late.'

Turning from her, he mounted his horse with an athletic grace that did not surprise her in the slightest. She would have expected nothing less from this arrogant lord.

'You will find the shortest route back to Mulberry

Hall is to ride through the park which belongs to my brother, Lord Cardell. Although if you do so, I must warn you that you could be apprehended for trespassing. But worry not,' she said, when his expression became one of surprise. 'I am sure Richard would show you more tolerance and leniency than you have just shown to Mrs Ruskin.' She switched her attention to his mount pawing its hooves on the ground, clearly impatient to be off. 'You seem to be having difficulty controlling your horse, sir. Is it not time you taught it who is master?'

'I assure you he knows who is his master.' He looked at her closely. 'What a firebrand you are, Lady Juliet Sinclair. It appears to me that you are in need of some mastering yourself. Should your brother fail to do so, I would be honoured to put myself forward. Teaching a lovely young female how to behave like a lady should be—interesting. I would use the same tactics as I would at taming a horse. I would soon have you doing my bidding and swooning at my feet.'

His hollow chuckle held a note of mockery. A flush of anger spread to the delicate tips of her ears. 'Why, you conceited, unmitigated cad...'

'I get the gist,' he said, cutting her short with a low laugh, noting the icy fire that smouldered in her deep amber-coloured eyes.

Suddenly he seemed to relax in the saddle and his lips curved into a smile, taking Juliet by surprise as she stared at him. It was the most engaging smile she had ever seen, the smile of a man who finds the whole world a delightful place to be. It was a smile that lit his eyes and caused her heart to flutter.

'You are arrogant if you believe I would ever swoon at

your feet. Thank God I am not afflicted by such weakness.' She stepped away from him and his horse, finding his closeness and the way he towered over her a little intimidating. 'Be on your way, sir.'

Not yet ready to be dismissed, he hesitated. 'At least allow me to escort you to Endcliffe House.'

Her chilled contempt met him face to face. She stepped back. 'I am quite capable of taking myself home. Go away and take that vicious beast with you,' she snapped, glancing irately at the bay stallion that had begun to snort and stamp impatiently, its vigorous temperament reminding her so very much of its master.

'Aren't you taking a risk? You might be set upon by footpads or worse. Anything could happen to a woman travelling alone.'

'It just did, and I am of the opinion that I'm in less danger of being set upon by footpads than I am from you. At least they may have better manners.' Turning her back on him, she hoisted herself up into the trap, taking up the reins.

He sighed, feigning disappointment, slowly shaking his head. 'Such ingratitude.'

'Ingratitude?' she gasped. '*You* call *me* ungrateful after the distress you have caused Mrs Ruskin by accusing her husband of poaching your rabbits?'

His eyes gleamed with amusement. 'Have it your way. You know, Lady Juliet, I cannot believe that here we are crossing swords in this undignified manner, two sensible people arguing about rabbits. If there has been a misunderstanding, then I will apologise to Mrs Ruskin and her husband most sincerely. Rest assured, I shall look into the matter immediately.' He pulled on the reins and turned his restless horse about. 'I sincerely hope that when next we meet, this unpleasant issue will have blown over and we behave as acquaintances should. I am certain that as neighbours, we are going to get on famously.'

'Really? You are sure of yourself, sir—and conceited if nothing else.'

Juliet's voice held a note of reproof that finally penetrated Lord Cardell's intensity. He gave her a startled glance, then a disarming smile and impudent honesty.

'Not always. Only when I see a lovely young woman I would like to know better.'

'I see.' Juliet lifted a disapproving brow. 'And you hope to make a good impression, I presume.'

'It had occurred to me.'

'Then you will be disappointed that you have not, sir.'

'So, am I to understand that calling on your brother is out of the question?'

'That's right—at least not until your manners improve. Good day to you.'

'And good day to you too, Lady Juliet.'

He kicked his horse into motion. His laughter drifted back to her, his mockery infuriating her yet further. Urging her pony on she glared after his retreating figure, muttering all kinds of threats under her breath. She had never met a man who had irritated her as he had just done, and it chafed her sorely to consider his flawless success.

Riding away, Marcus halted his horse and turned and looked back. He watched with a brooding attentiveness in his eyes and not without a good deal of interest as Lady Juliet Sinclair travelled in the opposite direction towards Endcliffe House. Hostility from ladies in her position was not something he had encountered before. Most young ladies were more than eager to be amiable to him—although perhaps she'd had good reason not to be in her defence of Joe Ruskin. He was, after all, one of her brother's tenants and Lady Juliet was convinced of his innocence.

Perhaps she was right and his accusation had perhaps been a little hasty, but having been most put out on receiving a letter from his mother forbidding him to bring Adele, his six-year-old daughter who was a sensitive child, to Mulberry Hall until he was more settled and had put his mind to finding himself a wife and mother for his daughter. Adele would remain with her in London for the time being or at the Cardell estate in Sussex.

Continuing his journey back to Mulberry Hall, he became thoughtful. He'd spent a little time in London before coming to Surrey. As soon as word got round of his return, invitations to social events had rained down on him. Before his marriage, his potent attraction to women had been a topic of much scintillating feminine gossip, but marriage and his military career had taken him out of the public eye. Now he was back, a widower and about to take up residence at the fabulous Mulberry Hall estate—a draw for any aristocratic family with a bevy of unmarried daughters.

But age and his experiences in Spain had changed him. Now he possessed a haughty reserve that was not always inviting and set him apart from others in society. He was always careful to choose a mistress whose company he enjoyed. She had to be intelligent and sophisticated, who would not mistake lovemaking and desire with love, and moreover, she had to be a woman who made no demands and expected no promises.

He missed his military life and his fellow soldiers. Since arriving at the house, he realised he would have to give himself up to the day-to-day running of the estate. He had called in the bailiffs to give an account of their management, accounts gone in to, acres of land ridden over and meetings with his tenant farmers. Alone in his elegant house, he restlessly wandered from room to room, unable to escape the throbbing emptiness and his longing to make it a family home once more.

His mother was right. Now he was home he must put his mind to remarrying, his wife, Elizabeth, having died giving birth to Adele. He had been fond of Elizabeth and had mourned her passing, but he had not loved her in the romantic sense. Desire, he understood. It was a more honest emotion. Passion and desire were easily appeased—fleeting—and easily doused. When he chose a woman to be his wife, he would be careful to choose a woman from a good family, whose company he enjoyed. But the most important thing of all was that she would be a good mother to his daughter. Adele was his priority. This was non-negotiable.

With Mulberry Hall within his sights, Lady Juliet drifted back into his thoughts, and a faint sensual smile quirked his lips. Her features had an aristocratic cast to them, and she had an air of good breeding. She had a face of unforgettable beauty, with high delicately moulded cheekbones, a perfect nose and generous lips. It was a strong face but essentially feminine. She had the kind of looks which few men failed to respond to with interest and some women with envy. She had worn a bonnet, but what he had seen of her hair, it was the colour of burnished gold. She was vibrant, vital and bold, but there was also about her a mysterious, almost sweet and gentle allure. Her form was slender and appealing. He smiled, looking forward to their next meeting, for as close neighbours, it was inevitable that their paths would cross in the future.

As for this matter concerning Joe Ruskin, maybe his keeper had been mistaken after all. He would look into the matter.

As Juliet travelled the well-worn path back to End-cliffe House, she was determined to cast Lord Cardell from her mind. The man was obnoxious, she decided, and not worth thinking about, although he was terribly handsome—she would grant him that. There was also an uncompromising authority in the set of his jaw and an arrogance in the tilt of his head that was not to her lik-ing. But considering the remarks he had made regarding her brother, there was more than a ring of truth in what he had said. She prayed constantly that Richard would exchange the bustle of London for the grace of Endcliffe House. Since the death of their parents, their mother just one year before their father, Juliet had learned not to expect any form of duty from her brother, who was wrapped up in his own self-indulgent world of gambling and all the pleasures London had to offer.

At twenty-one years old Juliet was younger than Rich-ard by three years, but she had always been the sensible, practical one, while he was somewhat reckless and fool-hardy and liked to live life to the full and in comfort. She had soon learned that where Richard was concerned, her own wishes were not to be consulted, and she was forced by circumstances to live in genteel poverty, to be the keeper of Endcliffe House and to put all her youthful energies and her loneliness into their home, where she was responsible for all the household matters and the staff—of which only a handful of the old retainers remained. On Richard's last visit to their home, she had confronted him, begged him, as she had done countless times in the past, to give up his reckless, expensive way of life and return to live in Surrey, for if he did not heed their situation, then ruination would soon be knocking at the door.

Whenever she had broached the subject, Richard was at once defensive and would become angry, finding her persistence to try to reform him extremely irritating. London, with its splendour and corruption, its squalor and excitement, thrilled and entertained him in a way his provincial home in Surrey had never done. His taste for pleasure and his capacity for enjoyment lifted his spirits in the restless, teeming city.

But enough was enough. After his last visit to Endcliffe House, discovering that the only valuables remaining in the house—their mother's jewels—had disappeared, and knowing Richard must have taken them, and knowing exactly what he intended to do with them—that he would sell them in order to pay for his gambling, she knew they could not carry on like this. An inexplicable weariness and pain lay heavy on her heart. If they had to sell her beloved home, it would tear her apart. She would fight tooth and nail to hold on to it.

Ever since their father had died, leaving them in dire straits, with Richard away in London, she had come up against so many obstacles and had almost worn herself out in the bargain. She was to travel to London shortly to attend a prior engagement. It would be the perfect opportunity to confront her brother. She would try again to make him see the error of his ways, but she did not hold out much hope of success.

As she neared Endcliffe House, she thought how different her life would have been had she married Thomas. The image of his handsome laughing face flashed before her. Everything about him had drawn him to her. She'd been young and with the naivety of a girl who'd had a sheltered, loving upbringing, and being a man from a family with great affluence and a proper lineage, Thomas had been the epitome of everything she wanted her future husband to be.

She remembered the first time they had met at a soiree in London. They had spent the entire evening in each other's company. They met on several occasions after that night. Her eyes would light up when he came into a room, and she would hang on his every word with a rapt expression on her face. He told her she was the most beautiful woman he had ever seen and that he had fallen in love with her the first time he'd laid eyes on her. She remembered the rapture she had felt when he had taken her in his arms and kissed her, then the blessed relief when he'd asked her to be his wife. Both families were in favour of the match, and she'd accepted him gladly, but her happiness led to heartache when, as a young commissioned military officer, he departed for the Peninsular with Wellington's army.

He'd left with the sun shining on his hair, standing with one hand on his sword in the attitude of a Greek god, appearing to Juliet unbearably heroic. They would have been married by now had he not been killed at the Battle of Albuera in Spain just a few months ago. She would never forget the day when the tragic news had come to her and all the pain and desolation that had come with it. Never had she believed she could feel such pain, such anguish that went deep—deeper than anything she had ever known.

His death had coincided with the death of her father, and with this, combined with the worry that they might lose the Endcliffe estate that had been in the Sinclair family for generations, she had continued to carry on. Richard had suggested she should seriously consider seeking an affluent man to marry to solve their problems. Even though she had a sense of responsibility towards Richard stronger than it should be, it was there and was an intrinsic part of her. But she was unwilling at this time to be made a sacrifice. It was one of the few times she had lapsed into self-pity. She would rather marry a man she had chosen than one forced on her.

Whatever the outcome, she was determined never again to feel for any man the way she had for Thomas, that no man could ever take his place. She had hardened her heart, resolved that no man would ever breach it.

Chapter Two

It was a week after her encounter with Lord Cardell that found Juliet riding alone in the lush green water meadows, interlaced by a network of silvery streams off the winding river where moorhens and swans were gliding gracefully between the rushes and reeds. The day was hot and sultry, and on a day such as this, Juliet had only one purpose in mind. The small lake surrounded by trees was her own secret place, a place where, when things were bad, she could escape to. After making sure that she was quite alone, kicking off her shoes and removing her thin cotton day dress, she waded into the lake, the water bathing her flesh beneath her petticoat like a soothing cool balm.

Dipping below the surface of the warm, clear water she began to swim, stretching her body to its full length. It was a simple exercise, requiring little thought, although she was well aware that if she should be observed indulging in such outrageous behaviour, it would be considered unacceptable and her reputation would be in ruins. But now, with the sun on her back and in dire need of respite from the many problems that beset her and having no wish to marry in the foreseeable future, she thrust these thoughts away. Here she could be herself. It was her secret pleasure.

Only the subdued call of birds and the lazy drone of a browsing bee disturbed the silence of the woodland as Marcus rode slowly along the dim chequered path. He came out of the trees and on to the edge of the small lake. It basked in the benign warmth of the sun, and long tendrils of willow brushed the surface. Aware of the seclusion of this place, taking a moment to enjoy his surroundings, dismounting, he tethered his horse to the branch of a stout tree and strolled beside a slow, meandering stream, watching the clear water as it tumbled lazily over its rock bed.

The day was hot and the water looked cool and inviting. Resting his back against the trunk of a sturdy beech, he stood and gazed at the vista before him, beautiful and tranquil in its simplicity and natural state. The lake shone like glass beneath the sun and, momentarily dazzled, he failed to see the bobbing head in the centre of the lake until it came closer to the edge. When his eyes came to focus on it, it took a moment for him to register that someone was out there swimming. And it was a woman at that, for her long hair trailed behind her as she swam with strong, sure strokes.

Marcus continued to watch as she lifted herself effortlessly out of the water and began to wade back to the shore. She was too absorbed in wringing the water from her hair to notice him. That was when he realised the swimmer was none other than his neighbour, Lady Juliet Sinclair. As slender as a wand, her perfectly rounded breasts rose in two delectable white hemispheres above the lace of her petticoat. Saturated, it clung to her, outlining her body, her hips arching from her small waist, and the perfect shape of her legs. Her breathtaking beauty quickened his soul and stirred his mind with imaginings of what further loveliness lay concealed beneath her flimsy attire.

Marcus was riveted. Vibrant and vital, she had a freshness and a delightful simplicity that captured his attention. In those first dazzling moments, he acted as any hot-blooded male would, and all he could do was stare as a thrill of excitement ran through his veins. But Marcus Cardell was no ordinary male and he recovered at once.

Suddenly her back stiffened and she became still, like a young animal that has caught the scent of danger. She spun round and her gaze flew directly to where horse and rider stood. Eyes narrowed, with a proud lift to her head she waded out of the water and moved towards him, seemingly not in the least embarrassed at confronting him in her sodden petticoat. There was indignation in the thrust of her chin and anger in her eyes. Stopping a short distance away, her feet were luminously white on the green grass. How small and slender they were, like a child's, Marcus thought. Her eyes were heavily lashed and tilted, almost feral, a warm shade of amber, and her honey blond hair clung to her shoulders in long silken skeins. Something that had lain dormant for many years stirred inside him. There was something about her, the boldness in her eyes, the tilt of her head, that attracted him.

As immobile as a lizard, Juliet stood in front of her neighbour who was staring at her with an intensity she could feel, and inside her, something started to tremble, a tiny quiver of alarm that somehow managed to make itself felt despite her dislike of this man and the numbness inside her. He seemed to fill the space around her, his presence almost overwhelming. Her nerves vibrated. It was as though she were awaking from a long sleep, and she suddenly felt extremely vulnerable and exposed. She was determined not to let him see how his sudden appearance affected her.

'Lord Cardell! We meet again,' she said in a voice as calm as may be, her manner unwelcoming. 'I was unaware that I was being spied on.'

Lifting her chin haughtily, Juliet met his light blue eyes that were observing her with frank interest—far too much interest, she thought as he scrutinised her with a thoroughness that made her feel more undressed than she already was. His gaze moved over her unabashedly. She stiffened with indignation. No man—not even Thomas—had looked at her in quite that way before. Her pride had been pricked, and after their disastrous meeting the day before, she was in no mood to forgive this impudent lord for being at hand when she was so scantily clad.

'I trust you've had an edifying look, Lord Cardell. Not satisfied with tracking down poachers, you also ride about the countryside on the lookout for defenceless ladies.'

White teeth gleamed in a reckless smile as Lord Cardell responded. She was like a kitten showing its claws. Again, his gaze slid from her moistened lips, following the line of her throat down to the tantalising orbs of flesh exposed to his view above her clinging wet petticoat.

'You? Defenceless? Now you do exaggerate. Something tells me you are afraid of no one.'

His voice was a lazy drawl, his manner calm, deliberate. His light blue eyes were cool, his wide, beautifully shaped mouth held in a stern line. As on their previous meeting, there was no warmth, no humour to soften those perfectly chiselled features. She sensed he was a hard man and that he could be utterly ruthless if the need arose. The skin was stretched tautly across his high cheekbones, and his rich dark hair was ruffled from his ride. He was wearing brown boots, snug tan breeches, and a thin lawn shirt beneath his dark green jacket.

His sudden appearance only seemed to exacerbate Juliet's temper. 'Have you nothing better to do with your time?' she said, going to where her dress was draped over a bush and beginning to pull it on over her sodden petticoat. Any other day she would have lain on the soft grass to allow her clothes to dry before doing so, but her impatience to be away from her neighbour was paramount to that.

'Since you are only recently ensconced at Mulberry Hall, I would have thought you had better things to do with your time.'

'I suppose I could find something to occupy me,' he replied easily, seemingly amused as she struggled to put on her dress, 'but I can't think of anything more pleasurable just now than looking at you. I was merely out riding. The day is too pleasant to remain indoors.'

'I see. Then it is time you consulted with your steward regarding the boundaries of your land, otherwise you would know that you are trespassing. This is private land.'

A slow appreciative smile worked its way across his face as his eyes raked her from head to toe once more and then came back to her furious eyes. 'I do apologise, but my crime, if that is what it is, was well worth it,' he said smoothly.

'My brother has been known to prosecute trespassers.'

'Is that so?' His eyebrows arched and his eyes gleamed with sardonic amusement, which seemed to infuriate her all the more as she sat on the ground and began pulling on her stockings.

'There are notices.'

'I'm afraid I didn't see them.'

'You would have—had you kept to the paths.'

'Forgive me, but it is not every day I come across a young woman cavorting nearly naked in a lake.'

Unashamed of her behaviour and resenting his inference, she threw back her shoulders and lifted her head haughtily. 'I was not cavorting. I was swimming—which I do quite often when I have the time. Besides, no one ever comes here, so it is quite safe for me to do so.'

'*I* came, Lady Juliet.' Stepping away from her, he gazed at his surroundings. 'These water meadows belong to your brother, is that right?'

'Yes. Why do you ask?'

'No reason.'

She glanced at him sharply. 'They are not for sale.'

'I didn't imagine for one moment that they were. Whenever I came to visit Mulberry Hall with my brother as boys, we used to come to the water meadows. This lake was one of our favourite spots to swim.'

Juliet looked at him and could envision a tall youth with shining black hair wading through the water. She smiled tightly, not feeling too generous towards him just then. She was still put out that he had forgotten all about their meeting when she was a child. Half her hair was damp and hanging limply about her shoulders. Her dress was rumpled and damp from her undergarments. She brushed the damp tendrils from her face and took a deep breath, willing herself to maintain some semblance of calm.

'And what else did you do when you came here?'

'The usual thing boys do—rode through the woods kicking up leaves, took off our boots and followed the stream all the way to where it joins up with the river. But most of all we used to daydream. Of course that was in the days when our families were friends as well as neighbours, and no one would dream of accusing the other of trespassing.'

'No, I don't suppose they would,' Juliet said, having tugged on her boots and impatient to get on home to remove her wet petticoat, which was most uncomfortable beneath her dress. 'However, times change. Nothing remains the same. Now if you will kindly step out of my way, I will leave you. Since you are familiar with the lake, you might like a swim,' she said on a note of sarcasm. 'You have my full permission to do so.'

Lord Cardell raised a sardonic brow at her tone and contemplated her snapping amber eyes. 'Thank you, but I will forgo the opportunity to do so today. That's quite a temper you have there.'

'Yes. It can be quite ferocious when I'm provoked.'

'Now, why would I want to do that?' he said smoothly, an almost lecherous smile tempting his lips. 'I would

much rather we progress to something of a more intimate nature.'

Juliet eyed him warily, unconscious of the vision she
presented with her clothes clinging to every delectable
line of her body. He was far too close for her peace of
mind and automatically she took a step back. His eyes
mocked her cautious retreat, but he made no comment on
it. 'What do you mean?'

'That I wouldn't mind finding out what it is like to
kiss those sweet lips, although I have the distinct impression that would be stirring a volcano and that it would
erupt in my face.'

All Juliet's wrath came rolling back and she faced
him with the molten blaze in her eyes. 'Why, you conceited ass. Kiss you? Why on earth would I want to do
that? I'd as soon kiss a mule.'

'I assure you that it wouldn't be nearly as much fun
as kissing me,' he chuckled infuriatingly, the sound low
and deep in his chest. 'A mule, being a sexless beast,
wouldn't kiss you back.'

Juliet stared at his arrogant features, at the mocking
light in his enigmatic eyes, realising that he really did
want her to take the initiative and kiss him. Silently she
cursed herself for being so stupid as to try to get the better of this man, who was way beyond her sphere in both
age and experience.

Directing a glance of wry humour at her, Lord Cardell's
eyes narrowed and he said, 'Tell me, Lady Juliet. Are you
normally hostile to everyone you meet, or is it just me?'

Her chilled contempt met him face to face. 'It's just
you.'

'Do you mind if I enquire as to why?'

'You can ask, but I'm not obliged to answer.'

'You have certainly none of your mother's good manners,' he remarked. 'As I recall, she was always a delight to be with.'

Juliet paled at his mention of her mother. He was quite right. Her mother had been goodness and patience personified, and no matter how hard Juliet had tried to model herself on her throughout the years, she had failed miserably. 'Thank you—yes, she was. My mother was quite exceptional. Now please excuse me,' she said, taking hold of her horse. 'I am not noted for my patience—which you will have observed.'

'You also have plenty of cheek, I'll say that,' he chuckled softly.

'Say what you like,' she retorted, her defiant chin elevated to a lofty angle. 'I do not care.'

'Hostile too. I don't usually encounter such hostility from young ladies.' He cocked a dubious brow. 'However, I find it hard to believe that your brother allows his sister to indulge in such wanton abandonment.'

Juliet tossed her head haughtily, stepped onto a log, hoisted herself up into the side-saddle and adjusted her skirts. 'What my brother does or thinks is none of your business. Now please go away. Not only are you a trespasser, you are offensive.'

'I apologise if that's how I seem to you, Lady Juliet,' he said, placing his hand on her horse's neck. 'But I have to say that you are the rudest, most impudent young woman I have ever come across, and I have every sympathy with your brother,' he told her calmly. 'And why your parents didn't take you in hand before their demise, I can't imagine. My father would have had you locked in your room with nothing to eat and drink but bread and water for a week.'

For an incredulous moment Juliet was speechless, then, forgetting her intention to ride away, she glared down into his far too handsome face, with authority and arrogance stamped all over it. That was the moment she decided he was detestable.

'Then I can only thank the Lord that he is not *my* father, who was more civilised. Now, kindly remove your hand from my horse and stop bothering me so that I can be on my way.'

Lord Cardell grinned affably and removed his hand and stepped back. 'I think I like bothering you, Lady Juliet, and I shall enjoy bothering you a good deal more before I'm done.' Inclining his head politely, his eyes doing one last quick sweep of her delectable body, he said, 'Good day,' and turned away to go to where he had left his horse.

Juliet rode back to the house, but suddenly the brightness of the day and the breeze held a bitter chill. What a dreadful, dreadful man their new neighbour was, although she had to admit that her manner towards him had been less than ladylike. Her mother would have been appalled with her for showing such rudeness to her neighbour, having held Lord Cardell's relatives, who had lived at Mulberry Hall previous to this new lord, in the highest regard. Juliet really should learn to guard her tongue, especially where this particular gentleman was concerned. Since they were neighbours, it was in both their interests to reach an amicable acquaintance.

And yet she could not stop her curiosity about him getting the better of her. Despite his self-assurance, she sensed a sadness about him, something frozen and with-drawn, and that he gave of himself sparingly. The only thing she knew about him was that he was a military man. She also knew he had been married and that he had a young daughter. His wife had died early in their marriage apparently. Juliet wondered about her, what she had been like. Did Lord Cardell still mourn her pass-ing, and what kind of a relationship did he have with his daughter, having spent several years in Spain fighting the French with Wellington's army?

She was bemused by him and their meeting and prey to all the emotions churning inside her. She could appre-ciate his virile good looks, his seductive scamp's eyes and sensual mouth, but that was where it must end, she told herself severely. And yet, despite this, perhaps an apology would be in order on their next meeting. On that thought, she put Lord Cardell from her mind and concentrated on her forthcoming journey to London to confront her brother.

Marcus watched Lady Juliet go, a gleam of interest in his eyes. Aware of his worth and used to being much admired by the female sex, he did not know whether to be amused or insulted by her hostile attitude to him. One thing he did know was that he wanted to get to know her better, and her imperviousness only whetted his appetite. It roused the hunter within him. Having her resist was a novel occurrence for him. He was unable to remember a time when he had turned on his charm and a female had made it so plain that his advances were not desired.

A smile tempted his lips, anticipation stirring inside him. He was going to have to work hard to turn her re-sentiment to desire—and he thought he was going to enjoy the chase immensely. But first he had to journey to West Sussex to see his daughter and to persuade his mother to let him bring her back with him to Mulberry Hall.

It was late when Marcus passed beneath the broken sign of the unwelcoming inn on his way back to London from West Sussex. Going to Cranswick Hall had been a wasted journey. His mother and Adele had left for London a day before he had arrived. They must have passed each other on the road.

The taproom was small and low-ceilinged, and if the hour had not been late, he would have travelled on to look for another. He was met by the nauseating reek of tobacco smoke and alcohol combined with the unappetising odour of cooked food. The tables were occupied by what he would only describe as a drunken rabble. Two soldiers in a similar state, in uniforms of scarlet coats and tight white breeches, clearly having seen much service and which were creased and unwashed, were obviously on their way home from the Peninsular War, their cocked hats and sabres on the bench beside them.

Marcus sat at a table away from them, and a young serving girl came to him. She was small and lacked the lusty sensuality of the other serving girls. He observed that she had caught the eye of one of the soldiers, who reached out to try to touch her as she moved past his table. His advances were unwelcome, and swiftly she darted away. As Marcus ordered food and a room for the night, her pretty young face beneath the starched white cap was scarlet with embarrassment and shame, and her large liquid-brown eyes held the same kind of fear he had seen in those of a frightened young doe facing death.

After he had eaten, he settled into the corner of his seat, slowly savouring his brandy, shutting out the coarse, drunken singing and shouting, and his thoughts turned to Lady Juliet Sinclair. In fact, he had thought of little else since leaving for West Sussex, and how bewitchingly lovely she had looked when he had come upon her in the water meadows.

He sat in deep reflection, sternly attacking his sentimental thoughts until they cowered in meek submission, but they refused to lie down. His attraction to Juliet Sinclair was disquieting—in fact, it was damned annoying. If he wanted an affair or diversion of any kind, he had a string of some of the most beautiful women in London to choose from, so why should he feel this insanely wild attraction to a woman he had met only twice?

Since their parting at the water meadows, he had tried to put her from his mind but failed miserably in his effort. He cursed with silent frustration, seized by a strong desire to call on her and cauterise his need by holding her close and clamping his lips on hers. Instead, he watched the flames in the hearth as they danced against the fireback and forced himself to think of his daughter. Under normal circumstances this was a simple matter, for nothing gave him greater pleasure than being with Adele, but slowly, a face with a pert, dimpled chin, a lovely and expressive mouth with soft, full lips, cheeks as flushed as a peach and thickly fringed amber velvety eyes crept unbidden into his mind—teasing him, tantalising him, laughing, beckoning him.

His attention was again drawn to the young serving

girl, who was still trying to avoid the clawing hands of the soldier. Marcus studied him. He had the superior attitude and the trimmings and facings on his uniform of a young officer. His thick pale blond hair fell in a heavy wave over his boyishly handsome face and his eyes were grey with heavy lids, giving him a lazy, insolent look. His fleshy pink lips were parted as he leered and groped at her.

At first Marcus watched with amusement as the young girl eluded his clawing hands, but gradually he became irritated and then angered by the distress the soldier's persistence was causing her. Suddenly, with a shout of triumph, and much to the glee of everyone present, the soldier at last succeeded in pulling the girl onto his knee and thrusting his hand down the front of her low-necked dress. With a wordless cry and unusual strength for one so young, the girl pushed his hands away and scrambled from his knees. Reaching out, she grasped his tankard full of frothing ale and flung it in his face before turning and fleeing from the inn.

Silence fell and all eyes became fixed on the young soldier. His manner changed immediately and his eyes became splintered with ice. It was clear to Marcus that here was a young man who was not used to being rejected or bested by someone he would consider his inferior.

The inn suddenly erupted in a volley of shouts and coarse jokes as the soldier rose, his hair dripping with ale, which he made no attempt to wipe away. His voice, full of a desperate violence, thundered above the din.

'I wager any man here that she's a virgin, and I'll tell you now that I intend to find out.'

A roar of approval went up, and the soldier staggered drunkenly towards the door, dragging one of his legs, which indicated that he had been wounded in the war with France.

Marcus watched and listened, suddenly remembering the fearful look he had seen in the eyes of the serving girl, thinking she could not be more that sixteen years old at the most, and as he was all too aware of the soldier's evil intent, it wasn't long before he followed him outside.

The night was dark and cold when he stepped into the yard but he paid no heed to it. Hearing the strangled cry of the girl pierce the air, it was cut off as if a hand was clapped over her mouth. He turned towards the sound and quickly went across towards the stables, where a light spilled out from the open doorway. The soldier had seized the terrified girl and dragged her inside, where he had brutally flung her on to a pile of straw, crashing on top of her and began tearing at the thin fabric of her dress. Though she screamed and managed to struggle frantically against him as if her very life depended on it, she was no match for the soldier's brute strength, his muscles honed to perfection on the battlefields of Spain. At first her resistance surprised him, but then it excited him and he laughed, a low merciless sound.

'Fight me all you like, my little beauty. I like a girl with spirit.'

The girl's last reserves of strength were almost exhausted when Marcus's tall shadow fell across them from where he stood in the doorway. In surprise the soldier paused for a moment and turned, favouring him with a mocking grin, a glazed expression in his eyes. 'Come to watch the sport, have you? You can have her when I'm done.'

'Enough,' Marcus said with an ominous coolness, noticing the mute appeal in the girl's terrified eyes. Something in his tone made the soldier turn again and look at him.

'Indeed, it is not,' he growled. 'Enough, you say—for what reason? I do not care for anyone to interrupt me in my pleasures. So, whoever you are, be gone. Find your own amusement or wait until I'm done.'

Undeterred, Marcus stepped closer, glowering down at him. 'Then allow me to introduce myself—Marcus Cardell, at your service, and I told you to release the young lady. She has made it quite plain that your over-amorous advances are not welcome.'

Recognising the refined tone and that each word was enunciated slowly and carefully, the soldier staggered to his feet, his clothes dishevelled and his expression deadly. He stood and faced Marcus, several inches taller than himself, who was making a visible effort to control his anger, a faint, scornful smile on his lips that only added to the soldier's rage.

'This is not your affair and I resent your interference.'

'Really?' Marcus mocked. 'But you are bothering the young lady and I am making it my affair.'

'Young lady?' sneered the soldier. 'She is nothing but a common trull.'

There was a faint, animal-like whimper from the straw as the girl, as pale as death and shaking from head to foot, struggled to her feet, modesty causing her to pull her torn skirts together. The soldier turned as if to go back to her.

'Touch her again and I'll break your neck,' drawled Marcus.

The threatening quality in his voice caused the soldier to look at him again, anger blazing from his eyes, and suddenly, unable to restrain himself, he sprang at Marcus with clenched fists. Perhaps, if his brain had not been fogged with drink, he might not have missed his target, but as he raised them to strike, Marcus deftly sidestepped and struck out, hitting the soldier on the side of the face. His eyes rolled in his head and he staggered and fell to the ground, his face bleeding from a cut caused by the blow. All vestige of pride was stripped from the soldier, who was enraged to find himself so humiliated. His body shook with the intensity of his rage, and sheer hatred blazed from his eyes.

'Now get out,' Marcus said, his voice like steel.

The soldier struggled to his feet and in the doorway he turned. 'If ever I have the misfortune to meet you again, I'll make you pay for that. I'll get even—I swear.'

'I doubt our paths will cross again, but perhaps you'll think twice the next time you are intent on raping anyone.'

Muttering curses beneath his breath, the soldier turned and stumbled out into the night, dragging his injured leg behind him.

Marcus turned and looked at the girl. 'Are you all right?'

She nodded, smiling at him gratefully, too shocked to speak. A woman suddenly appeared by her side.

'Oh, Sal…' and, taking in her torn clothes, she looked at Marcus in alarm. 'Is she all right?'

He nodded. 'I came in time.'

She sighed with relief. 'Thank the Lord. Come on, love. I'll take you home.'

The following morning, Marcus continued his journey to London.

Juliet arrived in St James's Square at the Sinclair residence—for how long it would remain so was a constant worry. Her father's gambling and Richard's affliction to the same, might force them to sell it. The house was of modest proportions but tastefully furnished. It was early afternoon and Richard was nursing a frightful hangover, having spent most of the previous night losing heavily at the tables. He had risen from the bed in which he had fallen into a dissolute, drunken slumber.

On seeing his sister looking unnaturally calm, her face pale through worry and lack of sleep, his face fell, telling her he wasn't particularly pleased to see her. There was only a slight resemblance between brother and sister. They had the same shade of hair, but there the resemblance ended. Juliet was like a piece of thistledown with a finely structured face, where Richard was six feet and stockily built, with a strong square chin and green eyes.

'Good Lord, Juliet!' he groaned, falling into a chair. 'What are you doing here? And you come alone, without your maid, I see.'

'I had to let her go, Richard,' she said, shocked by her brother's appearance. He looked thoroughly broken, his handsome face creased with deep lines of anxiety, his clothes and hair dishevelled. 'We could no longer afford to pay her—along with some of the other servants. When I discovered you had taken our mother's jewels to pay for your gambling, I had to come. Besides, we are to attend Lord and Lady Wyatt's dinner party tomorrow night—although perhaps with all this going on, you have forgotten about it. Our situation is desperate, you know that. You must stop before it is too late and we have nothing left to sell or gamble but this house and the estate—such as it is.'

'It might be already too late,' he grumbled. 'If things don't improve, then I will have to consult my lawyer.'

Immediately, an icy hand gripped Juliet's heart, and her feeling of dread deepened as she feared the worst.

'We are in a devil of a fix, Juliet.' Richard drew himself up in the chair, staring with a stricken look out of bloodshot eyes at his sister. 'What's to be done? How are we to be saved,' he cried, looking at her as if she knew the answer. 'You really should consider what I suggested. If you were to marry a wealthy man, it may go some way to solving our problems. Our family name still stands for something in the scheme of things. There will be some of the cream of London society there when we attend the Wyatts' dinner party. With any luck, you might attract the attention of an affluent gentleman who is looking for a wife.'

Juliet was aware of a deadening of her senses, and her heart was pounding so hard that she could scarcely breathe. All around them the house was silent. When she looked at her brother, a bitter taste filled her mouth and she wanted to shout hurtful words at him for bringing them to this, this state of ruin and degradation. But when she saw the look on his face, her conscience smote her, and the cruel words died on her lips. What could she say, anyway, that would hurt him? He knew only too well what he had done and it was killing him.

'I have made my feelings plain about that. I refuse to marry a stranger for his money. Besides, your reputation as an inveterate gambler might well deter any prospective bridegroom. There has to be another way.'

'What have I done? That I should have brought us to this.'

The appeal in his voice went straight to Juliet's heart. Without thinking how they could survive, she went to her brother and put her arms around him. Her eyes were soft and tender, and she spoke impulsively, lowering her cheek to his.

'Together we'll think of something. There has to be a way. Something will come up, you'll see.' As she spoke those words that were meant to reassure him, she knew in that moment that there was not even the suspicion of a hope that something would happen to save them.

For the rest of the day, Richard moped about the house in a state of deep depression. She managed to persuade him to put off fetching the deeds to his estate from Surrey and presenting them to his lawyer until a later date, in order to give them more time. She must do all in her power to find a way of keeping the estate and would not recognise defeat. She paced her room, desperately trying to sort out in her mind what she could do. There must be someone who would lend them the money. But then, if someone did lend them the money, how could they ever hope to repay it?

Chapter Three

The following day Richard's carriage was only one of a glittering array that rattled and streamed through the Portland stone gateway of Wyatt House. How she hated these dinner parties which they were invited to attend while in London. They did so because she knew their mother, who had been a popular socialite in her time, would want them to maintain their place in society. Amid the shouting of coachmen and the jingle of the harness, the carriage came to a halt, waiting for the ones in front to discharge their occupants at the foot of the steps to Wyatt House. Slowly their carriage edged its way along, and Juliet leaned her head against the soft upholstery, thinking with longing of the quiet solitude and leafy green meadows of home.

With Richard by her side, they eventually entered the splendour and opulence of the house, ablaze with lights shining from every window. From somewhere inside, the musicians were already playing, their music filling the rooms, dipping and rising, sweet and sublime, which at any other time she would have found soothing. But not tonight. The strains of the violins matched her nerves, which were as taut as their strings. As she entered the glittering world of fashionable London society, where chandeliers blazed and baskets full of flowers scented the air with a lovely fragrance, she thought, wistfully, how different it would be if Thomas were here to share it with her.

They were greeted by Lady Wyatt, brimming over with her usual exuberance. She was a desirable asset to London's social scene and one of the most popular hostesses at this time—in fact, probably one of the most favoured in London society—giving the most elaborate and brilliant parties, surpassed only by those given by the Prince Regent at Carlton House.

Juliet liked Lord and Lady Wyatt. They had been good friends of her father for many years. Lady Wyatt was a clever, astute woman with an amazing wit. If somewhat domineering and bossy, she was no fool, and her guests could always be assured of some high-level, interesting conversation covering a wide range of topics at her crowded dinner table.

'Why, Juliet,' said Lady Wyatt, taking her gloved hand in her own and squeezing it with affection, while Richard turned away to speak to her husband, 'How lovely you look. I'm so glad you were able to come. Your father would be so proud of you. You do him credit. Now, off you go, my dear, while I talk to your brother. Lydia Davenport was looking for you earlier. She's just dying to tell you about her visit to Brighton. We'll chat later.'

Juliet smiled gratefully, knowing Lady Wyatt was well aware of Richard's overindulgence where both alcohol and gambling were concerned and would be sure to keep a watchful eye on him while he was under her roof. Juliet turned and went in search of Lydia. This was supposed to be an even grander affair than usual, given in honour of the Prince Regent, but Juliet didn't really care. All she was concerned about was getting through it as quickly as possible.

As Juliet made her way down the long gallery, she failed to notice the man standing apart from the rest, leaning casually against an overlarge statue with a calm but bored expression on his darkly handsome face. But then he saw Lady Juliet Sinclair. The glamorous woman who had given him his pedigree was strolling casually through the houseful of wealthy elite. For the first time since arriving in London two days ago, all his senses became alert.

He found himself watching her as she moved with a serene grace along the gallery, her figure swaying slightly as she walked, and he stared, fascinated against his will, remembering the day he had seen her dripping wet in her revealing petticoat when she had emerged from the pond in the water meadows. Forcing his gaze slowly over her figure, coming to rest on the small, high bosom, he could not look away as the most lascivious urges passed through his mind. Good Lord! Had he been *that* long without a woman?

He continued to watch her. With the light from the chandeliers bathing her in a golden glow, she was beautiful in a lavender silk gown, beneath which he could discern all her alluring curves and imagine all the hidden delights of her slender body. The effect was stunning. She aroused envy in almost every woman present and admiration in the eyes of the men, although none could have said whether it was given to the proud beauty of her face, the pale gold hair coiled expertly about her head, or to the exquisite perfection of her body.

Marcus watched her smile and offer words of greeting to people she passed, but her smile was pinned to her face and her actions mechanical—a façade. She appeared remote and detached, totally uninterested in everything that was going on around her, which aroused all his curiosity. Growing tired of watching her, he shoved himself away from the pillar and began his approach.

Juliet was surprised to see Lord Cardell here this evening. The memory of their angry altercation on their previous encounter was still very much on her mind. She stiffened her spine and raised her chin when she saw him heading her way. She looked at him fixedly. Had she wanted to look away, she could not have done so. Never had she seen a figure of such masculine elegance. There was no denying that Marcus Cardell was a gorgeous male with a commanding presence and a potent sexual magnetism that was like a palpable force. She was acutely aware of that force.

Few women would even try to resist a man like this one, she thought, and she was scandalised by the sensations stirring inside her at the mere sight of him. His movements, his habitual air of languid indolence, hung about him like a cloak. He wore no wig, and his own hair was brushed smooth. He looked every inch the well-heeled landowner—and a great deal more dangerous than the average country gentleman. There was something primitive about him, and she felt that his elegant attire and indolence were nothing but a front meant to lull the unwary into believing he was a civilised being while disguising the fact that he was a dangerous savage.

Unlike the other gentleman, who were dressed like peacocks in a multitude of the customary bright colours, the perfect fit of his dark blue coat and the tapering dove grey trousers accentuated the long lines of his body. It was impossible not to respond to this man as his masculine magnetism dominated the scene. A slow half-smile curved his lips and she saw him give a careless shrug and raise his fine, dark eyebrows at some remark. He completely ignored the young women eyeing him with encouraging, flirtatious glances over their fans. Where other women might have succumbed to the irresistible pull to see behind the cool façade and start uncovering the man beneath, Juliet could feel the palpable danger around him. She was a rational person and had the good sense to heed the warning.

Unable to avoid a confrontation, she stood her ground and braced herself as he bowed graciously.

'Lady Juliet! How delightful to see you here tonight. I am surprised.'

Juliet looked at Lord Cardell's shuttered eyes. She could find no trace of gentleness or kindness anywhere in his tough, cynical features. His slashed eyebrows were more accustomed to frowning than smiling, and he had a hard mouth. It was a face that said its owner cared nothing for fools, and in the light blue of his dark lashed eyes, silver flecks stirred dangerously, like small warning lights.

'Lord Cardell! You take me by surprise also. I'm flattered that you remember me,' she said testily.

'You are not an easy person to forget.' He sighed. 'I

don't know why you always give me such a hard time when we meet.'

Determined to appear calm and unaffected by their previous encounter and not indulge in a public display of temper, Juliet forced a smile to her lips. 'I've tried to forget our less than pleasant encounters, Lord Cardell, but it is difficult.'

'Then I can only hope that you will succeed, given time.'

'I will,' she bit back. 'You are acquainted with Lord and Lady Wyatt?'

'They are long-standing friends of the family. Are you enjoying the occasion?'

'My brother and I have only just arrived, but I always enjoy attending Lord and Lady Wyatt's dinner parties. They go to a lot of trouble to satisfy their guests, and the food is always exceptional.'

'No rabbit on the menu?'

'No, I don't expect so…' Her words trailed off when she saw the mischievous twinkle in his eyes and the curve of his lips. She laughed softly. 'I see you are teasing me, Lord Cardell.'

'Do you mind?'

'No, but since our meeting at Mr Ruskin's house and again at the water meadows, I trust you have seen the error of your accusation.'

'I have. I am aware that many a rabbit or a pheasant finds its way into a family pot, but the offence is more serious when deer are killed on a large scale, the ill-gotten gains sold further afield. I now know that Joe Ruskin is not guilty of poaching my game. My keeper admits he was mistaken, and I have since apologised to

Mr Ruskin and his wife for any distress my misjudgement may have caused.'

'I am glad to hear it.'

'This is the first social event I've attended since returning from the Peninsular.'

'You were a soldier I understand, having seen many years of active service in Portugal and Spain.'

'You understand correctly. I've only recently returned.' He looked around at the guests without much enthusiasm. 'I almost didn't come here tonight, but I grew bored watching the world go by in my family's townhouse in Grosvenor Square, so I came to see if the sights were any better here.' He spoke with slow deliberation and the corners of his lips twitched with amusement. His eyes gleamed into hers as he added softly, 'I am happy to report they far exceed my expectations, and I'm glad I came.'

Juliet turned aside, giving him a cool glance askance. 'Have you nothing better to do than ogle the ladies, Lord Cardell?'

'It might look like that, but in truth I was watching just one.'

Juliet ignored the remark, but she could not ignore that seductive lowering of his eyelids or the quickening of her heart. 'The gaming tables will attract a good many gentlemen after we have eaten,' she retorted tightly. 'Why don't you try that?'

'Because I find talking to you more enjoyable than anything else I could come up with. I saw you arrive with your brother. I must renew our acquaintance, not having seen him since we were in our youth. I've heard he is not averse to a game of cards or dice. It's a wonder he hasn't disappeared into the card room before now.'

Juliet stiffened, considering his remark concerning Richard to be in bad taste. 'Lady Wyatt has set rules, Lord Cardell. No gambling until after her guests have eaten.'

'Then, if he has a penchant for the gaming tables, he will probably be the first in the queue.'

Juliet looked to where Richard stood speaking to a close friend of his, James Hockney. They were so heavily engrossed in conversation that they were not aware that she was watching them. Deeply unhappy, she forced a smile to her lips, managing to keep her anxiety hidden. 'Not this evening, Lord Cardell. Tonight, he is to refrain from any form of gambling. He has promised to be a passive observer, nothing more.'

'Very wise, Lady Juliet, if I may say so. Do you believe him?'

'He is my brother. He would not lie to me.' Even as she said the words, which she knew to be untrue, she would not give this arrogant lord the satisfaction of saying so, or give him any indication that they were facing financial ruin because of Richard's gambling.

'Then you fool yourself, Lady Juliet. Take my word for it, if he is as keen a player as I have been led to believe, he will weaken eventually.'

'And you would know that, would you?'

'I've met a lot of men like that—reckless young fools— prepared to risk evething over a game of cards or the throw of dice.'

'I am perfectly well aware of that, Lord Cardell,' she responded sharply, 'but that does not mean it applies to Richard.'

'Are you a gambler, Lady Juliet?'

'No, of course not.'

'Pity.'

'Why do you say that?'

'Because I would wager a large sum of money that your brother will find his way to the card tables before the evening is over.'

'Then it's a pity I am not a gambler, Lord Cardell, because you would be out of pocket.'

'Nevertheless, it's a very wise person who knows when to stop.'

Juliet glared at him. 'You really are the most provoking man alive and quite insufferable.'

Instead of being insulted or angered, he looked at her with amusement and shook his head. 'What were you expecting, Lady Juliet? A socially accepted gentleman? A rake or a dandified fop? I am none of these.'

'I have not known you very long, Lord Cardell, but I know exactly what you are. Now if you will excuse me, there is someone I wish to speak to.' Bobbing a stiff curtsy, she turned and walked away, having seen Lydia at the far end of the gallery. For all his devil-may-care attitude and forthright disposition, Lord Cardell was a very intelligent, very perceptive man. Being with him was always stimulating. Her senses seemed to heighten and seemed to be more alive. It was his energy and his vitality, she assured herself. One couldn't help but respond to it.

Lydia smiled broadly on seeing her and hurried towards her. They had become firm friends some years ago when they had both attended Lady Margaret's Academy for Young Ladies here in London. Lydia had been the one good thing about coming up here. She was small with an abundance of glossy auburn hair, which her hairdresser had arranged into fashionable Grecian curls. Lively brown eyes danced in her small elfin face with a smattering of pale gold freckles. She was generous and warm-hearted, and had been a great comfort when Thomas was killed, but she was also vivacious and a terrible flirt, constantly surrounded by a lively circle of friends—especially male friends, whom she not only encouraged but also seemed to thrive on their attention. Juliet was glad of her company tonight and that they were placed together at dinner.

While they were waiting for the first course, Juliet glanced up the table loaded with long-stemmed crystal glasses and gold and silver plates. Richard was seated next to the opulent Lady Melbourne, the two already engaged in lively conversation. Juliet's heart sank despairingly. Her brother's face was already flushed crimson from drinking too much wine. She tore her eyes away from him, praying he wouldn't drink much more, but she knew this was futile. If he didn't gamble, then he would be well and truly drunk when they left. She became desperately anxious for the night to end.

Looking in the opposite direction, she noticed the increasingly popular young poet Lord Byron, his face pale and surrounded by a riot of chestnut curls, his whole attitude tonight being one of disdain. She let her eyes wander to the lady seated beside him, recognising her immediately as being the outrageous Lady Caroline Lamb, whose scandalous behaviour and indiscreet affairs had made her the most notorious, talked-about woman in London, to which she didn't object in the slightest—in fact, she adored being the centre of attention, positively thriving on it.

Sitting right next to Lady Caroline Lamb was Lord Cardell. He was looking directly at her, his eyes unnerving. A crooked smile curved his lips, and Juliet noticed his long and slender hands toying with his napkin on the table. There was no fuss to his dress, and yet there was no denying that he had exquisite style. His presence formed a stark contrast to all the other gentlemen present, who seemed to fade into insignificance beside him. There was an air of complete assurance about him, and he seemed curiously out of place among all this gentility, the overdressed dandies and frills and flounces of Lord and Lady Wyatt's party.

Immediately she dropped her gaze and tried not to look in his direction again, but she was so conscious of him, her nerve endings so raw, her body so primed and aching for something she was too inexperienced to understand, that it was difficult to keep her eyes off him. As each course arrived, she tried to ignore him, uncomfortably conscious of his eyes on her constantly, burning into her flesh.

'That gentleman next to Lady Caroline Lamb looks at you a good deal, Juliet. Are you acquainted with him? He's terribly handsome. If you are, I wouldn't mind if you were to introduce us.'

Juliet shoved the strawberries around on her plate, a faint flush spreading over her cheeks. 'I think you exaggerate, Lydia. It must be you he's looking at.'

Lydia smiled mischievously, her eyes dancing merrily. 'Come on, love. He hasn't taken his eyes off you all night. And you mean to say you don't know who he is? Why, you must be the only person here who doesn't. That's Marcus Cardell, the son of an earl, although as a second son, he's not likely to inherit.' She leaned closer to Juliet, whispering confidentially, 'He was a military man, having distinguished himself in the Peninsular with Wellington's army. Rumour has it that he's now looking for a wife.' Gazing down the table, Lydia shamelessly flashed him a dazzling smile. 'Isn't he wonderfully virile—despite that polite exterior? I wouldn't mind if he chose me, I can tell you.' She sighed dreamily. 'He's as handsome as Narcissus and, I've heard, as rich as King Midas.'

'And we all know what happened to them,' Juliet quipped drily. 'Narcissus was so vain that on gazing into a pool, he fell hopelessly in love with his own reflection and, being unable to endure to possess and yet not possess himself, he plunged a dagger into his heart.'

'Oh dear! And King Midas? What happened to him?'

'After nearly starving to death because everything he touched turned to gold—including his food—and then being given ass's ears, unable to live with the disgrace, he died miserably. No, Lydia. I wouldn't liken Lord Cardell to either of them.'

'Perhaps not, but you can't blame me for wondering what could happen if he were looking at me instead of you. Oh, Juliet, don't you ever dream that one day—'

'No,' Juliet cut in crossly, her expression hard, suspecting that Lydia was about to embark on one of her daydreams about love and romance. 'I don't dream any more, Lydia. I stopped dreaming of romance when Thomas died. He took my heart with him to the grave and there it will remain.'

When she saw Lydia's eyes fill with remorse, she regretted her somewhat harsh and thoughtless words, although Lydia had never shared her own admiration for Thomas. In her opinion, Thomas had been selfish and egotistical, and she had made no secret of the fact. Juliet had never been able to understand why she felt that way about Thomas. She had wondered if Lydia was jealous of her relationship. After all Thomas was one of the most popular, handsome men in town before he had gone to the Peninsular. Being so deeply in love with him herself and not caring much for Lydia's opinion or Richard's, come to think—for had he not voiced his dislike of Thomas on occasion—she had thrust their disparaging comments aside, allowing nothing to cloud her happiness.

Reaching out, Lydia squeezed her hand. 'I'm sorry, Juliet. I didn't mean to hurt you. It was unforgivable of me.'

Juliet sighed and smiled weakly, placing her free hand over Lydia's. 'It's all right, Lydia. It's not your fault that I'm so edgy tonight, but it's not just thinking of Thomas that hurts—it's Richard.' She glanced in his direction just in time to see him pour another glass of wine down his throat.

When the meal was over and some of the guests began to drift towards the rooms where card tables had been set out, and it looked as if Richard—swaying slightly and clutching a glass of liquor—was about to go with them. *Why does he have to drink so much?* she thought angrily. If he has to gamble, then why can't he do it with a clear head? At least then he might stand a better chance of winning some of his money back.

For the next hour, Lydia and other friends and acquaintances claimed Juliet's attention. Having lost sight of Richard, excusing herself, she went in search of him, her instinct taking her in the direction of the card room. Here the noise was curiously muted so as not to distract the players. Small tables for dice, whist, French hazard and other games that took the guests' fancy had been set up. Juliet's eyes scanned the groups of people clustered around the tables, where several games were in progress. The players were obscured from view, but on seeing James Hockney standing in a small group, she moved towards him.

James turned and immediately took her arm and drew her away, but not before she had seen her brother sitting at one of the tables, his body taut and a wild, concentrated gleam in his eyes, which only gamblers had when intent on winning and they could see nothing except the cards in front of them. Shaking off James's arm, Juliet moved towards where Richard was playing.

'Stay back, Juliet,' James said softly. 'Richard won't be pleased to see you in here.'

'I do not care. I am well aware that any self-respecting female with a place in society would be disgraced for all time, but with so much at stake, the ethics of the matter do not concern me. Our situation is desperate—you know that, James. Richard must be made to stop before it is too late and we have nothing left to sell or gamble but the estate, such as it is.'

'I know that, but he is determined. He will not be stopped.'

'Have you tried?'

'Yes, but you know what Richard is like when he has his head set. He will not listen.'

'I will speak to him. He must listen to me,' Juliet said in desperation, making a move towards the table.

'Wait,' James said, putting a restraining hand firmly on her arm. 'Leave him. It may surprise you to know that Richard is winning. He will not thank you for interfering.'

'Winning?' Juliet exclaimed in surprise. 'By how much?'

'Three thousand guineas.'

Juliet gasped, astonishment mingled with relief flooding over her, unable to believe what she was hearing, her mind already racing as she calculated what could be done at Endcliffe House with such an enormous amount of money.

Through a gap in the people crowding round the table, Juliet saw once more her brother's flushed, handsome countenance and his sleek, ash-blond hair falling untidily over his brow. There was a glazed set to his features and a grimness in his eyes. He looked blindly in her direction, his eyes registering surprise and then anger, and his lips curled in disapproval, but he refused to allow himself to become sidetracked from the game in hand by an angry sister who should have known better than to enter the card room. Looking at the table once more, he uttered disappointment when his partner rose, having lost the game and being reluctant to play on.

Juliet was swamped with relief, sure that Richard would finish and come away. But another man came and sat opposite him, putting one of two packs of cards on the table with slender, flexible fingers. She froze on seeing the identity of his partner, for it was none other than Marcus Cardell. She studied him, struck by how different he was to Richard. This man was no fair-haired young man with the face of a choir boy and the manner and air of the privileged. Not one bit. This man with his lean tanned face and a devil-may-care demeanour, wore his impeccably cut clothes with a careless elegance and didn't seem to care a damn.

She felt something inside her plummeting. She couldn't really understand what she was feeling—it seemed to be a terrifying moment of prescience, for she suddenly saw her brother rendered wanting in the presence of Lord Cardell. The man had a way of making everyone he was close to appear somewhat lesser than him even if they were not.

'Why does Richard not stop?' she whispered to James, who was looking on with deep concern. 'No doubt he will blame me if his luck turns.'

'If he loses, it cannot be blamed on you. Not when he is playing Lord Cardell.'

'He's a gambling man?'

'Yes, although he doesn't often come into society, being a military man and only recently back from the Peninsular. He is known for being extremely skilful at cards, and a great number of people have lost whole fortunes to him. His personality is so strong that with a lift of one of his arrogant eyebrows or a flare of a nostril, it is not unknown for his opponent to tremble with fear and drop his cards. He is hard and ruthless and enjoys winning at any form of gambling—and cares little for those who suffer as a consequence.'

'Why is he so unpleasant?'

'It isn't that he's unpleasant. In fact, he can be quite

charming, especially to the ladies, who drool over him, and it's not difficult to see why with his looks.'

Juliet didn't tell James that she was already acquainted with Lord Cardell. Richard, too, having made his acquaintance in the long and distant past, but she was beginning to think that the game of cards Richard was about to play had become something personal for Lord Cardell. That he was about to prove to her that had she taken him up on his wager earlier, she would have lost. Instinct made him look up, as if sensing her gaze. There was a strong, arrogant set to his jaw, and his face was as hard and forbidding as a granite sculpture, his fingers handling the cards with expert ease were long and slender. His eyes locked onto hers, compelling and piercing, and Juliet saw a tightening to his features as his eyes narrowed and swept over her. A confident *I told you so* smile curved his lips before he lowered his eyes to pay attention to the game at hand.

Knowing exactly how the game would end, Juliet was tempted to walk away, but she stood her ground, determined to see it out to the bitter, humiliating end.

They began a game of piquet. It was a game for two people which offered excellent scope for both intelligence and judgement, something Richard would have risen to had his head not been fogged with the fumes of alcohol. Every card he played and lost would have many repercussions. She could feel them now coming at her like ripples when a stone was thrown into a pond. Looking up, he met her eyes, unconcerned by her reaction. Then he looked away, already intent upon the game. She was furious with him. At that moment she was nothing more to him than the cards he played and to be set aside.

Both men became intent on the game, which followed the classic pattern with Richard winning a little, then losing more and more, until he ceased to win anything at all as his partner, who, unlike Richard, was completely unaffected by alcohol, raised the stakes higher and higher. With a mixture of languor and self-assurance, his eyes on the cards did not stir.

For the next half hour, Juliet watched every move of the game with a sinking heart, the tension becoming unbearable as Richard lost more and more of his winnings to Lord Cardell, who presided over the game like a predatory hawk. Her anger was growing by the second, but she tried not to show it. She saw Lord Cardell was experienced, and the more Richard lost, the more Lord Cardell incited him to go on playing, to bid higher and higher. He must have been able to see Richard was drunk and not in possession of his right senses. He would have to be blind not to, but he lounged indifferently across from him, his expression bland as he coolly regarded her brother, whose flushed face and nervousness clearly betrayed his emotions.

When Richard had lost his former winnings, pushing a pile of banknotes into the centre of the table, Lord Cardell raised the stakes yet again by one thousand guineas, and Juliet could not believe it when Richard, in an agitated state, accepted the bet, knowing all he had left to stake were the deeds of Endcliffe House.

No longer able to stand by and watch his friend lose every penny to his name, James stepped forward.

'Don't be a fool, Richard,' he said softly but firmly in his ear. 'You cannot cover the bet if you lose. After losing what you have won tonight, you no longer have one thousand guineas to your name.'

Richard shot him a look which told him not to interfere as he put his signature to a chit and placed it with Lord Cardell's money in the centre of the table. 'I will take the bet and aim to win it back on the next hand.'

Lord Cardell seemed irritated by the interruption, noticing Richard's slight hesitation. 'Do you continue?' he asked curtly.

'I continue,' Richard replied firmly.

Juliet flinched, trying not to look at Lord Cardell's glacial expression, but her anger was also directed at Richard. How could he go on playing when he knew what it would mean if he lost? She continued to watch with the sickening knowledge that because of his reckless stupidity, they were about to lose everything they owned. She turned and left the table just as the last hand was being played, no longer able to watch. No doubt the money Lord Cardell had won was a modest sum to him, whereas to herself and Richard, it was a fortune. Not until the game was over did she turn back to see Lord Cardell rise from the table.

'Thank you. That was an excellent game,' he said as Richard quickly signed the IOU for the money he owed. Richard handed it to him, and Juliet watched Lord Cardell pocket it as her brother slumped in his chair, the knowledge that they would have to face the enormity of his loss quite overwhelming.

Chapter Four

When Richard finally emerged from the card room and came to stand beside her, Juliet caught all of Lord Cardell's attention. He was conversing with Lady Wyatt. Juliet placed a hand gently but firmly on Richard's arm and spoke softly.

'Come, Richard. It's late. I think it's time we left.'

Only then did he become aware of her presence, and he scowled at her, his red eyes full of displeasure and annoyance. 'I can't leave yet,' he said belligerently, slurring his words. 'The hour is not late.'

'Yes, we can—we must, Richard,' Juliet persisted.

'Run along, Juliet. I will not be dictated to by you. I'll leave all in good time.'

Obstinately, Juliet stood her ground, and it was the anger he saw spark in her eyes that prompted Lord Cardell to move towards her, Lady Wyatt following in his wake. The last thing she wanted was a scene.

When Lord Cardell suddenly appeared and introduced himself to Richard as his new neighbour at Mulberry Hall, Richard looked at him, a trifle nonplussed, unable to understand how a man who could ruin him at cards could then behave as if nothing untoward had occurred. 'Neighbour, you say?'

'I am. We have met—on a couple of occasions when I visited my aunt and uncle at Mulberry Hall many years ago.'

'Ah, yes,' Richard murmured. 'I do recall the occasions. We were visiting with our mother.'

'Lady Juliet and I have already become reacquainted.'

Richard's gaze swung from Lord Cardell to Juliet and back again. 'You are? How?'

'We met before I came to London. I had only recently taken up residence at Mulberry Hall. We encountered each other whilst out riding. Is that not so, Lady Juliet? We shared a somewhat…pleasant few minutes before going our separate ways. I had no idea I had such a charming neighbour.'

His voice was as deep and as smooth as silk, and he exuded a potent masculine allure that was almost impossible to ignore, and, however much Juliet told herself she was immune to it and despite all her efforts, she could not prevent the colour from tinting her cheeks. He must have noticed, for one corner of his mouth lifted in a slight smile, which Juliet found infuriating. How could he behave as though what he had done to Richard was a mere trifle? Had the man no scruples?

'Yes,' Juliet said tightly, inwardly fuming. 'We have met.'

'Humph—oh, I see.' Richard looked accusingly at his sister. 'You never told me.'

'I saw no reason to. The meeting was brief and of no importance.' She turned her attention to Richard. 'I think we should leave now, Richard.'

'Juliet is right, Richard,' Lady Wyatt said. 'The hour is late and our guests will all be leaving shortly.'

'Nonsense. There are a good few hours left yet.'

'I'm afraid not,' she said softly. 'Go home, Richard. Juliet looks quite worn out. Is that not so, Juliet?'

'Yes,' she replied, joining in on the conspiracy. 'I have a headache coming on. Come along, Richard.'

Casting a message with her eyes to one of the footmen when he was close, she asked him to escort Lord Sinclair out to his carriage. Juliet would have liked to follow him as he went down the steps, but the tall figure of Marcus Cardell barred her way. She turned to Lady Wyatt. 'Goodnight, Lady Wyatt, and thank you for a lovely evening.'

'Lovely?' she said not unkindly, reaching out and touching Juliet's arm in an affectionate gesture. 'I think not, Juliet. At least not for you. I know just how painful these parties are for you, having to watch your brother throw more of his money away while all the time your heart is pining to be back in Surrey. And you, Marcus,' she said, turning to Lord Cardell, 'you should have known better than to draw him into a game when he can ill afford it. Lord Sinclair has a hopeless passion for gambling, and if Juliet weren't here to keep an eye on him, then he'd have nothing left.'

Lord Cardell looked at Juliet, his expression suddenly serious, his look questioning. 'It is as bad as that?'

Deflated and unable to deny the truth, she nodded. 'I'm afraid so, Lord Cardell. It is unfortunate, but there it is.'

'But—anyway,' Lady Wyatt said, glancing sharply from one to the other, 'I'm glad you two have met. Might put a sparkle back into her eyes, Marcus, having such a charming neighbour. Juliet has far too many worries for

one so young. It's not good for her. By the way,' she said,
eyeing him quizzically, seeming reluctant to let either of
them go. 'What are you doing here in London? Aren't you
supposed to be settling in at Mulberry Hall?'

'I'm here to see Adele—my six-year-old daughter,'
he said by way of an explanation to Juliet. 'At present,
she is with my mother. I would like to take her back to
Mulberry Hall with me when I leave, but my mother obstinately refuses to part with her.'

'I'm sure she will relent. It will be good for the two
of you to be together. Now, all you need is a wife to
take care of you both, and if you run true to form, you
shouldn't have any difficulty finding one. If my memory
serves me correctly, women never used to be a problem.
Rumour has it that this is the reason why you are here
in London—to look for one.'

'No. That is only one of the reasons.'

Lady Wyatt gave an exaggerated sigh and looked at
Juliet. 'If only I were younger, Juliet, and not already
married to Henry, but you,' she said, smiling, a mischievous twinkle dancing in her shrewd eyes. 'Now, you
would make someone like Marcus an excellent wife.'

'But perhaps Lady Juliet does not wish to marry anyone,' said Lord Cardell, his smile challenging and his
light blue eyes darkening to a deeper blue, resting on
Juliet's face.

She had listened to the brief interchange between
them and was neither shocked nor surprised. She was
not at all disconcerted by Lady Wyatt's words, whose
laughter made light of them. But Juliet was no fool and
knew what lay behind them, that Lady Wyatt thought
it high time she stopped thinking of Thomas and what

might have been and began looking to the future. Perhaps she was right. Again, she looked directly at Lord Cardell, at the merry gleam dancing in his eyes, one of his winged brows arched as he waited expectantly for her reply. She looked at him with new interest and found herself remembering Lydia's words and her reference to King Midas, and wondered if he really was that rich. She told herself to stop it, not to think like this, but she couldn't help it, and the reply was already on her lips before she realised what she was saying.

'Lord Cardell,' she said coolly, 'I would marry the devil himself if he would settle the debts on Endcliffe House.' She saw the startled look that appeared on his face, quickly followed by a thin smile curving his lips, and she caught a glimpse of very white teeth. 'Now, if you will excuse me, I will bid you goodnight.' And without further ado she turned, following her brother down the steps to the waiting carriage.

'Well now,' said Lady Wyatt, a smile of approval for the way Juliet had responded to their teasing curving her lips. 'There's a challenge if ever there was one. A challenge not to be ignored, I'd say.'

Watching the Sinclair carriage drive away, Marcus nodded thoughtfully. Her reply had been brief but to the point. And it had certainly given him food for thought. It was as if she had thrown down a gauntlet, and he was forced to pick it up.

'You're right, Lady Wyatt,' he replied, having reached the most monumental decision of his life. 'I have no intention of ignoring it.' Come hell or high water, one way or another, he would make Juliet Sinclair his wife.

Lady Wyatt smiled broadly, well satisfied that her words had not fallen on deaf ears. 'No, Marcus. I didn't think you would.'

'How well do you know her?'

'I've known the family for years—her mother since we were children. It was a sad day when she died a couple of years ago, Juliet's father a year later.'

'What's she really like?'

'You've seen her. Surely that should speak for itself.'

'I know, and she's quite a beauty—there's no denying that. But I want to know what she's like beneath that.'

Lady Wyatt smiled slowly. 'This is not just a passing interest?'

'No. She impressed me a great deal and I wish to know more about her.'

'Well, I will tell you all I can and will begin by telling you that she is not like her father—or her brother, for that matter. Her father was a notorious lover of pleasure. He preferred to live in London rather than in Surrey, which he found suffocating. In their time, her father and mother were like a pair of social butterflies, always popular, their presence at any event much sought after. Unlike her father and brother, Juliet deplores London and likes nothing better than to bury herself in the country with her horses, although I believe circumstances have forced them to sell most of them. Most of the young ladies of my acquaintance are sweet-natured, always stitching samplers or dabbling in watercolours or music, a trouble to no one, which cannot be said of Juliet.'

'No? And how is she different?'

'Well, she is quite extraordinary, highly intelligent and enduringly devoted to those she cares about. As a girl, she was defiant of all restrictions and rebellious of all convention. She was complex—untameable, hot-tempered and truculent when she failed to get her own way, and an angel when she did. Her parents despaired of ever making a lady of her, but she has mellowed some-what since their demise. There was a young man she was to have married—the second son of a baron. They had known each other for years, and devoted to him she was, although I never cared for him myself. Too much of a gad about town for my liking, but she was so deeply in love with him that she was blind to any of his faults and would hear no wrong said about him. He was reported killed at Albuera—which you will know all about, being a military man yourself. It hit her hard at the time, but she's young. She'll get over it.'

So that was it, thought Marcus, understanding at last the reason why Lady Juliet looked so distant, a mournful solemnity in her lovely eyes. She was suffering from a broken heart. But he had no intention of being deterred by this and believed that time would heal her wounds. She had built up a resistance around her inner core, and he had every intention of breaking it down.

'Nevertheless, Lady Wyatt, the man must have been someone quite exceptional to have inspired such love. But what did you mean when you said he was reported missing?'

'His body was never found.'

'So many were killed at Albuera—a bloodbath, it was.'

'We heard. Eyewitnesses have reported seeing him shot down. His father received a letter from his com-manding officer, informing him that his son had fallen on the field of battle—seen it himself. Unfortunately, it could not be ascertained whether or not his body had been buried along with many others who had fallen, nor was his name on the list of prisoners.'

'I see,' Marcus said calmly. 'Then there is a possibility that he might not be dead, that he might have been picked up by peasants or the partisans?'

Lady Wyatt nodded. 'There is that possibility, but I doubt it. I believe something would have been heard before now.'

'Then tell me, why does Lady Juliet come to London if she dislikes it so much?'

'Because if she didn't keep an eye on Richard and his gambling, they'd have nothing left and, if rumour is correct, she has cause to be worried. They're heavily in debt. Since the death of her mother, Juliet has had nothing but heartache, and to add to her worries, she now has poverty staring her in the face. But—if my judgement of her is correct—she will fight tooth and nail to keep Endcliffe House, because if that goes, it will break her heart. No, I feel nothing but admiration for the way she has coped with the arduous task of Richard and his gambling. I am sure she'll come through in the end. She is a very resilient young lady.'

'Yes,' he said, trying to sound casual, but Lady Wyatt could tell that she had caught more than his eye.

'And is it right that you are home to look for a wife?'

'It is one of the reasons. I'm going to have my work cut out getting to know Adele. Lord knows I've missed enough of her young life as it is. My mother's done an excellent job, but it's time she was living with me. A wife would make it a hell of a lot easier, but I have to make sure I marry the right woman.'

Lady Wyatt nodded, understanding. 'If you decided to pursue Juliet, then I approve of your choice. You'll not regret it.'

'Even though it would be like paying court to a powder keg?'

She laughed. 'Even that. She may be nursing the hurt of her betrothed's death, but she's young, she'll get over it, and if I know anything, you're just the man to make her forget. It may cost you a pretty penny though, but I have no doubt you can afford it. Yes, it will be a perfect match, and I guarantee you'll never be bored. Whoever gets Juliet Sinclair will be a lucky man indeed.'

Marcus was conscious of a strange jolt in the region of his heart. Lady Juliet aroused emotions that he had never experienced, not even during his marriage to Elizabeth had he experienced that, which confused him. He was unaware that she and her brother had hit on hard times. Yes, he had known of Richard Sinclair's weakness for gambling, but not to the extent that Lady Wyatt pointed out. Had he known, he would never have drawn him back to the card table when he had been on a winning streak.

On his part, he had wanted to feel nothing but the satisfaction of extracting a measure of revenge because Lady Juliet had been so certain her brother could not be persuaded back to the tables. Marcus had wanted to prove her wrong. It was unsettling knowledge, and there was a faint frown on his forehead as he returned to his home. There was something about Juliet Sinclair that twisted his emotions and made him want to put things right between them.

* * *

Not until they were in the carriage did Juliet or Richard speak, Richard being the first to do so, enraged by his own foolishness.

'I should have taken James's advice and left the table when I was in front.'

'Yes, you should.' Juliet felt the seriousness of the situation had not hit him yet, but when it did, it would be with the force of a hammer blow. 'You promised me you wouldn't gamble tonight, Richard. The whole evening has turned into a disaster. Perhaps if you hadn't drunk so much in the first place, you might have retained a little of what you had won.'

'If Lord Cardell hadn't been there—blast him—I would have won more. Hell and damnation! Just when things were going well for me. It had nothing to do with the drink—it's just that his skill at cards is not to be matched by anyone I know.'

'Then why did you allow yourself to be drawn in by him?'

'Must you always disapprove of everything I do, Juliet?' Richard remarked petulantly.

'Of course I disapprove. I cannot condone your private life or your behaviour. Oh, Richard, how could you?' she accused him bitterly. 'How could you gamble away almost everything we have left?'

'We'll find a way out of it. We always do.'

'How can you say that?' Juliet admonished harshly. 'Don't be stupid. This time we can't. Things are bad, very bad. In fact, they could not be worse. We are in a hole and I cannot see any way out—unless we throw ourselves on Lord Cardell's mercy and persuade him to tear up the IOU. It would bide us a little more time, although it is not enough to save us from ruin in the long run.'

Richard was clearly shocked by her suggestion, which no gentleman would even consider. 'That is quite out of the question, and besides, Lord Cardell would refuse. But if I don't honour the debt, I will be thrown out of my club and spend the rest of my days staring at the walls inside a debtors' prison. I couldn't bear that, Juliet. The shame would be unbearable.'

'Better that than we lose everything. You do realise we will have to sell Endcliffe House, don't you, Richard?' she said despairingly, the mere thought that their home would be gone forever bringing tears to her eyes. 'There is no way we can obtain enough money, and I doubt the bank will grant us a loan.'

As if ashamed of his recklessness and the hurt he had caused Juliet, Richard's expression became contrite. 'Forgive me, Juliet. I do realise that we're in the deuce of a mess. I suppose we could sell this house—although I'd be loathe to do it.'

Juliet looked at him sharply. 'So would I. Mother loved this house. It was where she loved to socialise when she came to town.' She sighed deeply, knowing it might have to be considered if they didn't find a way out of this mess. 'How long before the debt must be paid?'

'A week.'

'As soon as that?' she whispered. 'Then we must work something out.'

As she prepared for bed, she could think of nothing else other than that they might lose everything. She felt weak and defenceless, at the mercy of fate, and then something steely came to the fore. She wasn't going to let it go, not if she could help it. Her mother had told her she was strong, so had her father. Some of that strength came to her aid now. She felt a hard resolve replacing the panic. She wasn't going to let this defeat her.

Two days after Lord and Lady Wyatt's dinner party found Juliet in Mr Marsden's second-hand bookshop in a busy alley just off Paternoster Row. She had come in the hope of obtaining for a few pence a book by William Collins of sentimental lyric poetry, a style that Mr Collins and others had first made fashionable in the middle of the last century. She was also glad of the opportunity to be out in the fresh air, to be alone for a while so that she might think.

She wanted nothing more than to stay at Endcliffe House and never have to leave, but Richard's gambling had made their situation virtually impossible. He hadn't left the house since Lord and Lady Wyatt's dinner party. Realising the seriousness of their situation had aged him ten years. He looked thoroughly broken, his face creased with lines of anxiety. Not possessing a plethora of relatives they could turn to in order to bail them out, she knew that it would require all their brains and ingenuity if they were to survive.

A bell tinkled pleasantly overhead when she entered Mr Marsden's shop, where the smell of ink, paper and leather-bound books assailing her nostrils was surprisingly pleasant. Like many other establishments, Mr Marsden's shop stocked items other than books, bookselling alone was rarely sufficient to make a prosperous living. The hour was early and apart from two well-dressed matrons who sat gossiping and an elderly gentleman carrying a small parcel of books he had just purchased, the shop was quiet. Juliet loved the bookshop and visited it at every opportunity when she was in town. A table of dusty bargain books invited one to browse. Mr Marsden was unpacking some pamphlets and looked up when she entered, smiling brightly. She told him what she was looking for.

'Let me see, I should have a copy somewhere. You browse, Lady Juliet, while I have a look in the back.'

Happy to wander among the narrow aisles crammed with sagging, dusty shelves of books ranging from classics, educational, drama, romance, prose and many more, she examined books by Fielding and Defoe with avid interest, having read most of them. She picked out *Clarissa*, a book written by Samuel Richardson that was a particular favourite of hers. She had read it several times and agonised over poor Clarissa Harlowe's fate on finding herself in the clutches of her abominable persecutor, Lovelace.

She became lost in the print as she flicked through the well-thumbed pages. She was about to move away from the shelves when a man's heavy tread sounded in the shop, growing closer. He stopped and spoke in a calm, casual voice, unmistakably the voice of a gentleman, a voice she instantly recognised.

'Well, Lady Juliet, here we are again.'

Juliet whirled round at that familiar deep voice and looked into the face of Lord Cardell. For some inexplicable reason, her heart set a wild beat. His face was still, but his eyes were a brilliant, quite dangerous pale blue. He lounged indolently against the bookshelves behind him with the ease of a man discussing nothing more serious than the weather. The remembrance of their previous encounters, all of which had been angry and bitter experiences, touched her deeply. And now he was smiling at her, a friendly quizzical grin.

Taken off guard by his appearance, she started. Ever since their meeting at the dinner party, she had tried not to focus her mind on him, but now that she was facing him once more, her panic increased and she could hardly believe what she had said to him—that she would marry the devil himself if he would settle the debts on Endcliffe House. No doubt Lord Cardell considered her far too outspoken, that what she had said had been foolish in the extreme. She had acted impetuously, rashly and unthinkingly and most importantly without common sense in Lord Cardell's eyes. His name spun through her mind with a combination of anticipation and dread, and now she told herself she would rather do a deal with the devil than her illustrious neighbour.

And yet the feelings she had experienced on the last occasion when they had met took some understanding. She fixed him with a cool, indifferent stare. He was dressed in a tan jacket, buff-coloured breeches and highly polished brown riding boots. The man possessed a commanding presence and was built with all the magnetism and virility of an ancient Greek athlete, with long limbs and powerful shoulders. He seemed to belong to another world, one where the wind and sun had turned his skin the colour of bronze, one that was wild and exciting and far removed from her village in Surrey. Her heart lurched, surprise holding her immobilised for a split second. He seemed to set the whole atmosphere inside Mr Marsden's bookshop vibrating.

'You take me by surprise, Lord Cardell. I did not expect to see you in a bookshop.'

'And why not, pray? I happen to read extensively—when I have the time. I haven't been home very long and there is much to be done at Mulberry Hall. I am on an errand to see an acquaintance of mine and saw you enter the bookshop.'

'And you followed me?'

'Yes. You are recovered from the dinner party, I trust.'

'Recovered? You seem to infer that I was ill. I enjoyed the evening and suffer from no ill effects. Did I look like I was?'

'Not in the slightest. You handled yourself beautifully and with perfect poise.'

'I do my best,' she retorted.

'There's no need to be so defensive. I was merely trying to pay you a compliment. Apparently, I'm out of practice.'

'Apparently you are.'

Idly he inspected the titles on the spines of the books that lined the shelf, selecting one at random. 'Do you mind that I followed you in here?'

'If you had genuinely entered the shop to look at books, then no, but since you admit to following me, then yes, I do mind—although I am sure Mr Marsden who owns the shop will be glad of the custom of such an illustrious gentleman as yourself, Lord Cardell.'

'The informality of my doing so was not meant as an offence, Lady Juliet, and if I offended you when last we met, then I apologise most humbly.'

'You did not offend me, Lord Cardell, although I wish you had not drawn Richard into a game of cards. But worry not. What he owes will be paid before the week is out.'

'That is the procedure, although now I have been made aware of your circumstances, I regret doing so.'

'As much as accusing Joe Ruskin of poaching?' she bit back, unable to stop herself. But she was hurting, and it was a relief to hit out at someone, even though she reproached herself for doing so. Having considered the occurrences on every situation since when they had met, she had to admit Lord Cardell had done no wrong. Of course he had to investigate the poaching situation on his land, and again when he had come upon her swimming in the water meadows and she had accused him of spying on her. He had not been there deliberately to watch her swim. He had come upon her by chance. As for taking four thousand guineas off Richard at the tables, only Richard and his weakness for gambling could be blamed for that.

'I'm sorry,' she conceded. 'I do understand why you acted as you did, and I apologise for accusing you of spying on me at the water meadows. You couldn't have known I would be there. I just wish you had considered the facts before upsetting Mrs Ruskin.'

Watching her closely, Lord Cardell nodded. 'So do I. Where I am concerned, I would like to forget the matter altogether.'

'Yes, I too would like to forget it.'

'And me too I expect.'

'Yes,' she murmured. 'You too.'

He chuckled, unoffended. 'Most of the ladies I meet are more than eager to be amiable to me because of who I am, but you have the unique distinction of being the only woman I have met who is honest enough to tell me to my face that, having met me, she is eager to put me from her mind.'

'Really? And you are not put out?' Juliet asked drily, thinking that what he said must be true, that if he was as wealthy as she had heard he was—and with his kind of looks—he must have women falling at his feet like dominoes in a row, all rendered quite helpless when confronted by his charm and allure.

'Not in the slightest. In fact, I find it a refreshing change. Tell me, are you a frequent visitor to this bookshop?'

'Yes, when I come to town,' she answered, suddenly beginning to feel slightly uneasy. She did not like the way he had followed her inside Mr Marsden's bookshop, nor did she like his easy manner and the steady, unsettling gaze of his penetrating light blue eyes. He was the most lethally attractive man she had ever met, and she would have to take care not to be drawn in by him. Swiftly she raised her defences. 'I do not pretend to be knowledgeable about books, but I do enjoy reading.'

'Has anyone ever told you that you resemble your mother?' he said suddenly, softly, thumbing through the pages of the book.

Juliet stared at him, surprised by his comment. 'You knew my mother?'

'No, not really. I saw her from time to time. I did not often come to Mulberry Hall to see my aunt and uncle— my mother's brother—but there were occasions when your mother came to call on my aunt. As young as I was, I recall she was unforgettable.'

Juliet said nothing to this. The blue-eyed gaze when

he turned to look at her was disconcerting, and she was miserably conscious that he had caught her dishevelled from the morning's work of sorting out items of furniture in the attics she and Richard might sell to raise the money to clear his IOU. 'Yes, she was. Tell me, Lord Cardell,' Juliet said, his comment about her mother throwing her for a moment, but not placating her so easily, 'have you caught any more poachers on your estate recently?'

'I've put the matter into the hands of my stewards. They are always vigilant, and there have been no incidents of late. Hopefully, whoever they are, they will have moved on.'

'I sincerely hope so.'

'Has your brother been affected?'

'I... I don't believe so, although it is not unusual for the odd rabbit or pheasant to be taken. It happens.'

'Since the demise of my uncle, there has been no one in the family to oversee the estate for some considerable time. It has been laid wide open to poachers. My uncle might have turned a blind eye to it, being in poor health, but I am no pushover and will not be laughed out of what is rightfully mine.'

'Poachers are usually people who have fallen on hard times and are desperate to feed their families. Does that not concern you?'

'Of course it does, but don't be fooled, Lady Juliet. It does not stop at rabbits or the odd pheasant. When deer go missing, along with sheep and cattle from the home farm, it cannot be ignored. There's a question of money involved.' He placed the book back on the shelf before giving her his full attention once more. 'Since your brother and I are neighbours, let us understand each other,' he said carefully. 'The poaching fraternity—or thieves, as I prefer to call them—is tightly knit, and they keep to their own rules. Certainly they make a living out of what they do—a good living. They are highly organised and they do not stop at the Mulberry Hall estate. Perhaps you should look to your own, Lady Juliet. Your brother's negligence may be seen as an opportunity for the thieves to divest you of some of your own livestock. It is your loss.'

The coldness of his words touched Juliet like ice. With great deliberation she turned away from him, thinking about what he had said. She could not ignore it. The unpleasant thought that there were people out there making a living off their land when they were struggling to keep afloat, she had never considered.

'They—the poachers—they make money out of it?'

'I'm afraid so. They get a good price from butchers in towns farther afield. Your brother should look into it. In this matter, we may be able to help each other. Can you afford to turn a blind eye?'

She shook her head. 'No. You are right, Lord Cardell. Although Endcliffe House needs money so badly that the miserable pounds we might secure is hardly worth thinking about.' She looked down at the book in her hand, tracing the groove of the title with her fingertip. 'Don't you see that once a stage of need is reached, a little money saved here and there does not put a new roof on the house or repair the walls and keep the damp at bay? It would be such a small part of what we need that it wouldn't even begin to patch it up.'

Lord Cardell's eyebrows lifted and his features relaxed. 'Let me see the book that has caught your attention,' he said on a change of subject. He took the volume she was holding. Reading the title on the spine, he raised his eyebrows in surprise. '*Clarissa*! It would not be my choice of good reading, but I can quite see why it appeals to the ladies.'

'No matter your opinion, Lord Cardell, the book has met with considerable success and is a fine work,' Juliet was quick to say in defence of one of her favourites. 'I cannot see why you should pour scorn on it.'

He smiled. 'Clarissa is a nervous young woman of excessive sentiment and sensibility. I confess to having read the book, but she did not endear herself to me in the slightest.'

'And how do you define "sentiment and sensibility," Lord Cardell?'

'As an expression of intense human feelings, of which the heroine in question is in possession to excess. The two words are often confused. *Sentiment* is ruled by the human heart, which is the centre of all emotions, whereas *sensibility* is the key to bodily sensations—touch and such things,' he said softly, his eyes filling with amusement when she flushed and lowered her gaze at his definition and the hidden connotation of the words. He smiled, knowing exactly the effect he was having on her. 'Clearly, you enjoyed the book?'

'Yes,' she replied, wishing she had not asked him to define the two words because she knew she was blushing at the intimacy of his tone. There was altogether something too explicit and intense in his eyes. However, she refused to be deflected. 'So much so that I have read it several times. I confess I was much moved and felt a great deal of sympathy for Clarissa—being pursued and persecuted so cruelly by the abominable Lovelace.'

'Ah, but she did throw herself on his mercy.'

'She accepted Lovelace's offer of help because she was quite desperate to save herself from a dreadful marriage, only to find herself in a worse situation than she was before.'

'And you have an affinity to Clarissa, have you, Lady Juliet?'

Juliet smiled with a faint trace of cynicism. 'Oh, I believe there is a Clarissa in most women, Lord Cardell—just as there is a Lovelace in most men.'

'Perhaps you are right, but we do not all have to resort to kidnapping to engage the affections of the ladies we desire,' he said slowly, meaningfully, in a voice low with seduction that made Juliet think improper things. It was a voice few women would be able to resist, especially not if the man speaking happened to look like Lord Cardell—over six feet tall and built like a Greek god.

She looked at him, suddenly beginning to feel out of her depth, unable to answer his question, and sensing a wave of hot colour burn her cheeks under his close scrutiny. She was relieved when Mr Marsden chose that moment to come shuffling along the aisle towards her.

'I must apologise, Lady Juliet, for taking so long. I thought I had a copy of Mr Collins's poems, but I was mistaken.'

'That's all right, Mr Marsden.' Juliet smiled. 'Thank you for taking the trouble to look.'

When he had moved away, Juliet looked up to see Lord Cardell eyeing her with some amusement and a hint of mockery, his eyelids drooped down over his glorious blue eyes giving him a lazy, sleepy look.

'William Collins! A book of sentimental lyric poetry that was fashionable when first published and much sought after in some circles, I believe.' His smile widened. 'I salute your taste, Lady Juliet—a veritable catalogue of sensation. Perhaps Mr Marsden might order it for you if you are so desirous to obtain it.'

'I'm sure he would. I will give it some thought for another day.' Taking Clarissa out of his hands, she placed it back on the shelf. 'And now, if you will excuse me, Lord Cardell, I must be on my way. I have much to do and little time to do it in.'

Juliet pushed past him and, after bidding Mr Marsden good day, marched out of the shop, relieved that he had not mentioned her parting words at Lord and Lady Wyatt's dinner party, that she would marry the devil if he would settle the debts on Endcliffe House. Having thrown down a challenge, she hoped he had thought no more of it—and yet, did she? She felt a rush of righteous indignation when she recalled how he had drawn Richard into that game of cards and beaten him.

Chapter Five

It was mid-afternoon, St James's Park attracting all manner of people at this time of day. The sun was pleasantly warm, with people strolling along the paths or lounging on the grass in groups, rosy-cheeked children playing all manner of games. Juliet was accompanied by Daphne. Of medium height, dark-haired and with an easy manner and sunny disposition, she was employed at the London residence and had a willingness to turn her hand to any chore. Juliet usually dispensed with a personal maid, but when she was in London, she pressed Daphne into her personal service.

Today they walked side by side, enjoying the day's warmth. Juliet carried a small bag of bread, intending to feed the ducks on the pond. Fallow deer roamed free and were a constant delight to the children, in particular, who loved to feed them. Soldiers, resplendent in their colourful red-and-blue uniforms, paraded at Horse Guards, which was one of the main attractions of the park during the afternoons.

Juliet almost didn't see the group of four people coming towards them—a man and two women and a young girl. Having just replied to something amusing Daphne had said, which had brought a smile to her lips and a sparkle to her eyes, she suddenly noticed their approach, and her smile froze as her gaze became fixed on them.

One of the women, whom she thought to be in her mid-sixties, was quite tall and statuesque, with a regal bearing and strong, handsome features, her gloved hand placed lightly on the gentleman's arm. The other woman, plainly dressed and quite young, Juliet assumed to be the lady's maid. She held the hand of the child, her dark hair arranged in ringlets, which bounced delightfully from beneath her bonnet when she moved her head. But it was the gentleman who caught Juliet's eyes and held them, for it was Lord Cardell.

Both parties stopped, leaving several paces between them. For some inexplicable reason Juliet experienced the depth to which her mind and body were oddly stirred whenever she was in Lord Cardell's presence. His face was still, but his eyes were a brilliant, quite dangerous pale blue. The remembrance of their previous encounters, some volatile and the one at the bookshop not so volatile, touched her deeply. He wore a plum-coloured cutaway coat and buff knee breeches tucked into highly polished black riding boots, and his neck linen was sparkling white.

'Lady Juliet,' Lord Cardell said, 'I did not expect to find you here.'

'I cannot imagine why not. I enjoy walking and the park is so pleasant.'

'I couldn't agree more,' the older lady said, looking at Juliet. Interest kindled in her eyes. 'Come, Marcus. You must introduce us.'

'Of course. Mother, allow me to present to you Lady

Juliet Sinclair of Endcliffe House, a close neighbour of mine. Lady Juliet, my mother the dowager Countess of Cranswick.'

Juliet dipped a curtsy.

'Sinclair?' the Countess said. 'Of course the name is familiar to me. I believe I met your mother on occasion when she visited my sister-in-law at Mulberry Hall. Is that not so?'

'Yes, they were friends as well as neighbours.'

'This is indeed interesting. I learned of your mother's demise some time ago, followed so soon by your father. My condolences, my dear, although it is a little late, I know, but I mean it most sincerely. Are you to return to Surrey?'

'I am staying with my brother at present, but I hope to return to Surrey in the next week or so.' Juliet looked down at the child half hiding behind the other woman's skirts, peering shyly up at Juliet.

'And who is this young lady?' Juliet said, smiling down at her. The little girl's shy awkwardness touched a hidden chord in her, reminding her so much of herself at that age.

'This is my daughter, Adele. She is always shy with strangers,' said Lord Cardell.

Adele took a step towards Juliet a little hesitantly at first, regarding her seriously, and she noticed that she bore a remarkable resemblance to her father, but unlike her father, Adele's eyes, which were wide and as darkly grey as a winter's sea, were from a different strain. There was something rather timid about Adele, dainty and fragile. There was also something cowed about her, contrary to the normal exuberance of children. Juliet prayed silently for acceptance. On impulse she reached out and took her small hand in her own, and bending low, so that her face was on a level with hers, she smiled warmly into her eyes.

'I'm so pleased to meet you, Adele, and what a pretty dress you are wearing. I do hope you're enjoying your walk in the park. There is so much to see, and I always bring Daphne with me for company.'

Adele made no attempt to pull away, and a little smile began to tug at the corners of her mouth. She seemed to be assessing her, and when her eyes ceased to regard Juliet so seriously and her smile gradually broadened, which was a delight to see, it brought a relieved smile to Lord Cardell's features, and he seemed to relax, which told Juliet how apprehensive he was about introducing his daughter to strangers. When Adele's gaze lighted on a small bag in Juliet's hand, Juliet opened it and showed her the contents.

'I've brought some bread to feed the ducks on the pond. Would you like to help me?'

'Oh, yes please,' she said with a bright, eager light shining in her wide eyes, her face taking on a look of enthusiasm, no longer seeing the beautiful lady as a stranger.

Juliet stood up straight and looked at Lord Cardell and his mother. 'Forgive my imposition, but I really have come to feed ducks. Would you permit me to take Adele?'

'Of course,' the Countess said, more than happy to comply. 'I'm sure she would love to. What do you say, Marcus?'

Frowning, Lord Cardell looked down as his daughter.

'Please, Papa,' Adele whispered tentatively. 'Will you let me feed the ducks?'

'Very well,' he conceded, 'it's a wonderful thought.' His eyes lit on a bench close to the pond. 'We'll sit and wait over there.'

Clearly enjoying this exciting moment, holding Juliet's hand, Adele skipped along by her side. Daphne following several paces behind.

For Marcus, watching his daughter happily throwing bread to the ducks with Lady Juliet, it was a moment of complete enchantment. He began to smile, for their laughter as the ducks noisily competed with each other for their share of the bread was infectious. His face was soft and his eyes were warm. He had a strong sense of responsibility and felt a deep affection for his daughter. It worried him greatly that she was growing up without the influence and love that could only come from a mother.

Equally moved as she watched her granddaughter give way to joyous laughter, his mother said, 'Lady Juliet is a personable young woman, Marcus, pretty too.'

'Yes,' he agreed, watching his daughter as her ringlets bounced against her back and seeing that a rosy glow had sprung to her cheeks as she had skipped alongside Lady Juliet. Skipping! He could not recall seeing her do that. Her bonnet had fallen back off her head and was being held on by the ribbon about her neck. 'She is also the most controversial and unconventional woman I have ever met.'

His mother gave him a quizzical look. 'I see. You must have become well acquainted with her to have formed an opinion.'

'We have met on a few occasions, not all of them amiable.'

'Well, I like her. In fact, I think I recall seeing her at Mulberry Hall when she was quite small, her brother also, although I also seem to recall there was some controversy after one of our visits,' she said, speaking absently. 'Something about Lady Juliet missing for some considerable time...' She shook her head. 'Not that it matters now. It was all so long ago. Clearly, she was found safe and unharmed. Lady Juliet has an easy manner. I like that. Adele seems to be quite taken with her also.'

Marcus glanced at his mother sharply. 'I can see that.' A frown deepened on his brow. 'What are you getting at?'

'You know what I'm getting at, Marcus, so don't pretend you don't. There is nothing that would delight me more than to know you have found someone to marry, a young woman who possesses the requirements of birth and breeding enough to make her worthy of marrying into the Cardell family.'

'I know, Mother, since you never tire of telling me at every opportunity.'

'You are now Lord Cardell, the Earl of Ashleigh, of Mulberry Hall, so you must marry well for duty's sake. I know you would prefer not to remarry at all, but you are not getting any younger, and you must secure an heir for the Mulberry estate and a mother for Adele. My own family is thin on the ground, as well you know, which is why you are in the position you are now. You cannot go on postponing the inevitable any longer. Besides, it's about time you gave me another grandchild.

Your brother and his wife had two sons in the first five years of marriage.'

'You seem to forget I've been in the Peninsular for the past eight years fighting Bonaparte, with little time spent at home.'

'Which is why it's important for you to find yourself another wife. I'm no longer a young woman, Marcus, and your brother and his wife have their hands full raising their own children—with another one due shortly. Adele needs guidance and a loving family of her own.'

Marcus didn't argue the matter. He was a widower who had seen little of his family in the past because of his military career. As a young man with a lust for adventure, he'd had little time for marriage and affairs of the heart after Elizabeth's death. Certainly he yielded to the desires of the flesh as much as the next man. Many women had passed through his life. Some had faded from memory and a few he had felt affection for, but he'd never doted on any, not even his wife.

Their marriage had been arranged by their two families. He had been fond of Elizabeth and had grieved when she had died. But it was the army that had been of the utmost importance to him. While the military campaign was ongoing in Spain, he concentrated on developing his mind and spirit for action on the field of battle—until his daughter was born. It changed everything. On inheriting Mulberry Hall, he had resigned his commission.

It was important to him that he got to know his daughter and married again to provide an heir for the Mulberry estate, but he refused to be browbeaten by his mother.

'I am well aware of that, Mother, and I intend to put my mind to it.'

'Well,' she said, a warm gleam in her eye as she looked at her son. 'I do not think you will have far to look.'

Marcus hardly heard his mother's words as he watched Lady Juliet bend down and place her arm protectively about Adele's shoulders, preventing her falling into the water in her excitement, her cheek resting on the child's dark head. Mesmerised by the lovely picture the woman and child created, his expression softened. Looking on, he felt as though he were an intruder, a stranger, and that his daughter belonged to someone else. He was determined to change that. When the last of the bread had been thrown, they slowly made their way back.

He listened intently to Lady Juliet talking to Adele in a way that seemed to come quite naturally to her. Adele looked up at the face of the woman with something akin to adoration, responding to the warmth in her voice. Both the scene and Lady Juliet's words bewitched him and reached out to some unknown part of him that he had not been aware he possessed. It touched and lightened a dark corner for a brief instant, and then it was gone. He wondered what it was about her that he found so appealing. She was lovely—beautiful—but there were many kinds of beauty, and the most obvious didn't often appeal to him. There had to be something else, something more than the colour of her eyes, the perfect loveliness of her face and the delectable curvaceousness of her body, though as a red-blooded male he wasn't hypocritical enough to deny this appeal.

'There,' Lady Juliet said, still hold Adele's hand, 'all

the ducks have been well and truly fed. Did you enjoy feeding them, Adele?'

'Oh, yes,' she replied softly, reluctant to let go of her hand. 'Will you come to the park again?'

'While I am in London, I come to the park most days.'

'And can I see you again?' she asked hopefully, 'Can I, Papa?' she asked her father beseechingly.

Marcus smiled down at her. 'Certainly, should we encounter Lady Juliet. Hopefully she will bring more bread for the ducks.'

'I will,' Juliet confirmed. 'It's been lovely meeting you, Adele. You too, Lady Cardell,' she said, bobbing a small curtsy. 'I won't detain you any longer.'

'It's been a pleasure meeting you, Lady Juliet. Perhaps you will call on us when next we are at Mulberry Hall?'

'Yes, thank you. I would like that.' As Marcus made his way out of the park, he stopped every now and then, his eyes glancing back at the young woman walking in the opposite direction, unaware of the little satisfied smile playing on his mother's lips.

When he had seen her gliding soundlessly over the grass towards him, slender and long-limbed, Marcus had been enchanted by her, his eyes making an instant appraisal. She really was a remarkably beautiful young woman, and it was as if he were seeing it for the first time in his life. Juliet Sinclair was a natural temptress, alluring and lovely. The appeal of this young woman he found hard to explain. His attraction to her was beneath her beauty, it was something else entirely.

As Adele trotted along beside him, it was Lady Juliet he saw dripping wet after her swim in the water meadows. Courageous and lovely, it was Lady Juliet who had faced him squarely at the Wyatts' dinner party, telling him she would marry the devil himself if he would pay the debts on her beloved home. On all their encounters, he'd had no idea she was in such dire straits. She'd been too proud to let him think otherwise, and he admired her for that.

Since returning to England and seriously considering remarrying, when he tried to think of a suitable candidate to be his wife, it was Lady Juliet Sinclair's image that lingered the longest in his thoughts. Yes, she was indeed lovely, but she was much more than that. Highly intelligent, she was proud, wilful and undisciplined. She was also gentle, brave and innocent. She projected a tangible magical aura, and he could almost feel her vibrant inner energy and appetite for life. Her beauty in her home setting had fed his gaze and created a warm hungering ache that would not be easily appeased by anything less than what he desired.

She was different from any other woman he had ever known, but today the smooth skin of her face was marred by mauve shadows circling her eyes, which, he suspected, were the result of worry and sleepless nights. His admiration for her ran deep. As young as she was and dealing with the burden of her ancestral estate while her brother gambled his way through the distinguished halls in London, to keep Endcliffe Hall off the auctioneers block as well as taking care of the servants who remained, she had learned to deal with adversity while holding her head high. He admired her stoicism, her determination to face her trials head on and to deal with them as best she could. Unfortunately, she was running out of options.

But one thing had not changed about her, and at this he felt a pang of dismay. There was still no warmth in those glorious eyes, which stared out of her pale face with a solemnity that touched him. But instinctively he knew that no matter how sad she was, her sorrow only enhanced her magical power that was capable of enslaving him forever.

When he had been close to her, the faint, heady scent of crushed rose petals had come to him, a scent he would associate with her for evermore. They had looked at each other steadily for a long moment, and Marcus had realised then that if he was to take a wife, then he wanted Lady Juliet Sinclair to be that woman. He wanted her, but more important was the fact that he wanted her to want him, and if he hoped to win her affections, then he was going to have to hold his emotions under restraint, which—not a man known for his patience—would be no simple matter.

As a soldier, he listened to his head and not his heart in all things. Nothing in his life was accidental or unplanned, and everything was carefully thought out. But this was one time when he did not pause to understand the reasons for what he was about to do. He wanted her, and that was reason enough.

Having made a decision to propose marriage to Lady Juliet, Marcus sought Richard Sinclair out in the hallowed rooms of White's, the gentleman's club in St James's. The room was cloaked in the quiet, restrained ambience redolent of the masculine smells of sandalwood, leather and cigars. He scanned the room, his gaze coming to rest on Richard Sinclair. In a sombre mood, he was morosely staring at a goblet of brandy—no doubt nursing his wounds inflicted over his losses at the tables. When Marcus approached, Richard looked up at him, his boyishly handsome face etched with pain.

'May I?' Marcus said, sitting opposite before he could object. Signalling to a servant to bring a decanter of brandy and two snifters, he studied the man opposite.

'If you have come to propose another game of cards Lord Cardell, you can forget it. I'm all cleaned out.'

'Be assured that I did not seek you out for that purpose. I apologise if I have chosen an inopportune time, but what I have to say is of the utmost importance.'

'If you have come to collect on the debt, I still have a couple of days to settle. No matter what your opinion is of me, Cardell, honour my debt to you. Because of my irresponsible behaviour, I have brought shame and dishonour to my family name and ruined whatever chance my sister has of making a decent, respectable marriage in the future. When I have settled my debt to you, with creditors already on my back and the estate mortgaged up to the hilt, I may very well be forced to put it on the market.'

'And you are prepared to do that?' he asked, picking up the decanter and pouring them both a drink.

'Of course. Nothing I can say can excuse my own part in what has happened, and I have reproached myself many times for it. I am to blame and I am deeply ashamed of my past conduct. I have nothing to say in my defence.'

'At least you are man enough to admit that. However,

I am here to put to you a proposal—one which, I hope, will benefit us both.'

Lord Sinclair looked at him with the beginning of interest lighting his eyes. 'A proposal?'

Marcus nodded, swirling the brandy around and letting the delicate fumes rise in the air. 'I am well aware of your financial situation. Rents and income from your land are still provided, but it comes in at a trickle and is not sufficient to get you out of the hole you have dug for yourself. I have a bargain to put to you which will wipe out your debt to me and give you some breathing space.'

He had captured all Lord Sinclair's attention. 'I am not a man to turn away a bargain. Let me hear it.'

'It concerns some of the Sinclair land—the water meadows to be precise.'

Lord Sinclair stared at him with astonishment. 'Good Lord. What have the water meadows to do with anything? Although if you intend on making an offer for them, then we could negotiate.'

'That's good to hear. I am interested in coming to an arrangement.'

'You are aware that they are prime pasture?'

'Which is precisely why I have selected that particular stretch of land. Come, Lord Sinclair, think about it. You have just told me that when you have settled your debt to me, with creditors baying at your door and your house mortgaged up to the hilt, you will have no choice but to sell. I am offering you a solution—it is a temporary situation, and it is up to you and your will to stay away from the card tables.'

'You have it all worked out, don't you, Lord Cardell?' Richard said, settling back in his chair.

Marcus nodded. 'They will provide more pasture for livestock on the home farm. According to my steward, the tenant farmers are forever complaining there isn't enough.'

'And what of my own tenant farmers?'

'I'm sure we can come to some arrangement. There's enough pasture to accommodate both.'

'And I pay rent to you—for land that I once owned?'

'Like I said, we'll come to an arrangement satisfactory to both of us.'

Lord Sinclair sat back in his chair, watching as he swirled the amber liquid around the bowl of his glass before looking at Lord Cardell once more. 'An arrangement you say. It seems a queer kind of arrangement to me. It is by no means a fair exchange. I owe you four thousand guineas, Lord Cardell. The water meadows cover fifteen acres. By my reckoning, at roughly fifty pounds an acre, that will leave you out of pocket by something like three thousand guineas. You are either being over generous, or you have something else up your sleeve.'

'I might have. But I ask you to seriously consider the offer.'

'It would seem you leave me with little choice, although how I am going to confront my sister with this, I shudder to think.'

'Come now. You are desperate, are you not, Lord Sinclair? Your present financial situation leaves you with no choice. Settle your debt to me with the land, and you may be able to keep afloat a while longer.'

'You are asking me to sell precious acres, Lord Cardell. It is a difficult decision for me to make.'

'Then let me make it easier for you. Should you agree

to my proposal, then I will work with you to help your situation improve. We are neighbours, after all. Your parents were close friends of my uncle and aunt and frequent visitors to Mulberry Hall. That counts as something to me. As you know I have only recently taken up residence at Mulberry Hall following years of military activity in the Peninsular. Managing an estate this size is daunting, but I look forward to the challenge. I also intend to increase my investments in my family's business ventures. I have a flair for business that will guarantee the prosperity for future generations of Cardells. Which brings me to another proposition I would like to put to you.'

'Ah, I thought there might be a catch. Which is?'

'Your sister.'

Lord Sinclair was unable to conceal his shock. 'Juliet?'

Marcus nodded. 'If you will allow me to offer marriage to her, it will benefit us both. I am a widower with a six-year-old daughter. I wish to remarry and settle down.'

'But why Juliet? Forgive me, Lord Cardell—I applaud your taste—but I can't help thinking that if I were to consent to your proposal, it would be like feeding her to the wolves.'

'Do not underestimate your sister. I strongly suspect that she has the courage to pit her will against any man, including me. I choose your sister to be my wife, and in doing so, I confess that I do not make this decision lightly. I know this is sudden, but I have met her on several occasions, and I have discovered she has a temper, is wilful and of an unpredictable disposition, but beneath that, I sense a softer side to her nature.'

'I agree with what you say. She does have a temper and is rebellious, which is our father's fault. He indulged her every whim and allowed her far too much freedom. Mother and I warned him, but he would only laugh and tell us not to worry, that his little Juliet would turn out to be so beautiful that no one would care how stubborn and wilful she was. She will need gentling with a firm hand by the man she marries, should that man be you.'

A smile tempted Marcus's lips. 'It would be a sin to tame such a prize. It is her spirit that I admire most. May God help me if I do anything to change what's inside her.'

'I'm relieved to hear it. She is naive and innocent and refreshingly virtuous—unhampered by caution or wisdom. You ask my permission to marry her, but having just turned twenty-one, she is of an age where she does not need my permission, although I wonder with some trepidation how she will react when she discovers what you intend.' He cast an apologetic glance at him. 'She has no dowry, which is an embarrassment to me.'

'That is immaterial to me. My desire to marry her was not inspired by thoughts of fortune. I am a wealthy man, wealthy enough to keep my wife in the manner to which she is accustomed. She has even met my daughter in the park. They fed the ducks together and Adele has talked of nothing else since.'

'You are aware that she was engaged to be married, that her betrothed was killed at Albuera.'

'I know she was betrothed but not the identity of the man she was to marry. Who was he?'

'Thomas Waring, the son of a baron. Like you, he

was a second son who made his career in the army. Did you know him by any chance?'

'I knew of him, but I can't recall meeting him.'

'The family's ancestral home is also in Surrey, just ten miles from my own.'

Marcus nodded. 'There are three sons I believe, somewhat wayward.'

'Thomas was that,' Lord Sinclair said, unable to conceal his dislike of the aforesaid gentleman.

'I sense by your tone that he did not come high in your esteem.'

'No. The truth is that I disliked him intensely. He was never without female distractions. His attitude to love and women had always been easy going, take it or leave it. It was his father who insisted that he marry Juliet. The baron is a fiercely proud man and would not have the ancient line of Warings sullied by having any of his sons marry just any woman. Juliet was the daughter of his good friend—my father. She was the kind of woman he wanted Thomas to marry, to bear his grandchildren, not one of those unsavoury doxies he kept company with in London.'

'He was as bad as that?'

'Absolutely. Thomas took his father's advice and also took advantage of Juliet's naiveté and innocence and courted her, admitting that his father was right. Thomas boasted that she would make a perfect wife, the daughter of an earl. No doubt he thought she would be the perfect wife he could keep tucked away in the country while he continued to enjoy the kind of life he had become accustomed to in London and pursue his military career.'

'Did you not try to dissuade her from marrying him?'

'Yes, constantly. But it was useless. She was hell-bent on marrying him. Her ears were deaf to any criticism.'

'As strong minded as your sister is, I can understand that.'

'Absolutely.' His expression became grave. 'You must want to marry her very much.'

'I do. We have only known each other for a short time, but I have developed a high regard for her. I pray she will accept my proposal.'

'Then, what can I say? I have no objections, but you must realise that in the end, the decision is hers to make. She is not easily persuaded. She has also some idealistic notions concerning marriage, and love plays a prominent part, although the circumstances are such that it will leave her with no choice but to marry you. But what if she doesn't? My debt to you will still remain.'

'I would not like your sister to feel obliged to marry me simply to get you out of a hole. That is the last thing I want. Are you able to settle the debt?'

Lord Sinclair became silent, thoughtful as he mulled over his options. 'Yes,' he said at length. 'Yes, I can.'

Marcus nodded slowly; his eyes narrowed. 'Forgive me. I thought you were—'

'What? Penniless. Not quite. I still have the house in St James's Square.'

'You would be prepared to sell it?'

'If I have to. I realise it would only be a temporary solution to settling my debts, but it would be a start and give me a little more time to try and get my house in order. Should Juliet turn you down, then that is what I will do. I love my sister dearly, Lord Cardell. I would not like her to think I was forcing her into a marriage that was not agreeable to her.'

'Then the decision is hers. I will not force her into anything, but should I be fortunate and she accepts my proposal, I promise you that I shall woo her like her most ardent suitor and strive to behave impeccably. I have it on good authority that you are seeking to wed yourself, Lord Sinclair, which tells me you are looking to the future.'

'That is correct. There is a lady who is very dear to me, but my financial situation does not extend to marriage at this present time.'

'Your future will not look so bleak should your sister become my wife. I will do what I can to help you, but you must give me your word that you will keep away from the card tables in future.'

'I know that and I will. I have learned my lesson. Let me assure you that I intend giving the matter of the water meadows serious consideration.'

'I would appreciate that. Now that the most pressing issues have been decided upon, the marriage—should she consent to my proposal—money and business arrangements will be handled by our lawyers.'

Marcus and Richard took their leave of each other, Marcus accepting Richard Sinclair's invitation to dine the following evening to discuss the future with his bride-to-be.

It was early evening when Daphne knocked on Juliet's bedroom door and told her that Lord Cardell had arrived and that he was ensconced in the drawing room with her brother. Having been told by Richard of his meeting with Lord Cardell the previous day at his club and that Lord Cardell had a proposition to make regarding the settling of his IOU, one he hoped Juliet would be in favour of, he had invited him to dine. She told Daphne to inform her brother she would be down shortly. Casting all melancholy thoughts aside, with a firm resolve inside her, she prepared herself to face Marcus Cardell and what he had to offer squarely.

As she went down the stairs, she felt like an actress on the eve of a new performance, all her senses concentrated on making it a success, for on that success, her own and Richard's survival depended. She had to make it the performance of her life, and her instinct told her that if she kept a level head, she could do it. And survival was a question of instinct. *Dear Lord, let it serve me well.*

She entered the drawing room quietly, and although the candles had been lit, the heavy curtains were not yet drawn. Lord Cardell was staring out at the street, his hands joined loosely behind his back. Richard stood by the fireplace raising a glass of brandy to his lips. The soft rustle of her skirts betrayed her presence and Lord Cardell turned sharply. For all the room was quite large and high-ceilinged, his tall broad-shouldered frame appeared to make it smaller. He was as immaculately dressed as he had been at Lord and Lady Wyatt's dinner party with the exception that his long muscular legs were now encased in polished black knee boots. He was standing perfectly still, watching her.

Something in his expression made the breath catch in her throat, and the spell was broken, but the effect of that warmly intimate look in his eyes was vibrantly, alarmingly alive. She did not know this man very well at all, and yet even now he was watching her with a look that was much too personal—and possessive. In the candle-light, his tanned strikingly handsome face had taken on a curiously softer look that she remembered from two days before. But despite this and his polite, correct manner, Juliet sensed something purposeful and intent about him, which troubled her and made her feel uneasy.

'Ah, you're here at last,' Richard said, placing his glass on the mantelpiece.

'I apologise if I've kept you waiting,' she replied, her manner stiff.

'Lord Cardell and I were just reminiscing about the times when he visited his aunt and uncle at Mulberry Hall, Juliet, although Lord Cardell's memory is some-what vague about the couple of times we were there with Mama.'

Marcus nodded slowly as he tried to recollect. 'My memory is not as vague as I thought, although I confess it is still somewhat hazy,' he said, looking at Juliet. 'I remember a young girl—I assume that was you.'

'Yes, it was. I was four or five, I think.'

'Your sister took an aversion to me when we met recently on my arrival at Mulberry Hall. I cannot for the life of me think why.'

Richard laughed. 'Can you not? Then let me enlighten you. I think it stems back to a game of hide and seek when you shoved her into a cupboard. Unfortunately for her, she couldn't get out. The game ended and you went home. It was hours before we found her. She was terribly upset and never forgot it. She still refuses to sleep in the dark. It was a foul thing to do.'

Marcus looked mortified as the memory of the incident came flooding back. 'Yes, it was, but please believe me when I say it would not have been intentional. I have just a vague memory.' He looked at Juliet. 'Was that you?' She nodded. 'You must have been very scared.'

'Who wouldn't be? Locked in a cupboard for hours in the dark.'

'I didn't lock you in.'

'I discovered that afterwards,' Juliet said quietly. 'The door stuck. You were at Mulberry Hall with your brother and a couple of friends. You hardly noticed me, but I did so want you to involve me in your games.'

Marcus frowned, looking at her hard. 'I do remember now. We were on the point of leaving for London when something went wrong with the coach—a wheel came off or something to that effect—so we decided to have a game of hide and seek while it was being fixed. I remember you looking for somewhere to hide—you were excited and keen not to be found, which was when I shoved you into the cupboard, not realising the door would stick. I can imagine your ordeal, your terror.'

'I couldn't believe you had left me in there. It was very dark, and I couldn't get out no matter how hard I tried. I shouted, but no one came. Everyone was taken up with you leaving. I thought someone would miss me and come looking for me. Even a little time in that place was terrifying. Richard found me three hours later.'

'Good Lord! As long as that? I am so very sorry, Lady Juliet. Little wonder you were hostile towards me when we met. How could you not be afraid to be shut up in that place?'

Richard poured a glass of wine and handed it to Juliet. 'Dinner will be announced shortly. In the meantime, I think we should discuss Lord Cardell's proposition, Juliet. I pray you will be in favour of it.'

'So do I,' she replied, sitting on the sofa and taking a sip of wine before placing it on the small table in front of her. Folding her hands in her lap, she looked from her brother to Lord Cardell expectantly, unable to ignore the look of caution that passed between them and beginning to feel decidedly uneasy all of a sudden. 'Well, which one of you is going to enlighten me?'

Lord Cardell glanced at Richard. 'You haven't told her?'

'Er, no, not yet.'

'Then perhaps you should do so—now.'

Juliet stared at her brother. 'Told me? Told me what? Come, Richard. You know how I hate subterfuge of any kind. If there has been a development, then it concerns me. It's not right to keep it from me.'

Somewhat reluctantly Richard began telling her about Lord Cardell's offer regarding the water meadows, how he was prepared to exchange Richard's IOU for ownership of the fifteen acres.

Juliet listened patiently, hardly able to believe what she was hearing. She stared at him through eyes enormous with disbelief. Suddenly, through the turmoil in her mind, something penetrated, something so awful and humiliating that she fervently hoped neither Richard nor Lord Cardell would confirm it. It was a picture of lush green meadows full of strawberry roan cows munching contentedly on the grass. That Lord Cardell was prepared to buy them in exchange for Richard's IOU was indeed a generous offer, but there was something not quite right about it.

'I see,' she said when Richard fell silent. 'It is indeed generous, but isn't it a bit one sided? The water meadows are worth far less than what you owe Lord Cardell, unless…'

'Unless what?' Lord Cardell said, crossing the room slowly and looking down into her upturned face.

'Unless there is something else, something you haven't told me.'

'Yes, there is,' Richard said, giving her a nervous smile before looking somewhat desperately at Lord Cardell to help him out.

'And?' she asked without taking her eyes from the man looming over her.

'I would be honoured if you would agree to be my wife,' Lord Cardell said softly, watching closely for her reaction.

For a moment Juliet's mind went completely blank. She stared at him in confused, disorientated shock. What colour remained in her face drained away. When the words finally sank in, shock and horror brought her surging to her feet. Her eyes blazing, she glared at him, and when she spoke, her voice shook with the violence of her outrage.

'Of all the conceited, vile, despicable, underhanded… Oh!' she seethed, unable to think of any more expletives to portray her animosity. 'You ask me to be your wife in exchange for—let me see—after the price of the land has been deducted, it will be going on for three thousand pounds.'

'Juliet…' Richard said, clearly cursing perverse fate for making what had already been a difficult situation into one that looked fit to worsen. 'Please listen—'

'Listen? Listen to what?' she flared, glaring at her brother. 'I do not feel particularly complimented by Lord Cardell's intentions and even less flattered by the manner of his proposal.'

Richard frowned, clearly disappointed by her reaction. 'Do not be too hasty in your rejection of Lord Cardell. This is a great opportunity. What matters is that he wants to make you his wife. He has a large estate, and you would still be close to Endcliffe House. You would find him most generous.'

Juliet glared at her brother in disgust. 'Good heavens, Richard, you make it sound as if I'd been offered a kingdom. I care nothing for his wealth,' she told him, sounding harsher than she had ever sounded when she addressed her brother. But considering the circumstances, it was important that her feelings had to be made plain to Richard so he wouldn't browbeat her into marriage to Lord Cardell. 'I want nothing from him but the settlement of what is owed by you. Next you will be telling me that the matter is already settled.'

'Well, of course I gave him my permission to go ahead and court you.'

'I am of an age where I no longer need permission from you, Richard. But how could you agree for me to marry a man who was almost a stranger to me until not so very long ago without consulting me?' She looked again at Lord Cardell, who had remained infuriatingly calm so far. 'I find the manner in which you have hatched this plot to secure the water meadows and to marry me behind my back, arrogantly expecting me to fall in with your wishes without argument, both insulting and degrading. You must want to marry me very badly if you are willing to *buy* me,' she retorted, her face a stiff mask as she fought the anger and shame churning within her, and the unbelievable hurt that this might be so.

Lord Cardell cocked a handsome brow as his eyes locked on hers with a frowning intensity. 'Well, you certainly know how to turn a man down, Lady Juliet.' He looked at Richard. 'Would you leave us? I would like to speak to your sister alone.'

Richard looked relieved. 'Of course.'

Battered, humiliated and deeply hurt, Juliet watched him leave the room before looking once more at Lord Cardell, feeling the full weight of her misery, her foolishness and for the time she had wasted trying to understand the turbulent, all-consuming emotions this man always managed to arouse in her. At Lord and Lady Wyatt's dinner party and again at the bookshop, she had felt protected and full of a cool self-assurance, but here, in the intimate privacy of the drawing room, where the only sounds to be heard were the clatter of carriage wheels out in the street and the somnolent tick of the clock on the mantelpiece, she was uncomfortably conscious of the overwhelming presence of this man who had come so suddenly into her life at a time when she was lonely and so very vulnerable, when her spirits had sunk to such a low ebb that it would be so easy for her to turn to anyone who offered comfort.

Suddenly Lord Cardell laughed, a soft, velvety sound. 'You're not afraid of being alone with me, are you?' he asked, his eyes and voice challenging.

Juliet looked at him steadily for a long moment, at his darkly handsome face. Fate was moving quicker than she had anticipated. 'No, I'm not afraid of you, Lord Cardell.'

'Thank goodness. I apologise if my proposal has taken you by surprise. I've been too long in the Peninsular, where we do not always stand on ceremony. Perhaps now that we are alone, we can discuss this matter in a civilised manner.'

Juliet's trembling chin raised to a lofty level as she eyed him coolly. 'I do not think much of your methods of procuring a wife. What you did was vile and contemptible. Your deviousness and deceit do you no credit,' she told him bluntly. 'I want nothing from you—absolutely nothing,' she said tonelessly, the repetition with which she issued this statement already beginning to ring a note of insincerity in her mind, the weakening increasing her anger. Her eyes speared him like shards of steel. 'I will not be paid for—certainly not by a man whom I know will demand value for his money. I have my pride, Lord Cardell, and when it comes to the truth of the matter, I consider myself above the price of fifteen acres of land and three thousand guineas.'

'You are wrong if you think that.'

'Am I?' She raised her brows. 'Richard is to give you his water meadows in part exchange for his debt to you. My own part in this sordid affair is far greater.'

'Believe me when I say that I was not comfortable taking your brother's money. When I proposed a game of cards, I was unaware of his colossal debts. Afterwards, I wanted to make reparation without taking away his dignity.'

'At my expense. Well, it appears you have gotten your wish. I suspected you had your eye on the water meadows when we met that day.'

He nodded. 'Your suspicions were correct. I have gotten my wish, but it is the matter of my proposal of marriage that interests me more.'

The husky sincerity in his deep voice was beginning to make Juliet feel most uncomfortable. The fact that she could even consider entering into a marriage with a man she barely knew was quite outrageous. The fact that she found him far too attractive for her own good roused fresh resentment inside her. She had felt herself being drawn to Marcus Cardell against her will by the compelling magnetism he seemed to radiate, and the memory of his smile and how he had looked at her in the bookshop, how his incredibly light blue eyes had hardly left hers for a moment and the intimacy of his lazy gaze, made her tremble and heat course through her body. She was always stimulated at the way they engaged in a casual repartee she was not accustomed to from her male admirers—not even Thomas, who had been easily bored to converse at length with her on matters that were of interest to her. This had both annoyed and upset her, but she would never have dreamt of saying so.

She reminded herself that Lord Cardell might be the most handsome, exciting man she had ever met—more handsome, even, than Thomas, but then she told herself that he was too conceited, too self-assured by far. He was both these things and more, and she must keep reminding herself of this so that she could keep the fires of resentment alive.

But did she want to? She didn't know that either. The more she delved into the exact nature of her feelings for Marcus Cardell, the more she began to compare him with Thomas and to criticise her former betrothed. Feeling the way she did, it not only seemed silly but wrong and childish to go on resenting Marcus. And why should she? Apart from the poaching incident and the fact that a long time ago he had locked her in a dark cupboard and forgotten about her, he had done nothing to deserve her bitterness and animosity. When the memory of Thomas flashed into her mind and how appalled he would be at a match between herself and the man who was almost a stranger to her, it had a distinctly sobering effect of her but didn't last. Thomas was dead and she must go on, and if marrying someone else who was wealthy would ensure that she could go to bed at night and sleep peacefully without having to worry about money, knowing Endcliffe House and Richard were safe, then she would do it.

He was watching her intently. He smiled, and Juliet was caught up in the powerful charm of his expression. *Dear Lord!* she thought. Her wits must truly have fled if a mere smile from him could bring this spurt of pleasure.

With no small amount of admiration, Marcus watched Juliet struggle to maintain her dignity as she moved away from him, trying hard to hold on to her composure. He should have known that a defiant Juliet Sinclair, with an infuriating stubborn streak and unpredictable disposition, would resent and oppose a proposal of marriage having been made secretly between the prospective suitor and her brother instead of quietly accepting and letting the betrothal run its course until the wedding. Clearly it had been an affront to her pride, and her pride would force her to retaliate by making the whole ordeal as difficult as possible for him.

'Will you at least consider my proposal and what it

would mean for both you and your brother? Can I not persuade you?'

'I care little for your methods and even less for your kind of persuasion. You insult me, Lord Cardell—fifteen acres of land and me thrown into the bargain. I consider myself to be worth more than that. Richard should have negotiated a better deal.'

Despite her haughty stance, Marcus saw that her beautiful amber eyes, which were blazing scornfully at him, were also full of hurt. 'You're right,' he said gently. 'Anyone knowing you would agree that you are worth much more.'

'When you told me you were looking for a wife, I had no idea you would choose me,' she said, looking at him steadily.

'How could you? I didn't even know myself then. It was too soon.'

'Yes, it was. It was arrogant of you to assume I would accept a proposal of marriage made in this manner. I do have a mind of my own.'

His eyes captured hers and held them prisoner. 'I know. That is one of the things that attracted me to you in the first place.'

'And I am more than capable of taking care of myself.'

Marcus moved closer to her. Her wide amber eyes came to meet the mocking smile in his. 'Were you able to do that, Juliet Sinclair, you would not be in the situation you are now,' he pointed out. As clearly as she obviously wanted to throw the statement back in his face, he knew that she could not. Her hauteur faded and was replaced by an expression of pained sadness.

'You think that you know me, Lord Cardell, but you

don't. You have much to learn.' Her voice was small and oddly strained. 'I take objection to anyone who believes I can be bought.'

Refusing to believe that all his romantic plans were about to be demolished, Marcus folded his arms across his chest and perched his hip on the arm of the sofa, arching his brows as he looked at her. 'When I decided to ask you to be my wife and approached your brother, I was not buying you, Lady Juliet. If you believe that, then condemn me for it if you must, but I beg you to pardon me afterwards. I was clumsy and in too much of a hurry. I should have approached the subject of marriage between us more cautiously, not rushed in without consulting you first. Clearly my mishandling of the situation has put your back up, and I cannot, in all fairness, say that I blame you for being angry. I confess to being drawn to you on our first encounter. I tried to discount it and put it down to infatuation, but when I met you again in the water meadows and again at Lord and Lady Wyatt's house, I had to finally face the truth—that I wanted you to be my wife.'

'I cannot for the life of me imagine why. You can have no idea of what marriage to me would mean.'

Going to her, he gently placed his hands on her shoulders, his eyes grave but calm. 'Oh, I believe I do,' he said softly, relieved that she did not pull away from him. 'And please believe me when I say that it was not my intention to pry into your circumstances. Apparently, it is no secret that since your father's death, your brother has squandered money in every direction, leaving you hopelessly in debt, and that in order to survive, you will have to sell that which you hold most dear—Endcliffe

House. I did not know that at the time when I sat down with your brother to a game of cards.'

She nodded dumbly. 'No, I see that now. There will be no dowry, you do know that?'

'That is immaterial to me,' he said, his gaze lingering on the stubborn set to her jaw. 'I know it is the custom for a bride to bring a dowry to her marriage, but it is something I'm not happy with. As a man, it is my responsibility to provide for you, not the other way round. I mean that Juliet,' he said with cool finality. 'You don't mind me dropping the formalities and calling you by your given name?' She shook her head. 'And you must address me as Marcus.'

'I can see you do mean what you say, Marcus. However, I think you carry the issue of pride too far, but since you feel so deeply about the matter, I will let it rest for now.'

Marcus decided there and then that his bride was going to be a challenge if her defiance was anything to go by. 'It is the woman I marry, not what she might or might not bring to the marriage. I recall you saying that you would marry the devil himself if he would settle the debts on Endcliffe House. Did you mean it?'

'Yes, at the time. I realised afterwards that it was a silly thing to say.'

Looking down into her eyes Marcus searched their depths. 'But you were driven to it, I can see that now. In the eyes of the enemy when I fought in the Peninsular, I was likened to the devil many times, but I hope you never have cause to see me as such. Would you prefer to remain as you are—struggling to pay creditors and eventually losing all you hold dear—or marriage to me?

I am offering you a chance to be happy, a future that is secure. I promise you that if you marry me, I will secure your home, since it is so precious to you and if it is to be a condition of your acceptance.' He saw relief flood her eyes and sighed. 'I'm right, aren't I?'

She nodded. 'Yes. Thank you. It means everything to me.'

'Marry me and Endcliffe House will be on your doorstep. I promise I will do all in my power to help your brother get back on his feet and make the Endcliffe estate one to be proud of once more.'

Juliet's eyes widened. There was a softening in their exquisite depths, and he could see some of her belligerence fading.

'You would do that?' she whispered.

'Yes, but your brother must change the way he lives his life. I will neither fund nor advise a gambler.'

'Richard takes after our father, I'm afraid.'

'He was a gambler also?'

'Very much so. Much of what has happened was down to him. His profligacy and lack of judgement had already squandered much of the family fortune before Richard was born. He borrowed money from his friends and was unable to repay it. And so it went on. But Richard has promised me he will change his ways. He understands that and has sworn to me that he will give up gambling. Indeed, there is a lady—the Earl of Bainbridge's daughter, Amelia—they live in Berkshire. Richard is enamoured of her, but her father refuses to consider his suit until he mends his ways, which is another incentive for him not to gamble. But why me? Why do you want to marry me?'

'Because I need a wife.'

'But there are thousands of women in London. Why me? With all my debts, I can only be an encumbrance to you.'

'Because you are the only one who interests me. The only one I want—debts and all. I want to make you smile, to laugh, and I want you to savour all I have to offer.'

'I must be frank with you, although I suspect you already know what I am about to tell you. After all, you do seem to know everything else about me,' she said not unkindly. 'But until a short time ago I was betrothed to someone I loved dearly. He—he was killed in Spain, shortly before we were to have been married,' she finished softly.

Marcus nodded, noting how her face changed when she spoke of him, bringing a softness, a mistiness in her wide eyes, and he felt a sudden rush of resentment towards this past love of hers. His face remained impassive when he next spoke. 'Yes, I did know. But time is a great healer, Juliet. You were both very young. You will forget.' Immediately he regretted saying these words, for her eyes were suddenly charged with anger.

'I may not have the benefit of your experience, but I loved him more than life itself, and I know that I shall never forget him.' Her anger melted and she sighed, lowering her eyes. 'I shall probably never love you, Marcus. I shall probably never love any man, so if,' she said, her face pale and tense, 'knowing this, you still want to marry me, and if you will promise to secure the Endcliffe estate, then I accept. However, you must realise that whatever it costs to get the estate back on its feet, it must be considered a loan. Richard, I am sure, will pay it all back, given time—and good harvests and investments.'

Marcus understood what she was saying and was full of admiration for her steadfast loyalty to the man who had brought her to near ruin. But Richard Sinclair was her brother, and whatever he was guilty of, she would cloak his sins and utter no words that would dishonour him in any way. He smiled a strange, crooked smile and placed his fingers gently beneath her chin, tilting her head, forcing her to meet his gaze. 'I am sure he will, Juliet, but believe me when I say that marriage to you will be payment enough. However, there is something I should mention, and do not think too ill of your brother. He told me that should you decide against becoming my wife, he intends on selling this house to cover his debt to me.'

Juliet stared at him aghast. 'He—he said that?'

'Yes. You see, he doesn't want you to feel under any obligation to me. So, Juliet, you do have a choice.'

Shaking her head, she tried to absorb what he had said. 'But—but we have discussed selling the house and Richard decided against it at this time. I—I had no idea he would do this.'

'Despite his weakness for gambling, you are his sister and he loves you enough to not force you into an unwanted marriage. Knowing this, will you still agree to marry me?'

Lowering her head, she turned from him, biting her bottom lip as she considered this new turn of events. Marcus watched her, praying she wouldn't change her mind. At last, she turned and looked at him, her mind made up.

'I am indeed grateful to Richard—that he would do

this for me, but no, it makes no difference. Selling this house would be a mere drop in the ocean to what he owes his creditors. I have made my decision. I will marry you, Marcus. Indeed I will be happy to be your wife.' Her lips trembled into a smile. 'We hardly got off to a good start, and I made my resentment towards you quite plain.'

He grinned. 'And the reason for that, your brother has just explained to me. I did not lock you in that cupboard. I thought I was doing you a favour. I merely closed the door so you would not be found, and it stuck.'

'And to make matters worse, you forgot about me and went home without another thought for me.'

'For which you have my most profound apology.'

'When I recovered from the ordeal, my mother told me I would forget it. The memory would fade. It was like a nightmare, but it was not real, though for a long time I dreamt I was still in that cupboard.'

'I regret my thoughtlessness for being to blame for you having to endure such a terrible experience. You were a quiet, shy child as I recall, a little like Adele is now.'

'I enjoyed meeting her in the park. She is such a charming little girl.'

He nodded, a troubled look entering his eyes. 'She is and I love her dearly. Unfortunately, I have been apart from her too long. My mother has had full charge of her since Elizabeth, my wife, died. It is my intention to make up for the time we have both lost, and to do that I must spend as much time with her as I am able. I am impatient to involve myself fully in the running of the estate, but my mother refuses to let me take Adele to Mulberry Hall until I have found myself a wife.'

'I see. I am beginning to understand your hasty proposal to me,' Juliet said, her tone resentful once more.

'I would have proposed marriage to you regardless of my mother's demands.'

'You would?'

'Yes. You are an original, and I find you considerably more interesting and amusing than any of those simpering young ladies who were present at Lord and Lady Wyatt's dinner party.'

'Is that a compliment?'

He nodded, smiling. 'The first of many. But I have to ask you how you feel about becoming Adele's stepmother. She was quite taken with you when you met in the park, which is unusual for Adele. She has never reached out to anyone the way she did to you that day. Her care is my concern, and it would help me a great deal knowing that the person who will share her upbringing with me is someone I can trust. Of course, a governess will be found for her in due course. Looking after Adele, worrying about her, wearies my mother, and finding the right nursemaids to care for her has often proved a problem in the past. You may find looking after her demanding, and it will require all your patience.'

'What can I say other than I will do my best to take care of her and make her happy? Children have never played a part in my life, but I am sure we will get along just fine.'

'So you will accept my proposal of marriage?'

She nodded, lowering her eyes. 'Yes,' she said softly. 'It would be foolish of me to refuse.'

'I couldn't agree more. Now,' he said, drawing her

closer, 'I think a kiss is in order to seal the matter. Do you not agree, Juliet?'

Tilting her head, she looked at him, her eyes wide. 'Yes, I have no objections.'

Something clenched painfully in the region of Marcus's heart as he took her hands and lowered his head to hers, having wanted to kiss her since they had met at the Ruskins' house. His lips captured hers. Her mouth was soft and the texture beyond his imagination. He had wondered what it would be like, suspecting that her lips would be sweet and warm, but he could never have guessed at the powerful desire it would awake within him the moment his mouth touched hers.

She gasped and removed her hands from his, her fingers gripped his shoulders. Her entire body responded to his kiss as instinctively she arched closer. Her mouth clung to his, causing his blood to race in his veins, and warmth flooded through him. Marcus had never felt such explosive desire before, and a warning bell rung in his brain. If he did not bring to a halt this sweet moment of desire, he would be unable to stop, and before he knew it, he would have gone too far. One thing he did know was that she desired him as much as he desired her and that she would not be a reluctant bride. He tore his lips away from hers.

'Dear Lord, Juliet, what are you trying to do to me? That,' he said, his voice low and husky, 'was not what your brother left us alone for.'

Juliet sighed and disentangled herself from his arms. 'No, it wasn't, but at least the matter of our marriage is settled now. Richard will be pleased.'

Her brother took that moment to return to the room.

'Time to eat,' he said, rubbing his hands, looking expectantly from one to the other. 'Please tell me the matter I left you to discuss is now settled and we can move on.'

'Yes, Richard. You will be relieved when I tell you that I have accepted Lord Cardell's proposal of marriage, but you really should have told me that should I have refused, you were prepared to sell this house.'

He grinned sheepishly. 'I wanted you to have the choice, Juliet. It was the least I could do. I am pleased you have agreed to wed, that we will be neighbours as well as brother and sister. Now,' he said, rubbing his hands with glee, for things could not have turned out better, 'let us go in to dinner and we can discuss the details.'

'Of course,' Marcus said quietly, his gaze settling on Juliet's face. 'It is my intention for the wedding to take place as soon as possible.'

Juliet glanced at him. A serious note had entered his voice, and he wasn't smiling any more as his eyes held hers. Startled by his frankness, curiously she felt her nervousness subsiding despite the doubts she felt over becoming his wife. She wasn't at all displeased by his suggestion that they marry as soon as may be. And why should she be? she thought wryly. Wasn't this just what she wanted, an opportunity to hold on to all she held most dear?

Marcus Cardell was conscientious and considerate, a man with a strong responsibility for his estate and his daughter, whom he clearly adored and wanted only the very best. He had proven to be the solution to all her worries, yet it was imperative that she keep all her wits about her. Thoughts of Thomas stirred powerful, painful memories and emotions, especially now when she had decided to relegate him to the past.

When they had become betrothed, she had thought he would come back from Spain and they would be married. She realised now she had been living in a fool's paradise. Nothing had turned out as she had hoped. Now she had to think about making a new home for herself— a stepdaughter and connections and what each partner could bring to a marriage as their relationship developed. She would be mistress of Mulberry Hall. Many women would be thrilled to be in her place. She knew what she had to do. She could not sacrifice her brother because of her own selfish reasons of wanting love as well as marriage. For a moment she felt as if she were suffocating. It was like being back in that cupboard.

Chapter Six

In the dining room, the three of them were seated at the table in the centre of which was a bowl filled with pink roses, each one soft and velvety and perfect, giving off the most gentle, heavenly scent. Marcus was both polite and attentive throughout the meal, keeping the conversation impersonal. The more Juliet relaxed, the more she looked at him, letting her gaze linger.

She was beginning to feel all the power of his gaze when he looked at her, and although she had sworn never to become romantically involved with any man again, she was not immune to Marcus's dazzling good looks and strong personality. But she did wonder if it was his urgent need to find a mother for Adele rather than his desire for a wife which had prompted him to propose marriage to her. But whatever the reason, she was committed to the decision she had made, and for all she held dear, she would abide by that no matter how much heartache it brought her in the future.

After the meal, she walked with him to the door, where he turned and took her hand. 'Thank you for the meal, Juliet. I want to assure you that Mulberry Hall is a place that will be worthy of you, and you will be able to visit your old home whenever you wish. I don't want to give you any reason to regret marrying me.'

She nodded as she looked at him, feeling strange emotions stirring in her breast. 'I don't think you'll do that. I only hope I don't give you cause for regret. I do promise to make you a good wife and pray that we shall be tolerably happy.' She smiled wryly. 'After all you've done for me and my brother, the last thing I want is to prove a poor investment.'

Marcus looked at her sharply and his eyes suddenly flamed with anger, at which Juliet immediately regretted her thoughtless, impulsive words, and for the first time since she had known him, she felt fear in her heart. He took both her hands in his own hard grip. His eyes were dark and compelling, forcing her to look into them, and his voice was stern when he spoke.

'Tolerably? An investment? I intend for us to be more than tolerably happy, and I never for one moment considered you an investment. I am not given to pretty speeches, Juliet, and unlike your former betrothed whom you professed to love more than life itself, at this point in our relationship, I cannot offer you that, but what I am offering you is a home, wealth and an estate to be proud of.'

'And I am indeed grateful, Marcus,' she said softly, wishing he had not made that reference to Thomas. Wealth and an estate were all very well and meant that she would live in comfort for the rest of her life without having to worry about how to make ends meet, but they were not at the top of her list when it came to marriage. What she wanted was loyalty and respect, to love and to be loved by her husband, and she could only hope and pray that this would come in time.

'You must understand, Juliet, that I asked you to be my wife because it was you I wanted and for no other reason. The fact that your brother was hopelessly in debt was unimportant. You have told me that you will never love me, that your heart went with the soldier to whom you were betrothed to the grave, and I accept that for now, but time heals many wounds, including the invisible ones, and when it does, you will love again. When you become my wife, when you bear my name, which to me is proud and noble, I shall expect some affection from you and respect, but more than anything else, I want you to be happy.' His voice softened when he looked at her sad, downcast face. He placed his fingers gently beneath her chin. 'Look at me, Juliet.'

Slowly she raised her eyes to his, the candlelight shining into their amber depths. Despite himself, he was touched by the grief he saw there, which brought a bitter taste to his mouth. He sighed deeply, shaking his head slowly, his eyes never leaving hers.

'I am a fool,' he murmured, 'and I have a distinct feeling that I am going to make an even bigger fool of myself where you are concerned, but you cannot live your life searching for something that is gone, that is dead. It is like chasing the wind. You have to let go, Juliet. Do you think you will be punished if, instead, you look for happiness among the living? That you will have to pay penance? For I can tell you that no amount of tears can bring back the dead.'

Juliet stared at him, lulled into a curious sense of well-being by his words as a rush of warmth and gratitude completely pervaded her and her lovely eyes became blurred, shining like stars with her tears. 'I really do not deserve you,' she whispered, 'and I know you are right, only…it's not that easy to let go.'

'Then perhaps this will help,' he murmured, and very slowly he lifted his lean brown hands and placed them on either side of her face. His eyes darkened as he leaned forward, and at his touch Juliet trembled slightly, with nerves or excitement, she didn't know which, but she did not draw away from him as he placed his mouth on her soft, quivering lips, cherishing them with his own slowly and so very tenderly. His gentleness kindled a response and a warm glow spread over her, but also a fear began to possess her, a fear not of him but of herself and the dark, hidden feelings he had aroused.

When he finally drew away, she remained unmoving, as though still suspended in that kiss, her lips moist and slightly parted. She gazed wonderingly into his eyes, and for the first time since she had met him, the grief was gone from hers, which were very bright with unshed tears. 'How do you think your mother will feel about a marriage between us? She might not take too kindly to you marrying your penniless neighbour.'

'My mother will be delighted. She was not only impressed by you when we met in the park but the way you interacted with Adele and she with you. In fact, my daughter has spoken of nothing else since.'

'Really? I look forward to meeting her again and getting to know her. I—I must insist on a modest wedding, Marcus. I don't want any fuss.'

'It suits me perfectly. The sooner we leave London, the better I shall feel.'

'Then what can I say. I hope I shall be worthy of Mulberry Hall, and I promise to do my best to make you a good wife and stepmother to Adele.'

Marcus's lips twisted in a thin smile. 'I am sure you will, but I have to admit that it does nothing for my pride or self-esteem, knowing it's my wealth and not my charming self that you want. However, I do think we both have something to give.'

His face suddenly became a hard, inscrutable mask, and something Juliet could not recognise flickered behind his eyes, and again she sensed in him something purposeful, something vital that made her feel uneasy, and it came to her that Marcus Cardell was not a man to run afoul of. Ignoring this moment of insight and preferring to think instead of the kindness he had shown her and her brother and his obvious sincerity, she fixed him with a steady gaze. Yes, she would marry him. With everything collapsing about her ears, it was the perfect answer to the many problems that beset her.

But how different it had been when she had loved Thomas, with all the passionate intensity of her youth. How she had yearned to marry him, to learn all the overwhelming joys that love had to offer. But this was to be a different kind of marriage—positive and cold. It was to be a union of two people drawn together by circumstances. She wouldn't think about what would come later but would be content for now, knowing the Endcliffe estate and her home was safe.

Marcus's news of his forthcoming marriage to Juliet Sinclair was warmly welcomed by his mother. The fact that Adele liked Lady Juliet and was happy to be in her company was an added bonus and a great relief to her. She had a few qualms about the part Marcus was to play in assisting Lord Sinclair to clear his debts, but she was sure this would be overcome in time should the young man abide by his promise to keep away from the gaming tables.

When Juliet arrived at the house to be presented to her once more, she received her warmly. Attired in a hyacinth blue gown, Juliet stood watching her future mother-in-law, pale with apprehension. Marcus sighed with relief as his mother smiled to put her at her ease, her eyes tender, for she was determined to befriend this lovely young woman who had brought her son once again to the brink of matrimony. Although he wondered how his mother would feel if she knew that beneath Juliet's pleasant exterior, with her soft feminine elegance, there was a will every bit as strong and stubborn as his own.

Juliet entered the Cardell townhouse with trepidation. She was surrounded by wealth: oil paintings of ancestors and country scenes on the walls, carved furniture gleaming with polish, marble underfoot and chandeliers above.

'I am delighted to welcome you into the family, Juliet, and look forward to getting to know you better.'

'Thank you,' Juliet replied a little shyly, seeing she need not have worried about meeting the dowager countess once again, and finding her kindness comforting. She was so gently solicitous that she found herself warming towards her. 'You are very kind.'

'And you are extremely lovely, my dear.' The dowager countess's eyes twinkled. 'Now I begin to understand how impossible it was for Marcus to resist you.'

Juliet flushed, embarrassed by her words, and a frown

of disapproval appeared on Marcus's face at his mother's outspokenness, but she laughed lightly, well used to her son's disapproving looks and knowing how to temper them. It was clear to Juliet that she was not in the least sorry that her words might have caused either of them to feel a sense of awkwardness.

'Marcus has made me aware of the circumstances of why you are to marry, of your brother's unfortunate situation and Marcus's willingness to forgo the debt your brother owed him in exchange for some land and to help set him on his feet, Juliet,' she said on a more serious, gentle note, 'which is unfortunate, and I have to say that where marriage is concerned, I cannot countenance such behaviour. I know how forceful Marcus can be, and I do hope he has not made you feel that you are under any obligation to marry him.'

Juliet flushed as she strove to answer the question. 'Why, I—I—no, of course I'm not. He has been most generous.'

'I'm relieved to hear it. Time presses, however, and it is not for me to sit in judgement or to interfere in something which is entirely between your two selves. That is your affair. But I do hope you feel deeply enough about each other to marry in these circumstances.'

Juliet's gaze met Marcus's, but she could read nothing in it. The dowager countess's remark spoken in a quiet, imperious tone would have been enough to daunt even the strongest heart, and Marcus was no exception. Although not the type of man to be easily intimidated by a woman, and had it been said by anyone else, he would have launched a bitter attack. But this was his mother, whom he loved and respected, and he took her gentle reproach lightly, prepared to be tolerant, and Juliet suspected that his mother would not overstep the mark by antagonising her son.

'Is the sermon over, Mother?' Marcus asked tersely.

A smile lit up her face and she laughed easily. 'Absolutely. I promise. It only leaves me to wish you both every happiness. Marcus tells me he is to take you to Mulberry Hall immediately after the wedding, Juliet. Is that not so, Marcus?' she said, looking once more at her son, her seriousness of a moment before having disappeared.

'That is my intention. It is to be a modest affair, but when news of the marriage gets out, it is bound to create a stir. It is my wish to avoid the inevitable curiosity and questions. Besides, I am anxious for Juliet and Adele to become better acquainted—the sooner the better.'

'I agree. You will like living at Mulberry Hall, Juliet. It's a lovely old house, although as you are already acquainted with the place, you don't need me to sing its praises, but the estate has been in my mother's family for generations. When my brother died without issue and with Marcus's elder brother William already ensconced at Cranswick Hall, and with more titles than is good for any man, it seemed only right that Mulberry Hall should pass to Marcus. Adele is adorable, but unfortunately, I cannot spend as much time with her as I would like to. She is a quiet, shy little girl, but she is young and will soon warm to you. Being many years younger than myself, you might understand her better than I do.'

With a maid in attendance, Adele entered the room quietly. At first, she only had eyes for her adored father, who swept her into his arms and gave her a fierce hug, inhaling the sweet innocence of her before setting her on her feet once more. Marcus's pride as he looked at his daughter could not have been more evident. It was plain for Juliet to see that he loved his daughter and felt a profound need to protect her. Taking Adele's hand, he drew her forward.

'There is someone I want you to meet,' he said gently to the little girl. 'This is Juliet. You remember meeting her in the park? She is to be my wife—your stepmother.'

Adele's face broke into a wide smile when she saw Juliet. Marcus had told her that Adele couldn't remember her own mother and would be unsure what a stepmother was, but at that moment, when Juliet smiled and moved towards her, it didn't matter. As Juliet became reacquainted with Marcus's daughter, looking beyond her to where his mother sat, watching the proceedings closely, Juliet saw her eyes were bright with tears—of gratitude or thankfulness that the child would be well cared for. Juliet thought she saw a lightening of her spirits, as though a great weight had been lifted from her shoulders.

Unable to believe their good fortune, throughout the days leading up to his sister's wedding to Lord Cardell, Richard walked with a new spring in his step. His relief in knowing his estate would not have to be sold after all was enormous, and he lost no time in making it quite clear to Juliet that he thought she had done well for herself. Better, he told her, than if she had married Thomas Waring. His feelings regarding her one-time betrothed had been far from favourable.

However, she would be devastated if she knew what

Richard had discovered from an acquaintance he had met at his club, that Thomas had not perished in Spain after all but was still alive. Apparently, he had been wounded and taken prisoner by the French and rescued by the partisans, where he had lingered in the arms of a dark-haired beauty who had made his time spent in their camp pleasurable—so much so that he had been reluctant to be parted from her.

May God and Juliet forgive him, but he could not tell her, not until after she was safely married to Marcus Cardell. He would pray that Thomas, who, according to his acquaintance, had gone directly to his home, Amberley Park, in Surrey to see his parents, was in no hurry to come to London. But Richard's instinct told him that what he was doing was right. It was far more advantageous to him that Juliet married Marcus Cardell, and she would be far happier with Marcus than she ever would be with Thomas.

If Thomas had been anything like decent, he would not be deceiving her in this way, and besides, he thought as renewed anger possessed him when he remembered how he had not even bothered to write to inform Juliet that he was still alive, it would serve him right when he finally condescended to come to town and found Juliet had married someone else, someone richer even that his own arrogant, conceited self.

The wedding was to take place the following day. Having written to Lydia to inform her of her forthcoming marriage, she arrived to help Juliet prepare for her big day. She swept into the house, her bunches of ringlets bouncing wildly as she moved, her bright eyes shining. Juliet hugged her warmly.

'Thank you for coming, Lydia. I can't tell you how glad I am to see you.'

'And I can't tell you how astounded I was to learn you are to marry the exquisite Lord Cardell. I couldn't believe it,' but then she held Juliet at arm's length. 'It is true, isn't it? You're not jesting?'

Juliet laughed, taking Lydia's hand and leading her into the drawing room. 'Would I jest about so serious a matter?'

'I guess not.' Lydia sighed, a kind of wonder in her eyes as she looked at Juliet, hardly able to believe that what she had told her was true. 'But I recall you saying that after Thomas died in Spain, you'd never marry.'

'I know. I said a lot of things when he was killed, and I meant every word I said—then. But now I have the future to think about. However distasteful the prospect, I thought that if I must marry, if it is not for love, then it must be to someone I could respect. But the most important thing is that he must be rich. Marcus Cardell is all that. Tell me you understand, Lydia.'

'Of course. I can understand that. But to think that you were on the point of penury and now, well, look at you. Your position is most enviable.'

'Oh, Lydia, no one is more shocked than I am at the speed with which everything has happened.'

'Where is he?'

'Who?'

'Why, the exquisite Marcus Cardell, of course.'

'I don't have the faintest idea. I won't see him again until I arrive at the church. But I am so lucky, Lydia.

Just think, I will be living close to Richard and End-cliffe House. I'm going to miss living there, but I know it will be well taken care of with Richard and his future wife—if her father agrees to his suit once he has found his feet. Hopefully my dear brother will become a re-formed character and he will have no objections. I have a lot to thank Marcus for. What he has offered me is a lifeline. I have to take it. He's been so kind, so consider-ate, and I believe he is genuinely fond of me. Why else would he have asked me to marry him?'

'Why else indeed? You know, you've changed, Juliet,' Lydia said on a more serious note.

'Changed? I dare say I have changed a little. You see, I've made up my mind to put the past behind me and look to the future. My marriage will not be clouded with romantic thoughts—at least not for the present. I've been a captive of my emotions once and I vowed never again, and yet,' she said, a soft flush mantling her cheeks when she thought of Marcus and the times when he had kissed her. 'To feel like that—well, I must confess that it was quite wonderful, and I wouldn't mind in the slight-est if I could experience it again. But for the present all my aspirations must be realistic. It is important that I marry someone I can trust, someone I can lean on, and if Marcus can do that for me, then I shall try very hard to love him, although I have to admit that marriage to him scares me a bit.'

'You'll soon get used to it.'

'I do realise how lucky I am, but everything has a price, even happiness, and if I have to leave Endcliffe House in order to preserve it, then I am ready to pay that price.'

* * *

The day of the wedding dawned sunny and warm. The ceremony was scheduled for midday, and beyond the occasional moment of panic, Juliet felt a strange detachment as Lydia and Daphne fussed with her appearance.

Dressed in a simple gown of champagne-coloured silk gauze and a small flowered headdress, Juliet married Marcus Cardell. Because she had wanted as little fuss as possible, the wedding party was small. The only people present in the church were close family and just a handful of close friends. Richard walked her proudly down the aisle to meet the man who would be her husband. Marcus's brother, William, the Earl of Cranswick, who had come up from West Sussex to see his younger brother married, acted as Marcus's groomsman. His wife, Alice, had not accompanied him since she was close to giving birth to their third child. A serious-minded man, not as tall as Marcus, William had a pleasant disposition. Welcoming her into the family, he had shown her courtesy and friendliness, putting her at her ease at once.

Looking terribly handsome and resplendent in a claret coat and grey trousers, Juliet was aware of nothing but Marcus's close proximity and his firm hands when they'd slipped the gold wedding band gently but firmly on her finger, and for the first time since entering the church she'd met his eyes, darkly serious and intent. She had to quell the ache that rose inside her when she remembered her dreams of how her wedding day would be if Thomas had not disappeared so quickly and tragically from her life.

There was nothing romantic as she had always imagined, nothing but a seal on a promise that must be kept. When Marcus placed his hand over hers, she felt herself possessed. To this man she had committed her life and there would be no going back. But then, becoming aware of his power, his strength, a feeling of wanting to belong to someone, to be cherished almost overwhelmed her. Feeling herself falling under some kind of spell and resentful of it, she was tempted to flee from the church, anything to escape these new, alien feelings Marcus had brought to life inside her.

She knew he was trying to snare her—it was like a clarion warning in her mind—and she knew it would be wise to flee, but she simply couldn't. It was as if her feet were made of clay. Standing there, his hand holding hers, she suddenly realised that she didn't want to run away, that without Marcus, there was an emptiness in her life that she did not want to admit. Her own lack of discipline and restraint frustrated her, but she wasn't entirely certain whether to blame it on him or herself. She liked him to touch her and welcomed his attentions—and the heat and craving he awakened in her.

When the cleric pronounced them man and wife, with the collective eyes of all those present anticipating his next move, Marcus leaned forward to place a light kiss on her lips so as a seal to their union. His mouth was gentle on hers, as befitted the formal occasion in front of witnesses. Their duty done, they departed in the waiting carriage to St James's Square for a private wedding breakfast.

Alone in the carriage with Marcus, Juliet felt as if the whole day had taken on an air of unreality, and she found it almost impossible to believe that the man sitting next to her was now her husband. She had married him but did not know him well. She glanced obliquely at him, telling herself how fortunate she was when she gazed at his clean-cut profile and proud, handsome features. Turning her mind to the physical side of their marriage, of her duty, and all that would come later, she experienced a curious mixture of terror and excitement.

She remembered how, when he had kissed her, he had made her feel suddenly alive, rekindling desires she had suppressed for so long. Desires that she had told herself she would never experience again after Thomas, which proved how little she knew her own body. The memory of those kisses brought colour flooding to her cheeks, and she looked away, but too late, for at that moment Marcus looked at her and laughed softly. Taking her hand in his own, he lightly touched the narrow golden ring on her finger before raising it to his lips.

The simple act of reassurance released her from her anxiety and she began to relax. The cold numbness that had gripped her from the moment she had left for the church began to melt, and the feel of his lips on her fingers sent a strange thrill soaring through her.

'Tell me what you were thinking. What made you look away?'

'Oh, nothing really. I was only thinking how fortunate I am.'

'Are you happy?'

She nodded. 'Yes. Yes, I am.'

'No regrets?'

'No, none that I can think of.'

He contemplated her for a moment, and Juliet was riveted by his gaze. 'Did I tell you that you look exquisite?'

'No, not yet.'

'Then I will tell you now. You are beautiful, Juliet, like some perfect work of art.'

She laughed, a soft flush on her cheeks. 'I'm sure every groom says that to his bride on their wedding day. I am no more beautiful than any other.'

His eyebrows rose. 'I think I should be the judge of that, and perhaps they don't all mean it as sincerely as I. It is no simple passion that torments me, Juliet, but an ever-increasing desire to have you with me every moment.' Drawing her close, his eyes darkened as they fastened on her soft lips, moist and slightly parted, revealing her small white teeth.

His voice was husky when he spoke, which sent a tremor through Juliet. His breath was warm and close to her ear. She could not remain unmoved by the deep, ca-ressing tone that was like a seductive whisper. Looking into his eyes, warm and liquid with desire, she saw what was in them, and she was moved and excited by it. Over the last couple of days, she had thought of him constantly, wondering what it would be like when she was his wife in the true sense, and now that he was close to her, he was more attractive, more desirable than ever, and the ur-gency to be even closer to him was more vivid than it had ever been. She swallowed, feeling her body grow warm.

'Would you mind if I kissed my wife now that we are alone? For I fear that when we arrive at the house, I shall not have you to myself for—let me see—at least seven or eight hours.'

Juliet's eyes widened in mock amazement and her mouth formed a silent O. 'That long?' and she smiled softly. 'Then in that case, I think you should.'

Sliding his hand around her waist, he pulled her towards him, his eyes dark and full of tenderness. He did not kiss her at once but studied her face, close to his, with a kind of wonder, his eyes gazing intently into hers before settling on her parted lips, which he at last covered with his own, his arm about her waist tightening, drawing her closer, until their bodies were moulded together and Juliet could feel the hardness of his muscular body. Her heart was beating so hard that she was sure he must feel it. His lips, moist and warm, caressed hers, becoming firm and insistent as he felt her respond, kindling a fire inside her with such exquisite slowness, a whole new world exploding inside her. She raised her arms, fastening them around his neck, returning his kiss, her lips soft and clinging, moving upon his in a caress that seemed to last for an eternity.

Marcus's lips left hers, and he buried them in the soft hollow of her throat. 'I want you, Juliet. You can have no idea how much.' His voice was a soft murmur, a gentle caress, his mouth close to her own once more. He heard the sharp intake of her breath, but she did not pull away from him, and when he lifted his head and looked at her, his eyes burned with naked desire.

Never had Juliet been as aware of another human being as she was of Marcus at that moment. Each of them was aware of a new intensity of feeling between them, a new excitement, both of them victims of the overwhelming forces at work between them. They stared at each other for a second of suspended time, which could as well have been an hour or two, and Juliet had a strange sensation of falling. She saw the deepening light in his eyes and the dark, silken lashes. She saw the defined brows and wanted to touch his face, to know him. She trembled inside, feeling as if she was on the threshold of something unknown, which caused fear to course through her but also something else, a longing so strong that she wanted to pull him towards her, for him to kiss her with all the savage intensity of his desire.

Then slowly, almost haltingly, Marcus lowered his mouth to hers once more in a kiss that warmed her to the centre of her being. Parted lips, tender and insistent, caressed hers, moulding and shaping them to his own while his arms wrapped round her. She had been kissed before by Thomas and then again by Marcus, but never like this. Those kisses had not aroused the passion that the kiss she had just experienced did, a passion so primitive, which swept through her. A passion almost beyond her control, evoking feelings she had never felt before, and this new awareness of her own desire shook her to her very core.

Seeing the hunger in her eyes, Marcus sighed deeply. 'So, I was right.'

'Right?' she whispered. 'What do you mean?'

'That the first time I saw you, to me, a stranger, you seemed to have everything and, I imagined, every young man in London at your feet. But you seemed remote, as if only part of you was alive. There was also a wilfulness about you, a stubborn tenaciousness that told whoever got in your way to have a care. You became an enigma to me, Juliet, and I was determined to get to know you better, convinced that behind that cool façade you presented to me and the world, there beat the heart of a warm and passionate woman. And, it seems, I was right. I hope you will never have cause to regret your marriage to me.'

'How could I? You have given me everything I could possibly want.'

His dark brows knit together as he considered her thoughtfully, a shadow of doubt darkening his eyes. 'Everything?'

Just for a moment her eyes clouded, but quickly they became clear, as if she had suddenly come to a decision, and then she looked at him directly, a determined tilt to her chin. 'Well, almost everything.' Smiling, she leaned forward and kissed him gently on the lips, just as the carriage came to a halt outside the Sinclair townhouse. 'Companionship, loyalty and love are important in a marriage, Marcus. It's what I want—what I consider important between two people who are to spend the rest of their lives together, and I am certain that will happen between us with time.'

On leaving the church, Marcus had allowed his gaze to linger on Juliet's features, unable to put his feelings into words. His throat constricted at the picture she presented as his bride. He observed how young she looked, how pale and exquisite her face was against the upholstery, making him realise that it would be virtually impossible to keep his hands off her now she was his wife. Pray God, he thought, let me be worthy of her. Before today she had been lovely, but today, as his bride, she was exquisitely perfect.

When he had swept her into his arms in the carriage, he had kissed her slowly, feeling her lips open under his own. In that instant he felt the suppleness of her body, her breasts pressed against him, and when he felt her surrender, a melting sweetness had flowed through his veins. When he finally raised his head, her eyes had lifted to his, and the gentle yielding he saw in their amber depthsd melted his heart. Already he was anticipating the time when all the guests had departed and they would be alone.

On entering the Sinclair house in Henrietta Street, Lydia, who had been following close behind the newlyweds with Richard, hugged Juliet.

'Congratulations, love, and to you too, Lord Cardell. I sincerely hope you will be happy together. 'You made a lovely bride, Juliet.'

'Seconded by me.' Richard pecked his sister's cheek and shook Marcus's hand.

The wedding breakfast was a prolonged and happy affair, the hired butler and extra staff presiding over the proceedings and making sure everyone was taken care of. The food was exquisite, the champagne cold and delicious, the toasts numerous. Juliet chatted and graciously accepted the congratulations given her by the guests and Marcus's brother, all the time aware that the moment when she would be alone with her husband was drawing closer.

Marcus's mother was clearly satisfied and highly delighted that her second son was married again.

'With your brother in charge of the estate, Juliet,' she said when she managed to get the newly-weds alone, 'your dear mother would have been well pleased. I shall look forward to visiting you at Mulberry Hall, but not too frequently. I want you and Marcus to get to know each other and familiarise yourself with the house without me breathing down your neck.'

'You will be welcome always,' Juliet said.

'I know I will, my dear,' the dowager countess said, looking fondly at her new daughter-in-law. 'I hope you will like living at Mulberry Hall. It is natural that you will be filled with trepidation, but you will soon settle down and grow to love the place.'

'I'm sure I shall,' Juliet said, smiling.

Marcus looked at her, his eyes warm and full of affection for his bride. 'And she will love it all the more because I am there,' he teased softly. He arched a brow, amused when Juliet gave him a feigned look of exasperation.

'Why, I see your conceit has not diminished now you are a married man, Marcus,' she chided playfully.

'You're not impressed?'

'Not in the least. You're a complete rogue.'

Marcus gazed at her, his eyes amused. 'I do not deny it. But it cannot bother you too much, otherwise you wouldn't have fallen so readily for my irresistible charm,' he teased, and he smiled, the kind of smile that would melt any woman's heart.

Juliet returned his smile a little shyly. 'I am beginning to see that I was a complete fool to get involved with you. You're quite outrageous.'

'Absolutely,' he grinned.

'He always was,' commented his mother in complete agreement.

As they moved among the guests, Marcus was charming, regaling them with fascinating stories of his time in the Peninsular, taking care not to dwell on battles fought which had taken so many men's lives on both sides. They chatted and laughed until, replete and exhausted, the time came for the guests to depart.

Juliet and Marcus were to spend their wedding night at the Sinclair residence. Tomorrow they would leave London for Mulberry Hall. When the time came for the Countess and Adele to leave for the Cardell residence, Marcus had no intention of going with them, until Adele became tearful on being parted from her beloved father. She implored Marcus not to leave her. Concerned that the day's excitement might have proven too much for her, he gave in to her childish appeal and agreed to accompany her, promising Juliet he would return as soon as she had been put to bed.

Seeing Richard hovering in the doorway, seeming undecided whether he should leave for his club so that the newly-weds could be alone, realising she had hardly exchanged a word with him all day, Juliet went to him.

'The day has gone well, Richard, don't you agree?'

'Absolutely. As you know I intend to make myself scarce so you and Marcus can have the Sinclair house to yourselves. I am to reside with a friend for the time being who has put his house at my disposal.'

'Before you leave, come into the sitting room with me, Richard. It's the first time we've had a chance to be alone together all day.'

Juliet relaxed on the sofa, watching Richard with concern as he sat opposite, sipping a brandy. That he wasn't quite himself was obvious. He fidgeted with his cuffs and crossed and uncrossed his legs, which he always did when nervous. They made small talk for several minutes about the wedding and other unimportant matters, until Juliet could stand it no longer.

'What's wrong, Richard?'

'Wrong?' he asked, somewhat surprised.

'Yes, something's amiss. I can tell.'

He laughed nervously, taking another gulp of his brandy. 'Nonsense. Nothing's wrong,' he replied, trying to sound casual.

Juliet studied his face closely. 'Come, Richard. It's me, remember? I know you too well. I always know when something is not quite right. You cannot deceive me. You've been on edge ever since we left the church. What is it?'

He shrugged. 'Nothing. But if you think I've been on edge, then it's probably just the excitement over the wedding and what your marriage to Marcus means for our future.'

'Are you sure that's it?' asked Juliet, not convinced. 'And that it doesn't concern me?'

'You. Of course not.'

Juliet shook her head and sighed. If there was something wrong and Richard didn't want to tell her, then she couldn't make him. 'Well, if you're sure.'

'Yes, I am sure. Don't trouble your head about me. You have other things to think of now. Your husband, for one. You're so lucky.'

'Yes, you're right. I am lucky, aren't I? And you will be too, when Amelia's father agrees to your suit. My marriage to Marcus will make a difference, I am sure of it. But although you say otherwise, I am still not convinced there isn't something you have to tell me.' Hearing a carriage out in the street come to a halt followed by loud knocking on the door, she sighed. 'Whatever it is will have to wait. I think we have a visitor. More than likely, one of the guests forgot something.'

Getting to her feet, she crossed to the window and

drew back the drapes a little, peering out at the gathering dusk, noticing the long shadows cast by the surrounding buildings. She sighed, about to turn away, but her eye was drawn to a large carriage in front of the house. The horses were lathered and the carriage travel-stained, indicating that it had come a long way. Juliet suddenly turned icy cold when she recognised the familiar coat of arms emblazoned on the door panel. It was the Waring crest.

She stared at it, unable to believe what she saw, but then she told herself that it must be some relation of Thomas's, his father, even, and she reproached herself for not having written to tell him of her marriage. Letting the curtain fall back, she turned and faced the door. A footman stood aside to allow the visitor to enter.

'Lord Thomas Waring, my lady.'

Juliet froze, one hand rising to her throat, the colour draining from her face, her lips, and her eyes fastened on the man who had entered the room sporting a gold-knobbed walking cane. He was quite tall, with a languid, aristocratic grace, his attire elegant. He wore a dark blue coat, and there was white linen spilling from his neck and wrists.

Juliet stared at him, unable to believe her eyes, remembering so vividly the pale blond hair falling in a heavy wave over his forehead and the handsome features, the cynical smile on his lips and hooded lazy grey eyes. She must be dreaming. It could not be true. How could fate play such a cruel trick? Thomas was dead and she was married to someone else.

Chapter Seven

Thomas looked at her and smiled lazily. Juliet felt all the blood drain from her face and with one hand frozen at her throat she watched, feeling an agonising wrench in the region of her heart, as he moved farther into the room. Then she knew her eyes were not deceiving her.

'Thomas,' she breathed, a hazy mist floating before her eyes, darkness threatening to engulf her. 'It—it cannot be you. They told me you were dead.'

He raised his brows in mock surprise. 'Did they really? I assure you, Juliet, that—as you see—I am very much alive.'

It was then that Juliet gave a desperate cry and crumpled to the floor.

Alarmed, Richard hurried to her and fell to his knees beside her, taking her cold hand in his while raising his face to Thomas Waring, utter dislike blazing from his eyes. 'Why did you have to come here? Why couldn't you leave her alone?'

Very slowly Thomas smiled, a thin, cruel smile, his eyes like ice. 'I shouldn't have thought it necessary for me to have to explain my reasons to you, Richard, and, besides, Surrey is a trifle dull just now. Why did you not tell Juliet that I am alive?'

'I didn't want her to know. I hoped and prayed she'd never find out. My God, man! She's better off without you.'

'How could she not find out? This is London, Richard, and gossip spreads like quicksilver. Anyway, shouldn't she be the judge of whether or not she's better off without me? I doubt she would agree with you,' he drawled.

Reassured that Adele was suffering no after effects from the excitement of the wedding, Marcus had returned to the Sinclair townhouse and was going to join Juliet when he heard her strangled cry and halted in shock. Seeing the door to the sitting room open, he hurried inside to find her lying in a crumpled heap on the carpet with Richard by her side. His face clouded with concern.

'Juliet?'

'She's all right,' Richard said quickly. 'She's fainted, that is all.'

Marcus picked her up effortlessly, cradling her in his arms, her head resting against his shoulder. It was only as he straightened up that he became aware of the presence of someone else standing across the room. At first, taken unawares, Marcus was startled by the man's presence, and it was when their eyes met that recognition came to each man simultaneously.

'Permit me to introduce you,' Richard said, his face ashen.

'I think the social distinctions can be ignored, thank you, Richard,' Marcus said tightly. 'We are already acquainted, although his name escapes me.'

'I don't believe we were introduced,' Thomas said, his cold grey eyes narrowed with murderous fury. 'So, it is you. The man I had the misfortune to encounter on my journey back to London.'

'The same, and I observe you have discarded your uniform.'

'Temporarily, I assure you,' he replied, his voice like steel. 'We have an account to settle, you and I. You cannot have forgotten.'

'I have not, and neither have I forgotten the sordidness of the situation in which we met, and I have no doubt you are still the same black-hearted villain who tried to force himself on a defenceless young woman. As I recall, the account was settled. Now, it appears Juliet has received quite a shock. I suggest you leave this house before I do something I would not regret.'

'Wait,' Richard said as he was about to turn away, his face a picture of confusion. 'Marcus, have you no idea who this is?'

'No, nor do I wish to.'

Richard ignored his cutting remark. 'It is Thomas Waring. Thomas, this is Marcus Cardell, Lord Cardell the Earl of Ashleigh. Thomas was betrothed to Juliet before he went to the Peninsular and was reported killed.'

The tension inside the room was ominous, an eerie silence wrapping itself about them.

With anger pouring through his veins like acid, Marcus did not reply at once. He just stared at Thomas Waring, showing neither shock nor surprise, his face a hard, inscrutable mask, the muscles tight. 'Dear God,' he said when he finally did speak, his voice not without contempt. 'How unfortunate for Juliet.'

Still holding Juliet, who was beginning to stir in his arms, he gently laid her on the sofa and stood looking down at her, relieved to see that some of the colour had returned to her face. He was well aware of all the torment, the suffering she would feel when she came to, and it tore at his heart.

The first person Juliet saw when her eyes fluttered open was Marcus, his dark form staring down at her, his eyes full of pain and concern but also something else, which puzzled her—understanding and pity. An anxious Richard stood beside him. Juliet blinked her eyes to clear the mist, wondering what she was doing lying on the sofa, and then she remembered Thomas and that he had come back to her, and her heart leapt and began racing as her eyes moved around the room, searching for him.

Thomas stood, seeming very much at ease at the far side of the room. She stared at him, unable to speak for what seemed to be an eternity, and her eyes shone with the unbelievable comfort of knowing he was alive, and yet why, when he looked the same, did she feel that she was looking into the face of a man she did not know— a stranger?

Seeing her open her eyes, Thomas moved towards her, ignoring Marcus, whose face wore a hard mask of disapproval. With Richard, he stepped back to observe the reunion between his wife and her one-time betrothed.

Aware of and slightly amused by his audience, arrogant in his demeanour, Thomas dropped to one knee beside the sofa and took Juliet's hand in his own. Slowly she reached out with the other and gently touched his cheek with the tips of her fingers to convince herself that it really was him.

'It is you,' she whispered. 'It really is you.'

'Yes. I apologise if my sudden appearance gave you a shock, but I came as soon as I was able.'

'Of course you did,' Richard uttered, unable to conceal his scorn at this barefaced lie. 'But you were reported killed.'

'That I didn't know until later.'

'What happened?' Juliet asked. 'Please, tell me.'

'It was during the battle at Albuera that my horse was shot from under me, and afterwards grapeshot shattered my leg. I was also injured in the chest. I lost consciousness, and I knew nothing else until I came to, only to find myself a prisoner of the French.'

A deathly pallor spread over Juliet's face. So often she had pictured him lying wounded on some battlefield or other, his life's blood ebbing away. She couldn't bear to think of it. 'How did you get back to your regiment? Did you escape?'

'No, it was later, when I began to recover, that I was rescued by the partisans. They came under cover of darkness and freed several prisoners. They returned me to my regiment, but it was only to find that most of it had been wiped out.'

'How dreadful. Are you going back?'

'Yes. I was sent home to recuperate and shall return when the officers who returned with me to England have recruited fresh men.' He smiled down at her. 'Did you miss me, Juliet, as much as I missed you?'

'Yes. Yes of course I did.' Even as she said this, she was vividly aware of Marcus standing behind Thomas as if turned to stone, his hands clenched by his sides, but she did not look at him—she dared not.

Taking her hand, Thomas raised it to his lips and

kissed her fingers. 'Would you agree for us to be married before I return to Spain?'

Before she had time to reply, Marcus's voice lashed the air like the crack of a whip. 'That is enough.'

Juliet glanced at him, at his taut face and the thin line of his lips. It was clear he was unable to watch a moment longer this intimate, touching scene and the possessive way Thomas was holding her hand.

'And I would be obliged if you would take your hands off her.'

Thomas turned and stood up straight, fixing him with a cold stare. 'I am baffled as to your presence here, sir. Are you a friend of Richard's? After all, he has a reputation of keeping an odd collection of friends. Juliet and I were betrothed before I left for the Peninsular. We are to be married.'

Marcus stepped forward and he smiled, an absolutely chilling smile, his eyes gleaming with a deadly purpose, his voice cold and lethal. 'I think not. Juliet is no longer free to marry you. She is my wife. We were married today.'

Marcus's words hung like a pall in the air. An unearthly silence fell on the room. The moment was tense. The expression on Thomas's face did not change, but his skin paled and a tiny muscle began to throb at the side of his eye. There was a cold glitter in his eyes when he fixed them on Marcus.

'You lie,' he spat.

'I am not in the habit of lying.'

Thomas spun round on Juliet, who had risen to a sitting position on the sofa, and his eyes, when they rested on hers, were merciless, his tone cutting. 'Is this true?

Is this—this man your husband?' When she hesitated, his voice rang out impatiently. 'Come, Juliet, what have you to say?'

She nodded, gazing up at him, all her wretchedness and pain staring out of tear-filled eyes. 'Yes,' she whispered. 'It is true. But I thought you were dead.'

'Dead or alive, I can see you lost no time in filling my place. How long has it been? Nine or ten months? Were you in such a hurry to be rid of me? The next thing you'll be telling me is how much you love him,' he sneered, 'how you couldn't wait a decent interval of at least a year to marry. For God's sake, spare me that.'

'Thomas, please,' Juliet cried in a terrible anguish, rising to her feet, one hand stretched out to him in her need to make him understand. 'You don't understand—'

Cutting short her protestations, Thomas dashed away her hand. Marcus stepped towards them. The tone of Juliet's one-time betrothed had been deliberately offensive and had provoked his anger further, and he was torn by Juliet's piteous defencelessness.

'Whether he understands or not is of no consequence. The time he has been missing is neither here nor there. You were not married to him, so what does it matter? Juliet is *my* wife.'

Thomas's face was set hard, and a terrible hatred and jealousy directed at this stranger smouldered just beneath the surface to burst like a raging volcano, but an inborn caution seemed to tell him to stay calm, to overcome the overwhelming lust to reach out and tear the man apart with his bare hands. 'Damn you for forcing your attentions on her, knowing she was spoken for.'

'To all intents and purposes, you were dead,' Marcus drawled flatly. 'Or so everyone thought.'

'As you see, I am very much alive.'

'The devil has a way of taking care of his own, and if you intend to remain that way, then I suggest you stay away from me and especially Juliet. So let that be an end to it.'

'An end to it? As far as I am concerned, there will never be an end to it. You have offended my honour. I have a mind to call you out. I want revenge, and I will stop at nothing until I have obtained it.'

Juliet gasped with horror at his words. 'No, Thomas, please, you must not.'

Both men ignored her pleas and their eyes clashed with all the violence born of hatred.

'Honour?' Marcus scorned. 'I dispute that. There isn't an honourable bone in your body, and do not try and fool me. We both know that the revenge you talk of is not, as you would have me believe, for my marrying Juliet. As I remember, you have the disgusting morals of a tom-cat, and you make me sorry I didn't kill you when I had the chance. Your sort can only go one way, and I thank God that by marrying Juliet, I have prevented her from being dragged down into the mire.'

Juliet's eyes passed from one to the other in puzzlement as she tried to comprehend what they were talking about. None of it made any sense. That they should feel prejudice towards each other was understandable, but Marcus was talking of another matter which had nothing whatsoever to do with her or their marriage.

'You know each other, don't you?' she asked in shocked disbelief.

'We have met,' Marcus replied. 'But I shall not offend your ears by telling you of the unsavoury circumstances.'

Tell me, Juliet, Thomas had said, *would you have married him if you had known I was alive?*

The echo of his words lingered in the stillness of the room as all eyes became riveted expectantly on her. It was a question she had preferred not to ask herself because she could not endure knowing he might have refused her when he discovered she didn't have penny to her name.

'I—I don't know,' she faltered. 'Please, don't ask me that.'

Slowly and with a deadly purpose, Thomas sauntered to where Richard stood, his limp not quite as pronounced as it had been. Considering the severity of his injured leg, he was lucky in the fact that he had kept his where others had lost theirs. He fixed Richard with a cunning stare, fully aware of what the impact his next words would be.

'Why didn't you tell your sister, Richard? Why didn't you tell Juliet that I was due to come to London? That you spoke with an acquaintance known to both of us, who informed you that my intention was to come to see her just as soon as I had been to Amberley Park to see my parents?'

Juliet's heart suddenly missed a beat and she thought she was going mad. She stared at Richard. 'Tell me it isn't true. Tell me Thomas is lying.'

Richard squared his shoulders, meeting her gaze unflinchingly. 'No. He is telling the truth.'

'So,' breathed Juliet, 'that is what you've been keeping from me. I knew there was something.'

Thomas's lips curled with derision. 'And you are supposed to be her brother, with her best interests at heart.'

Richard looked at him steadily, reading the mockery on his face, but his gaze did not falter. 'You are right. I am her brother,' he said coldly, 'and I have always done what I consider is best for her. That is precisely why I did not tell her. You are a liar and a cheat, Thomas, and many more things besides. I couldn't begin to list them all. You are a man without morals or principles, and you dishonour the very name you bear. You could have written to Juliet, letting her know you were still alive. You had your chances, and then when you returned to London, you could have written or come here, but you chose not to.' His eyes glittered with contempt. 'I don't know who it was that kept you occupied for the time you were a prisoner, but I hope she was worth it.'

Richard heard Juliet gasp and moved towards her. 'God knows, I wanted to tell you, Juliet, but I couldn't. I truly believed—and I still do, I might tell you—that he would have brought you nothing but heartache. For you to marry the likes of him would be like casting pearls before swine.'

'Stop, stop, please stop,' Juliet cried, covering her ears with her hands. 'I cannot bear it. Oh, Thomas, you should have written. You cannot know what it was like for me, the anguish I suffered day after day. I have lain awake night after night, not knowing whether you were alive or dead. Thousands were killed or wounded, yet I heard nothing of you, never a word. All I could do was wonder and pray and—and then your father…he…he wrote and told me you had been killed. I had to come to terms with that. You must understand.'

'You came to terms with it a mite too quickly for my liking, Juliet,' Thomas said with brutal sarcasm. 'However,' and he turned from her sharply, 'I do realise the impropriety of my coming here today. I am well aware that this is your wedding night, and I should hate to rob you of a single minute, so I shall leave you to get on with it.'

'But—but we cannot leave it like this, Thomas,' Juliet cried as he turned and strode towards the door. 'We—we were betrothed. I cannot bear to think I've hurt you. We will meet and talk—not tonight but soon.' She looked imploringly at Marcus, her eyes bright with tears. 'Marcus, please…' But there the words froze on her lips, and she suddenly felt very afraid. His face had paled and his narrowed eyes held a frightening glitter, and she realised that what he felt for Thomas went deeper than anger, deeper even that hatred. It was something she did not recognise and therefore could not understand.

But Marcus had read her mind, and the look he gave her was hard and unyielding, his tone low with contempt. 'No, Juliet. You should know better than to ask that of me. It is inevitable that at some time you will meet socially, but there will be no private meetings between you. He can go and rot in hell for all I care.'

Thomas laughed, a light, brittle sound, but there was no hiding his underlying tension. 'Worry not, Juliet. I will not be far away. You know where I live when I am in town, and should this husband of yours not reach your expectations, then you will know where to find me.' Flinging open the door, he walked out into the hall.

Juliet noticed his limp and was brutally reminded of all he must have suffered in Spain, and her tender heart went out to him. A tearing sob broke from her.

He couldn't leave, not now that she had found him again and, gathering up her skirts, she hurried after him, avoiding Marcus's hand when he reached to stop her. 'Thomas, wait. For pity's sake, please wait.'

He stopped and turned, and she came to a halt in front of him, her face awash with tears. 'I'm sorry,' she gulped. 'I know how much I must have hurt you. Please, you must forgive me.'

He looked at her hard for several moments, and his eyes travelled with a lazy insolence over her wedding gown, from the warm glow of the pearls around her slender neck down to her slippered feet before coming to rest on her face. 'Tell me, Juliet, is that the dress you would have worn at our wedding?'

She stared at him in horror. 'Oh, no—no. That would not have been fair.'

'Fair on whom?' he said scathingly. 'Me or the man who is now your husband?' He looked back at Marcus, a cynical curl to his lips. 'As you will know I am a gambling man,' he said slowly, 'and I will lay odds that Juliet will come back to me in the end.'

Marcus's sleek black brows rose mockingly. 'I am a gambler of some skill myself, and I would not bet on that.'

'Oh, I would. You see, I hold the trump card.'

'And that is?'

'It is me she still loves. Think of that when you lie with her tonight. I shall have her in the end.' With a satisfied smile, he turned and left the house.

Juliet watched him go without a smile or a word of affection or even farewell, and she bowed her head, thinking that he might as well be dead to her. The sound of the closing door and his feet dying away down the steps was like a death knell to her already breaking heart. She stared at the closed door for several moments until, filled with panic that she might never see him again she hurled herself forward. She couldn't let him go, not like this.

'Thomas,' she called, crushed with misery, but suddenly hands caught her, holding her in a firm grip, pulling her back, and she was enraged to find herself helpless.

'Juliet, are you out of your mind? Let him go,' Marcus commanded sharply.

'No,' she cried, whirling round in his arms, a wild expression in her eyes. 'I have to make him understand why I married you. I cannot let him go like this. I might never see him again.'

'And for that I will thank God,' he snapped.

'That's unfair, Marcus,' she said, her voice quivering with anger. 'We were to have been married. Can you blame him for being angry, coming home after what he's been through only to discover that the woman he should have married has married someone else? I don't know what he's done to make you speak of him as you do, but whatever it is, it cannot possibly justify this terrible hatred you feel for him.'

Marcus remained silent, his expression hard, his hands clenched by his sides. 'I met Waring in the most unsavoury situation. I could tell you what took place between us, but I do not want to be the one to shatter your illusions.'

Juliet looked at Marcus, her brother hovering in the doorway to the drawing room, her eyes full of pain and accusation. 'You deceived me, both of you. You should have told me.'

Richard came forward. 'I wanted to—you've no idea

how much—but I couldn't. Do you really believe Thomas would have married you, that his father would have allowed him to, when he became aware of our circumstances? He wouldn't. He would have dropped you like a stone.'

Juliet's lips curled scornfully. 'What a low opinion you have of him, Richard. What can he possibly have done to make you hate him so? And yes—yes, I tell you—he would have married me, but you tricked me, both of you, and you had no right. I shall never forgive you for keeping this from me, either of you. I had a right to know so that I could choose for myself.' With a choked sob and a swirl of skirts, she turned sharply and fled up the stairs to seek the sanctuary of her room, but not before Marcus had seen fresh tears shining in her eyes.

Marcus entered Juliet's room. Still attired in her wedding gown, she was standing by the hearth with her back to the door, her body taut, her hands clenched by her sides. She didn't turn as he moved to the centre of the room. Taking a moment to look at her, his throat constricted with pain on seeing her desolation. As she stood there in the flickering golden glow of the fire and candlelight, her hair caressing her shoulders, he thought no one in the whole world was as lovely as she, and he cursed Thomas Waring with every fibre of his being. His very presence had withdrawn her a distance of a thousand miles, and what was in Marcus's heart was like death itself.

Aware of her suffering, rage rose inside him against Waring, and he wondered what manner of man he was that could inspire such a love as hers, but also so much devastating misery. He let his gaze wander around the essentially feminine room he was to have shared for this one night, their wedding night, before they left for Surrey on the morrow but, he thought bitterly, that was unlikely now. He would not make her his wife in the true sense of the word until she had cleansed her heart of Thomas Waring.

Becoming aware of his presence, she turned and looked at him. Her eyes were filled with the pain inflicted on her, her face pale with anger. 'I'm surprised you have come, Marcus. I thought after what has just transpired, you would have left.'

'And why would I do that?' he uttered with a trace of sarcasm, her anger inciting his own. 'Do I have to have a reason for entering my wife's bedroom?'

'Wife?' she scorned, feeding her anger with her words. 'I might not be your wife if you'd been honest with me.'

'Explain what you mean by that?'

'You know perfectly well what I mean. No wonder you were in such haste for the wedding to take place, having me believe it was because you wanted to return to Mulberry Hall when all that time, it was because you knew Thomas was alive and he—'

'Enough,' he snapped harshly. 'Have the grace to hear me out first. Your accusations are unjust. I do not deny that I met him just the once, but I swear to you that I did not know who he was until today, and I will not offend your sensibilities by recounting the sordidness of the situation in which we met.'

'Am I expected to believe this?'

'Believe what you like, but as I told him, I do not lie.

What a low creature you must think me, Juliet, but not as low as Thomas Waring. But this I do know. Richard spoke the truth when he said Thomas was a cheat and a liar. The man is utterly corrupt, rotten to the very core, and this worthless libertine is the man you say you love.'

Without taking her eyes from his face, Juliet moved towards him, beside herself with fury. 'How dare you make the one thing I have loved so vile?' she flared. 'I will not listen to your accusations. I do not believe you.'

'Because you don't want to believe me. You cannot get it into your head that your beloved Thomas is anything other than what you know of him, which, it seems, is very little.'

'I knew him well enough to say I would marry him.'

'I doubt that, but just supposing you had married him, do you believe for one minute that he would have loaned Richard the money to save his assets, your home, which you profess is important to you? If you think that, then you are a fool.'

Juliet held her ground while Marcus walked past her to the hearth. Turning, she looked at him. He stood with his back to her, his hands resting on the mantelpiece, his head bowed, his shoulders taut. The cold disdain with which he had uttered the words was like having icy water thrown in her face, and she was suddenly reminded of all he had done for her and was full of contrition. She realised he was just as devastated as she was. He had offered her strength, security and understanding, which she had accepted gladly. She couldn't throw it back at him.

Sighing deeply, some of her anger receded. Nothing could be heard but the rustling of her skirts as she moved towards him. She came to a halt a few feet from him, pausing to gather her wits before she spoke, trying to think where to begin, and because she was so overwhelmed with emotion, she said the first thing that came into her head.

'You're angry, Marcus, and you have every reason to be.' She saw his shoulders stiffen at the sound of her voice, and when he brought himself up straight and turned and looked at her, his expression gave her no reassurance.

'You're right,' he bit out, his mouth set in a bitter line, his black brows drawn in a straight line. 'It would appear that you are already regretting your marriage to *me*.'

Juliet flinched at his enunciation of his last word, which rang with a hollow note. 'But I'm not. Oh, I no longer know what I think. But I am sorry. And perhaps I am a fool. You must think me extremely ungrateful.'

'I did not marry you for your gratitude,' he said coldly. 'That is the last thing I want.'

'Is it true? That you didn't know Thomas was alive?'

'Yes.'

'But Richard knew. He could have told me.'

'Richard loves you, he is your brother, and he would not hurt you intentionally. Because of his past knowledge of your so-called betrothed—which, I might add, seems anything but honourable—he considered that what he was doing was right. He must have gone through hell keeping it from you, but he truly believed he was doing it for your own good.' Smiling crookedly, he moved away from her, paused halfway to the door and turned to look at her again. 'You should thank me, Juliet, for by marrying you, I have saved you from an infinitely worse fate than death. Although I have no doubt you are thinking that you had no need to marry me after all. How could I have been so naive, so stupid? With all my experience and as old as I am, I should have learnt my lesson.'

'Please don't say that, Marcus. You do not understand.'

'What is there to understand? It's simple enough. Before I met you I had only myself and my daughter to take care of. Now, with a wife and a penniless brother-in-law foisted on me, I find I have extra responsibilities I could do without.'

The vicious meaning of his words cut Juliet to the heart. With a surge of genuine anger, her jaw jutted with belligerent indignation, and tension twisted within her as she quickly asserted herself. 'Since you see us as pitiful nuisances—'

'Your words, not mine,' he interrupted harshly.

'Nevertheless,' she seethed, her voice like splintered ice as she took up a stance in front of him, 'that is what you mean, what you were implying. If that is how you see us, then I shall remain in London. You can go to Surrey by yourself.'

'Like hell I will. I will give you a warning, Juliet,' Marcus said in a terrible voice. 'Do not even consider a separation between us. You are my wife, and you will come with me to Surrey when I leave. Is that clear?'

Fury was quick to flare in Juliet's eyes. Moving forwards, she planted her hands on her hips and leaned towards him. 'How dare you, Marcus Cardell! I do not need your permission to do anything, and if I wanted advice, I would not ask you.'

'Then don't. But from now on, you will apply discretion and forethought in your behaviour. I realise how devastated you must feel on finding Waring did not die on the battlefield, and you have my sympathy, but you will never speak with Thomas Waring again. Is that clear?'

Juliet stared at him with hard eyes. 'I shall speak to whomever I choose.' Despite her arrogant words, she felt a spark of fear at the look in her husband's eyes.

'By my faith, Juliet, all I ask is that you do not speak to him, do not make contact with him.' His soft voice was infinitely more intimidating than a raised one. 'Your loyalty is to me, so let that be an end to the matter. You are my wife, little though I can believe it at this moment. I will have you act your part. You will compose yourself and call upon your dignity. The sooner you accept your position, the better it will be for both of us. You will be accountable to me for your actions. Is that understood?'

Juliet didn't even recoil from his quivering anger. Fury rose up like flames licking inside her, her face as uncompromisingly challenging as his. 'I own no man my superior, least of all you. Ever since I was a child, I have been accountable for my actions to one person or another, being told that women don't have choices, that men make choices for them, but no more. I will not be accountable to you for what I say or do.'

'Yes, you will. Someone should have taught you some sense and tempered that wilful pride of yours years ago,' he said, the anger pouring through his veins making him carelessly cruel. 'Do not defy me, Juliet.'

To her consternation and fury, suddenly Juliet felt close to tears. Rather than let him see her flagging courage and refusing to be humbled, she raised her chin and assumed an expression of remote indifference. 'And if I do?' she ground out in a low voice.

In the face of her defiance, Marcus moved closer and leaned forward until light blue eyes stared into amber from little more than a foot apart. 'You will rue the day. Heed me and heed me well, Juliet. As my wife, you will conduct yourself with proper decorum and never discredit the name you now bear. I am not an unreasonable man, but I can become very unreasonable when I am angry.'

'You are a loathsome, overbearing monster, Marcus Cardell.'

'Yes, I think I have the picture,' he said, stepping away from her.

His eyes narrowed and a murderous glint shone out at her. There was a deep and dreadful silence, a silence so menacing, filled with an unwavering determination of the two to hurt, to destroy one another, that the tension was palpable. 'Do not goad me further, Juliet.'

'But, where are you going?' she asked as he turned away from her.

'I'm leaving. And you needn't worry. I will not be bothering you tonight. I'll spend the night at my home in Mayfair. Tomorrow we'll leave first thing for Surrey. Be ready.'

'What do you mean?' she whispered in bewilderment.

'What I mean,' he said, turning and looking at her once more, his eyes gleaming oddly and one sleek black brow raised, 'is that you can keep your chaste sanctity, my dear. Do you think I would stay with you tonight as, I might remind you, is my right, lie with you, touch you, all the while knowing you were wishing it was your precious Thomas who was beside you?' He looked at her long and cool. 'It is obvious by the way you rush to his defence that you still care for him a great deal, so until the time when it is otherwise, I will bid you goodnight.'

Marcus went out, leaving Juliet staring at the closed door, feeling so utterly bereft, thinking what an awful mess everything was.

A merciful numbness filled her mind as she listened to his footsteps dying away on the landing, and she wanted to go after him, to appeal to his emotions, but she knew that while Thomas was uppermost in her heart, he would remain implacable. He would not yield from his cool verdict and she would continue to sleep alone.

He had been angry and with good reason, and as she stared into the dying embers of the fire, she took stock of all that had happened that day, suddenly so very tired and drained of all emotion. Her feelings towards Thomas were confused and her mind seemed to be going round circles. Why had she been so ready to believe he was dead? Why hadn't she waited before rushing into marriage with someone else? But she told herself, she couldn't have waited if she'd wanted to. Not with Richard's creditors baying at the door.

Her thoughts turned to Marcus. Of her own free will she had married him, nothing could change that and, she thought sadly, it was too late to weep for Thomas and what might have been. She and Marcus were man and wife, and she would honour that, but what her feelings were towards him, she couldn't say, only that they were different from those she felt for Thomas. Marcus had asked her if she believed Thomas would have married her knowing her circumstances, without a dowry and with the added shame of Richard's debts and that they might lose the Endcliffe estate. Would Thomas have secured the estate as Marcus had done? She doubted his father would have agreed to this.

With her heart and mind ravaged by divided loyalty, for her own peace of mind, she had to know so that she could put things right, and to do this she must see Thomas tonight. Marcus intended to leave for Surrey in the morning, so tomorrow would be too late, and if Thomas was to return to the Peninsular, then she might never see him again.

Wishing to avert questions from his mother should he return to his family home in town on his wedding night, Marcus decided against leaving. Occupying another room in the house, lying fully clothed on the bed and hearing the door to the street open and close and a carriage drive off, he went to the window and, looking out, saw the dark silhouette of a carriage disappear. He was filled with a dreadful suspicion that Juliet was inside it.

Cursing softly, he hurried to her room and flung the door wide open. On finding it empty, his eyes darkened until they were almost black, his scorching anger burning a flame in the centre of each one. He knew without doubt that his wife was going to see Thomas Waring. He paused only to enquire of the hired butler the location of the Waring townhouse and to order a horse to be saddled.

Chapter Eight

Juliet was admitted to the Waring house. On being told by the butler that Lord and Lady Waring were not in town, hearing the clink of glass coming from the drawing room, without waiting to be announced, she crossed the hall and pushed open the door and went in. Occupied with pouring himself a drink, Thomas turned. On seeing Juliet, his eyes widened, but then he smiled thinly, a smug, self-satisfied smile, and setting his glass down, he sauntered to where she stood.

He looked untidy without his jacket. His shirt was open at the collar, the fine white linen stained with alcohol. Juliet was disappointed. She had never seen him like this; he had always been so immaculate in the past. It came as some surprise to her to find he had lost some of that magical power to stir the old attraction that had kept her love attached to him for so long. He had also drunk a considerable amount, for his eyes were bloodshot, his aristocratic countenance flushed. She had always been aware of his capacity to absorb large amounts of alcohol, but this was the first time she had seen him lose some of his dignity. When he spoke, his voice was slow and a little thick. He gave her a profoundly mocking bow.

'Why, Juliet, this is a pleasant surprise. I did not expect you quite so soon.'

His lack of elementary politeness irked her somewhat. 'Why were you so sure I would come?'

'Because I knew you would be unable to resist the temptation of seeing me before I left London in the morning. But isn't this a little irregular? I mean, isn't it supposed to be your wedding night? Or is it that your husband doesn't live up to your expectations?'

'Please, Thomas, don't do this. Marcus has no idea that I'm here.'

'Of course he hasn't, otherwise you wouldn't be. But why are you here?'

'You know why.'

'No. Tell me. Is it because now after finding out that I am alive, you are sorry you married Marcus Cardell? Perhaps if I had been dead, it would have saved you the embarrassment of your betrayal, your treachery.'

She gasped, angered by his accusation. 'Treachery? No, never that.'

He moved closer to her, his narrowed eyes fixed on her face. 'I find it hard to believe how easily you forgot me, Juliet.'

'I never forgot you,' she said emphatically. 'You have no idea how I wanted so much for the reports of your death to be untrue. I tried not to believe it, and you can have no idea how I dreamed of your coming home so that we could be married. But...' She sighed, lowering her eyes. 'What's the use in talking now? I am no longer free.'

A cunning glint appeared in Thomas's eyes. 'A sermon doesn't make a marriage. You can be free of him.

The wedding can be annulled if you swear it has not been consummated.'

For a moment she dispassionately studied this man she had once sworn to love forever and shook her head slowly. 'No, Thomas. Nothing is the same as when you left. I am not the same, although I am only now becoming aware of it. My marriage cannot be annulled. The vows I made are sacred. I married Marcus of my own free will, and I will not betray him. He is my husband in the sight of man and God.'

At her words, there was a sudden change in Thomas's manner, and his features became taut with a strange glow in the depths of his eyes. Juliet began to feel uneasy. She moved away from him, remembering why she had come, the question she must ask for her own peace of mind.

'There is a reason why I had to see you, something I have to know. Since coming home, what do you know of my circumstances?'

'What do you mean?'

She looked at him directly. 'Would you have married me without a dowry?'

He looked nonplussed. 'Dowry? What has that to do with anything?'

'Before you went to Spain, you were aware of Richard's passion for gambling—be it cards, dice or anything else he could put his money on. Unfortunately, we have creditors demanding money. Indeed, our situation is so bad that there is the possibility that the estate will have to be sold.'

A look of genuine shock and amazement spread over Thomas's face. 'Good Lord! I had no idea. I knew he had

debts—what gambler doesn't?—but to be fool enough
to lose everything…'

'Yes. Everything. So, Thomas, what I want to know
is, would you have still married me penniless and with
the shame of what Richard has done? I need to know.
Did you love me enough to do that?'

He was taken aback by her question, and for a moment they looked at each other as if both were carved
from stone.

'Marriage,' he murmured at last. 'Good Lord, why
of—of course I would…' But his voice died away, flat
and unconvincing.

Juliet wanted to believe him, but she knew with a
sickening sense of reality that he was lying, and the face
that looked into hers was not that handsome beloved
face it had once been. That was a sweet fantasy, a cherished illusion that had been shattered forever. Thomas
did not love her, had never loved her, not in the way
she had wanted to be loved. He would have used her to
serve his own interests, nothing more. It should hurt,
but strangely, it didn't, and if it didn't hurt, then could
it be that she didn't love him either?

She smiled bitterly. 'Don't try and fool me any more,
Thomas. I can see the truth in your eyes. You wouldn't
have married me, even if you had wanted to, and I very
much doubt that now. Your father would never have allowed you to marry me anyway.'

He remained silent, looking at her hard, swaying
slightly on his feet, the unspoken truth staring from
his eyes. She turned from him, eager to leave, to get
back home as quickly as possible—back to Marcus. She
prayed he would never find out that she had come here

tonight. He would never forgive her. Thank goodness he had decided to spend the night elsewhere.

'I don't think there's anything more to be said between us.' She moved to the door, but in an instant, Thomas covered the distance between them, blocking her path, a dangerous, threatening glint in his eyes. She could not repress the icy fear that crept through her. When he spoke, his voice was low and each word he uttered precise, but underlying them, she could sense the violence that threatened to erupt at any moment.

'Before you go, Juliet, tell me about Cardell and how it was that he came to marry you. Did you have to lie about your circumstances to him?'

'No, I didn't have to. Marcus and I have always been perfectly honest with each other. He has loaned Richard enough money to secure the estate.'

For a moment his face did not change its expression, but suddenly, what she had told him caused him to laugh mirthlessly. 'You mean, he bought you?' he sneered. 'You sold yourself to the highest bidder?'

'There were no other bidders,' she told him harshly. 'Only Marcus.'

'And he promised to pay all your brother's debts for your own sweet self,' he scoffed. 'How very touching and how unworthy of you.'

'Unworthy? No, I don't think so. I had no choice. It is fortunate that his family on his mother's side owns the Mulberry Hall estate, which adjoins Endcliffe House, so I won't be far away from Richard.'

'Then I wish you a happy life together—while it lasts. Perhaps I shall visit you there one day.'

'Our life together will be a long and happy one at

Mulberry Hall, and I think you know that you will not be welcome there.'

'And do you love him?'

'He—he has been very good to me.'

'I asked you if you love him,' he persisted.

'He is a wonderful man.'

'But you don't love him,' he said with an odious smile of triumph, with such finality that she stared at him unbelievingly, noting the immense satisfaction he derived from this knowledge, and she wished with her whole heart that she could have said otherwise, but her feelings for Marcus were still nebulous.

'Move out of my way, Thomas. I wish to leave.'

'Not until I am ready. I am not your husband to order about. You are beautiful in temper. Does your husband tell you that? I've never wanted a woman as much as I want you, Juliet.'

'Why, Thomas? Because you cannot bear the fact that I now belong to someone else? Someone you've clearly had unpleasant dealings with before.'

The meaning of her words and the force with which they were delivered hit home. Thomas's veneer of sham politeness crumbled, and the smile on his face disappeared as he thrust his face close to hers. 'That is true. Cardell and I have a score to settle, and what better way to do that than to take his woman? Why should I let you return to Cardell—the man who has taken the woman I would have married? I will tell you this, Juliet, our last night together will be one to remember. I know you still love me, not Cardell, who you've so foolishly married.'

Juliet paled. Marcus was Thomas's objective, she knew that now, and he would harm her to get at him.

She didn't know fully what warped loathing Thomas harboured against Marcus, but she knew that whatever rebuff Marcus had given him must have festered inside his head and that he was dangerous. He moved closer to her, and she could feel his breath hot on her face. She went numb when she met his gaze. The charismatic façade that had once attracted her was now arrogant, saturnine and cruel, and the cocksure smile had acquired a malevolent twist. She stepped back, her face showing revulsion.

'What you suggest is an adulterous love. The sort I despise.' She smiled scornfully. 'You talk of love, of my love, of not being loyal and accuse me of treachery, but what of your love? Not once in all the time I have known you have you mentioned that.'

'Have I not? Then permit me to show you. I'm going to love you, Juliet. I'm going to make you so happy that you'll never want to leave me to go back to your husband.'

'Never,' she cried angrily. 'I wish to leave now. Let me go.'

'No.'

'Do you intend to hold me here by force?'

'Only if I have to.'

Panic and fear overcame Juliet, and she began to tremble. He noticed and smiled with smug satisfaction.

'Why, you're trembling. Come, Juliet,' he drawled, his voice thick with passion, 'you think I don't love you, but I do.' He placed his hands heavily on her shoulders, looking deeply into her eyes. At his touch, she struggled to free herself from his grip, but his fingers tightened, refusing to relinquish their hold. 'So,' he hissed, 'you want to fight me? Well, all the better. I like a woman with spirit—one to match my own.'

Juliet was suddenly overcome with fear, but it was a different kind of fear from any she had ever known. Never, in all the time she had known him, had Thomas been anything other than charming, and she had always believed that nothing could touch him, that nothing mattered. But as she faced him, his expression dark and ruthless, she knew that at last something had touched him enough to bring about this ill-mannered, drunken stranger. She was now in no doubt that it was Marcus who had brought about this change and, whatever had passed between them that first time they had met, it must have been something terrible. She knew with a sinking heart that she could have married anyone, and Thomas wouldn't have cared one iota, but because it was Marcus, it was a different matter. Thomas would destroy her if he could to get back at him.

The full consequences of what she had done by coming here swept over her. Thomas saw her fear, but he only laughed, a deep mocking sound that curled his lips, and a look of madness filled and dilated his eyes, which told her that his mere triumph over her, her very resistance, excited him much more than all her passive docility. He wanted her whatever the odds.

A fierce, merciless struggle began between them. Now that she was faced with the terrible prospect of being raped and possibly killed, renewed strength surged through her, and she fought as if her life depended on it, like a wildcat turning on its tormentor. In a blind fury, her nails raked his face, his eyes, anywhere she could see his flesh, feeling an immense, unholy satisfaction when she drew blood. He laughed, a fierce, demonical sound that sent a chill through her.

'That's it. Fight, my beauty,' he hissed, pushing her down onto a sofa. 'Fight all you want. I shall soon have you crying and pleading for mercy. I shall enjoy teaching you to obey me, breaking that stubborn pride of yours.'

Savagely he tore at her clothes. She was finding it harder and harder to defend herself, reality slipping further and further away, and despair overpowered her as she reached the limits of her strength and her struggles became feeble.

And then, abruptly, something happened, and his weight left her. There was a dull thud, and she ceased struggling, trembling in what remained of her clothes. Through a mist, she looked up and discerned a terrifying, faceless figure looming over her. Instinct made her draw her defiled body into a ball, quivering like a terrified child. In the wild tangle of her hair, her eyes, enormous and full of fear, accentuated the transparent whiteness of her face.

She peered up at Marcus, who was in a towering rage, his face contorted out of all recognition as he glared down at her, beside himself with fury. Juliet did not ask herself by what miracle he happened to be there, to save her from what she had been about to suffer at Thomas's hands—it was enough for her than he had come, regardless of the fury and anger he would be sure to vent on her.

Marcus glared down at her dishevelled form bitterly. The spectacle of the vile and contemptible Thomas Waring forcing his attentions on his wife and the pitiful state he had brutally reduced her to made him feel physically sick. In the flickering glow of the candles, she was still lovely, although now tragically so, and he knew the sight of her should sicken him, but it didn't.

'You little fool,' he uttered quietly, his concern for her coming to the fore. 'This was a senseless thing to do. You should not have come here looking for him. Did you think I would not find out? What did you imagine would happen when that animal got his hands on you? You could ask for nothing better—believe me.' His eyes took in her soft flesh showing through the tattered remnants of her bodice, and quickly he removed his cloak and gently draped it over her.

Straightening up, he looked at Waring, who had gotten up from the floor, where, in his rage, Marcus had thrown him. He stood glowering at Marcus, his fists tightly clenched by his sides, and the scratches of Juliet's fingernails that she had left on his face trickled blood.

'Damn your filthy hide, Waring,' he spat, his voice like a naked blade. 'Can't you get it into your head that Juliet no longer has anything to do with you?'

'Perhaps not, but she did come looking for me, like a bitch in heat.'

Pure madness flamed in Marcus's eyes, and he sprang at his adversary, grasping the front of his shirt and pulling his face close to his own, full of revulsion. 'And you should know all about that, being the dog that you are. Your methods of seduction leave a lot to be desired. I could kill you now, but I will save that pleasure for a later date.'

Waring's lips twisted in an arrogant sneer, his eyes spitting venom as he knocked Marcus's hands away.

'Why, you are jealous—jealous because she preferred my bed to yours. But then, why shouldn't she? And how do you know she hasn't shared it with me before?'

Marcus eyed him with unconcealed scorn. 'Judging by what has occurred here tonight, I doubt very much she would come back a second time.'

'Ah, but you don't know that for certain. How could you? Unless you have pre-empted your wedding vows and taken her yourself.'

For a moment Marcus stared at him in silence, a flicker of doubt entering his eyes as he hoped to God there was no truth in Waring's words. 'What a vicious, callous individual you are, Waring.'

Satisfied that his words had hit home, Thomas smiled smugly. 'I see I have cast the seed of doubt, Cardell. At least I have given you a wedding night to remember. You must have paid quite a price to get her to marry you— debts and all. Perhaps after tonight you'll consider she wasn't worth it.'

Marcus looked at him coldly. 'That doesn't concern you, Waring. You belong to one of England's most noble families, yet you are out of your class. You haven't a noble bone in your body. You are a low, brutal animal not worthy of the blade with which I shall kill you.'

An ugly smile spread across Thomas's features. 'No, it is I who will kill you. I who have been wronged. Had Juliet waited and married me, I would not have had to buy her as you have done.'

Disregarding Waring's insult, Marcus turned back to Juliet, who hadn't moved, and pulling her towards him, wrapped his cloak about her trembling form before again facing Thomas Waring. 'I'm taking my wife home. I would like to say I very much hope our paths do not cross again, but if they should—'

'Oh, they will, Cardell. You can be sure of that. You and I have a score to settle. I demand satisfaction for this night's work.'

Marcus's features tightened. 'You shall have it.'

'It will give me immense pleasure to kill you. I shall not be cheated by you a third time.'

'Don't be too sure. Whatever you might think, having spent several years in the Peninsular myself, I am an expert with both pistol and blade, and I aim to make damned sure you assault no more defenceless women— whether they be high or low born.'

Riding behind the carriage carrying Juliet home, Marcus didn't have the chance to speak to her until they reached the house. They went directly to her room, where Marcus seated himself before the fire. He leaned indolently back in his chair and crossed his long legs at the ankles.

Juliet watched him, waiting for him to speak to her, her very stance defiant, her exquisite features clouded with resentment. She had imagined Marcus would be icy, angry, anything but this cold self-possession. A look had entered his eyes she did not recognise and she felt awkward. She swallowed, shrinking under his scrutiny. Anger had sustained her so far, now fear and something else, something she could not identify, began to nudge. Struggling to steadfastly keep her thoughts on what was happening and aware that in her breast her heart was thumping far too fast for her to claim a mere tolerance

of him, surreptitiously she took a step back to mini-
mise contact.

'I imagine you are now ready to explain your behaviour tonight, Juliet.'

The tone of his voice made Juliet's heart contract.
No hint of softness showed in the marble severity of
his face—no hint of anger, either—which she suspected
was stirring just beneath the surface, which was infinitely more disturbing. Anxiety abounded in her heart.
After all, what did she know of this husband of hers?
She forced herself to remain calm, not to appear ill at
ease, not to show the unnerving effect being alone with
him was having on her.

'Well?' he demanded impatiently. 'I should like to
know precisely what happened between you and Waring before he went off to Spain. As your husband, I have
to ask you just how far his attentions have gone. And do
not lie to me, Juliet. If there is nothing else, there has to
be truth between us from the start.'

Understanding his meaning, Juliet felt the flush start
somewhere deep down and rise upwards over her chest
and face, and then anger, full-bodied and fortifying, pro-
pelled her forward to stand over hm. 'Of all the loathsome, arrogant...' she erupted furiously. 'Despite what
happened tonight, which I suspect was brought on by
disappointment at my marriage to you, Thomas's behaviour towards me had been impeccable.'

'Thank you for that edifying piece of information,'
Marcus remarked coldly. 'And am I to believe that you
weren't lovers?'

Juliet was stung by his unjust accusation and the contempt in his voice, and some of her fighting spirit rose

to the fore, and her eyes met his, flashing defiance. 'We were never that, but you can believe what you like,' she fumed, stepping back. 'I speak the truth.'

Marcus's face became taut, his eyes boring into hers, plumbing their innermost depths, searching for some sign that would tell him she was lying, but there was none. This woman, his wife, was not only beautiful, she was proud, and her pride would make her oppose him if she thought him unjust. She was also courageous and stubborn, but she was no liar. He believed her, and as he continued to watch her, it was clear to him that after all Waring had meant to her, she was feeling utterly broken by what had happened to her at his hands tonight. She stood in the centre of her room, still clutching his cloak about her like a shield of armour, as if afraid to let it go.

He was suddenly overwhelmed with compassion. He wanted to go to her, to open his arms and gather her to him, to hold her and never let her go, but he couldn't. Not yet. It was hard to swallow what she had done and he could not yet forgive her for going to Thomas Waring. The memory of this night would live with him for a long time, longer than the sight of her bruised and broken body. Her act of betrayal was hard for him to bear.

Getting to his feet, he strode towards the door, and she became alarmed.

'Marcus? You're not leaving?'

He turned and looked at her, his face immobile. 'There is something I have to take care of.'

He watched as his words penetrated Juliet's tortured mind and realisation of where he was going and what he intended dawned on her. Looking sick with horror, distraught, she flung herself across the room. Her eyes were full of desperate pleading. 'No,' she cried. 'I know what you are going to do. Please don't give Thomas the satisfaction of fighting a duel. I beg of you. I have to prevent this happening. It's—it's madness, don't you see?'

'Madness? You should have thought of that before leaving this house to go to him.'

'If I have to, I will get down on my knees to entreat you not to do this.'

A ripple of something stirred in Marcus's breast, and he marvelled at her courage. She might be stricken and feeling at her lowest ebb on finding that Thomas Waring had not been killed as she had been led to believe, but this wilful young woman had certainly not parted from her temper. Marcus felt a rush of blood through his veins and a hammering in his chest. Like a dangerous illness that desires a desperate remedy, he refused to back down. Before this day was out, he would force her heart to forget Thomas Waring.

'You can't fight a duel,' she persisted. 'One of you will be...'

'What, Juliet? Killed? And which one of us would you prefer to live?'

'Both of you.'

'I intend it will be me.'

'Please, I am begging you, Marcus.' She breathed as if she couldn't inhale enough air. 'How do you expect me to live with you as your wife, to respect you as a wife should, if you take Thomas's life? Don't you understand? Don't—don't make me hate you.'

Marcus looked at the proud beauty and saw the despair that was tearing her apart. When he saw the tears and the fear steal into her luminous eyes, he was beset by a twinge of conscience, which he quickly thrust away. He caught the note of anguish in her voice, which tore at his heart. She was right and he was deeply sorry for the hurt this duel with Waring would cause her, but it was too late to change anything now. It would be a long time, if ever, he thought, feeling a pang of regret, that she would be able to love him as she had loved Thomas Waring, but it would be a long time before he would be able to forget that she had gone to that man on their wedding night. And yet he knew he must if they were to have any sort of life together as man and wife.

'I know you will hate me a good deal more before I am finished, but you appear to forget that it is Waring who has instigated this, not me.'

Lifting his brows, he gazed at her with enigmatic eyes and an impassive expression for several endless, uneasy moments. Her hair lay on her shoulders like a gleaming golden mass. Having thrown off his cape, his gaze dwelt on her torn gown—her beautiful wedding gown. His cool gaze warmed as it rested on her. She was very lovely, this obstinate, spirited young woman he had married. So lovely, in fact, he could almost forgive her for her defence of Thomas Waring.

'Do you know, Juliet, you are one of the very few women who verbally attacks me. The majority of your contemporaries usually find me quite charming. I might even say that some have a great affection for me.'

'Perhaps that is because they have not had the pleasure of being married to you.'

Marcus look at her with disdain. 'The ferocity with which you defend Waring is touching, Juliet.'

'I know how much I must have hurt you, Marcus, but what can I say other than I am sorry. Everything happened so fast. I wasn't thinking. Do not forget that Thomas and I were formally engaged. I foolishly felt that I had to speak to him. We are to leave London tomorrow and he is to return to Spain very soon. I may never see him again.'

'I sincerely hope not.'

'I know you want to settle a score with Thomas, and after seeing the true nature of the man I would have married, I cannot blame you, but do not underestimate him. However confident you might feel about your own prowess, Thomas is a superb marksman and an expert with a sword.'

Marcus looked down at her, a cold glitter in his eyes. 'Don't try and stop me, Juliet. I have to do this. Waring has issued a challenge that cannot be ignored. You are my wife and it is my duty to defend your honour. What you have done, going to another man's house on our wedding night, is beyond the bounds of respectable behaviour.'

He was being uncompromising, he knew, but he was still shaken by what had almost happened to her. Stiffening her spine and with her head held high, as impressive as a tropical storm and a fierce challenging pride on her face, she took a step back imperturbably. She looked as if she were about to do battle, ready to do battle, ready for anything Marcus would aim at her. He impaled her on his gaze, leaving her in no doubt that he intended to seek satisfaction in a duel.

'Promise me you will not kill him. Whatever he has done, he does not deserve that.'

'No? Then perhaps you should have thought of that before you went looking for him.'

'How did you know that I had gone? I—I thought you had left the house.'

'Having no wish to concern my mother, I changed my mind. If she knew there was discord between us already, then she would be reluctant to part with Adele. I cannot risk that. I heard the carriage leave the house. When I found you weren't in your room, I knew you were in that carriage, and where else would you be going if not to Waring? The fact that you have betrayed me, have incurred my displeasure, does not seem to matter,' he said with heavy irony.

'Of course it does, and you have every right to be angry, but I did love him once—only I realise now that I did not know him, what he was capable of. I—I was so afraid.'

'Of course you were, when you discovered to what depraved depths he would sink to get his own way. If anything has been achieved by tonight's events, it is that all romantic thoughts of that man will at last be banished from your mind.'

'Yes, you are right. I had no idea he would behave as he did. It was as if some kind of monster had been unleashed.'

'And yet you want him to live.'

'Yes, of course I do,' she said, her eyes blazing with anger. 'Even though I pity him, if the events of this night have taught me anything, it is that his soul is a cold quagmire of cruelty, deceit, selfishness and wickedness. I loathe him, and to think I would have married him.'

'I am sure his feelings for you have not changed, but

your circumstances have. You are my wife in name, and soon to be my wife in fact, should you need reminding of the vows you spoke earlier today. Juliet, that man has abused you and damn near destroyed you. Don't ask me to ignore what he did tonight. I would rather hang.'

'And hang you shall if you kill him.'

He looked down at her, feeling her hand clinging to his arm with all her strength. Unsmiling, he looked at her seriously for a moment, one eyebrow lifted almost imperceptibly. 'The minute he walked through the door, he addled your wits. If you had known he was still alive, would you have married me? Tell me, Juliet. I have a right to know.'

'I cannot answer that. The truth is I don't know,' she replied miserably. 'Truly.'

'Now that you have seen him again and know what he is capable of, do you still have feelings for him?' he went on remorselessly.

'I told you. I hate him for what he has done this night. Whatever feelings I had left for him, he killed tonight. He is a brute, and I would like to see him punished for what he has done, but I beg you not to fight a duel. I no longer love him, but I cannot be the one to bring about his death. All this has come about because of my foolishness, and I have no wish to have the death of either of you to be the result of me making the wrong decision. If you kill him, I shall blame myself as surely as if I had pulled the trigger or wielded the sword. I shall have killed him, and I cannot live with that. The guilt would be too heavy for me to bear. Please,' she whispered softly, 'if you kill him, his death will stand between us forever.'

The anguish and pain on her pale face had their effect, touching some hidden chord deep inside him. Marcus didn't know how to react to this display of grief, but he had to acknowledge the sense of her words, fully aware that he had allowed his hurt masculine pride and anger to cloud his judgement.

'Has it not crossed your mind what will happen if you do kill Thomas, that despite being who you are, you will be arrested? I cannot bear to think of the punishment that will be meted out to you. It is too horrendous to imagine.'

He considered her intently and nodded slowly. 'Yes, I have thought about it. But put it another way, Juliet. What if Waring proves to be stronger than me? Has it not occurred to you for one moment that *I* might not return? Have you thought what will happen if he kills me?'

At his words, she stared at him, mortified. 'I have indeed thought of this, but believing you are stronger and more proficient than Thomas, I have tried not to dwell on it. Tonight my feelings have undergone a considerable change so that I no longer know what to think. But, dear God, not that. After all that has happened, after all I have lost, I could not bear that—to lose you. It would break my heart.'

Deeply touched by her words, Marcus's heart swelled with thankfulness that she should feel this way. 'Very well, Juliet. Should I gain the upper hand, I promise you that I shall not kill him. Merely teach him a lesson he will not forget. But he should not go unpunished, leaving him free to assault other innocent women. He is to return to Spain in the near future. Perhaps army discipline will knock some of the wickedness out of him.'

On that note Marcus turned on his heel. At the door he hesitated and looked back at her. 'Goodnight, Juliet. I trust tomorrow we can put this behind us.

Juliet stood and looked at the closed door through which her husband had disappeared, his face set in such lines of implacability that it left her feeling thoroughly chastened, stupid, and what little fight she had left within her drained away. Her behaviour had caused a hidden force to erupt inside him, and she was seeing a side of him she hadn't known existed. Could that cold, angry stranger be her husband? The man she had married, who had promised her and Richard so much for the future?

Crushed by the full weight of responsibility for her stupidity, her gullibility that had wreaked such havoc, she sank onto a chair. The hideous events of the night had unleashed in Marcus all the fury of his passionate nature. Within the past twenty-four hours, her life had been torn asunder, and she prayed fervently that Marcus would return to her unharmed, for she had come to depend on him like the very air she breathed and whose quiet strength she valued a great deal.

Feeling bruised and defiled and weighted down with terrible misery and despair, the thought that she had to go on living beyond this night was inconceivable. Covering her face with her trembling hands, she wept, silently praying for his safe return.

Chapter Nine

Marcus's anger died the moment he entered his room. Throwing his jacket on the bed and moving to the fireplace, he rested his arms on the mantelpiece, his mind going over the night's events as he stared down into the flames. He could not find words to describe his defiant young wife. He was enraged by her attitude, yet at the same time, he could not help but admire her courage. She had spirit, too much damned spirit, he thought. He didn't know another woman who would stand up to his wrath as she did. She had stood up to him from their first encounter, and then angered him by taking it upon herself to visit Waring at his home.

Juliet wasn't a woman he could wrap around his finger and charm with an irresistible smile. With her back straight, head held high, her hair caressing her spine and her eyes flashing a desperate amber, she had faced up to him. He was intrigued by her eyes, for they would glow with fervour, and at other times they were quiet, looking inward and sad, and it mattered to him. He thought about everything she had said, how vehemently she had expressed her feelings. For a long time he stood there, knowing he must try and make amends for all the wrongs he had caused her, before her hurt really did harden into hatred.

Perhaps his anger had made him hasty. If he was honest with himself, then he had to admit that he didn't want to kill Waring. He was a villain and he despised him, and it was right that he should be punished for what he had done, but he did not deserve to die for it. The last thing he wanted was his death on his conscience. He would prefer to put the whole ugly episode behind him.

But that was before one of the servants brought him a note that had just been delivered to the house. It was from Thomas Waring, and the short missive told him that he would meet him at dawn in Hyde Park, where they would settle their differences with swords. Marcus uttered a sigh of resignation. So, he had no choice. He would have to fight. If he did not meet him, he would be branded a coward, and that was unthinkable.

It was just before daybreak that he went to rouse Walter, his valet of many years, urging him to get dressed quickly and meet him in the hall. After briefly informing Walter what was required of him, they did a short detour to collect his sword from his home before riding in the direction of Hyde Park. Initially he had considered asking William to be his second, but finding the mere thought of explaining to his brother the sordidness that had brought about the duel and not wishing to cause his mother undue concern should she get wind of it, he had decided against it.

The world as the two men rode through the park in a thick blanket of grey cloud was cold, everything about them dormant, gripped by a beautiful desolation. A slight breeze snaked its pathway round the trees, pointing their leaf-covered branches up to the sky.

Grim-faced they rode hard, the only sound being the heavy breathing of their horses and the rhythmic pounding of their hoofs. As they approached the desired spot where the duel was to take place, it was oddly silent and deserted, the park hereabouts deeply wooded. They entered a circular glade, slowing their pace. They scanned the dark shadows not only for Thomas Waring and his second but also for others, for the constables, for if the law had got wind that a duel was to be fought, then it would spell disaster for them all.

Waring and his second were already there. Accompanied by a physician he had had to pay well for his services, they rode out of the dark shadows as they entered the glade. Quickly they all dismounted, Marcus divesting himself of his cloak and handing it to Walter, eyed Waring carefully as he moved closer. In the cold light of dawn, there was no trace of the drunken creature of last night, when the fumes of alcohol had clouded his mind. Now he met Marcus's gaze coldly.

'I trust you slept well,' he said with sarcasm, 'and that you said farewell to your bride, for I doubt you shall see her again on this day or any other.'

'No, I did not, for I do not expect to die.'

Waring smiled almost pleasantly. 'Then you were too confident, for I promise you, you will not live to see another dawn.'

'We shall see,' Marcus said, taking off his jacket and throwing it on the ground.

The two men faced each other in shirts of fine lawn, and Marcus read clearly the evil intent to kill in Waring's eyes. Both men loosed their swords, freeing the naked blades from their sheaths.

Waring saluted his opponent with a sardonic smile. *'En garde.'*

They circled each other warily before their blades engaged, ferociously slicing the air. The swords clashed, and at first, neither bore the initiative, but they fought with all the violence born of hatred. Both men were evenly matched, although Marcus was the taller and appeared the most powerful of the two with his strong, muscular frame, but Waring possessed a lithe agility and fought with all the skill of an experienced duellist.

It was only after Waring stumbled slightly on stepping back, his weakened leg letting him down, that Marcus seized his chance and immediately took the initiative, lunging, pressing home his attack. Enraged at finding himself at a disadvantage, Waring fought like a man possessed, and their blades clashed faster and faster. A fierce, determined light shone in Marcus's eyes, but not a muscle in his face moved as his sword flashed, the clash of steel on steel rending the air. With everything to lose, Waring began to fight dementedly, but however hard he tried to attack, he could not penetrate that unwavering guard and was constantly driven back as Marcus proved the stronger, his blade fiercely hissing through the air.

Pure cold fury filled Waring's eyes at being held constantly at bay, and in desperation, he began lunging wildly, carelessly, while Marcus retained his calm. And at last pressed home his advantage, sliding the point of his sword through the soft flesh of Waring's right shoulder.

Waring's eyes opened wide in absolute surprise, his sword slipping from his hand, bright red blood staining the white purity of his shirt as he stumbled and fell, crumpling onto the ground. Marcus stepped back and stared down at him.

Waring cursed softly and attempted to get up but, his chest heaving, the effort proved too much and, smiling bitterly, he looked up at Marcus. 'Well, what are you waiting for? Aren't you going to finish me?'

'I shall not kill you, but only because before I came here, Juliet begged me not to. It is she you have to thank for your life, though God knows why after what she suffered at your hands. But be under no illusion, because it would give me immense pleasure to finish you for good.'

'Then do so,' hissed Waring, 'because I swear that while ever there is breath in my body, I shall hunt you down. I shall be avenged. I swear it! You shall regret not killing me. This I promise you.'

Marcus's eyes were like cold pieces of flint as they met his adversary's. 'I doubt that. When we parted on our first encounter, I was aware of your insane hatred, but I did not know what such bitter resentment might lead you to do until I met you again last night. And now this. If I ever catch you on my property or in close proximity to my wife again, I will arrange your judgement day to come sooner than you expect.'

'You…threaten me?' Waring's tone was mockingly incredulous. 'Don't be too sure about that, Cardell. It's your life and all you hold dear hanging in the balance, not mine.'

'I am stating what our future relationship will be,' Marcus said coldly. 'We have fought a duel. I won. You had your chance to get rid of me and failed. You are a sad excuse for a man, Waring. I pity you.'

Thwarted of triumph, Waring's fury burst. 'Pity? You

pity me? His face darkened with rage as he watched his adversary begin to move away.

'That is what I said.' Marcus stepped back. 'Come, Walter, our business here is done. Waring is not dead and it was a fair fight. Whatever he threatens, I doubt he will bother us again.'

And without paying further attention to the recumbent figure with the doctor ministering to his wound, he turned and strode away, firmly believing as he did so that he would never set eyes on Thomas Waring again.

Back at the house Marcus found Juliet in the drawing room pacing up and down as she waited anxiously for him to return. When he entered the room, he paused for a moment and looked at her, so still that she might have been carved out of stone. Her face was white, one hand at her throat as she waited, taut with suspense.

'Marcus,' she uttered softly. 'Thank God you are safe, that you have returned to me unscathed, haven't you?' Hope that this was so was mirrored in her eyes, plain for him to see.

'I am unharmed.'

'I was—I was so worried. I could not have borne it if… You are telling me the truth, Marcus? Thomas did not hurt you?'

'Cease your worrying, Juliet. I come back to you in one piece.'

She swallowed hard. 'And Thomas? Is he—is he dead?'

Marcus saw that she trembled slightly with fear at what he might tell her, and the intonation of his voice when he spoke was cold and distant as he replied, 'You will be relieved to know that I spared him. When I left him, I regret to tell you he was very much alive.'

At the relief that flooded her eyes, his face hardened and he was conscious of a sudden surge of anger.

'Thank you. Was—was he badly wounded?' she whispered, her voice dying away into the silence of the room.

Marcus looked at her incredulously. 'You astound me, Juliet. Does it matter to you so much? Is it possible that after all the harm he has done, you can still feel compassion for Waring?'

'It is natural for me to feel concern.' She looked down at her hands despairingly. 'How can I make you understand the torment I have been through since you left? How can I make you believe that I never want to see Thomas again—ever? But that neither do I want him to die at the hands of my husband. And how can I make you believe that after much soul-searching, I realise that if one man had to forfeit his life during the course of the duel, then I would rather it have been Thomas?' She stared up at him, and as she met his gaze miserably, she said, 'This has been the most terrible night of my life. I shall never forget it as long as I live.'

'Then you must forget it. For your sake as well as for mine,' he said. 'And I will tell you this, Juliet. I never want to hear the name of Thomas Waring mentioned again. Do you understand? You are my wife now and I expect you to behave as such. I will fight no more duels on your behalf. I have Adele to consider. She has already lost her mother. I cannot risk leaving her an orphan.' He turned from her. 'And now perhaps you would be good enough to be ready to leave for Surrey as soon as possible. I have to go and collect Adele. William is to leave for Sussex with my mother, to welcome a new addition to the Cardell family, I expect. With such a long journey ahead of him, my brother will not thank me if I am late.'

'Yes—yes, of course. I have instructed Daphne to begin packing my things.'

Following him out of the room, with her head held high, she proceeded up the stairs. Marcus watched her, aware of the wretchedness she must be feeling and detesting himself for venting his anger on her, knowing that the manner in which he had spoken to her was unforgivable. On reaching his house, he strode quickly into the dining room cursing angrily and, taking a decanter, poured a generous helping of brandy into a glass, but not even when he drank deeply, feeling the fiery liquid course through his veins, did it lessen his self-loathing.

Juliet was glad to be leaving London for Mulberry Hall. Daphne had completed the packing and, to Juliet's delight and relief, had agreed to go with her to the country to act as her maid.

When Juliet considered what her life would be like from now on, she felt that it would be like spinning about in some great vortex without the stable influence of Endcliffe House, on which she had always depended and from which she had been wrenched, and she was totally unprepared for the scale of misery that engulfed her.

Adele, who was supposed to be travelling in the coach behind with her nursemaid, Daphne and Marcus's valet, became fractious and tearful to find she was to be separated from her adored father.

'Adele can surely travel with us,' Juliet suggested, hoping Marcus would agree, because Adele's presence in the coach would go some way to alleviating the tension that existed between them.

Adele immediately caught on to the suggestion, and

her little face became alight with hope. 'Please, Papa, let me go with you.'

Marcus looked down with concern at his daughter and his expression softened. 'If she's going to be difficult, then I suppose she must.'

Juliet was pleasantly surprised when he reached down and lifted Adele into the carriage.

The little girl was clearly delighted to be travelling with her father and her new stepmother. A happy smile stretched her pink lips as she nestled as close to Marcus as was possible, which made him smile.

He cocked a dark brow at Juliet as she settled herself opposite, waiting for the nursemaid to join them. 'How I wish I could pacify all the women in my life as easily as I can my daughter.'

Juliet responded with a wry smile. 'Perhaps if you didn't go around with such a stern expression on your face all the time, you wouldn't find it such a problem,' she dared to say, amused when she turned her head away and heard him chuckle softly.

It was late afternoon, and the clouds were gilded with sunshine when the carriage passed through a huge stone gateway with the heraldic bearings of Marcus's mother's family. They travelled slowly up a hill, the drive lined with giant beech trees, offering a cool, gentle shade. Adele had drifted off to sleep before halfway through the journey and was cradled close to her nurse. Before they topped the rise, Marcus ordered the driver to stop the carriage. He climbed down, holding his hand out to Juliet.

'Come, I'll show you Mulberry Hall.'

'But I've seen it many times, visiting it when I was a girl, if you recall, and on the occasions when I ride out.'

'I know that, but I want to show it to you myself.'

Holding her hand, he led her to the top of the rise. Touched that Marcus wanted her to see it with him, without realising she was doing so, Juliet held her breath when she gazed in wonder at what she always thought must be a dream. The gentle sweep of the valley unfolding before her eyes, the acres of fields and woods stretching almost as far as the eye could see and the pastures full of cattle never failed to move her. Seeing it with Marcus filled her with enchantment. This was her husband's domain, and when her eyes rested on the house, the stones of which it was built glowing rose-pink in the late-afternoon sun, her heart swelled. The house rose stately and supreme in timeless splendour, like a jewel beneath the dark shade of tall oaks and elms, surpassing the quiet beauty of her own Endcliffe House.

Watching her reaction, Marcus smiled slowly. 'It's beautiful, is it not, Juliet?' he said with pride.

'Yes,' she breathed, 'it is quite splendid.'

'I think this is the best spot to see the house. It never changes,' he murmured. 'It smiles, it beckons, it invites and welcomes. I have loved it since I was a child. There is nowhere quite like it.'

'Has it always been in your mother's family?'

'Yes. It was my great-grandfather who gained favour from Queen Anne and acquired the earldom, then built the house. It was only after many trials and adversities that he at last achieved success and created a rich estate—the one you now see. One to be handed down with pride to his descendants. Sadly, over the years, the family were not blessed with male heirs, hence my own ascendance to the title and estate.'

'But your brother William? Should it not have passed to him?'

'William has titles and properties enough on the Cardell side. Knowing this, my grandfather bequeathed Mulberry Hall and the title to me on his demise.' Marcus looked down at her. 'It will be handed down to our children. All this is yours now, and I want you to feel for it as I do. I want you to be happy here, and not miss Endcliffe House too much.'

She smiled up at him. 'I don't think that will be too difficult.' At that moment she had no doubt that Mulberry Hall was part of her destiny, that she belonged here, that she could be happy here. She told herself that these thoughts were fanciful, but she truly believed it was possible. 'Endcliffe House was my home for too long for me not to miss it, but Mulberry Hall is my home now. I'm sure I shall be very happy here. Indeed, who would not be? It is a beautiful house. How did the house get its name?'

'My great-grandfather was something of a botanist. He cultivated the mulberry trees for their berries. The leaves can also be fed to livestock. The trees grow to quite a height, so they need pruning. '

'Are the berries not excellent food for silkworms in the silk trade?'

'I believe the leaves of the white mulberry are. The Romans first brought the trees to Britain. The leaves are said to have medicinal purposes, but they became most prized for their succulent berries.'

'Have any of the trees survived that your ancestor planted?'

'Several, I believe, though they are somewhat gnarled now, but they still bear fruit.'

'Then I shall look forward to seeing them—and tasting the berries.'

'I sent word on ahead, so we are expected. I am sure you will be familiar with some members of staff since they are from the locality. Having run Endcliffe House since your mother's demise, you will be no stranger to what is expected of you, but don't worry. You'll soon get used to it. The housekeeper, Mrs Cherry, who has been at Mulberry Hall for some years now, will familiarise you with everything. I mean to entertain quite often—local dignitaries and such like. But you can rest assured that I have no plans to entertain anyone for the present, and nothing too strenuous will be required of you.'

'I have no worries about that. It will be no different to running Endcliffe House, but on a larger scale.'

'Come,' Marcus said, turning and slowly escorting her back to the carriage. 'Let us be on our way to the house.'

The two coaches pulled up in front of the house. What seemed like a dozen servants suddenly appeared and began unloading the baggage while the occupants entered the house. The large hall was surprisingly cool, with doors leading off to other rooms, all tastefully furnished.

Juliet hadn't visited Mulberry Hall since she was a child, but it was much as she remembered. As soon as she entered the house, she was greeted with unaffected warmth. The magnificence and antiquity with which she was surrounded overwhelmed her. She had the strange feeling of passing into another world and that life would never be the same again. She could feel the past closing in on her, wrapping itself around her, but it was in no way threatening or unpleasant; in fact, it was quite the opposite, for it gave her a warm, welcoming glow deep inside. It was a house where courtesy and mutual affection ruled in perfect harmony. As she absorbed the atmosphere of the great house, it seemed alive but dormant, quietly waiting for the return of a family to fill its rooms with the voices and laughter of children, to make it a home again.

The staff had gathered to welcome them home. Some of them who came from the surrounding area Juliet already knew. Adele was whisked off to the nursery, and Mrs Cherry, who had been housekeeper since before Juliet was born and remembered her mother, escorted her up the long flight of stairs, pointing out the merits of her new home. The long gallery, crossing the width of the house, was of tremendous proportions. Its floor was of polished oak and its walls supported a huge vaulted ceiling of decorative plaster. Set in rows along the walls and giving the visitor the impression that they had stepped into the presence of gathered nobility were paintings of Marcus's ancestors on his mother's side—men and women who had coloured the exclusive world of Mulberry Hall for generations, all housed in elaborately gilded frames. Her bedchamber, which was one of gracious elegance, sumptuous in both design and colour, was decorated in delicate shades of green and ivory.

'I can't tell you how happy I am to have you here, Lady Juliet,' Mrs Cherry said warmly. 'Your dear mother would be happy for you.'

'Yes,' Juliet replied softly, 'yes, she would. She always loved visiting this house.'

'You have brought your own maid along with you I see.'

'Yes, Daphne. She has been employed at the house

in London and is a highly competent and capable young woman. Having spent all her life in town, I was so pleased when she agreed to come with me to Mulberry Hall.'

'I'm sure she will soon settle down. I hope the room is to your liking. Facing south, it gets plenty of sun, and it overlooks the deer park and the lake.'

'Yes, I like it very well, Mrs Cherry. It's perfect.'

The heavy brocade curtains moved gently with the soft, refreshing breeze blowing in through the open windows. There was a door connecting Marcus's room to hers, through which he could come to her any time. It was only then that Juliet, staring at the large bed, felt a sudden dart of panic when she thought of the nights Marcus would share it with her.

Mrs Cherry departed when Daphne came in, unable to suppress a gasp of delight at the extravagance of her new surroundings. She flitted about the room, inspecting the dressing room leading off from the main bedchamber and delighting at the wardrobe space where Juliet's beautiful gowns would be hung.

Impatient for her mistress's trunks to be brought up so she could unpack them, Daphne made herself scarce when Marcus entered.

'I see the bed has given you pause for thought, Juliet. Does it displease you knowing we will occupy it together?'

She spun round, startled by the sound of his voice. 'No—no, of course not,' she stammered. 'Only, I—I thought—'

'Thought what?' he said brusquely. 'That because of the unpleasantness that followed our wedding I didn't wish to share a bed with my wife? Well, whatever thoughts might have passed through that pretty head of yours, I can tell you now that I find the possibility quite appealing. Although it seems that I will have to wait, for I will not make love to my wife, or any other woman, come to that, while her heart lies elsewhere.' He threw her a mocking smile. 'Rather like having three in a bed, don't you think?'

He moved to the window and stood looking out. Juliet stared at his stony profile, his jaw set firm. With a sudden surge of longing to go to him and run her hands over the broad set of his shoulders welling up inside her, she didn't move. His relaxed, easy manner when they had stood together to look at the house had gone. She swallowed hard, sensing the tension inside him. She thought back to all that had happened since their wedding, which now felt as if it had happened in some other lifetime. But one thing was clear to her: they couldn't go on like this. They would have to talk, to bring down this invisible wall he had erected between them. She had sensed a softening in him when they had stopped to look at the house, but the reticence was back.

She moved towards him. 'Please, Marcus,' she said softly. 'We have to talk. We can't go on like this.'

'No, you're right, we can't.'

Juliet watched as he lifted one hand and massaged the taut muscles in his neck, his expression becoming darker and more ominous as his mind went over what had occurred. He was deeply troubled, Juliet could see that, and naturally so, with everything that had transpired. Weren't things difficult enough between them without the added pressure of Thomas standing between them?

In a desperate attempt to make things right, Juliet moved closer to his side.

'I'm sorry about all this, Marcus. Believe me, if I could change things, I would.'

He turned his head and looked down at her, barely concealed doubt cloaking his eyes. 'Would you, Juliet? Would you really?'

'Yes, of course I would. There was a time, not so long ago, when I could never have imagined being close to any other man but Thomas. But times and emotions change, and they have changed me. When will you realise that I no longer love him?'

'Then tell me,' he said, his voice low and controlled, 'why did you go to him last night? I have to know, Juliet.'

He had told her he never wanted to hear Thomas's name mentioned again, and since leaving London neither of them had, but she knew the man remained uppermost in Marcus's mind.

'I have already told you why. Do we have to go over it all again?'

'Tell me again.'

'I went to him,' she said quietly, 'because I had to know if he would have married me when he became aware of my circumstances. I had to know—it was important to me—before I went away, for my own peace of mind.'

Marcus turned sharply and looked at her, and she cringed inwardly at his cold expression. 'And would he?'

She shook her head. 'No.'

'Then it was fortunate for you, after all, that I came along when I did, wasn't it?'

'That isn't fair,' she gasped, stung by his words. 'You

knew my situation when you asked me to marry you. I made no secret of what my feelings were for Thomas.'

'Of course,' he said, his lips twisting with sarcasm. 'You must forgive me for forgetting. But do you expect me to believe that you went to him on our wedding night for no other reason than to talk to him?'

'Yes, I do,' she said, moving closer to him. 'As far as I am concerned, Thomas is dead, and if we are to find any happiness in our marriage, then he must be dead for you too. Nothing can change what has happened, so we must learn to put it behind us. I no longer love him—I realised that before I went to his home to see him—and in fact, I don't know if I ever did. This I have told you, so why can't that stubborn pride of yours let you accept it?' She sighed deeply, her anger of a moment before leaving her.

Aware of his indecision and that he continued to doubt her words, she moved closer to him. 'Please listen to me,' she pleaded fervently, gripping his arm. 'I find it hard to see myself as I used to be—living my life believing Thomas would be a part of it forever. That was another lifetime. Then I was somebody else. I want to discover a different life—with you and Adele here at Mulberry Hall. I cannot conceive of anything different.'

'I am touched by what you say, Juliet, and more than anything, I want to believe you. In the beginning, I did wonder how you could ever respect me as a wife should—a man who had virtually bought your affections, and yet when you spoke your vows, I hoped you had truly put Thomas Waring behind you.'

'I fully intend to do that,' she murmured, placing her hand timidly on his arm. Summoning up all her courage, she gazed beseechingly into his eyes. 'Have you made up your mind to hate me all your life? How much longer will you continue to spurn me? Can you not find it in your heart to forgive me? None of this has been easy for me either.'

Marcus tried hard to shove her away with hands that secretly asked nothing more than to hold on to her. She had taken the first step toward a reconciliation, and she expected him to take the next, which, after all that had transpired within the past two days, he found difficult. Despite having told him otherwise, he suspected that deep down, Juliet still harboured tender thoughts for Waring, and he could not bear the thought of making love to her while she was thinking of someone else.

He looked into the imploring softness of her eyes, so bewitchingly beautiful, and he was moved in spite of himself, wanting nothing more at that moment than to atone for his sharp words and win her forgiveness. With some concern he noted the dark smudges beneath her eyes.

This is not good, he thought, despairing. *We can't go on behaving like enemies.*

She looked so piteous, so defenceless, and she spoke so passionately that the hard gleam went from his eyes and there was a softer tone to his voice when he spoke.

Taking her hand from his arm, he tenderly drew her close. 'I don't hate you, Juliet—don't ever think that. No man in his right mind would spurn you intentionally. You are far too lovely for that. I know that none of this is easy for you, that it is far easier for me than you.' He smiled slowly. 'I've been a selfish brute, haven't I? You deserved better after what you've been through.'

Juliet smiled with relief at the tenderness filling his eyes, and she trembled with a quiet joy. 'Then we are friends again?'

'More than that, I hope. But how does it feel to know you have the power to make me suffer, to make my life hell? You have bewitched me, Juliet. No other woman has done that.'

'I—I'm sorry, Marcus.'

'What for?'

'My stupidity. Did I hurt you very much?'

'More than you will ever know, but you are right. We will put all that has happened behind us. We must not allow it to poison our happiness, and besides, the days ahead—of settling in to living at Mulberry Hall and building on your relationship with Adele, will be difficult enough for you without that. Having made a hasty marriage, I regret there was no time for courtship, but it is not the first time that virtual strangers have found themselves married to each other.'

'Not entirely strangers. We had met before.'

'You were a child, Juliet. A long time has passed since then, and I have been away fighting a war. While all this is strange and unfamiliar at this time, we have our whole lives to learn to know each other.' Gazing down into the magnificent amber depths of her eyes, he raised her hand to his lips, feeling desire surge through him, and he was impatient for the night to come when he could make her his wife in flesh as well as in name. But however soft and inviting the large bed looked, now was not the time. 'Much as I would like to remain with you at present, I have matters to attend to and you must settle in,' he said huskily.

Disappointment clouded her eyes. 'Yes, of course.'

'Later, we will spend time together. I promise,' he said, bending his head and brushing her soft lips with his own. 'Wild horses won't be able to keep me from you tonight.' He looked down at her, a wicked light dancing in his eyes. 'No objections, Juliet. It has been delayed, I know, but we will count this as our wedding night, and you are my adorable bride. I do not intend to waste one minute of it.'

'I do not object,' she murmured.

'That's what I wanted to hear. I will leave you to wash and change and I'll see you at dinner.'

Before joining Marcus in the dining room, Juliet went to check on Adele. After being confined to the coach for the journey to Mulberry Hall, the child was clearly thrilled to have been let loose at last and to explore her new domain. She had set about dragging toys out of boxes and cupboards and enthused excitedly over a particularly fine rocking horse. She insisted on showing Juliet her new playthings and in particular the books with stories of children's exploits, of fairies and elves and princes rescuing beautiful princesses, making Juliet promise to read them to her in the coming days. Leaving the nursemaid to settle her down for the night, Juliet went down to the dining room, where Marcus, washed and changed and looking terribly handsome in grey trousers and a dark blue jacket, which was stretched smoothly over his broad shoulders, was already partaking of a pre-dinner glass of wine.

'To us,' Marcus said as he handed her a glass of red wine.

'To us,' she murmured, raising her glass and gently

tapping his before taking a sip of wine, 'and to a new beginning.'

There was a pause as their eyes held for a moment, the peace between them unspoken but there all the same. It had been a while coming, and they both felt it deeply. She felt herself tremble with wonder, and the relief at being here with him surged through her entire body. But it was more than that. With Thomas receding into the past, Marcus had released what had been lost inside her, had set free her ability to feel the emotions that swelled her heart—her ability to love. She was ready to relinquish her guard, like a snake shedding its skin.

'What do you think of Mulberry Hall? Although having grown up in the grandeur of Endcliffe House and surrounded by the trappings of the nobility, perhaps it does not impress you as much as it would some.'

Juliet's eyes were alight with interest as she gazed at the pictures and furniture that harmonised perfectly. Turning to look at her husband, she realised he was awaiting her reaction. There was an expectant hope in his handsome face, and she could not deny him.

'On the contrary. I am impressed. It is very fine indeed,' she murmured, taking a seat by the hearth, 'and just as I remember. Few brides are presented with so much. Usually, it is the groom who receives what his wife brings to him as a dowry, which I have failed to provide.'

'I told you. None of that matters. You will find that I am a generous man in that regard.'

'What was she like, Marcus—your first wife, Elizabeth? I imagine she didn't enter into marriage as impoverished as I.'

'No. She came from an impressive, wealthy family.

Our families were friends of long standing. It had been in the cards for some time that we would marry. Elizabeth was young—no more than eighteen—simple and good and pretty.'

'Biddable?'

'Yes, she was.'

'Unlike me.'

Marcus grinned, capturing her gaze. 'Exactly. Never were two people less alike.'

'I see. And did you love her very much?'

Marcus looked at the glass of wine in his hand and swirled the liquid round in the glass, seeming to think how best to answer her question. 'I don't think love entered into it. We liked and respected each other—there was affection—indeed we were the best of friends, but love? Elizabeth wanted nothing more than to be my wife. For the short time we were together, she was content. She died giving birth to Adele.'

There was a husky rasp to his voice, an edge of sadness. 'I'm sorry,' Juliet said quietly.

'There's no need for you to be. It happened. I did love her in a way, but I wasn't in love with her. It was a long time ago. She is but a memory to me now.'

'Kept alive by Adele.'

He nodded. 'I can't tell you how important it is to me to be here, to take care of her. I returned home for a brief period when she was born, but the war in the Peninsular got in the way, and I was duty-bound to return. Now that I am home and she is with me, I will be able to devote more time to her.'

Their conversation was curtailed when a footman came to tell them dinner was ready to be served.

Chapter Ten

Attired in just her nightdress Juliet moved aimlessly to the open window, nervous but impatient for Marcus to come to her. As she looked into the distance, in the darkness she could imagine Endcliffe House. Part of her wanted to be back there but, she thought wistfully, if she were back there, then Marcus wouldn't be with her, and suddenly all those girlish dreams of Thomas and the bulwark of her security—Endcliffe House—began to slip into the past and didn't seem to matter now.

Suddenly, without her noticing, Marcus had become a very important part of her life. He had stood by her, offering her his name, risking his money and his reputation. No man would have done all these things for a woman he did not care about, and she knew she would rather be here with him than without him at Endcliffe House. But what did she feel for him? Did she love him? This she did not know. After Thomas, she would never trust her judgement again, but when she thought of him, of his darkly handsome face and flashing smile, her body trembled with an unaccustomed desire to have him hold her. To feel his strong arms about her and to rest her head on his broad chest—to have him love her. She was more than ready to become his wife in every sense of the word.

Her vigil was rewarded when she heard footsteps on the other side of the door that connected their rooms. With feverish anticipation she turned. Her heart began to beat quickly and her mouth became dry, the palms of her hands clammy, and then suddenly he was there, standing in the open doorway. His flame-coloured robe was partly open at the front to reveal the strong muscles of his chest, with its crisp matting of hair just visible. Broad-shouldered and with his dark hair curling about his face, his jaw lean and firm, with his wicked eyes and lazy smile, he would have made the most handsome pirate, she thought.

They stared at each other, the air crackling with unexpressed emotion. Marcus's awesome presence seemed to fill the room. She could sense his eyes on her, sense his penetrating gaze stripping her body bare. She watched him close the door and move closer with the same rapt attention a rabbit gives a stalking fox, feeling his presence with every fibre of her being. A growing warmth suffused her, and she was achingly aware of her own newly formed desires.

He cocked a handsome brow as he gave her a lengthy inspection. Her nightdress clung to her slender form and the pins had been removed from her hair, allowing the thick tresses free to tumble about her shoulders. 'I see you are expecting me,' he murmured, raising his hand and tracing her bare arm with his finger.

'Yes. I—I expected you sooner.'

'I apologise if I have kept you waiting, Juliet, but I want you to be sure you are ready to become my wife in more than name. After your ordeal at Waring's hands, I would like to make sure I will be welcome in your bed.'

She laughed lightly, touched that he would still be concerned how Thomas's assault may have affected her. 'Worry not, Marcus. What happened has not scarred me in any way. I know you would never harm me physically. I have no fear of what you will do to me. Indeed,' she said, flushing slightly as she anticipated the night to come with a tremor of excitement, 'it is quite the opposite. In fact, I am as impatient as you are to begin our lives together—already I am anticipating exploring the sensual side to our marriage.'

'Then I shall do my best not to disappoint you. Be assured, I shall be a proficient and considerate teacher.'

'Did you say goodnight to Adele?'

'I went to the nursery only to find she was asleep. She is quite exhausted, poor lamb.'

'I—I looked in on her earlier,' Juliet said haltingly, trying to subdue her nervousness. 'She is thrilled with her new toys, in particular the rocking horse.'

'I had it brought here from Cranswick,' he said, his fingers moving upwards to caress her shoulder. 'I intend buying her a pony of her own when she is settled. She loves horses.'

'She will like that,' she said, her heart pounding with a deafening beat as he bent his head and placed his lips where his fingers had gone before. She was tense and still as she allowed him to continue his caress. Closing her eyes, she tilted her head back, feeling delicious sensations stirring inside her. 'Marcus, please,' she gasped. 'Should we not wait—and—'

'Juliet,' he murmured, 'stop talking.' Looking into her eyes, he caressed her fingers with his mouth. He could feel her melting, feel it in the way her fingers trembled.

'But we—'

He stopped her sentence with his thumb gently pressed against her lips. 'Shh.'

The tone of his voice was so soft and inviting that for one mad moment, Juliet almost surrendered herself there and then. She felt herself tremble with the need that he always invoked in her when he was close.

Taking her shoulders, he drew her lithe form towards him, capturing her in a gentle embrace, his eyes feasting on the delicate creaminess of her face and her shining hair spilling down over her shoulders. The sweet fragrance of her body drifted through his senses, and the throbbing hunger to possess her began anew.

'You must learn to relax, Juliet,' he whispered, his mouth against hers. 'The attraction between us has been denied for too long. It is my hope that come daylight, we will have reached an understanding.'

'But there is nothing to understand.'

'There is, my love,' he said, his voice a ragged whisper as he slid his tongue across her lips. 'Let me show you.'

His voice had deepened. His strength and the heat of him were palpable. When he lowered his head, she lost sight of his eyes and fixed her own on his lips. They brushed hers, gently testing their resilience, teasing, savouring, then, with the confidence that there would be a welcome, he covered her lips assuredly. That kiss almost sent her to her knees. Sensations she had never imagined overwhelmed her. The feel of him, the smell of him sank into her flesh, into the bones of her. In response, she slid her hands up his chest to his shoulders.

The kiss ended and he drew back slightly, sliding his hands down her bare arms.

Taking her hand, he drew her towards the bed, seizing her lips once more, drawing her senses again into the heated depths of a kiss, devouring her sweetness, languidly coaxing and parting, his tongue probing and plundering the honeyed cavern, as if he had an eternity to explore and savour.

The sweet urgency of it made Juliet lose touch with reality. It filled her soul. The embers that had glowed and heated her rebellion in the early days of their relationship now burned with passion, her protestations having become raw hunger. It was a kiss so exquisite that whatever doubts had plagued her over the days before becoming his wife died as she became imprisoned in a haze of dangerous, terrifying sensuality over which she had no control.

His hand deftly slipped the narrow straps of her nightdress off her shoulders, revealing the cleft between the round fullness of her breasts. Her cheeks flushed scarlet at his boldness. Raising his head, he laughed softly. There was still so much of the girl in her at war with the assertive young woman, and Marcus had the knack of bringing it quickly to the surface. It was clear to Juliet that in this particular arena, he had absolute control.

Bending his head to pay homage to the soft flesh glowing like creamy pearls in the soft light, he placed his lips in the hollow of her throat where a pulse throbbed. The contact was a shock to Juliet, a delicious one. Heat blossomed and spread. But the heat building inside Marcus, fed and steadily stoked, was escalating into urgency. As he awoke from their kiss, his long fingers divested her of what remained of her nightdress. Her glorious body was a lustrous shade of pale gold in the wavering blur of the flickering candles. Juliet's throat dried. Marcus's gaze focused upon her figure and the ardour in his dark gaze was like a flame to her senses. She was unable to free her rational mind from the overwhelming tide of desire that claimed her, fuelled by a whirlpool of emotions she didn't recognise, much less understand.

'When you've finished ogling me, Marcus, kindly remember you're supposed to be a gentleman and take off your clothes too, unless you intend to make love to me with them on.'

Marcus continued to drink his fill, noting her shallow breathing, sensing anticipation rising like scent around them. Chest tight, eager to seize, to devour, to slake the lust that drove him, every nerve Marcus possessed stilled as slowly his gaze traced up the curves of her long legs, the gentle swell of her thighs, over her taut stomach and minuscule waist to her breasts, full and tipped with rosy peaks. Proceeding to remove his robe, he struggled impatiently with the restricting belt.

Surrendering to the call of her blood, impatient to resume contact between them, with nimble fingers Juliet undid the knot herself. She felt a tremor of alarm and embarrassed admiration pass through her as his body was exposed to her. He had the form of a tall, lithe athlete. His shoulders and thighs were firmly muscled, his belly flat and taut. He was splendid, magnificent, and as she stared at him, her heart gave a tremendous leap, unable to believe how handsome he was. He laughed when she flushed and averted her maidenly eyes away from his manhood, and his teeth gleamed white from between his parted lips as he threw back the bedcovers, and then they were together once more, locked in each other's arms. Never had Juliet been as aware of another human being as she was of Marcus at that moment. Each of them was aware of a new intensity of feeling between them, a new excitement.

'You are an inviting, haunting temptress,' Marcus murmured against her lips. 'And you are about to experience a night of passion and sensual delights such as you cannot have imagined.'

Juliet saw the deepening light in Marcus's eyes. She saw the defined brows and wanted to touch his face, to know him. Then slowly, almost haltingly, he captured her mouth once more in a kiss that warmed her to the core of her being. Parted lips, tender and insistent, caressed hers, moulding and shaping them to his own while his hand touched her bare skin, which felt like liquid satin, his lips following where fingers had gone before, wandering at will over the contours of her.

Juliet was on fire. With a low moan, she stretched alongside him and the hard pressure of his loins. So lost was she in the desire he was skilfully building in her that when his hand travelled along more intimate ground, her thighs loosened of their own accord and quivered beneath his questing hands. She almost drowned as wave after wave of pleasure washed over her.

Hesitantly she half opened her eyes and met her husband's intense gaze, hearing the drumming of her heart until her ears were full of the sound. Faintness drifted on the edge of her vision. She wanted him. She ached for him. And she clutched at him with the awkward desperation of inexperience. Anticipating the pain she would feel in the next moment, she stiffened her body, her arms going round him.

Sensing her apprehension, he gentled the moment of entry. The pain was mild, and when it had subsided, in its place was a hungering, throbbing ache. He filled her fully, touching all of her. It was incredible, something new that burst inside her, and as she slowly began to move as he moved and arched to meet him to the full, she was so carried along on a rapturous glow of passion by the driving force of his powerful strokes deep within her that she was almost delirious. When the explosion came, it broke in a wave of ecstasy and she felt her body soar.

When the weight of his strong body lifted off her, sated and happy, Juliet looked up at him, fighting her way back from oblivion. She sighed and closed her eyes. Marcus lowered his head and ran his tongue provocatively over her lower lip.

'Are you happy, my love?'

'Mm,' she breathed without opening her eyes.

'What are you thinking?' he asked with a tender smile, stroking her satiny skin.

On a sigh, like a kitten she nestled close beneath the sensual onslaught of his caressing hand and mouth. 'My thoughts are most unladylike, I'm afraid. I will not offend your ear by airing them.'

Opening her eyes, she saw the gleam of an ugly silver scar on his shoulder. She touched it with her finger, tracing its smooth line. Lifting her head, she looked at him, imagining the pain he must have felt on being wounded.

'How the war in the Peninsular has hurt you,' she whispered.

'Nay, Juliet. The scar is one of several. I like to think I gave the Frenchies as much as I received on the battlefield. I'm relieved you are not repulsed by it.'

As if to heal his scar, she kissed it before wrapping her arms around him. 'Is every night to be like this one?'

'It is my hope.'

'Then I shall be well satisfied.'

'You speak as if this one is already over and done with, sweetheart. If that is what you think, then you are mistaken,' he said and, as if to prove it, he took her lips in a devouring kiss, renewed desire already pouring through him as he proceeded to kiss and caress her into mindless insensibility.

Later, as Juliet slept, the silky mass of her hair draped about her, his mind still reeling when he thought of the flagrant sensuality of the creature lying next to him, Marcus lay on his side, resting on his elbow, the fingers of his free hand gently brushing strands of hair from her face. His eyes were drawn compulsively to her, and he looked at her with part reverence, part awe, unable to believe this woman, his wife, had succeeded in sending him to unparalleled heights of satisfaction and desire. A deep contentment engulfed him as he gloried in the sweet, wild essence of her.

Conscious of the languor that weighted his limbs, of the satiation that was bone deep, he realised that this state had been reached not by mere self-gratification, but by a deep contentment more profound than at any other time in his life. Juliet had succeeded in tapping the source of his well-being where every other woman he had known had failed.

He was engulfed in a swirling mass of emotions, emotions that were new to him, emotions he could not recognise and could not put a name to. His every instinct reacted to the fact that he had this woman in thrall, that he'd finally breached the walls and captured the elusive creature at its core. He had always known that when he finally made love to her, they would be a combustible combination, but what he had just experienced had been the most splendidly erotic sexual encounter of his life.

In the light of a single candle and the sanctuary of their bed, he had gloried in her beauty—her tiny waist and rounded hips and full breasts. He had lingered over his wife of two days as he had begun to seal their vows securely in a physical knot of passion, determined that he would make her body sing with rapture before he was done. But it had been no easy matter ignoring the urgent heat and throbbing in his loins, and as gentle fingers had shyly explored his naked body, slowly gathering courage, they had ignited too many fires for his rapidly splintering restraint.

When he had entered that most intimate part of her, she had gasped at his invasion, and with the blood pouring through his veins like molten lava, he had gloried in the joy of the woman in his arms, feeling her yield to his caress.

Juliet sensed the presence of a warm, naked masculine form pressed against her as she floated in a comforting grey mist, drifting in and out of sleep. Lying soft and acquiescent beside him, she could smell his skin, his hair, and he was drawing her to him like a magnet.

'Good morning,' Marcus murmured. 'I trust you slept well.'

Opening her sleepy eyes, she gazed up at him. His tousled hair was dark against the snowy whiteness of the pillows, and sleep had softened the rugged contours of his handsome face. She thought of the times that he had made love to her throughout the night. The first time he had loved her with wild abandon, but thereafter he had exercised more control, lingering over her, holding himself back while he guided her to peak after peak of quivering ecstasy, caressing and kissing her with the skill and expertise of a virtuoso playing a violin.

With these memories occupying her mind, she felt her lips, swollen from his kisses, part in a smile. 'I seem to recall you gave me little time for such luxury,' she answered, her voice low, throaty and warm. 'How long have you been lying there watching me?'

His smouldering gaze passed over her naked shoulders, lingering on the twin peaks straining beneath the sheet. 'Long enough to come to the conclusion that you are too much temptation for a man not long away from the battlefield and starved of a woman's company. In fact, my love, if you were not already married, after our night making passionate love, I would have to marry you,' he teased, kissing the tip of her nose.

'Then it's a good thing I'm a married woman,' she purred, trailing her finger slightly across his chest, 'although I shudder to think what my husband will have to say about it. Why, he might even insist on divorcing me.'

'You may strive at times to drive him to it, being the stubborn and temperamental female that you are, but I can promise you that he will never divorce you,' Marcus stated. His voice still held a hint of teasing, but his eyes were dark and deadly serious.

'What time is it?' she asked, stretching like a sated cat, her gaze going towards the window. Seeing the brightness of the sun penetrating a crack in the drawn curtains, she sat up. 'Heavens, it's daylight. I'm ravenous and ready for my breakfast.'

Laughing softly, Marcus swung his legs over the side of the bed. 'Then I will leave you to your ablutions and see you at breakfast shortly.'

Left alone, Juliet felt as if she were a different person from the day before. Marcus had awoken feelings inside her that she had not known existed. She was no longer a naive innocent but a woman, with a woman's wants and needs that could match those of any other, and she knew that only one man could fill those needs.

What she had felt for Thomas had not been like this. That had been warm and gentle and pure, whereas what she felt for Marcus she couldn't begin to analyse or understand. It was dark and mysterious and all-consuming, a highly volatile combination of terror, danger and excitement, and the force of it terrified her.

Last night he had come to her room to seduce her, to make her want him, and he had succeeded. Her face exploded in a blaze of scarlet when she thought of how she had lain with him and kissed him, had let him fondle her in the most intimate places, exploring her body with the sureness of an experienced and knowledgeable lover, and she felt the pleasurably wanton feelings tearing through her again at the memory.

The smell of his elusive scent still lingered, and she could still taste his kisses and remember how urgent and hungry his mouth had been on hers. Not even in her wildest dreams had she imagined that a man could make her body come to life like that, and she doubted that anyone else ever would but Marcus. It was instinct with him and, being a demanding male, with a dominating sensuality, it was the most natural thing in the world for him to make love.

She gazed at herself in the dressing table mirror, seeing her lips slightly swollen from Marcus's kisses, and her skin seemed to glow from his touch. At the transformation, a sense of triumph swept through her, for the face reflected in the mirror was the face of a woman, all trace of innocence having disappeared, and when Daphne tapped on her door and entered, smiling broadly, one look at Juliet's face, and she too noticed the transformation and welcomed it. Never had her maid seen her look so radiant, so happy.

Later, when Juliet was dressed, she went down to join Marcus in the breakfast room. She entered in a state of spiralling apprehension at the thought of seeing him again. In the cold light of day, how would they react to one another after the intimacies they had shared in her bed, and how could she appear calm and matter-of-fact when she could remember every intimate detail of what she had done with him? She found him already seated at the table. On seeing her, he rose.

'Ah, here you are, Juliet. I waited for you.'

'There was no need.'

'Yes, there was.'

Juliet found it difficult to hide her treacherous heart's reaction to the deep timbre of his voice. Why, she wondered desperately, did she feel different from the way she had felt yesterday? Why could she still feel his hands on her bare flesh and his kisses on her lips? Slowly, she walked toward him, trying to still the trembling in her legs. He seemed extraordinarily tall and broad-shouldered to her this morning, his face more striking and handsome than ever.

As he stood looking down at her, there was a small quirk of a smile on his lips, and though his gaze travelled leisurely from the top of her bright head, lingering meaningfully on her soft mouth, it lacked the roguish gleam that often brought a flush to her cheeks. She felt heat in her face, felt it spread at that naked, desirous look. It was a look that spoke of invitation and need.

'I was thinking of you. How lovely you look this morning. I was half afraid you were not real but a ghost of the night.'

Juliet laughed. 'I assure you I am flesh and blood.'

He nodded and smiled knowingly. 'So you are. Come and sit down,' he said, pulling out a chair. 'Cook has prepared a breakfast fit for a king, so I hope you will do it justice.'

Which she did. As she began to eat her eggs and delectable little mushrooms done in butter, she was amazed by how hungry she was. They made small talk until Juliet laid her napkin down after finishing her last piece of toast and slowly drank her coffee.

'I have certain important matters to take care of today, Juliet. It will be a good opportunity for you to familiarise yourself with the house and servants. It's a skeleton staff at present, but we can employ more when you have taken stock of things.'

'I will. I plan to speak to Mrs Cherry and ask her advice on staffing matters. I would also like to spend some time with Adele. I thought we would go for a walk.'

'She will like that. I expect she is eager to explore the house. When I was in Spain, I would think of Mulberry

Hall, remembering how much I loved the house when I was a boy. I want Adele to feel that way about it.'

'The war must seem very far away now.'

'It is. I spent a long time there.'

'What was it like?' she asked, taking a sip of her coffee as she tried to envisage him as a soldier, thinking how handsome he would look in uniform.

'Hot for the most part, dusty, although the winters, especially in the mountains, could be freezing. Food was frequently in short supply because resources failed to get through.'

'Did you see much fighting?'

'A great deal, as a matter of fact.'

'And did you suffer any injuries?'

'Several, minor ones. I was lucky.'

He hesitated. Thinking of the scar she had seen on his shoulder, Juliet was strangely sensitive to his thoughts and understood. 'You don't have to talk about it, Marcus. I have spoken to several soldiers who have returned from the Peninsular, so I do have a picture in my mind of what it was like.'

'Unless you were there, at Albuera or Badajoz, you can never know, and it's as well that you don't. Thank God we've almost seen the last of it. But there were times when I saw the real Spain, and at times like those, when the sun set over the brooding mountains and crimson lit the sky, like it does now, in a way that belongs to the radiance of late summer, we saw the beauty of the country and it felt good to be alive.'

As one day passed into the next and the wonderful shades of autumn began to colour the trees, Marcus was kept extremely busy with estate affairs and Juliet saw little of him during the daylight hours. He would ride off in the early morning with his steward or someone else, and she would often not see him again until late afternoon. On occasion he would ride over to Endcliffe House to see how Richard was managing his affairs, giving advice where necessary and reporting back to Juliet that he was working hard to put things right.

Juliet made a point of getting to know the servants and familiarising herself with the house, which was run efficiently by Mrs Cherry. She also spent a great deal of her time with Adele, realising that she had a talent for entertaining the child that surprised her. In spite of her lack of experience with children, she had no trouble winning her trust and arousing her eager curiosity for most things. Adele loved to draw and paint and play simple games. But her greatest love was to be outdoors. They would walk together in the grounds of the house and often go beyond to the surrounding deer park and sit by the lake and feed the ducks that clamoured for the bread they brought.

But there were times when Adele could be difficult. Often, she would be quiet for long periods and unable to concentrate for any length of time on any one thing. She was quite wilful, and there were tears if she could not get her own way. But on the whole, she brought much pleasure to Juliet.

It was Marcus who, knowing of her love of reading, proudly gave Juliet her first glimpse of the library. It was vast, a treasure trove of books, of precious tomes of history, religion and theology, the gems of poetry and fiction. It was as she perused these books that Marcus placed a small package in her hands. She looked at him in puzzlement.

'Is this a gift for me?' she asked.

'It is indeed. One more book to be added to the poetry collection, one I know you will like.'

She unwrapped it carefully, expectantly, gasping when it was revealed to be the book of sentimental lyric poetry by William Collins. She stared at it with delight.

'Oh, Marcus, how did you know?' and then she recalled the day they had met in Mr Marsden's bookshop, when she had gone there in the hope of purchasing this very book. She looked up at him, seeing in his eyes the pleasure it gave him to present her with this gift. 'You remembered.'

'I did. I managed to find it in another bookshop in London. I hope it will give you many hours of pleasurable reading.'

'It will. And thank you, Marcus. I will treasure it always—more so because you gave it to me.'

'I know you will, and who knows,' he murmured with a roguish quirk to his lips. 'What you read on the pages of Mr Collins's book of poetry just might spill over into our bedroom.'

Juliet laughed at his teasing audacity. 'Are you telling me that I need educating in the arts of making love, my lord?'

He smiled an amiable smile and lightly touched her cheek with his finger. 'You've learned a great deal. I am proud of you, my love. On the whole, you've been a marvellously satisfying student.'

'Are you saying that I have still more to learn?' she asked, her eyes sparkling with humour, thinking how wonderfully attractive he looked, his hair still a bit damp from his bath and smelling of pine-scented shaving lotion. He really was the most appealing man she had ever met.

'There are more delightful things you have to know, and between Mr Collins and myself, I am certain we can improve matters.'

'Thank you, Marcus. Every girl likes to be called inadequate.'

'You are never that,' he said, laughing quietly. 'And I guarantee you will not find your lessons too difficult a task.'

'I sincerely hope not, otherwise I shall be too exhausted to do my daily chores.'

'Then you shall have the day off.'

Tossing her head, Juliet laughed and walked toward the door.

'Where are you going?'

'To the garden to read Mr Collins's poems. His words happen to be more subtle than yours.'

'Ah, but not nearly as interesting,' he said, following in her wake.

'You, my lord,' she said, turning and poking him in the ribs with her fingertip, 'are outrageous.'

'Utterly,' he agreed, taking her arm and escorting her into the garden, where they would sit and together read Mr Collins's delightful and informative poems.

They had not been at Mulberry Hall a week when the invitations to visit neighbours began to arrive. And so began the endless round of social events as Juliet was swept along as if on a tidal wave. She never failed to look stunning, and Marcus proudly escorted her to all the events. They were the much sought after attraction at any event they attended and were received warmly. Never had Juliet believed she could be so happy.

The lives of the people in local society in which they mixed were varied and full. Most of them managed their estates, visited their neighbours, hunted, danced and gambled, making frequent visits to the city, and many of these privileged landowners also engaged in politics, dominating society and local government, the titled gentlemen taking their seat in the House of Lords. New to the area and committed to the management of his estate with the help of his stewards, at this present time, Marcus was not as deeply committed to British politics as some of his neighbours. This would come later.

Feeling restless and longing to stretch her legs and maybe ride out on one of Marcus's fine mounts, she entered the dim interior of the stables, the smell of hay, horses, manure and leather strong, though not unpleasant. Juliet observed several people at work. Her gaze became focused on a man forking straw out of one of the stalls. Her eyes opened wide. Tall and thin, the man was in his late thirties. He also had a wooden leg upon which he seemed to manage very well. She hurried towards him.

'Joe? Joe Ruskin—I am glad to see you have found work.'

Joe stopped what he was doing and looked at her, a wide smile breaking on his face. 'Lady Juliet! I can't tell you what a relief it was when Lord Cardell came to see me and set me on. It upset me, it did, when I was accused of poaching, but that was a mistake and His Lordship was quick to show how sorry he was to have believed the rumour and told me that I had you to thank for making him find out the truth of the matter.'

'I only did what I thought was right, Joe. I knew you were innocent.'

'Aye, I was, though it caused Rose a lot of grief at the time.'

'I know. And you are happy working here?'

'More than that. I love working with horses. That's what I was doing out in the Peninsular—taking care of the horses—until I lost my leg when I got too close to the battlefield. I thought I would never work again and shuddered to think what would become of Rose and the bairns. But Lord Cardell told me that since he was to expand his stable, there was always a need for an extra pair of hands.'

'I'm so happy to see you settled, Joe. You…are aware that Lord Cardell is my husband now? We were married in London.'

'I do know that and wish you both every happiness. It's good to know you won't be leaving the area.'

'Yes, that is one of the advantages.'

Having heard the voice of his wife, the man in the next stall jerked erect. 'Only one?' his voice rang out. 'I shall be interested to learn the rest.'

As Juliet turned her head, their eyes met instantly, and so abrupt was Marcus's appearance that Juliet started. Then she laughed. 'Marcus! I might have known you would be lurking somewhere. I've just been having a word with Mr Ruskin. I was surprised to find him working here. You should have told me.'

'It slipped my mind. Joe is a welcome addition to the stables—knows all there is to know about horses apparently, having looked after them for the army in Spain. Is that not so, Joe?'

'It is. Thank you, sir,' Joe replied. 'I was just telling Her Ladyship.'

Looking from one to the other, Juliet knew that because Marcus had given him this chance, Joe would be his servant forever. Grateful to Marcus for doing this for Joe, she regretted all the bitter words she had accused him of on their first encounter.

Walking into the stable-yard with Marcus, she said, 'Thank you for finding work for Joe. I am grateful to you for giving him a place, although now that Richard is home, and when things begin to improve at Endcliffe House, I am sure we could have found work for him.' Juliet looked at Marcus and smiled, meeting his gaze directly. 'You do realise that by treating Joe with courtesy, you have engendered his respect, and you can be assured of his lifelong devotion.'

'Which is what I strive to do with my wife,' Marcus remarked on a teasing note.

Juliet ignored his remark and averted her gaze. 'I came to see if I could find a suitable horse to ride. It's such a lovely day.'

'You should have said at breakfast. I will ride with you.'

'I know how busy you are, Marcus. Are you sure you can spare the time?'

'For my wife, anything.'

Chapter Eleven

Later that same day, after enjoying a vigorous ride with Marcus, with it being so lovely, she suggested taking a walk to the lake with Adele. Marcus was in favour of spending time with his two favourite ladies, even going so far as to suggest taking a hamper of food along with them and making an afternoon of it.

Adele gazed at the hamper her father was carrying with excitement. 'What's in that basket?' she asked. 'Is it a present for me?'

'Well, kind of,' Juliet replied. 'It's full of lovely food Cook has packed for us.'

Adele looked nonplussed. 'Why? Is it for the ducks?'

Juliet laughed, taking hold of her hand. 'Only a little bread is for the ducks. The hamper is filled with all sorts of nice things for us to eat. It's such a lovely day that your father and I thought we would eat it by the lake.'

'Do you mean we are going to eat outside?'

'Exactly,' Marcus said. 'It's a splendid idea, don't you agree, Adele?'

'Ooh, yes,' she replied happily, letting go of Juliet's hand as she skipped on ahead.

All the lazy heat of late summer was in the air as they

walked around the lake, which was fed by fast flowing streams at one end, swelling its banks before cascading over a weir at the other, where it fell into a turbulent deep dark pool. It was a dangerous place to be and was to be avoided by the unwary. Finding the perfect spot, discarding her bonnet to reveal the glorious, luxuriant hair upswept in glossy curls that almost took Marcus's breath away, unaware of the effect she had created with such a simple act, Juliet spread a large blanket on the ground. Adele helped her take the food out of the hamper and place it on a separate cloth, thinking it great fun.

'This is what I do when I give a tea party for my dolls,' she told them, happily kneeling on the edge of the cloth and helping herself to a sandwich.

As they talked and ate, Juliet was vaguely aware of Marcus's appreciative gaze on her animated face as she handed Adele a cup of lemonade. When the child had eaten and drunk her fill, she picked up some bread and ran off to feed the ducks on the edge of the lake.

'You have a way with Adele,' Marcus said. 'It's good to see her so happy.'

'She's an easy child to get along with.' Sitting beside him and tucking her feet beneath her, she looked at him. 'During the short time I have spent at Mulberry Hall, I have gained a deeper understanding of why you married me—your generosity towards Richard, how you are helping him regain his standing in the community. My attitude toward you has become more sympathetic and my thoughts more favourable. Of course you were furious when Thomas turned up on the day of our wedding, and in your place, I would have felt the same. But there are times when I really don't understand you. In the short time I have known you, you have gone from being an irritable neighbour to a considerate husband.'

His eyes slid over her face, trapping her in their burning gaze. 'Which is what I will always be, but I could never be indifferent to you. One must either love you to distraction or want to strangle you.'

'And what would you like to do to me, Marcus? Tell me.'

He grinned. 'I haven't made up my mind yet.'

'Then kindly let me know when you have.' Drawing up her knees and wrapping her arms around them, she watched Adele trying to make friends with a moorhen which skittered among the tall rushes skirting the lake. The day was perfect. They talked of ordinary and extraordinary things, about his childhood and his close relationship with his family and in particular his brother, of how his father had been killed in a riding accident during a hunt, and as he talked, his voice seemed to ring inside her head. When he fell silent, content to sit and watch his daughter, Juliet was miles away, thinking of nothing other than this incredible moment. Nothing could match this quiet joy she felt.

'This is such a wonderful place,' she murmured at length. 'Here by the lake and surrounded by wooded hills, one feels quite small and vulnerable—rather humble, in fact.'

Marcus's expression gentled, and a glint of amusement came into his eyes as he slanted her a wicked look. 'You couldn't be humble, my love, if you tried. You're unpredictable and quite outrageous, and you never cease to amaze me.'

She looked at him and laughed. 'And isn't that how

you want your wife to be? Predictability can be so dull—much more exciting for her to have many interesting and diverting contradictions to her character.'

'Not so many that she would take some keeping up with.'

'Then, what is your idea of an ideal wife? A woman who should lose her individuality completely and live only for her husband? To always be at his beck and call and spend her days carrying out her part of the marriage contract?'

Marcus stretched out on his back and closed his eyes, and the mobile line of his mouth quirked in a half-smile. 'Carry on, my love. It gets better all the time. I'm certainly in favour of a married woman knowing her duty is to take care of her husband, to cook his meals and to clean the house. And do not forget that the husband always likes his wife to be gentle and sympathetic to himself, to place him on a pedestal and be humorous, witty and cheerful at all times.'

Juliet was momentarily dumbstruck by his speech, then she burst out laughing at his teasing. 'While he doesn't always concern himself very particularly about the means to make and keep her so. And what are your opinions concerning an intelligent wife? Would that be acceptable to you, or would you be afraid that if she were too intelligent, she would be capable of perceiving the mind of her husband—should he be of lesser intelligence than herself, of course.'

Marcus opened his eyes and grinned up at her. 'Which he never is,' he uttered conceitedly, closing his eyes once more.

'Is that right?' she retorted with mock indignation.

'If women were more forthright and didn't appear to be dim-witted half the time, convincing their menfolk that they are smarter and wiser than we are, their egos would be well and truly shattered.'

'Then if that should prove to be the case, men would use their brute strength to gain supremacy over them in the time-honoured way.' A seductive languor appeared in his eyes when he opened them and looked at his wife, and it made her heart turn over. 'A man may treat his wife in any way he sees fit—within reason, of course.'

'But of course,' she scoffed, almost choking on the laughter that was bubbling up inside her. 'Like a possession, you mean!'

Marcus smiled, closing his eyes and nodded smugly. 'I could not put it better myself. However, I'd consider it necessary that my wife should be intelligent if she is to conduct my concerns through life, but not too intelligent, just enough to appreciate my own intellectual mind.'

'But you would allow her to have some freedom of her own?'

'The truth of it is that I would not have to permit my wife to do anything. In law you are my wife, so whatever is yours is mine also. I can, if I choose, treat you harshly and without consideration, and confine you to the kitchen and the bedroom.'

Unable to contain her mirth any longer, Juliet laughed out loud at the sheer arrogance of her husband, relieved since now that she had come to know him, she understood he was teasing her and enjoying every minute of it. 'You would not. You wouldn't dare. I would kill you first.'

Marcus linked his hands behind his head, staring up

at the blue sky dotted with white clouds. 'You have a beautiful laugh, Juliet. You should laugh more often.'

Wriggling herself into a more comfortable position, Juliet looked down at him. 'You're only saying that to change the subject. Please don't tell me you meant all that rubbish about wives being completely subservient to their husbands?'

Marcus half raised his eyelids and looked into her eyes, shining softly so close above him. 'I was just making a point—and a valid one at that. Many a husband would not allow you so free a rein as you have, my sweet.'

Juliet sighed, stretching out beside him and rolling onto her stomach. Cupping her chin in her hands, she feigned despondency. 'I am beginning to think I would be better off if I were a widow.' That said, she very quickly changed her mind as she let her gaze travel down the long, superbly fit and muscled body stretched out beside her.

'It's a good thing we have servants since I could not do all the things you would expect of me. You would be sadly disappointed. I've had no practice in the ways of a wife. I can't cook—at least I don't think I can since I have never tried—although I do know quite a lot about keeping house. I do have other interests and accomplishments, but I don't think they would be of much use to you.'

'Worry not, my love. I expect my wife to be happy with what I can give her. I would promise her that she will always have clothes to wear and food to eat and a roof over her head that does not leak, and if she loves me, she will accept that.'

Juliet's brow puckered in a thoughtful frown and she

turned her face away. 'Love? In truth, Marcus, I don't know what I feel. What I do know is that ever since you came into my life, I have been so confused, with my emotions all over the place. I—I have also come to have a strong attraction to you, which you already know.'

Reaching out, Marcus gently cupped her cheek to turn her face towards him. 'And I have an extremely strong and passionate desire for you, Juliet, and if we were alone, I would show you.'

She met his gaze steadily, strangely disappointed that he couldn't think of a stronger emotion to describe what was between them other than desire. 'Desire, as wonderful as it is, is not enough to base a marriage on, Marcus. It is only a temporary emotion, and I have no wish to become trapped in a loveless marriage.'

'It won't be, that I promise you. Do not forget that it was a mutual decision for us to take our marriage vows, Juliet. Honour and duty must run side by side with our emotions.'

In his expression Juliet saw a resolute determination that he would have his way. It was an expression she was coming to know quite well. 'I will not be your duty, Marcus. I want more from you than that.'

Adele chose that moment to come for more bread to feed the ducks.

'Here you are, Adele.' Juliet handed her more bread. 'They must be very hungry today—or just greedy.'

'No,' Adele replied. 'They really are very hungry,' she said over her shoulder as she went off to give the ducks more bread. Juliet began packing things away in the hamper when she suddenly found her wrist taken and looked up.

'That was not the most romantic thing I have ever said, Juliet. If I have hurt you by discussing our marriage in such a blunt fashion, then I apologise. Our marriage was not an ideal affair. I wish it could have been different.'

'So do I.'

'If you want the truth, I will tell you that in my eyes, you are as alluring and desirable as any woman I have ever known. I want you, and I shall go on wanting you. You are beautiful and vibrant, and you were made for love. On the nights when you lie in my arms, I find something that binds me to another human being more assuredly than anything else in my life. There is a sense of rightness to it, as if that is where you are meant to be. You have become a passion to me, and I cannot bear the thought of losing you. If I could, I would lay the whole world at your feet, and I have never been so serious in my whole life.'

Perhaps it was the way his head was slightly tilted to one side, perhaps it was a trick of the light, perhaps it was the yearning softness of his voice, but whatever the reason, Juliet had the impression that his face had changed. His features were relaxed, making him look younger, less hard and cynical. She had a momentary glimpse of the young man he must have been before he had gone to Spain.

'I don't want the world, Marcus. I will be satisfied for a very small and humble part of it, if it is somewhere we can call home.'

They sat for a moment in silence, each with their own thoughts. Juliet looked towards the lake where Adele was still feeding the ducks, feeling that nothing existed but the feelings of her body as she lusted for her husband with increasing desire. She was happy to be with him, satisfied that the unfortunate events that had clouded their wedding had been resolved between them. She could think of nothing but that glorious fact. The more they were together, they discovered things about each other that were entirely new. They both had such strong views on everything, and arguments flared easily, but they both agreed that a placid partnership would not have suited them, and they soon realised that it made the making up all the more passionate and exciting.

Juliet turned back to him, seeing how the sun caught his head in a halo of light. She gazed at his face and caught her breath at something she saw there. No man had ever looked at her quite like that before. She cursed herself for being unable to free herself from the sensual trap he had set for her.

She was falling in love with him. She knew she was.

It was an idyllic time for them, a time when they were suspended in some kind of dream, reluctant to let the outside world into their lives. But it was inevitable that it would intrude sometime, which it did when Richard took time off from his many duties and came to call. Juliet was amazed by the change in him and by the way he had taken over the running of things on the estate, without any mention of returning to his pleasurable pursuits in London.

His life had been taken over by work as he set about finding ways to increase the income of the estate, contracting better rents, which had been set some years back, without being excessive, and renting out more grazing land to the neighbouring farms to allow them to increase their herds and flocks. However, until things were seen to improve, economy had to remain a rule.

'I'm surprised I haven't seen anything of you since you came home, Richard,' Juliet said when he entered the drawing room with Marcus.

'There is much to be done on the estate, Juliet—as you well know—if I am to bring it back to what it once was. Your husband has been doing much to help me in that, for which I thank you, Marcus. I came to tell you that I'm off to Berkshire for a few days. Amelia's father, the Earl of Bainbridge, has invited me.'

Juliet gasped with delight. 'This is happy news indeed, Richard. Is he to consider your suit at last?'

Richard flushed slightly and smiled, looking a little bashful. 'It would appear so. If all goes well, then Amelia and I will be married at her home in Berkshire, possibly in the spring of next year. I do hope you will both be able to attend.'

'We shall be delighted. I doubt you will be able to keep your sister away,' Marcus said, pouring them both a glass of brandy. 'Do you not miss the London social scene?'

'Not really. Now that there is a chance that Amelia and I can be married, I am quite content to be at Endcliffe. I have not been drawn into a game of cards since I left town. You were my last opponent, and after that unfortunate experience, I have no desire for another.'

'I am overjoyed to hear that,' Juliet said, looking fondly at her brother.

Marcus sat down and crossed one leg over the other as he studied Richard. 'I'm glad you have seen the error of your ways, Richard, and decided to settle down to a more sedate and sensible lifestyle, which means less for Juliet to worry about. No doubt the delightful Amelia has had much to do with that.'

'She most certainly has,' Richard answered with a beaming smile, having observed that marriage to Juliet had certainly made his brother-in-law less formidable and more approachable. 'I have just seen Adele setting out on a walk with her nursemaid. She seems to be a happy little soul.'

Juliet laughed. 'And so she is. She's adorable. I think they are to walk to the lake to feed the ducks. It's Adele's favourite pastime, I'm afraid.'

'She really is quite delightful, but then, any child who is fortunate enough to have you for their stepmother would be.'

Marcus's face became set in serious lines. 'My sentiments entirely—in fact, Adele has begun addressing her as Mama, is that not so, Juliet?'

'Yes, she has. I am quite touched by it, but we have become close.'

'Your sister is a truly remarkable woman, Richard. She has become very dear to me. That game of cards, which was so disastrous for yourself, turned out to be a blessing in disguise for me—my salvation, you might say. Out of your misfortune came the luckiest moment of my life,' Marcus said quietly, his expression grave, intending to leave Richard in no doubt as to the strong bond of love that had grown between Marcus and his sister.

Juliet was always impatient for the days to end and the nights when Marcus would come to her room and take her in his arms. When at last a blissful aura broke over them, spent and exhausted, slowly they would drift back to earth, drained and incapable of any movement other than to hold each other close. Juliet sighed, the physicality of their lovemaking, her vulnerability and her implicit surrender sweeping over her as her hand caressed Marcus's chest.

They would make love until towards dawn, when at last they would fall into a short, blissful sleep, but before Juliet closed her eyes, curled within her husband's warm embrace. She knew with a feverish joy, as sure as night followed day, that she loved him. She accepted the truth with every fibre of her being. He was part of her, branded on her very soul, and she would never be free again. With this glorious revelation, everything she had found so difficult to understand suddenly seemed so simple. She wished to stay by his side for always.

Marcus was with his steward inspecting some land that was to be cleared of scrub to make room for more crops to be planted. The day had begun sunny and warm, but clouds were gathering overhead threatening a storm. At a loose end and deciding to take a walk in the grounds with Adele before the storm broke, Juliet summoned one of the maids to fetch Adele from the nursery. She was surprised when the child's nursemaid in a state of agitation came to inform her that Miss Adele was nowhere to be found.

Juliet stared at her in disbelief. 'But she cannot have disappeared. She might be hiding. Where have you searched?'

'Everywhere, but she seems to have disappeared into thin air,' the maid cried.

'When did you last see her?'

'Just after breakfast. She didn't eat much, said she wasn't hungry. I left the room for just a moment and when I returned, she wasn't there, and her breakfast plates were empty, so I assumed she might have eaten it after all and gone to see her father or you.'

'Lord Cardell is not here and I have not seen her. I'll summon the servants to mount a search,' Juliet said, not unduly alarmed, for Adele couldn't have wandered very far.

A search was mounted but without success. Going to the upper story herself, where some of the servants had their rooms, her eyes lighted on the large cupboard, a cupboard that was all too familiar to her. Immediately her mind went back to her own ordeal inside it when she was no more than Adele's age. She approached it with some trepidation, memories of that awful time flooding back. Gingerly she pulled the door open with effort. It was still stiff and would be impossible for a small child to open. With some trepidation she peered inside. Thankfully it was empty, but she decided there and then to have the cupboard removed from the house.

Going back down to the hall and being told that there was no sign of Adele, she became seriously worried. Outside she scanned the gardens and beyond, looking towards the lake. Thinking of what the nursemaid had said, that Adele had not eaten her breakfast and on returning to the nursery had found that both the breakfast and Adele had disappeared, she reached the conclusion that it was possible that Adele just might have taken what remained of her breakfast to feed the ducks. She felt sick at the thought of the child going all that way alone.

Juliet turned to find Joe Ruskin coming up behind her.

'Have you found her, Lady Juliet?'

'No, but I have a feeling she will be heading for the lake. I need to find her as soon as possible.'

'Storm's coming,' Joe said as lightning cracked and thunder rumbled in the distance. 'It'll be with us soon.'

Ominous grey clouds loomed overhead, and the wind was rising, buffeting the trees. Scanning the parkland and looking towards the lake, she was certain she saw the flash of something in the distance. Two figures, one tall, the other a child. The tall one looked like a man walking with a limp, and she saw that he was leading a child by the hand, heading in the direction of the calm, still water of the lake that was slate grey beneath the leaden sky. When the figures disappeared into a wooded area, at first, she thought her mind was playing strange tricks, but then she saw them emerge from the trees and stop beside the lake.

She stared in disbelief, sure they were about to step into the water, which was shallow there, until she saw them climb into a small rowboat that was one of three kept tethered to a small landing stage. The lake was teaming with pike, trout and carp, and the boats were frequently used by the gamekeepers to provide fish for the house.

'Goodness! I can see her, and she's with a person who is known to me. Thomas!' she gasped, her stomach twisting as she realised who it was that had Adele.

'I must go after them. Get help, Joe. Send them to the lake and tell them to hurry.'

Without stopping to think, Juliet began to run, her cloak dropping from her shoulders onto the ground. She ran as if her very life depended on it, taking air into her lungs, breathing in and out, putting one leg in front of the other. She was oblivious to the rain as it began to fall. The clothes she wore were not thick enough to shelter her from her nightmares of her wedding night and Thomas's vicious assault on her person, which rose to the surface of her mind to taunt her as she hurried onward, running harder, faster. Almost spent on reaching the edge of the lake, wiping the rain from her eyes, Juliet stared ahead, sucking great gulping breaths into her lungs. Suddenly there came another flash of lightning that pierced the sky, followed immediately by a deafening rumble that seemed to shake the very foundations of the trees. The storm had come.

Teeth gritted, bodily exhausted, she looked across the water at the boat. Thomas was manning the oars and Adele sat across from him, the waves tossing the little wooden boat from side to side. The child sat very still in her now sodden clothes, a frightened look on her young face as she clutched a small package to her chest, no doubt bread meant for the ducks. They were crossing the lake to the other side, where a variety of waterbirds collected.

Hearing the loud noise of the water as it cascaded over the weir at the far end of the lake into a deep whirling pool, Juliet was profoundly concerned for Adele's safety. There was a strong current in the middle of the lake that drew the unwary towards the weir. Looking to the other side of the lake where the road led away from Mulberry Hall was a carriage. It was stationary, and the awful thought of what Thomas intended—not only to abduct Adele but to secrete her away somewhere in retaliation for the humiliation he had suffered at Marcus's hands—was too much to bear.

'Thomas!' she called, waving her arms. She called out again, and Thomas turned his head and looked at her, making Juliet's blood run cold when she beheld the expression on his face. His eyes were as dark as the leaden water of the lake, his look one of madness, as if he had completely lost all reason.

With no other thought than to reach Adele before the boat was taken over the weir, she stepped into the water. If that were to happen, then Adele would surely drown, she thought suddenly, horror striking at her very soul. She must get help from somewhere. But how could she? There was no time. The house was too far away. By the time Joe had summoned help, it would be too late.

Without thought for her own mortal danger she stepped farther into the water and began wading out into the lake, shuddering when the cold water invaded her shoes. Her feet stirred up the muddy silt on the bottom, which clouded the water about her. With her eyes fixed on the boat, she shouted for Thomas to come back, but he carried on rowing, paying no heed to her entreaties.

Despite being hampered by her heavy skirts, reaching deeper water, she began to swim for all she was worth.

When Marcus returned to the house, he was aware of a strange quietness all around him. With a feeling of alarm, seeing an anxious-looking Mrs Cherry appear from the domestic quarters, he strode towards her.

'What is it? Has something happened?' he demanded.

Relief that he had come flooded Mrs Cherry's eyes. 'Thank goodness you're back, Lord Cardell. I'm afraid there is. Miss Adele has gone missing. The house has been searched, but there's no sign of her anywhere.'

All Marcus's senses became alert. 'Where is my wife?'

'She went to look outside in case she had wandered from the house.'

'What else has been done to find her?'

'Everyone is looking for her—inside and outside—even the stables have been searched. Lady Cardell was quite beside herself when she couldn't be found, and now she too appears to have disappeared. With rain threatening, she was wearing her cloak, but it was found on the drive and no sign of her.'

'I see. I'll see what's being done.' He left the house and looked around, taking stock of the indoor and outdoor servants searching the grounds. He looked at them hard, as if willing them to tell him what had happened, but he wasn't seeing anything. Something black and formless and terrifying in its secrecy had come alive inside him, almost stopping his breath and wrapping itself around his pounding heart. Joe Ruskin approached him as the first heavy drops of rain began to spear down on them.

'Have you seen my wife?'

'She's heading in the direction of the lake, said she'd seen a man leading a child in that direction. Told me to fetch help.'

Marcus stared at him. 'A man—with a child?'

'Yes, sir.'

'And what did this man look like? Have you a description.'

'No, sir, other than he looked like a gentleman and he had a limp.'

'A limp?' Marcus could think of only one man he knew with a limp, and that did not bear thinking about just then. 'And was nothing done to apprehend them?'

'Some of the grooms and lads from the stables have gone after them.'

'How long ago?'

'About ten minutes, sir.'

Marcus turned and began striding away, his eyes springing fiercely to life and his uncompromising jaw set as hard as granite as he looked in the direction of the lake, the rain slanting down as another flash of lightning forked across the sky in the distance followed by a hollow roll of thunder. A man with a limp? Thomas Waring was the only man he could think of, and remembering his parting words after that ill-fated duel they had fought, Marcus had no doubt that he was the man who had taken his daughter.

Richard, who had just arrived, was ashen-faced and came to stand beside him. 'I've just heard Juliet has gone missing?'

Marcus nodded, his face grim. 'And Adele. I have every reason to believe she has been abducted.'

'But I cannot think of any reason why anyone would want to abduct a child?'

'Can you not? There is one person who springs to mind, Richard. One person who wants to avenge me for marrying Juliet, along with an incident before that. He

is desperate and demented enough to go to any lengths
to exact his revenge.'

Richard blanched, swallowing hard, knowing after
one devastating, heart-stopping moment who he was referring to. 'You think it is Thomas, don't you?'

'Yes. I know it.'

'Thomas may be a libertine and accused of many
things, but I cannot believe he would resort to this. What
is the object of doing such a thing as to seize a child?'

'The man is so demented and determined on revenge
that I doubt he knows it himself. You are aware of his
dissolute reputation, Richard. Why, you were against
him marrying Juliet because of it, so to show any kind
of loyalty now is misplaced. He threatened revenge. He
is devious enough to resort to anything. Now come. We
must hurry.'

'Where to?'

'The lake.'

'Good Lord! Little wonder you are worried. But he
wouldn't stoop to—'

'To what, Richard? Murder?'

'He wouldn't.'

Marcus looked at him and their eyes locked in fervent
prayer to God that he was right. Waring's threats had
become reality. It would appear that Adele must have
wandered off and Juliet had gone after her.

'I'll head for the lake. Some of the grooms have already set off. Get more men together and come after me.'

Knowing without a doubt that his beloved daughter
was in the hands of Thomas Waring, he became like a
man in the grip of a nightmare, cursing himself for having shrugged off Waring's threat. Marcus knew what the

man was capable of, but he would never have thought he would stoop to anything as base as abducting a child. The thought of his daughter and Juliet, bewildered and terrified in the hands of a man who would go to any lengths to enact his revenge on Marcus for marrying Juliet, caused a violent rage to fill his being, which increased with each passing moment as ran swiftly to the lake, reaching it in just a few minutes.

Seeing the boat with his daughter and Thomas Waring heading for the weir, and his wife struggling to stay afloat, he flung off his jacket as he ran and pulled off his boots before entering the water. With powerful strokes, he began to swim out to Juliet across the lake, desperate to get to her, while he could see the boat with his daughter and Waring was being carried swiftly towards the weir. He could also see that men were already in situ at the head of the weir, ready to snatch Adele before the boat went over.

Chapter Twelve

Juliet did not see Marcus emerge from the trees, nor did she see the people running towards the lake from the house, or hear one of them calling her name in frantic desperation. Death stared her in the face as she went under the water, her legs, as they thrashed about, becoming entangled and held fast by long trailing weeds, resembling the long strands of her hair that had become unpinned. It was like a nightmare from which there was no awakening, and because of the water, she could not cry out.

She managed to surface briefly and gasp for air, at the same time seeing the boat being carried in the fast-flowing water towards the weir. Gradually she became unaware of the intensity of the cold seeping into her, of the numbness taking over her entire body. The last thing she saw before she closed her eyes was Adele's white face as she clung to the side of the boat, which was beginning to spin around with the force of the water close to the weir. Like a captive bird, she was visibly trembling, her eyes wide. But there was nothing Juliet could do. There was water in her mouth, her eyes, her ears, the force of it pulling at her, taking her farther and farther down to the murky depths of the lake.

It would be so easy to give way to weightlessness, so easy to surrender, to give herself up to the darkness waiting to claim her completely. A pleasant stupor stole over her and time lost all meaning, but from somewhere in the centre of her mind, the instinct for self-preservation made her fight the darkness in one last scramble for life. She flailed her arms, struggled to the surface and gulped for air as her head surfaced again, before darkness claimed her one more time.

Just when she thought all was lost, when she thought all the breath had been driven from her and her lungs would burst, she was sure she heard someone calling her name from up above, commanding her to live, and she felt herself being grasped and pulled upwards, strong arms encircling her waist. Again, her head appeared above the water, and this time someone was holding her, making it impossible for her to sink back into the slimy dark abyss of the lake.

Briefly her eyes flickered open and her heart soared when they became focused on Marcus's familiar beloved features. She was in no condition to ask what miracle had brought him to her when she needed help most, to snatch her from the very jaws of death. It was enough for her that he had come.

Barely conscious, she heard more voices as a boat was brought alongside and more arms reached out and pulled her up out of the water. Only when she felt the hard boards of the boat beneath her back did she realise she was safe. She felt her lips move, but no sound came for she was trembling too much. Hearing a buzz of voices coming from somewhere, her eyes flickered open for a brief moment, her vision obscured by mist, but she saw a blurred outline of someone bending over her. The excruciating terror of her ordeal had seeped into the deepest places of her mind and she was too weak, still too terrified to do anything other than shake, and giving a long shuddering sigh, she surrendered to the mist swirling all about her.

Marcus knelt beside his wife, cradling her head in his arms, unwinding her long sleek hair which had become tangled about her body. Her eyes were closed and circled with purple shadows, emphasised by the deathly pallor of her face. He called for someone to find something warm to wrap her in, and a blanket was quickly produced, which he wrapped around her, wiping her wet hair from her face before gripping her shoulders.

'Juliet, open your eyes. Please. I implore you.' He shook her in an attempt to get her to look at him, the hideous fear which had gripped him when he thought he might lose her beginning to recede when he saw she was breathing. 'Juliet, look at me. For God's sake, open your eyes and let me see you are all right.' He watched as she gradually came out of the darkness that had engulfed her and opened her eyes. 'Thank God,' he said, feeling that nothing could be compared to the joy he felt. His voice and the expression on his face gave evidence to the relief he felt at that moment, but he cringed when he saw they were wild with terror. Death may have receded, but fear would take longer.

Feeling a surge of deep compassion, he drew her into his arms, holding her tight in an effort to convey to her some of his warmth. His love. In her fear and desperate need for comfort, he felt her press against him.

'Be still, my love, be still,' he murmured, gently placing his lips on her brow, speaking the words naturally, for never would he know such anguish, such agonising pain, as he had felt when, on being told both his daughter and his wife were missing, his instinct as well as the last sightings of them had drawn him to the lake.

When he had seen Juliet swimming in the dark water struggling in pursuit of the boat, all the demons in hell had broken loose inside his head. If he didn't reach her in time, she would be lost to him forever. He had seen half a dozen of his outdoor workers congregated on the head of the weir to apprehend the boat before it could be swept over the edge, where it would be in danger of tossing its passengers into the swirling, frothing whirlpool below.

'I will take care of you. Don't be afraid. Come, calm yourself. You're all right now. You're safe. It's all over.'

'Adele…' she croaked, the wildness back in her eyes as she remembered why she had been in the water.

'Adele is unharmed and quite safe,' he informed her, having seen his daughter plucked from the boat before it went over the edge of the weir, its other occupant not so lucky. Men were trying to retrieve Waring from the churning waters. 'We'll get you to the house. There you will be tended to. Do you understand what I am saying?'

Juliet managed to nod her head, the mist receding from her eyes, making Marcus's face clear to her. She saw his clothes were wet, his shirt clinging to his skin and his black hair glistening with droplets of water. Her eyes left his and became fixed on the glassy, rippling water of the lake, so calm now the storm had passed, giving no evidence of the tragedy which had taken place within its depths just a short while before. When the boat reached the shore, she was lifted out. Marcus carried her to the waiting carriage which had been sent from the house, as effortlessly as if she weighed nothing at all. On the journey back to the house, she clung to him, shaking uncontrollably, trying to speak, but her words were disconnected.

As Marcus carried her up to her room, where he was met by an anxious Daphne and an anxious Mrs Cherry following in her wake, her terror and trembling began to lessen as she became comforted by his warmth, by his strength, which stole over her, giving her security.

When he turned to leave her and knowing where he was heading, she sat up in alarm. 'You will be careful, Marcus,' she begged as he shrugged himself into his jacket over his wet clothes. 'I couldn't bear it if anything should happen to you.'

'I will,' he said hoarsely. 'Waring planned his strike with evil cunning. After what he has done this day, he has much to answer for. I do not intend to let him escape.'

With Juliet safe, Marcus went in search of his daughter and the perpetrator of this vicious deed. He left the house as Adele was being lifted out of the carriage swaddled in a warm blanket and being carried by one of the grooms. Overwhelmed with relief, Marcus hugged and kissed her, trying not to imagine how he would have felt had she suffered the same fate as Waring. Having come to no harm except a soaking, her little face was smiling now, for the whole thing had turned into one big adventure she couldn't wait to tell her stepmother and her nurse about.

On reaching the weir, where the water tumbled over to the roiling depths below, he stood and watched the men at the water's edge trying to haul in the capsized boat that was bobbing about like a cork. One of his grooms turned when he saw the master.

'What's happening?' Marcus asked, having to raise his voice in order to be heard above the noise of the tumbling water.

'No sign of the man in the boat. It's thought he might be underneath, but until we can secure it, we can't be sure.'

'Has he surfaced at all?'

'Not that we know of. You can see for yourself how strong the current is. It will have dragged him under.'

Marcus stood and watched helplessly as his men worked frantically to overturn the boat. Eventually they succeeded and with poles with hooks attached, Thomas Waring was dragged from the water. He was laid on his back, his eyes wide open and staring, water trickling from his mouth. Marcus did not have to place his head on his chest and listen for a heartbeat that did not exist to know that Waring was dead.

Relief was clearly felt in the household when Juliet and Adele returned, mercifully virtually unharmed. On hearing of the events leading up to Adele's abduction, that she was taking her breakfast to the ducks on the lake when a gentleman had approached her and offered to assist her, after scolding her severely for going off and causing so much concern, making her promise that she would never wander off again without an adult, Marcus hugged his beloved daughter.

After removing her clothes and placing her in a hot mustard bath, her nursemaid put her to bed, where she was cosseted and pampered and fed by everyone, which

pleased her enormously. Fortunately, she suffered no af-
ter-effects from the ordeal, not even a chill after getting
a soaking from the rain and the spume of water overlap-
ping the boat, but the story of all that had happened to
her would be an adventure she would never tire of telling.

The day of Adele's abduction was like a grotesque
nightmare to Juliet. It was as though all the energy she
had concentrated on getting Adele out of Thomas's evil
clutches had drained out of her, and her spirits sank
to such a low ebb that for a while, as Daphne and Mrs
Cherry fussed around her, she almost ceased to function.

When she heard the news of Thomas's death from
Daphne, who had been told of it from one of the search-
ers, who called at the house with the news, she was
overcome with shock. When Marcus returned, he came
straight to her. The house was quiet now, everyone having settled down to their work after the worry and excitement of the day's events.

As she came towards him, her hands outstretched,
rage rose inside Marcus when he saw how deeply her
ordeal at Waring's hands had affected her. Her eyes were
enormous in her pale face, the dark circles of pain and
worry making them look even larger. He opened his
arms and she walked into them like a child seeking suc-
cour, but before she laid her head against his chest, he
saw her chin tremble and tears she could no longer hold
back brimming in her eyes and spilling over.

'Oh, Marcus, thank goodness you came in time.' She
wept, over and over again, with her face against his
chest, letting the violence of all the raw emotions that

would not come before now flow uncontrollably out of her. He held her for a long time, rocking her and kissing her hair, murmuring sweet, gentle words of comfort while she sobbed, quietly and wretchedly, waiting patiently until she had mastered her tears, aching with a love for her that was like a deep, physical pain.

He cradled her in his arms, holding her close while she poured out all her anguish and misery. Everything that had happened to her that day came out in a torrent of words, and he listened, knowing that it was good for her to talk like this, that it would help cleanse her of the evil Waring had perpetrated against her and Marcus and Adele. That it would help with the healing process later.

When she became still and quiet in his arms, feeling an unbelievable comfort of knowing he was holding her, that she was safe, she sighed, wiping her tears with her hands.

'My poor darling,' Marcus murmured, his lips against her hair. 'What has he done to you?'

'Nothing that won't heal,' she whispered bravely. 'I thank God that Adele is safe, that she is all right. According to Mrs Cherry, she has survived it well—better that I have myself, it would seem,' she said, smiling up at him through her damp lashes.

'Thank God.'

'I have been told that Thomas has drowned. Where is he? Where has he been taken?'

'He is here. Richard is taking care of everything. The carriage driver who brought him here is waiting. He is to write a letter to notify his father of what has occurred and have his body taken to Amberley Park.'

Juliet leaned back in Marcus's arms and looked up at him, her eyes luminous with tears. 'Thomas tried to destroy me, Marcus, to destroy us both—using your daughter to do it. If he had succeeded in getting to the other side of the lake, then I am certain he would have taken her away somewhere, and we would never have found her...'

Marcus's arms tightened around her. 'If he had succeeded in his vile plan, I would have found him, and he would not have escaped with his life,' he said hoarsely, his voice shaking with angry emotions. Taking her hand, he led her to the window seat, where they sat close together. He placed his arm around her, reluctant to let her go ever again. 'How are you feeling now?'

'Overwhelmed by a turmoil of emotions. It's a combination of relief, gladness and, at the same time, a feeling of horror mingled with some element of surprise, knowing that the man I once pledged to marry was the same man who would have let me drown in the lake, the same man intent on destroying our lives now dead himself. Oh, Marcus, I was so frightened when I thought I was going to die.'

Marcus held her tighter. 'So was I. When Joe Ruskin told me that Adele had gone to the lake with a man, I soon worked out that it had to be none other than Thomas Waring and that you had gone after them. You have no idea how my thoughts tormented me. What I went through.' Sighing, he kissed the top of her head where it rested on his shoulder. 'When I saw you in the lake, when you disappeared beneath the surface, I went through hell. I should have listened to Waring when he threatened to avenge me for all he had suffered at my hands. If I had, none of this is would have happened. I should have foreseen what he would do.'

'It wasn't your fault, Marcus. Neither of us was to know he would go to such drastic lengths.'

'You are very generous, but I cannot be acquitted so lightly, my love.'

Juliet stirred against him, raising her head and meeting his fierce gaze, seeing how much he had suffered on her behalf. 'Yes, you can. I think that my marrying you sent him to the far reaches beyond his control. I saw him in the boat which was heading towards the weir. The current was strong and he had lost control. He was looking at me, watching me as I struggled to get to Adele. There was madness in his eyes. He looked like a man possessed of the devil.'

'I would have had no compunction about killing him had I lost you.'

Juliet drew back and looked up at him, shuddering slightly on observing his taut features and the steely gleam in his eyes, knowing he spoke the truth. 'You would have done that for me?'

'I would do anything for you, Juliet,' he said achingly, unable to restrain himself, pulling her back into his arms. 'Never doubt it. I love you and cannot imagine my life without you. I adore you, Juliet.'

Juliet sighed, content to wallow in his doting gaze, having no doubts that he loved her—genuinely loved her. 'And I you, Marcus. I have come to love you dearly, and I cannot bear to think of my world without you in it.'

Marcus knew that the love between them would grow with time and supplant everything else in importance. He could see that in her eyes, and it made him ecstatically happy.

Epilogue

❧❦❧

Richard's marriage to Amelia Fortesque, the Earl of Bainbridge's daughter, in the spring of the following year at the Palladian Fortesque House, was a truly grand affair. Adele was so excited she could hardly contain herself as she accompanied the other bridesmaids in the wake of the bride. Juliet was relieved that her brother had turned his life around and that after all the years of neglect, the Endcliffe estate was showing signs of recovery.

Juliet was a vision of loveliness in a lavender gown, not quite as slender as she was for her own wedding to Marcus, due to the baby she was to bear two months hence. Her husband looked extremely handsome in a midnight-blue jacket, beneath which he wore an ivory satin waistcoat, his dark hair brushed smoothly back from his brow.

The ceremony was followed by a wedding breakfast, where the atmosphere was light-hearted, and Juliet would catch her husband's eye and a smile would move across his lean face, his eyes becoming more vividly blue over the rim of his champagne glass, silently informing her of his impatience for them to be alone later. The love they felt for each other was plain to see;

in fact, it was difficult to believe they were the same two people who had faced each other with so much rancour on their wedding day.

'Richard has done well for himself,' he told her softly when he managed to get her to himself for a brief moment. 'Things couldn't have turned out better.'

'And it is all down to you, Marcus. We would not be here now if you had not been there to guide and advise him. I'm thrilled for him. I have never seen him look more content, although I think Amelia has much to do with that. She's a truly delightful young woman, and it makes me happy to know she will be close enough for me to call on her and vice versa. She makes a beautiful bride, don't you agree, Marcus? Although I suppose all brides look radiant on their wedding day.'

'I only had eyes for the one,' he replied, his eyes caressing her upturned face. 'You were the most captivating young woman I had ever seen, and totally unaware of the effect you had on me.'

'And now?'

'Now that you are to bear our child, you look even more beautiful than you did that day.'

She smiled. 'I think you flatter me to tempt me, Marcus,' she teased.

'You are quite right,' he murmured, his eyes glowing with love and adoration as he gazed down at her. 'Are you complaining, Countess?'

'Not when I have such a passionate, attentive husband. But am I to believe you love me for my beauty alone?' she teased gently.

His features became solemn. 'No. I am not so stupid that I would have let your beauty alone make me love you. You have a multitude of other assets I admire and love. You are a rare being, Juliet. You are everything I dreamed a woman, a wife and a soon-to-be mother could be—and more.'

Juliet tilted her head up to his and could see he was perfectly serious. 'That is a compliment indeed, Marcus. Thank you.'

It was the greatest day Mulberry Hall had known for several decades when Marcus and Juliet's son was born, beginning a round of festivities suited to such an occasion. Happiness reigned over the great house, celebrating the new heir.

Marcus sat on the bed with his arm around Juliet, who was gazing at Adele looking adoringly down at her new brother sleeping in his crib beside the bed. He thought how changed she was. Happiness suited her. With the birth of their son her beauty bloomed with a new contentment and maturity as never before.

'What are you thinking?' she murmured.

'How lucky I am to have two wonderful children and such a beautiful wife—and how amiable you have become,' he teased gently. 'There is scarcely a trace of the contrary young woman I came to know in the early days of our acquaintance.'

'Do not be deceived, for she is still there, lurking somewhere in the background.' Juliet smiled softly, stirring within his arms, sighing and lifting her brilliant eyes to his, letting them feast on his handsome features. She adored this man, her husband, and everything about him, and she had come to know him like no other. 'She has not vanished. She is just waiting to be resurrected.'

'And you do love me, don't you, Juliet?'

'Absolutely. Have I not convinced you of it many times? When I have recovered from the birth of our son, I will show you how much.'

And she did, revealing the sweet anticipation of the rest of their lives to come.

* * * * *

The Truth Behind The Governess

Carol Arens

MILLS & BOON

Carol Arens delights in tossing fictional characters into hot water, watching them steam and then giving them a happily-ever-after. When she is not writing, she enjoys spending time with her family, beach camping or lounging about a mountain cabin. At home, she enjoys playing with her grandchildren and gardening. During rare spare moments, you will find her snuggled up with a good book. Carol enjoys hearing from readers at carolarens@yahoo.com or on Facebook.

Visit the Author Profile page
at millsandboon.com.au for more titles.

Author Note

Thank you so much for picking up a copy of my newest book, *The Truth Behind the Governess*. Your support means so much to me. Without you, there would be no stories.

This one is a story of things not always being what they seem, as the hero of our tale, Clement Marston, comes to discover.

You must gather by the title that there is a governess who has secrets to keep. But what is a lady to do when she is expected to become engaged to a marquess but has dreams of her own?

Vivienne Curtis does what any freethinking lady would do— she sneaks away for the summer in search of adventure before she must fulfill her duty to family and society.

In her guise as a governess, she finds a great deal more than adventure. As you will have guessed, she falls in love, not only with her employer but with his children.

I hope you enjoy discovering how Lady Vivienne and her employer, Clement Marston, find their way to one another.

DEDICATION

This book is dedicated to my dear friends
Sue Bruecker and Teri Feski.

Prologue

Liverpool—
March 1863

An insect, barely seen in the midnight shadow of the porch, skittered across the toe of Clement Marston's boot. He gave it no notice.

It was all he could do to find his next breath. To hold together when all he wanted to do was shatter.

The woman walking behind him was not holding together. Her soft weeping sounded as mournful as the ship's horn wailing in the harbour.

He glanced back over his shoulder at the house they'd walked away from. Saw the light in his sister's chamber window go out.

A fist grabbed his soul, squeezed with no mercy.

Alice Jayne would no longer need the lamp. His sister was dead.

'She is with her husband now,' he murmured, seeking to give and take what comfort was to be had in the thought. Alice Jayne had loved the man against society's approval. Three years past she had run away with her sailor, giving up the title that might have been hers except for love.

'Sir, let me take one of the babies,' the woman sniffled.

'Not yet, Miss Logan.'

His sister's girls were protected from the biting cold and rain under the coat draped over his shoulders. No need to expose them to the elements while walking to the carriage. He could not protect them from the tragedy of losing their mother, but he could protect them from the weather.

Miss Logan climbed into the carriage first, assisted by the driver. Once the nurse was settled he handed her one baby, then the other. The lady cooed over the infants while he settled on the other side of the carriage.

'Oh, Mr Marston.' The nurse, who only days ago had simply been the neighbour across the hallway from Alice Jayne, blinked wet eyes at him. 'What shall become of these sweet children?'

Clement was not certain.

At twenty-one years old he was ill equipped to be a father. But his brothers were even more ill equipped than he was. Duncan, having only recently inherited the title of Baron Granville, lived the loose life of a very wealthy society bachelor. So did his youngest brother, Eldon. Neither of them cared for anything beyond their next secret liaison.

'Your sister was my dearest friend, Sir.' Miss Logan patted the bottom of one blanket, her fingers trembling. 'I would like to ask…may I stay on as their nursemaid?'

He stared blankly at her. The woman was asking him to make a decision about the future of his sister's children as if he was the one in charge. As if he had some sort of plan.

As of two days ago, his plan had been to go to the Isle of Wight and search for insects. It was what entomologists did, discovered interesting things about unusual insects and then published their findings. Their names then became respected by their peers.

A nip of self-pity made him wonder if the ship's wail,

mournfully pressing against the windows while the carriage bumped over dock stones, belonged to the ship he had purchased passage on.

It would be at the harbour already, he knew, having planned every detail of the trip with great eagerness. It was to be the first step towards becoming a renowned entomologist. He had long dreamed of finding an insect which was the rarest of the rare.

One of his nieces whimpered. Miss Logan murmured to the baby which seemed to be the signal for the other one to whimper.

He reached across. Miss Logan handed one of the babies over to him.

Feeling sorry for himself was quite unworthy in this moment. It was, however, an easier emotion to cope with than crushing grief.

He had spent several days with his sister while she fought her battle against childbed fever. During it all he had not given a great deal of attention to the infants. Noticing how Miss Logan had cared for them with such devotion, he had asked if she would take the position of nurse until Alice Jayne recovered.

She had not recovered, though, and here the lady sat, waiting for his answer.

'Touch her cheek, she will suck on the tip of your finger, Sir. It helps sometimes.'

For a moment, perhaps. But at some point the girls would need to feed. He assumed Miss Logan had somehow taken care of it during the week since their birth. He had not heard them crying.

Clement touched the soft curve of the baby's cheek. She turned and latched on to his finger with more force than he'd guessed a tiny infant would have. Of course, when it came to infants, guesses were all that he had.

'How did you manage this past week, keeping them fed?'

Miss Logan closed her eyes, biting her lip while she shook her head. 'I do not dare say. If I do, you will send me away and I…' Hugging the baby close to her heart, she rocked it. 'It will break my heart, Sir.'

'Have you recently lost a child, then? Fed these in its place?' It seemed a logical conclusion.

'It is something of the truth, Mr Marston.' It seemed for a moment as if she would not go on, but then she did. 'I did lose a child, but not in the way you think. I was not wed, so…so I could not keep him, not if I wished for him to have a decent life.'

The only sound was of jingling tack and surf breaking against the sea wall while he gathered his wits in the face of her confession.

'I appreciate your forthrightness, Miss Logan. Do not fear that I will judge you. Truly, I am grateful you helped my sister and her children.'

'She was a dear friend to me, your sister. I see her in you, Sir. Both of you the very souls of compassion. But it broke her when her husband's ship went down with all hands lost…only five miles from the harbour, too. A wicked tragedy. All of Liverpool grieved. I wonder if it is why Alice Jayne did not find the strength to rally.'

'If you wish to feed the babies now, I shall look away.'

'Thank you. They are getting restless.'

He looked out of the window, watching the rain streaking through the light of a streetlamp and the dark, vague shapes of masts bobbing in the harbour.

Fabric rustled. 'Here you are, my sweet little dove.'

After a short moment Miss Logan said, 'We are covered up, now.'

All he could see of the child were her booties peeking out from under the blanket draped over Miss Logan's shoulders. She sounded utterly content.

The baby girl in his arms grew ever restless.

Never in his life had he felt as helpless as he did now.

'Did my sister name them?'

He ought to have known a thing like that.

'She would have, but the labour was long and when she was finished, she could not speak much. She held each of her girls, though, kissed them, but then, well…she did not know much after that.'

Such was her state when he arrived. He hoped his sister had felt him at her bedside, but could not be certain. The doctor had encouraged him to speak to her as if she might rally and answer. Still, they had both understood there was little hope she would survive.

'We shall call this one Alice, then.' He bent his head, kissed Alice on her smooth forehead. 'And her sister shall be Jayne.'

'Oh, Sir! Named for their mother! That is lovely.' Miss Logan began a new bout of sniffling.

He would join her in it, but he had decisions to make.

The first was leaving Liverpool for the family home in London…and then shortly after that, leaving London.

They exchanged babies so Alice could feed.

With neither him nor Miss Logan having anything further to say, the echo of his sister's last breath consumed him.

But, no…he must think ahead. Looking back only dragged one down into a pit of grief which was difficult to climb out of. He knew that well since it had been little more than two years since he and his brothers had lost their parents.

'I shall purchase a home in the country. Will you come and help me care for the children?'

'Oh, yes! You are a saint to take them…and me.'

He was not. Only a grieving brother. And a man without the future he had dreamed of.

Then he heard a sound, one he had never heard before. Contented coos and sighs issued from under the blanket draped over Miss Logan. Somehow it managed to poke a pinhole in his grief. As small as it was, it allowed a frizzle of hope in.

Life would be different than he'd pictured it, but it would be a life, just the same.

'Perhaps, Miss Logan, we will manage.'

Chapter One

◦◦◦◦◦

Whisper Glen, Cheshire—
June 1873

Lady Vivienne Curtis tucked this week's publication of *Whispering Times* under her arm, then set her camera on top of a waist-high tree stump. There was a particularly lovely bird who had perched in this very spot for three days in a row.

Sadly, photographing birds was ever so much more difficult than she'd thought it would be. Birds were quick, her camera was not. Perhaps she should develop a passion for photographing fruit baskets.

So far all she had managed to capture on the camera's glass plates was a blur which no one would guess had been a bird.

Still, the odds of capturing an image would be better here at her Great-Aunt Anne's estate than at home in London. The woods surrounding the manor house were alive with flitting feathered creatures.

Hopefully by the end of the family's week-long visit she'd have managed to take a few photographs.

There was a bush growing beside the stump which would make an adequate hiding place, being large and dense. She did not mind that it was somewhat scratchy because one expected a bit of discomfort while lying in wait.

Vivienne had a dream for her future, not that it mattered. She was as likely to obtain it as she was to get a bird to remain still for long enough while she took its photo. She might take a hundred of the most beautiful avian images anyone had ever seen and, still, no dream would come true for her.

Lady Vivienne Louise Curtis, daughter of the Marquess of Helmond, was destined for a prestigious marriage. Never, ever, in a million years, not for all her hoping and wishing, would she ever be the proprietress of a quaint little shop where she would sell her photos to admiring patrons.

Once she wed, her husband might forbid her to even go exploring with her camera. The day she wed, she would be chained to her new title. She could nearly hear the links clanking while huddling here in the shrubbery.

The very reason she and her parents were visiting Cheshire was to make a betrothal arrangement with Everett Parker, Marquess of Winterfeld, Great-Aunt Anne's stepson from her second marriage.

He was acceptable in every way…her father's equal in society, a widower with no children and a gentleman in behaviour as well as title.

Vivienne knew all this since she had been acquainted with Everett all of her life. She could not recall a time when he was not nearly a part of the family. She recalled being a small girl and chasing her puppy about the skirts of Lady Winterfeld's elegant wedding gown.

Everett had loved his wife deeply. The whole family had grieved when she'd died three years ago.

And now Vivienne was being pressed to wed him.

'Oh, feathers,' she mumbled, then opened *Whispering*

Times, seeking a distraction from her thoughts while she waited for the bird. 'I must marry someone.'

If she did not choose Everett Parker, she might end up with a stranger who turned out to be a wastrel who would leave her in poverty. Or a cad who would crush her soul.

It wasn't as if she had not seen that happen to a friend or two. What she'd learned was that it was best to put off marriage for as long as one could. Knowing a man for a long time before committing one's future to him was wise.

She had known the Marquess for ever. If she agreed to wed him, it would make her parents happy.

In the past it had been Grace, her obedient sister, making them proud. Vivienne had been the one causing problems with her uncommon opinion on what made a lady content. She wouldn't mind being their angelic child for a time.

She yawned, read for a moment and then gazed through the branches at a pond glittering in sunlight. There were benches placed at the water's edge which looked quite inviting.

Since there was no chance of getting the image of a bird from the comfort of a bench, she sighed and settled in for a long prickly sit and returned her attention to the news of Whisper Glen.

This was a quiet village, though, and there was nothing overly dramatic to read about. There was a man seeking a governess, one who was willing to travel to bucolic areas and care for a pair of ten-year-old girls.

Bucolic? It sounded charming.

'Lucky woman…' she mumbled. To be paid to travel? And all the lady needed to do in return was play with ten-year-old girls? 'I would do it in a moment, if only…

A whir of wings stirred the branches overhead. Apparently her bird had arrived, but now her attention was diverted because...why couldn't she be a governess who was willing to travel?

While she had never been a governess, she and her sister had bedevilled several of them while growing up. Indeed, having been a ten-year-old girl and having had governesses, she felt strongly that she would be qualified for the position. She could speak French. Sing in it, too, while plunking at piano keys. She was better at the harp and could teach her charges if the need arose.

While the bird chirruped Vivienne imagined herself on a great adventure, taking photos of all manner of fascinating things. Looked at in the right light, she had more to offer the children than merely instruction in ladylike behaviour. Wouldn't it be grand if she introduced them to the joy of capturing a moment in time on a glass plate?

A sudden movement made the bird take flight. Someone walked by at the edge of the pond. He sat on a bench. Ah, it was the widowed Marquess, Everett Parker.

He gazed at the water for a moment, then bent his head, folded his arms across his chest and crossed his long legs at the ankle. The poor man looked lonely. Would she make him happier if she allowed him to offer for her? Or would he recognise her reluctance to wed and feel bad for it?

Great-Aunt Anne, whom they both adored, had convinced Everett that he must find love again...and that he could find it with Vivienne if he looked hard enough. Seeing him now, Vivienne thought he had little hope of finding love again. Having loved his first wife so deeply, would he even be able to love another?

If he did propose to her, it would only be to make his stepmother happy. The same as her reason for accepting him, to make her parents happy. She must marry someone. He must marry someone. A man of his station was rather obliged to wed again. He was her father's age, yes, but not ancient. There was still time for him to produce an heir.

Being stabbed with an idea, she stood suddenly from the bush, picked up her camera and tucked it under her arm along with the newspaper.

'Good day, Mr Parker.' She called him Mr Parker because it was what she had always called him.

Ordinarily she would not sit on a bench with a man and begin a conversation—however, they were not strangers and there were things which must be said between them.

'Good day, Vivienne.' He called her that because he had done so since she was a child when he used to pat her on the head. 'Did you just pop up out of that bush?'

'Indeed, yes, I was…trying to get a photograph of a bird.'

'Rather quick creatures to be preserved on a glass plate, I would imagine.'

She sat down, putting the camera next to her, but pressing the newspaper to her bosom.

'It is incredibly discouraging.'

Small talk would not get them to the point of her sitting here so she pressed on. 'I assume you know why my family has come to visit your stepmother at the very same time you are also visiting her?'

If he was surprised by the blunt question, it did not show in his expression. He continued to smile at her.

'I do, of course. Tell me, though…do you not consider me too old for you?

She looked at him in a way she had never done before. As a friend of her father's, she had not paid a great deal of attention to him in the light of marriage.

Lord Winterfeld had deep lines etched at the corners of his eyes, put there by sadness, she supposed. The hair at his temples was beginning to turn grey, the same as Father's was.

'You do not seem so terribly old,' she said, trying to put him at ease over the great difference in their ages. 'But you must still see me running about in pigtails.'

'I will admit, I barely recall you from that time, Vivienne. When you were in pigtails I was a newlywed and my attention was only on my bride.'

'I am truly sorry for your loss. I cannot imagine how awful it must have been.'

A butterfly flitted about their heads. Everett reached a finger towards it, smiling.

'Pretty thing,' he said.

'The wings are pretty, but the rest of it is just an insect. I dislike insects.' Wicked nasty creatures which managed to creep into spaces they had no business creeping into and then springing out to startle one.

'Do you dislike me?' he asked.

Although the question seemed quite sudden, if there was ever a time to be forthright it was now.

'You mean as a husband, I assume?'

He nodded, gazing at the rippling surface of the pond. 'I would rather know it now if you do.'

'I do not dislike you in the least. But to be honest, if I had my way, I would not marry at all. I would open a little shop and...but never mind. As you know, I must wed for the good of the family name. Same as you must do. My parents will be happy at least, you know that. And Great-Aunt will be delirious with joy. She has strongly hinted at a union between us for some time now.'

He took a deep breath. 'May I speak with your father, then?'

With the briefest hesitation she answered, 'I believe it

is for the best…only, before you do, may I ask that you indulge me in one small matter?'

'But of course, my dear.' His tone felt very much as if, once again, he was reaching out of the past and patting her on the head.

'My sister and her husband are going on holiday to the Continent for the summer. I would like to go with them. I ask that we make the announcement of our engagement after I return.'

'Naturally a young woman like you will want a bit of freedom before she settles down to the responsibility of having a household and a husband. I shall speak to your father, my dear, and suggest it is my idea to wait on the formal announcement. He will agree if it comes from me.'

Everett Parker was a good man, one who did not deserve being told a half-truth. A pang of guilt nipped her conscience. It was actually less of a half-truth and more of a complete lie.

'I do thank you.' She rose from the bench, picking up the camera. She had the silliest urge to give him a hug, the same as she would have given her father when he granted her a favour. 'I have business this afternoon in the village, but I shall see you at tea.'

Hurrying away, she clutched the now wrinkled copy of *Whispering Times* to her heart.

With half a stroke of luck, she was about to become a travelling governess for the summer.

Come the autumn, she would settle into her life as an engaged woman, honest in all her dealings.

'What sort of father…?'

Clement watched the latest applicant for governess rise ponderously from the chair across the desk from him, her lips pressed thin, her grimace flat. She shook her head, making her double chin waggle.

'What sort of father, I repeat, allows children to sneak insects into a lady's hat?'

The insect in question—a speckled bush cricket, female and green as clover—scurried across the floor to hide under a basket stuffed with periodicals.

Clement pushed back in his office chair with a resigned but silent sigh. He escorted the woman to the front door, then watched her march down the drive.

Ah well, she would never have suited them anyway. He needed a lady who was fit enough to keep up with Alice and Jayne while they travelled.

He had mentioned travel in his advertisement, but he was certain this candidate had misunderstood the nature of the trip. There would be no luxury accommodations.

Unfortunately she was his last applicant, too. He was starting to despair that his long-dreamed-of trip of exploration would ever happen.

With a sinking heart he pictured the tickets lying on his desk. Four train tickets, four tickets for passage to the Isle of Wight for him, his ten-year-old terrors and the governess he now had little hope of engaging.

No governess, no voyage of adventure.

There was no question of leaving the children behind while he travelled. For his sister's sake, he could not. A stranger, no matter how well intentioned, would not care for the girls with the love a mother would…or, in her place, an uncle.

A movement caught the corner of his eye, drawing his attention to the bridge spanning the stream.

Ah, there those little pixies were, skipping over the

bridge, then dashing off into the woods. Having foiled his attempts to hire a governess, they would be off to celebrate.

He called back the curse making his tongue itch. Fathers did not curse.

If only Miss Logan had not married and gone off to begin a family of her own. The girls had loved their nurse. Apparently they saw the progression of governesses into their lives as intruders. In the three years since Miss Logan had left them, four haggard women had come and gone.

Now, when he needed a governess most, it seemed he would not have her.

Each and every one of the ladies he'd interviewed had fallen victim to his girls' mischief. His daughters, which of course was what they were to him, were highly creative in their pranks. At times he overlooked their antics, admired their ingenuity, even.

This was not one of those times. He set out after the girls. A lecture was called for.

His future as an entomologist was at risk. He was already familiar with every sort of insect inhabiting his own grounds. If he wished to publish his findings and have his name known, he would need to broaden his exploration area.

Since he refused to leave the girls behind, he must have a woman to care for them.

'It is time you learned to behave as young ladies,' he grumbled.

He had one foot on the bridge when he spotted a fascinating spider. He bent to have a closer look, then he heard a voice.

Straightening, he saw a woman coming up the path towards the house in great haste. She pressed her bonnet in place with splayed fingers. Sunny yellow ribbons streamed behind her.

'Oh, please do not say I have come too late.'

Too late for what? he wondered. She was not dressed like any governess he had ever encountered.

But what other reason would there be for her to be dashing up his drive unless it was to apply for the position? While it would have been proper to make an appointment, he was grateful she had not observed the formality.

What a boon! It was as if good fortune had dropped her here at this particular moment when Alice and Jayne were off on their premature celebration. He felt a grin rising. They could not run off a potential governess when they didn't even know she was here. Perhaps he would get the best of those adorable mischief makers this time.

He met the lady halfway up the drive.

'Please say you have not hired another woman in my place,' she said, her breath coming in short gasps because of the run.

In her place? This was encouraging.

'As it happens, I am still interviewing. Please come inside.' They walked back to the house. He ushered her inside, then led her to his study, indicating the chair opposite his at the desk. 'I will send for tea while you catch your breath.'

He hurried to the kitchen and ordered tea to be delivered to his study.

Returning, he found the lady had removed her modest, yet cheerful, hat and placed it on her lap.

Her appearance set her apart from the other women he had interviewed. There was no hint of dowdiness about her. Her gown was sunny...downright cheerful, if perhaps with a few years of wear showing.

Craning her neck this way and that, she gazed at the paintings of rare and beautiful insects hanging on the walls.

'Aren't they marvellous?' he asked, although he was certain anyone would think so.

'Vivid,' she answered cautiously, 'In every detail.'

They were and yet he still had the feeling that she did not appreciate the full beauty of the images.

He sat across from her, settled into his chair and tried not to look desperate. But leaping locusts, just when all had seemed lost, here she was.

First off, he must know what she expected of travelling with him and the girls. If she thought it would be a luxurious excursion, he would lose yet another potential governess.

More than that, though, he would need to be forthcoming about what she would be facing with Alice and Jayne.

It wasn't as if the girls were bad at heart. They were simply sweet, loving children...who were determined not to have a governess.

He, as their father, was even more determined that they would.

Folding his hands on top of the desk, he considered his words while studying this surprising applicant.

She did not resemble a governess, being younger than most and far prettier. Prettier in an uncommon way. She was a moth, he decided, rather than a butterfly. While butterflies were lovely and easily admired, moths were equally beautiful, only in a less flashy way. As far as Clement was concerned, the rosy maple moth was a match for the painted lady butterfly any day...or night, as it were.

This woman, with her rich brown hair and eyes the shade of amber, was a lovely specimen...of woman naturally, not moth. He had to wonder why she was not already wed. She was too young to be considered on the shelf. Why would she be seeking a position and not a husband?

It was not his business, he knew that; it was only that he was curious. But more than anything he was grateful she wished to apply for the post.

'I am Clement Marston,' he said, eager to get to the point of why she was sitting across from him. The sooner he hired her, the better. He could not be sure when Alice and Jayne would return so it would be prudent to keep the interview brief.

'A pleasure to meet you, Mr Marston. I am Vivienne Curtis.'

'It is lovely to meet you, Miss Curtis,' he replied. 'Thank you for your interest in the position.'

Chapter Two

V ivian hoped her aristocratic position did not show, having gone to some effort to disguise it. She had made sure to bring only older attire with her that she would normally only wear to go photographing birds. Nothing terribly drab, though. She had no wish to become depressed by wearing grey or brown, after all.

Her hair was done simply, without whirls and ribbons. If an acquaintance passed her on the street, she was certain they would not recognise her.

There was not much she could do about her well-bred manner of speech, however. But perhaps Mr Marston would not think much of it. Gently born ladies sometimes fell upon hard times, after all.

'The position sounds a most excellent opportunity.'

Luckily for Vivienne the flustered-looking woman who had charged past her on the road had clearly not thought so. She'd grumbled aloud about the children being a menace.

'Do you have experience with young girls?' Mr Marston asked.

She could hardly admit she had never had the care of a child, but… 'Yes, naturally, I was one myself…and I have a younger sister. I understand very well how their minds work.'

'What an unconventional answer. I've not heard it before.'

'No? I am surprised since it does seem an important aspect of performing the job well. Children must be understood if one is to relate to them. I believe it is important for them to be happy, but at the same time well behaved.' She emphasised that last bit because, according to the woman on the road, they were not. It was something she would need to deal with.

Mr Marston nodded his head ever so slightly.

'But how much actual experience do you have as governess?' he asked curiously. 'You seem rather young to have much.'

She had been raised by nannies and governesses all her life. What better experience could there be? However, once again, she could not tell him that.

'Not as old as some, I will admit. But it has been said that I have a particular affinity with children.'

Perhaps someone had said such a thing at one time. Just because she had never heard it did not mean no one had said it!

She gave him the most utterly charming smile she knew how to give. No one had ever said she had an utterly charming smile, she would wager, but it could not hurt to try.

Although charming was surely not a qualification for the position, who objected to a dash of congeniality?

'I am well able to instruct the children in reading, writing and arithmetic. I will also teach them to sing songs *en français* if it will amuse them.'

'I wonder…' he murmured thoughtfully, then tapped his fingers on what appeared to be tickets for travel.

'If it is a matter of my letter of reference…' She dug about in the reticule she had put on the floor beside the chair. She handed him an envelope. 'Here you are.'

He opened it then set it on the desk atop the tickets. It seemed to take a lifetime for him to read it. The clock on the wall ticked louder with each long, tense moment.

At last he looked up, nodded. 'It is quite adequate.'

It was not merely adequate, it was positively glowing. She had spent hours writing it last night.

'As you will know from the advertisement, your charges would be my ten-year-old daughters, twins.'

'Yes, what a lovely age.' It would surely not be too difficult to keep them entertained.

She folded her hands primly in her lap so that her nervousness would not show. Getting the position was only one of the challenges she faced. She must also convince her sister and her husband to keep the secret. When they discovered she was not going to the Continent with them, they would likely object…with vigour.

However, her sister had already expressed concerns about her having to marry a man so much older than she was. Grace wished for Vivienne to have all the marital happiness she had found with George. That would go in her favour.

Yes, it was probable that Grace would support her summer of freedom. Her brother-in-law would be the harder one to convince.

'The girls are my late sister's children, but I have raised them since they were infants. I love them, naturally, but at the same time I feel I must advise you that they can get into mischief.'

'Oh, but I am certain they are delightful.' It did not matter if they were delightful or not. She needed to be their governess.

'They have it in them to be and many times they are, but they have run off the candidates I interviewed before you.'

'Fortunate for me, then. I assure you, I shall not be run off.'

'My intention is to spend the summer travelling, which I also mentioned in the advertisement. You will not mind caring for my girls while I explore the wilds? I do not feel comfortable leaving them in Cheshire.'

'The wilds of where, may I ask?' Perhaps birds in the wild would be more amenable to having their images captured than they were here?

'The Isle of Wight.'

'The Isle of Wight? Where artists, poets and even the Queen go on holiday?'

'The very isle. But we will not be staying where they do, I'm afraid. It is into the less civilised areas for us. I am an entomologist and the island has some of the finest insects a man might find.'

She glanced again at the drawings on wall, trying not to flinch.

It was silly to worry that the insects were going to crawl out of the frames, creep up her stockings, and make her lose her composure during the most important interview of her life.

She knew they would not. Still, logic did little to keep her skin from prickling.

'You dislike insects?' Clement Marston touched his chin, thumb on one side of his jaw and finger crossing the other while he gave her a deep look.

The man had an interesting face. Not quite handsome and yet altogether agreeable. Anyone seeing the smile peeking from behind his hand would have a hard time looking away. It was wide and flat, but then took an amusing upward turn at each corner.

Just now he appeared bemused that she did not share his fondness for creepy crawling creatures.

Since she did need to become the governess to his lively girls, she smiled and lied once more. 'I adore them, of course. Who does not?'

'You do not.'

'Very well, you have caught me out. But I do adore little girls and it is them I am to care for, is it not?'

If his funny crooked smile was anything to go by, her honest answer satisfied him where her lies had not.

'I shall protect you from insects as best I can, but they do have a way of going wherever they wish to.'

'I shall be—'

Oddly enough, in that very instant she felt something… a tickling sensation on her ankle.

Her imagination. It had to be.

Discreetly, she lifted the hem of her skirt to be certain. To her everlasting horror there was a bright green creature creeping up her stocking! She could hardly scream and dash about the study in an effort to dislodge the small monster, not if she wished to appear stout-hearted enough to perform her duties.

She stood and stamped her foot. The insect hung on, digging its prickly legs into her stocking and climbing ever upwards. Surely this was a nightmare from which she would soon awake!

With each movement of the insect, she lifted her skirt higher, modesty forsaken in the moment. The insect reached her knee and seemed to have no intention of stopping. She spread her fingers to swat it, already dreading the disagreeable green stain sure to ruin her stocking and the sticky guts which would smear her hand.

'No!' Clement Marston leapt over the desk, sliding across the surface, scattering pens and papers. He caught her hand, but not his forward momentum.

She lost her balance and they both went down in a tumble.

'Oof,' he grunted, hitting the floor beside her.

She sat up, shaking out her skirt in search of the horrid insect…or a green smear.

Rather than offering an apology, Mr Marston gave her an astonished-looking frown.

'She is quite harmless, I promise.'

'You are acquainted with it, then?' How could he know the insect would not have bitten her?

'Acquainted with her kind.'

He glanced about, probably looking for a squashed bush cricket. Apparently reassured it had made an escape, he seemed to come to himself and noticed they were sitting on the floor.

'I beg your pardon. Please do forgive me. I confess, I get carried away now and again in my enthusiasm for particularly nice insects.'

It was all she could do not to point out that there were no nice insects.

A pair of reading glasses lay on the floor, cracked across the centre of one lens. They must have slid off the desk in the tumble. He picked them up, holding them up to a beam of sunshine coming through the window.

'Ruined,' he commented. 'But I believe the cricket made it safely away.'

Perhaps she ought to do the same. Unless she missed her guess, his daughters were not the only unruly members of this household.

Imagine putting the well-being of a cricket before her own! It might be that the man needed a governess as much as his daughters did.

Oh, feathers! She would not dismiss this position because of his overreaction to a cricket.

'I accept.'

'My apology…or the offer of employment?'

'The apology since you did not actually offer employment.'

'I was about to when our little miss made her untimely appearance.'

Our little miss? Heaven help her.

He stood, offering a hand.

Although she was capable of rising on her own, she took it.

My word, the man might be studious, but his hand did not indicate it. His fingers were strong and steady, helping her up.

'Miss Curtis, my voyage is for next week. I confess, I am desperate for a willing woman.' All at once he seemed to realise his questionable wording for lines suddenly creased his brow. 'For a governess, of course. Please tell me you accept the position.'

'I do accept, but there is a condition to it.' It would be unfair to carry on and not admit her limitation. She must bear in mind her promise to Everett. 'I can only give you the summer. After that I have another engagement I must fulfil.'

'I will gladly take whatever time you can give me.' Hmm, the man had interesting gold flecks in his green eyes. They were probably not glowing in relief, but it seemed so to her. 'Thank you, Miss Curtis. And I promise I will never put a insect's well-being over yours again.'

While his flat, turned-up-at-the-corners grin was not the polished smile of a society gentleman, she found it appealing…genuine rather than practised.

Genuinely confounding, too. Why would looking at his smile make her insides flutter in such a curious way? She had read of such feelings, naturally, but she had never experienced the sensation.

She was not certain she approved of it. The man was her employer, not her... Oh, dear, never mind that.

Three days before the ship was to set sail for the Isle of Wight, Vivienne stood at the head of the lane leading to the Marston home, waving farewell to Grace and George. She felt more than a bit victorious, having only just won a skirmish which, had she lost, would have ruined everything.

It had been a victory of the highest order convincing her sister and her husband to drop her off at the lane while they continued on with their holiday. They had objected, naturally, but Vivienne had been prepared to counter each protestation.

Although Grace had been stunned by what Vivienne was doing, it had not been so difficult to win her over. She and her sister had always been allies. As different as apples and oranges, but they always took one another's side.

'Your parents have entrusted you to my care and in it you shall remain,' her brother-in-law had argued.

To that, she crossed her arms over her bosom and shook her head. 'I take myself out of your care.'

'You are to be married. You cannot become a governess,' again from George.

'I already am a governess,' she parried.

'George, my dear. Surely you understand Vivienne's predicament? Would you not wish for a final summer's adventure if you were in her position?'

'I am a man. It is expected that we will have adventures before we wed.'

'Oh, indeed? And you had such an adventure?'

'Well, I... I did not.'

'Nor were you forced into a loveless marriage, George. Vivienne will have this time to herself before she commits her life to Everett.' George, clearly not convinced, shook his head at his wife. She patted his cheek as if dismissing his concern, then she gave her attention back to Vivienne. 'There is one thing, though. Our parents will worry.'

It wasn't as if she had not already considered that.

'It is why you must keep my secret.' Vivienne handed her sister a stack of letters she had written, to be mailed at different points of the Continental holiday.

'Think of it, George,' she said coaxingly. 'You and my sister will have a far better time without me.'

The glance George briefly shot at his wife, the smile lurking at the corners of his mouth, told her she had scored in her favour with that observation.

Still not convinced he should allow it, she and George had gone around and around while bumping along the country road.

Then Grace brought an end to it.

'We will keep your secret.' Grace gave her husband a look, one which Vivienne had seen her mother use on their father. 'We will, won't we, George?'

'While I do not condone this, yes, I will do as your sister asks.'

At last they had reached the point where the lane leading to the Marston home cut off from the main road.

With a bit more grumbling, George ordered the carriage to stop.

Then there had ensued another discussion because, no, George could not drop her off in front of the house. Nor could he meet her employer to judge his character and intentions.

Mr Marston was unaware of her being the daughter of

a marquess and if he knew, she would very likely lose her position. Ladies of her station did not seek employment.

Ten minutes had passed while Vivienne argued in favour of her employer's sterling character, which she actually believed to be true.

Finally bidding them goodbye, she had bestowed on them kisses and her good wishes for their trip…along with her promise to be home at summer's end to announce her engagement. With the experience of a lifetime ready to begin, she sat upon the lid of her trunk to gather her thoughts and calm her nerves.

This quiet moment to savour the coming adventure was lovely. Fresh air, warm and fragrant with jasmine, washed over her. She glanced about, curious to know where it was growing. With the woods being so dense, she could not spot it.

Some people might think it rash to go away with a man she had only met one time. Those people would be correct. It was why she had gone to the village of Whisper Glen to discreetly discover what his neighbours thought of him.

She'd learned that Clement Marston was the son of one Baron Granville. More than one person had pointed out that the baronetcy was very wealthy. The Honourable Mr Marston had an older brother who was now Baron and had recently married. He also had a younger brother who had not yet settled down. She already knew of the late sister whose daughters she was to care for.

Most importantly, she had learned that everyone thought highly of Clement Marston. He was considered a good neighbour and a man who loved his children.

She'd sensed this about him from their first meeting.

What she also knew of him from that one meeting was that, upon occasion, he valued insects at the cost of good sense…that he was studious, but not soft. Apparently the quest for interesting specimens kept him robust. He probably wore those dark-framed glasses, although she hadn't seen him use them before the lenses cracked.

He had a goal for his life. She envied him the freedom to pursue it. What impressed her most about him was that he not leaving his children behind while he travelled. It indicated a great deal of devotion to them, no matter if he was called uncle or father. She admired him greatly for it.

Although she was no longer under George's protection, she had every confidence that she would come to no harm while she was with Clement Marston.

An out-of-place noise rallied her from her thoughts. Vivienne had spent enough time in the woods of Cheshire over the past weeks, listening to bird calls and other natural sounds, to recognise when something was amiss.

She stood, stretched, giving every impression of being unaware of giggles and whispering from the woods. Unless she missed her guess, she was about to become acquainted with Alice and Jayne. Given that they had done their best to make their prior governesses leave, there was no reason for them to think they would not do the same to her.

Vivienne Curtis, they were about to learn, was one governess who would not fall prey to impish shenanigans. In expectation of battle, Vivienne had packed her weapons… lemon drops and peppermint sticks. She lifted the lid of the trunk, drew out the bag of sweets and slipped it into her skirt pocket.

Armed, she set off down the pretty lane. Strolling in the dappled sunshine of the leafy canopy overhead, she watched for interesting birds and listened to brush being crunched on either side of the path.

The girls did not seem to be terribly accomplished in

stealthy tactics. Of course, they were only ten years old. Vivienne, on the other hand was twenty-four and, as a lady negotiating society, had learned to be wily. Somewhere along this path the children would have laid a trap. Very likely it was something which would antagonise, but not cause harm. Only a little something to convince her they were not worth the trouble. How wrong they were. Given what she was getting in return, they were more than worth it.

She glanced above, scanning the branches for something which might spill down upon her. Nothing there, which was a relief. Children should not lay traps in tree branches, no matter what fun it might be. When it came to a contest between gravity and growing bones, gravity often won.

Moments later the footsteps stopped. This might mean the trap was nearby and they were waiting for her to fall into it. Ah, just ahead the ground looked disturbed. Leaves and twigs covered a shallow depression in the centre of the path.

Stepping to the very edge, she noticed a hidden mud puddle. Lifting her foot, she gave every indication that she would step into it. From each side of the path she heard excited gasps. Lovely. She held her foot above the trap for an exaggerated instant, then drew it back and stepped around the puddle.

To the left of the lane was a fallen tree. Using it as a bench, she sat down on the trunk and gave her skirt a fluff while giving thought to which weapon to unsheathe.

Peppermint. It was more easily seen than a lemon drop.

She withdrew the bag, setting it on her lap. Taking her time, she took out a stick, unwrapped it, then licked it with a sigh of delight.

'Please do come out of hiding, girls. Your scheme has failed.'

No response. Not that she had expected them to emerge at once.

'As you wish.' She let the statement stand for a moment and then, 'I offer you one of two outcomes. The first is that I will step in your puddle, jump about quite madly just to make sure my skirt and shoes are ruined. Then you may face whatever punishment your father sees fit to dole out. But you will have achieved your end.'

Silent for a moment, she let the thought settle.

'The other outcome is that you come out of hiding and join me for a treat. I have lemon drops and peppermint sticks. We will become acquainted one way or another. How we go about that is up to you.'

A little girl with a pair of sunshine-blonde braids draping her shoulders stepped out from behind a tree. She frowned at Vivienne with deep brown eyes.

'Are you Jayne or Alice?'

'Jayne.'

The other little girl came out of hiding. She was taller than her sister and also had blonde hair, but on the reddish side. She wore it in one braid down her back. Her eyes were identical to her sister's in colour and shape.

'I am Alice.'

'It is a pleasure to meet you both.' She patted the log in invitation. Hesitantly, they came forward, then sat beside her, one on each side.

What pretty children they were. Time spent outdoors had given their skin a healthy blush. Both of them had a dappling of freckles across their noses and cheeks.

'Which confectionary do you prefer, Jayne?' she asked the child who had called herself Alice. 'And you, Alice. Lemon or peppermint?'

They glanced at one another as if stunned that she had

figured them out. Poor babies were not nearly as crafty as they thought they were. It took all Vivienne had not to smile.

Alice chose the peppermint sticks and Jayne chose lemon drops.

'I am Miss Curtis. Given the manner in which you greeted me, I assume you knew it already.'

They sucked on their sweets without answering.

'I will admit, it was a creative trap.'

'Thank you, Miss Curtis,' Jayne said.

'I might have fallen for it if I had not known beforehand that you have undertaken such pranks before.'

The girls exchanged some sort of message with their eyes.

Vivienne smiled, liking them right off even knowing they were not ready to accept her…not yet. They would in time, she meant to see to it.

While it was true that the reason she had sought the position was to have a summer of adventure before she wed, she took her responsibilities to Alice and Jayne to heart.

'I do not believe that you are finished trying to get rid of me, just as you did my predecessors.' She nodded and smiled at Jayne, then to Alice. 'Please understand, though, I will not be driven away.'

Apparently they were not accustomed to having their mischievous intentions exposed so bluntly. They gave her wide, matching blinks.

'Come now, ladies, shall we let your father know I have arrived unscathed?'

Alice giggled, but probably by accident since she clapped her slender fingers over her mouth.

Clement looked up from the notes that he was jotting down regarding the newly hatched damselfly he had come across early this morning.

He glanced at the clock hanging on the study wall. Oh, curse it! It was nearly three in the afternoon! It was past time for Miss Curtis to arrive. He had meant to meet her at the end of the lane and walk her up to the house…to get to her before Alice and Jayne did.

Miss Curtis had assured him she would not quit her post, that she understood a young girl's mind, but she had yet to meet her charges. He had hoped to guide their first meeting, make sure it was without incident.

Dropping his pencil on top of his notes, he dashed out of the room and through the house. Out on the porch, he came up short. It could not be, but he was witnessing the sight firsthand.

There was Miss Curtis, flanked by his daughters…the three of them contently sucking on…sweets? No one was muddied. Miss Curtis did not appear to have insects in her hair or on her hat, praise the Good Lord for it.

'Good afternoon, Papa.' Alice said, her sunny braids swinging while she walked. 'You were late for meeting Miss Curtis so we did it for you.'

He gave them all a glance over. No one seemed the worse for it.

'Sometimes Papa forgets the time if there is an insect involved,' Jayne explained.

'I apologise, Miss Curtis, I ought to have been there to greet you.'

'What was it, Papa? A butterfly or a beetle? Please say it was a stag beetle!' Of the two girls, Jayne was the one who shared his interest in insects.

'An azure damselfly. I spotted it quite by accident near the stream. Unexpected discoveries are the best, Miss Curtis. It never fails to prove true.'

It was how he felt about the new governess. Just when

he had all but given up hope, there she had been, as pretty as said damselfly while she'd hurried up his drive.

For an instant he'd had the sensation of delicate wings batting about in his chest. It was a distinctly odd reaction to seeing a pretty face. Not that prettiness mattered, only that she had been hurrying up the drive and eager to be hired.

Now, seeing her standing in front of the house, a peppermint stick pressed to her lips, he could scarcely believe his good fortune. For the moment his daughters seemed accepting of her, but it might be because of the sticky sugar smearing their mouths.

'Where are your belongings, Miss Curtis?' Why hadn't the hired hack delivered her and her things to the front door?

'I had the driver leave my trunk at the entry to the lane. It is such a lovely day I wanted to walk.'

That made sense. It boded well for their excursion that she enjoyed walking and being outdoors. They would be spending a great deal of time in the open air. He wanted the girls to learn their lessons and sing in French, but not to the exclusion of fresh air and sunshine.

'Alice, dear, please run and ask Mr Chambers to bring the trunk to the house.' He tugged on both of her braids which was a special sign of affection between them.

Alice skipped away, braids swinging across her back.

'Jayne, love, let Mrs Simmons know that your governess has arrived. We shall have refreshments outside.'

Jayne stepped on top of his shoes and gave him a hug around the middle. This was their special sign of affection.

Clement wondered if he had thanked Miss Curtis heartily enough. For as much as this trip meant to him, he could not possibly leave his daughters behind. He knew parents who had no qualms about leaving children in the care of others while they travelled. His own parents had done so often. As far as Clement was concerned, the whole family had suffered because of their absence.

Perhaps had they not been gone so often, his sister would not have been as in need of affection as she was. She might have been more selective about whom she fell in love with and married. Everything might have been different.

One thing was certain—her children would never feel such a lack of affection. He loved them and would make sure they knew it.

'We shall go to Liverpool tomorrow,' he said while escorting Miss Curtis into the house. 'The day after, our ship will sail on the first tide. Will that be suitable?'

He could not imagine what he would do if it was not.

'Quite suitable. I look forward to it.' And then, to his everlasting relief, she added, 'Alice and Jayne are endearing girls. I look forward to getting to know them better.'

'You do?' She did?

'But of course.'

Since Miss Logan, no governess had said such a thing. Oddly enough, he believed her. There was no indication of insincerity in her eyes, no hint of it in her smile.

'I believe we are off to a brilliant start,' he said.

What he didn't say was that her presence was a gift, as if she'd been magically dropped from the sky. It was not true, of course. He had placed an advertisement and she had answered it. Still, it must be more than coincidence that a lady who thought his daughters were endearing had shown up in in his moment of need.

Vivienne was still awake long after anyone else in the household had fallen asleep. Even if she had not been too excited to sleep, she was in a new home in a strange bedroom.

The window was cracked an inch which let in all sorts of night sounds that she was not accustomed to. Insects, she imagined, singing their odd songs to one another. Crossing the room, she closed the window. Ah, that was much better.

Now that she was no longer concerned about what the strange clicking sound near the windowsill had been, she could think about what was uppermost in her mind.

Being a governess. She had an employer who counted on her to teach and guide his lively daughters. At the same time, those lively daughters would resist her attempts to teach and guide. She would need a few weapons in her arsenal which did not involve confectionery.

Books…that was what she needed. She wondered if Mr Marston had already packed them or if he meant for her to do it. Better to be prepared, she decided. A visit to Mr Marston's library was called for.

First, though, she sat on a chair, then took off her shoes and stockings. Giving her toes a good stretch, she sighed. This was one of life's delightful pleasures after a long, busy day. She plucked the pins from her hair, not quite certain how she would get it up again without her maid to do it.

A matter to deal with tomorrow, she decided. Tonight she must live up to her duty as a governess, even though she was not quite confident of all it would entail. Books, though—any governess she'd ever had carried one under her arm as a part of her attire.

Leaving her chamber, she walked down a long hallway, her bare feet silent on the polished floor. She remembered the way since her employer had given her a tour of his large, yet comfortable, home after dinner.

The only lamp still burning came from under Clement Marston's chamber door. He must be working late on his research. Would he be trying to peer though his broken spectacles or had he another pair? Although it was not his spectacles she was dwelling on as much as his eyes.

They were interesting eyes. Studious, to be sure, but she thought there were brief hints of humour in them, too. Mostly they reflected devotion to the children he quite clearly adored. Not quite green, not quite brown…yes indeed, he had very nice eyes.

Feathers, who was she to be noticing his attractive qualities? His governess, that was all…and a woman who was to become engaged at the end of the summer!

Around a corner, then down a hallway, she came to the door of the room she recalled being the library. The hinges squealed when she pushed it open. It was a lucky thing that the moon was bright since it was the only light in the room. She spotted a lamp on a corner table and struck a match to it.

The book-lined walls came to life with a golden glow. This was far more inviting than the library at home. It was cosy, whereas at Helmond House the library was vast. This place called for a person to sit and live within the pages of a book. Helmond's library was meant to impress guests.

She scanned the shelves, wondering what books she ought to bring to the Isle of Wight. There was great variety in the volumes. She picked a few on arithmetic and history. There were dozens on geography, so she took down a few of those, too. Best of all, she discovered several volumes of fiction she could read with them. Adventure was the very thing which would appeal to her charges, she thought.

There was a book on the shelf near the ceiling which had an interesting binding. In the dim light she could not read the title so she slid the library ladder over, then climbed up to look at what it was.

'The Fascinating Life of Queen Bees and Drones,' she read aloud. 'Hmm, what can be so fascinating about a bee?'

'Few insects are more interesting than bees, Miss Curtis.'

The voice coming out of nowhere gave her a start. Her balance wobbled. The book hit the floor with a hard thud. She would have ended up on the floor beside the book except that Clement Marston grabbed her knee, steadying her. With a gasp she clasped the ladder rail, clinging tight.

'I beg your pardon. I did not mean to startle you.'

She started down the ladder.

No man had ever touched her knee and Mr Marston had only done so to keep her from falling. She should read nothing into her reaction to his touch or the pressure of his strong fingers. No doubt the true reason her heart had skipped and stuttered was because she'd nearly fallen.

Or because she'd suddenly realised that from where he stood his gaze would be at the level of her bare feet. What a mortifying way to begin her employment.

'I was looking for books to bring to the Isle.' Hopefully he did not think she was snooping. 'To instruct the children.'

The man did not speak for a moment. He simply stared at her hair as if he had never seen unbound hair before.

If he felt uncomfortable, she was more so. Outside of her family no one had seen her hair unbound. This whole encounter left her disconcerted.

Why had she not remained sensibly in her room?

Then he blinked and gave her his wide, congenial smile which made her feel slightly less flustered.

'Ah, I am ashamed to say I did not think of bringing along any books. But Alice and Jayne will need them, won't they?'

'Books are the tools of a governess,' she announced as if she knew it from vast experience in the profession.

'Let me help you, then.'

With her hair loose and her feet bare? It would not do.

'I shall manage. It is what you hired me to do, after all.'

'Very well, just put the books you choose on the sofa and I will have them packed into a trunk in the morning. I do not know if I made it clear how grateful I am that you accepted this position. I had all but given up on my girls having proper guidance and instruction over the summer. I am relieved to know they will be well tended.' He held her gaze for an instant longer. She held his in return because…well, what was that expression? Recognition of her as a woman?

Certainly not! More likely he was making a valiant effort not to look down at her toes.

'Good night then, Miss Curtis,' he said at last.

'Good night, Mr Marston.'

With a nod, he turned to walk out of the library. She noticed that he had a smudge of ink on his thumb. So she was right about him being up late doing his research.

Once she had picked her books and stacked them on the sofa, she went back to her chamber. Not to sleep though. She would spend the hours until dawn remembering everything that her governess had ever said or done.

Or, she would be awake, recalling how her employer's hand felt bracing her knee. How his touch had been enticing and flustering all at once…

Chapter Three

The only one of them to have survived the ferry crossing in good humour was Clement Feodore Marston.

How the man could be grinning with rain pouring off the brim of his hat, while accompanying three females who had not done well with the rough seas, was a mystery Vivienne would never understand.

'Nearly there,' he announced, doing his best to steady an umbrella over the girls' heads. With the wind wild and contrary, it was a useless effort.

Alice was not likely to notice the rain, being as sick to her stomach as she was. Stepping off the ferry had done nothing to improve her condition. Vivienne and Jayne were queasy, but not as wretched as poor Alice was.

Through the dim light of late afternoon, made gloomier by the storm, Mr Marston pointed towards an inn. Please let it be the one he had reserved rooms in.

'It looks charming,' he announced cheerily. She wondered if he genuinely felt cheery or was just putting on a brave front for their sakes.

As far as Vivienne was concerned, any place with a warming fire and a solid roof would be paradise.

'Look, Alice,' she said, giving the little girl's hand a squeeze. 'Isn't it pretty?'

Alice gagged so they stopped for a moment, getting ever wetter while the child gathered herself.

Vivienne wished the inn was not so far from the nearest village. She had never been anywhere quite so remote. In the beginning it had felt civilised enough, but then the road had turned slick. The hired carriage had been forced to stop a quarter of a mile from their destination.

The driver had promised to return with their belongings as soon as the weather cleared, but for now they trudged along with only what they were wearing and an umbrella bent at odd angles by the wind. Vivienne reminded herself that she had come for adventure and this would certainly count as one.

Well…it would if Alice was not feeling quite so wretched.

Approaching the inn's drive, she heard surf crashing on a beach, but with clouds pressing close she couldn't see it.

Clement was correct about the place being charming. White paint made it stand aglow against the weather pressing on all sides. Smoke rose from several chimneys and seemed to wave a welcome.

'I am assured the food is excellent,' her employer declared.

Not the most excellent news for the three of them suffering the lingering symptoms of seasickness. He might as well have announced that the beds were damp for all the better it made them feel.

Coming up the front porch steps, Vivienne glanced though a large window draped with lace curtains. She spotted a fireplace with a wonderful snapping fire. A woman sat in a rocking chair beside it, knitting.

Mr Marston rapped twice on the door, then opened it and waited while the three of them filed in past him.

The lady in the chair rose at once and hurried towards

them. Her steps were quick given her short, round stature. She patted her grey hair as if to be sure the neat bun was presentable.

'Mr Marston, I assume?' Her welcoming smile did as much to warm the room as the fire did. 'I was afraid the weather would delay your arrival.'

Vivienne had an urge to embrace their hostess because of her resemblance to Great-Aunt Anne.

'It has delayed our luggage, Mrs Prentis, but here we are, no worse for the wear.'

No worse for the wear? Her employer did not see things as they were. Was he always so optimistic in the face of adversity? Or did he simply thrive in the face of it? As admirable an attitude as it was, it was a little hard to take right now. Alice was not thriving in the face of adversity. Judging by her expression, it would be a wonder if she ever ate again.

'Come directly to your rooms, my dears. Mr Prentis has already laid the fires in the event you made it through.'

A room and a fire. Nothing had ever sounded so inviting. The four of them followed her up the staircase to the third storey of the house.

'This room is for you, Mr Marston,' their hostess announced, opening the door to an elegantly appointed chamber with a large bed. It was appropriate for the brother of a baron.

The next door the lady opened had two beds.

'This is for you, my sweet young ladies.'

The room looked perfect for little girls. There were a pair of yellow rugs on the floor. On the wall was a mural of dainty blue flower bouquets with images of frolicking puppies scattered among the blooms.

Vivienne followed the girls inside, noticing that they were beginning to shiver.

'The doors at each end of this room connect all three. The room at this end is yours, Miss Curtis.'

Mrs Prentis opened the connecting door, indicating that she should go inside. 'I thought that you would enjoy a private space of your own so that you can shut the door on your charges when you wish to.'

Bless the woman. Perhaps she should hug her even if she was not Great-Aunt Anne.

A room in Buckingham Palace might not be as welcome as this small, warm space with its plush-looking bed. It did not matter that it was not as finely appointed as the other two rooms. She was the governess, after all, not Lady Vivienne. The truth was she would be blissfully comfortable in this snug chamber.

Leading Vivienne back into the children's chamber, the lady gave a look around, seeming to assure herself that all was as it should be.

'Now, sit and warm yourselves. I shall have Mr Prentis rummage about the attic for dry clothes. Dinner will be served in the dining room in an hour.'

With her guests' immediate needs settled, Mrs Prentis hustled out of the room, her skirts bouncing about her round hips.

Vivienne swung her gaze to her employer, surprised to see him frowning. As soon as he noticed her attention on him, he smiled.

'Well then,' he said, 'I shall collect you for dinner in an hour.'

As soon as his door closed, Vivienne began removing her charges' wet clothing. Pink and bare, she had them sit on the rug in front of the fireplace. She plucked blankets from the beds and draped them over the girls, tent style, until all that showed of them was hair, eyes and noses.

'There now,' she declared with a bright smile meant to rally their spirits. 'Dry clothes will be here in no time at all. We shall feel better once we have eaten.'

Vivienne's appetite was returning and Jayne's colour was looking better. Still, it would probably still be some time before Alice would eat.

'Miss Curtis,' Alice said, giving her an odd look. 'I am sorry I plucked the feather from that woman's hat on the train. I only thought it was unkind that she had it and not the bluebird it came from.'

Alice was quite correct about where the feather belonged, which in no way excused the child's behaviour. As their governess, it was up to Vivienne to enforce proper standards. Whether she agreed with them was neither here nor there.

'It is good that you recognise your mistake. I trust you will not repeat it.'

'Yes, Miss Curtis.'

Not exactly a promise of good behaviour in the future. Still, Alice had apologised for her crime and done it without being coaxed. While she had been contrite about that particular misdeed, there had been others.

The train ride had been stressful with hours upon hours of being tested by the girls. Sadly, as an inexperienced governess, she was not as canny as she might have been in catching them at their mischief.

There had been a moment when Vivienne had envied the titled ladies enjoying their leisure, their every need being anticipated and catered to. It had passed quickly enough when she remembered that she had her freedom for now, which they did not.

By the end of summer she would have photos and memories of adventures she would not have had, otherwise. She would also have the rewarding experience of teaching Alice and Jayne better manners…and balancing the teaching with carefree fun which children needed as much as the other.

'Miss Curtis…' Alice moaned her name. 'I feel like I am going to—'

Luckily the water basin was close at hand.

As it turned out, Clement and Jayne went down to dinner without Miss Curtis or Alice. Poor sweet Alice was not ready to face a dining room. Her governess did not feel she should be left alone. Vivienne Curtis might not have lengthy experience in the career, but she had an instinct for it, he felt. It was evident in the way she spoke to his girls, how she treated them with affection, but not indulgence.

Also, he'd already noticed a change in his daughters. Not that they had become angels overnight, but something was shifting in their attitudes towards Miss Curtis. Although Jayne and Alice might not realise it yet, they were beginning to respect their new governess. That had not happened since Miss Logan.

Clement had offered to bring dinner up, but Miss Curtis claimed she was not ready to eat. Perhaps not. But it might not be due to residual queasiness. He wondered if she had forgone dinner out of kindness to Alice. No doubt eating in front of his sick child would make her feel even worse.

Sitting down to dinner with their host and hostess, Clement found their company to be pleasant, but he was distracted with wondering what was happening upstairs with Alice and Miss Curtis.

During the conversation, Jayne had mentioned the reason for their visit to Isle of Wight. It was on his tongue to speak at length of the amazing insects he hoped to find along the shoreline.

But no. Surely Miss Curtis was getting hungry and hopefully Alice was, too.

After three-quarters of an hour he began to wonder how to dismiss himself and Jayne from the table without appearing rude. As a guest, he did not wish to misstep.

It had been ages since he'd had dinner in company, but he recalled from his old life in London, before the girls came into his life, that dinnertime could be endless.

He asked to take up dinner to Alice and Miss Curtis. Mrs Prentis assured him that the cook would have it already waiting. If Miss Curtis still had no appetite, she probably would soon. The meal had been worthy of society dining, but with a more homelike flavour.

Entering through his chamber, he and Jayne crossed the room, then he opened the door to the children's bedroom.

Vivienne lifted one finger to her lips, a signal for silence. She tipped her head towards the bed where Alice slept, a blanket tucked up around her chin.

An image formed in his mind. It made him feel warm all over. In it, Miss Curtis was tenderly tucking the blanket about Alice, giving the child a kiss on the forehead as his daughter's eyes dipped closed. It might have happened that way. His sister would have done so, had fate been kinder to her.

'To bed with you now, Jayne,' he whispered, then set the plates of food on a bedside table. 'It is late. Miss Curtis needs time to herself.'

He presented his feet. Jayne stepped on his shoes, gave him a hug, then she slipped under the bedcovers wearing the clean, dry gown Edward Prentis had brought down from the attic. The dress looked as if it belonged to an earlier generation. No doubt it had belonged to one of his children. Not that it mattered how old it was, only that it was clean and warm. Until their luggage arrived, he was grateful for anything dry to put on.

Jayne fell asleep at once.

'It seems I am too late to get Alice to eat.'

'Perhaps if she wakes soon she will have an appetite.'

'Perhaps. But come, Miss Curtis, eat your meal in front of my hearth. The fire is warm and the chairs are comfortable. We will leave the door open in case the children need anything. We can see them easily.'

She hesitated, clearly undecided on whether to do it or not.

Leaping locusts, he ought to have realised how inappropriate an idea it was. Respectable women did not spend time in gentlemen's bedchambers, no matter how sensible it was to do so.

'As tempting as it is, our chaperons are asleep.'

'I suppose I could put my chair in my doorway and you could put your chair in your doorway and we could speak to each other from across the children's beds.'

Miss Curtis cast a glance at the girls, her smile warm upon them. No one had looked at them that way since Miss Logan.

'This is the first bit of relief Alice has had since we boarded the ferry. It would be a shame to wake her, which speaking across the room would do.'

That said, she carried her meal into his chamber, then sat down in one of the chairs in the bay of the window. She lifted the napkin from the plate, breathed in deep, clearly appreciating the aroma.

'It is as good as it smells,' he assured her while settling into the other chair.

It was fascinating, watching her eat. She closed her eyes whenever she took a bite of something she found particularly delicious, giving a quiet sigh. He guessed she was a lady who savoured sensations, making them more intense by closing everything else out.

But what else was she? She spoke like a lady and she moved like one, too. Perhaps she was a vicar's daughter who had fallen on hard times? She might have married, though, and he wondered why she hadn't. She was lovely enough to attract a dozen beaus.

She had not enlightened him on her past situation and he would not ask. It was her business to tell him or not. His business was to attend to his studies, not dwell on the personal life of his children's governess.

Yet Clement found himself dwelling on her none the less. Perhaps he ought to look at the rain beating on the window instead of at the governess. Only the way her hair shone in firelight was too beautiful to glance away from. She had left it loose, probably to let it dry.

Given that he was not a worldly man like his brothers had been and had largely avoided society and its entanglements as much as he could, he'd not had occasion to watch a woman's unbound curls catch and reflect a fire's glow. It was fascinating watching copper glimmers within the dark strands. Made it seem like the fire was coming from the inside.

Lovely. If he did nothing but gaze at her for the rest of the evening, he would be a contented man…warmed at last after the cold trek to the inn.

Early fatherhood had limited his amorous adventures. There had only been two lovers. Odd that he should be remembering them now while sitting across from the governess while she ate her meal. But it was the way she savoured it which made him think of those other intimate moments. The second moment at any rate, not the first.

His first liaison with a woman had been at his brothers' strong urging. They'd insisted he was wasting away his youth with too much study so they pushed him towards an older, obliging lady. The matter of becoming a man had been accomplished in a shockingly short period of time. What he'd learned from it was that he was no less a man before and no more a man after.

He was rather certain that Miss Curtis was savouring her meal more than he had savoured that moment.

The second woman was one he had found on his own. He'd wooed her and believed for a time that they would be a match. In the end, though, he'd found it difficult to fall deeply in love with a lady who did not enjoy children or insects. Vivienne did not like insects either. But somehow her dislike of them seemed endearing, not pretentious. His governess and his former almost-fiancée were quite different women…so what was he doing comparing them?

He and Maisie Smith had bidden each other goodbye within six months. To his knowledge neither of them had shed a tear over the parting. Maisie's lips had never lingered over her food, chewing slowly and with great delight as the governess was doing. Nor had Maisie ever flicked out the tip of her tongue to catch a stray but tantalising crumb. Clement did not know for certain the crumb was tantalising, but the word certainly occupied the forefront of his mind.

He did not think Miss Curtis realised just how sensuous her movements were. But he was quite undone watching her enjoying her meal.

There was a valid reason why gentlemen did not entertain ladies in their chambers. Tantalising went to war with propriety every time.

* * *

Vivienne opened her eyes to find her employer giving her an odd look.

Feathers! Mother had warned her not to display overt pleasure while eating. It was not ladylike to sigh and smack one's lips. No doubt Clement Marston now considered her ill-mannered. He might even fear that she would teach his daughters improper behaviour.

She could not reassure him that she had been taught impeccable behaviour from the cradle…that her manners were so polished they shone…well, most of the time they did. If she admitted her station in life she was sure to lose her employment. The second son of a baron did not hire the daughter of a marquess. No one did, as far as that went. It was simply not done.

'The weather continues to be fierce,' she said. Weather was always a subject to engage in when one was unsure of what to say.

'Looking back on it, I ought to have sought us lodgings right off the boat. I am sorry to have dragged you out in it.'

'I hardly think you can take the blame for a storm which came up out of nowhere. Looking back on it now that we are dried out, it was a bit of an adventure.' The pursuit of adventure and photography was the very reason she had become a governess.

'A bit of one, yes. I only hope that, going forward, our adventures are not as wet.'

'I imagine rain makes it difficult to hunt insects.'

'Most of them, but there are some which thrive in moisture…roaches, silverfish and the like. It is easier to find them right after rain.'

How perfectly awful. She meant to keep as far away from those crawly creatures as possible.

'I wonder, Mr Marston—how do you wish for me to focus my time with the girls?'

So far they had not spoken of it in detail. She was to keep them safe, naturally, but what else? 'How advanced are Alice and Jayne in reading and arithmetic?'

'Their previous governesses had no success at teaching them, but I have worked with them on both subjects. They could do with some history and literature. I promise they are bright students when they apply themselves.'

'The academics, I have learned…' from her experience growing up '…are important. However, they must be balanced with free time. There is also much to be learned outside the classroom.'

'They will become proper young ladies one day.' He paused, looking thoughtful as if seeing them grown in a blink. 'For now, though, it is good for them to have a balance of study and free time.'

What a relief to know they were in agreement on it. Vivienne might never have been a governess before, but she did understand what made for a happy childhood.

'I want Alice and Jayne to join me in the field, to be a part of my research. Jayne will be eager, Alice not as much.'

Vivienne not at all. However, as their governess she would be required to be near her charges.

'What will you do with your research?' Surely there must be a point to it all.

There was a point to Vivienne's interest in photography. To capture the beauty of birds and share it.

Mr Marston grinned. He shuffled his chair sideways to face her. Eyes alight, he leaned forward as if he was about to reveal the grandest secret ever revealed.

His enthusiasm was contagious. She found herself leaning forward in her chair, as eager to know the secret as he was to tell it.

'I am going to write a book with drawings and descriptions of rare insects. My hope is to publish it and establish my name in the field of entomology.'

Vivienne sat up straight, struck by a thunderously grand idea, although she was repelled by it as much as she was drawn to it.

'Are there many in your field wishing for the same?'

'I know of several, yes. I suppose whoever makes the best find, perhaps a new species…or one that has not been seen in years…will win the publishing prize.'

'Clement… Mr Marston, that is.' In her excitement she nearly forgot that she was in his employ. 'If I may be so bold as to suggest something?' She did not wait to hear if she might be bold or not, but pressed on to make her point. 'Perhaps you need something unique to set your work apart, in case you do not find a rare insect.'

He sat back in his chair, cocking his head while he looked at her, brows raised. V-shaped lines etched his forehead. Was this how a rare insect species would feel under his intent speculation?

Probably not, since his specimens were usually dead, while Vivienne was alive…quite alive if the odd little sparks shivering her nerves were anything to go by.

'I wonder?'

'Wonder what, Sir?' She had not yet told him her idea so how could he be wondering about it?

'Out here, life is not strictly formal. The two of us sitting where we are right now is an indication of that. More, we each have Alice and Jayne's best interests at heart. Put those two things together, and it follows that our association would be more easy-going. If you do not mind, I would like to call you Vivienne. It didn't feel inappropriate just now when you called me by my given name.'

'As you say…here we sit quite informally.' How true it was that it had not felt inappropriate. Having permission to call him Clement gave her a ticklish smile inside. 'We shall be Clement and Vivienne.'

'Now, about my book.' He leaned forward again, elbows resting on his knees while he peered at her with his flat crooked smile. 'You mentioned something which you believe might set my work apart from others of its kind?'

'Yes, something unique. But may I ask, if you discover your new species, how would you prove you'd actually done so? It seems that anyone might make that claim.'

'I would describe it in words and then illustrate the creature in exacting detail. Come, I will show you.'

He rose quickly from his chair, then strode past the fireplace to a desk near the window. With a grin and a crooked finger he beckoned her to join him.

He turned up the wick on the desk lamp. A small circle of light shone on a leather blotter and a vase of yellow and blue wildflowers. The desk drawer squealed when Clement opened it. He cast a worried grimace at the doorway. Alice stirred, but did not wake up.

'Ah, here, we are in luck,' he said, keeping his voice low. He withdrew a sheet of paper, setting it on the desktop. Then he picked up a pencil and twirled it between his fingers.

'Let's say this is my journal and I have just discovered a unique wasp…'

'A butterfly, if you do not mind?'

He nodded, casting her a side grin. 'Will a Holly Blue do?'

She supposed so. Holly Blue sounded friendly and could not fail to be more pleasant than a wasp.

'So, just here.' He pointed to a spot on the desk above the paper. 'Imagine a jar containing the butterfly. I open it up and then put the insect on a square of black velvet.'

How interesting that his words, spoken softly so as not to disturb the children, sounded smooth like dark velvet.

He withdrew a pair of spectacles from his jacket pocket, then placed them on his nose. The lenses made his eyes look larger, his expression more animated.

'I inspect the specimen, consider the colour. Is it all one shade or does it change, light to dark? I look at spot patterns, measure her and then write down what I have observed.'

What Vivienne observed was the excitement in his whispery voice.

'After that…' he waggled the pencil '… I make an illustration of what I have seen.'

He began to sketch the imagined butterfly. His arm flexed with the strokes and shading he put on the paper. Fascinated, she leaned in close while watching him draw. In his enthusiasm he must not have noticed how his arm brushed hers once in a while.

For a bookish gentleman, he was well built. Even through his shirt sleeve she felt how firm his muscles were. Even though she should ignore the pure masculinity of him, she could not. Rather, she let it warm her heart, melt it just a little bit.

'That is beautiful, Clement. It looks as if it might flutter off the paper.' It really did. 'You are very talented.'

'Not really. It took hours of practice,' he answered with his head bent over his drawing, probably making certain every detail was accurate.

Vivienne peered over his shoulder, amazed at how he could recall the insect from his imagination and bring it to life on paper.

'No matter how you came by it, you do have a gift with that pencil.'

Turning his head suddenly, he looked back at her. His hair was curly on top and it tickled her nose.

My word, she had never smelled a man so close up. What mischief made her take a deep, appreciative breath?

Hopefully he had not noticed. She stood up straight, took a step backwards.

'But what if you discovered a new species and then a competitor accused you of fabricating it? Anyone might draw an insect and call it a new discovery.'

'I would have the insect in my jar. It would be labelled with the date and the location of the discovery...the time of day and even the weather.'

'Yes, but how long would it last in the jar?'

He answered with a one-shouldered shrug. 'Most of them keep well in alcohol or vinegar.'

'What if there was another way to avoid the question of your find's validity?'

He stood up, too, considered her with a thumb on his chin, a long finger crossed over his mouth.

'What is it you are getting at, Vivienne? I have not made such a discovery, nor has anyone attempted to discredit it.'

'I am saying you should have someone photograph the insects. Publish the photos along with the descriptions and drawings. Even with ordinary insects, it would set your work apart.'

'And where would I find someone to take these photos?'

'Here.' She spun one time in her borrowed, baggy and too-short gown from the attic, pointing at the button on her bodice. 'Me!'

For the longest moment he stood, silently staring while she tapped the button. Chances were he was not seeing the benefits of photography. If she had it to do over again, she would simply have dashed to her chamber and come back with her camera.

'I am a photographer. Or trying to be, but of birds. They are a challenge, of course, since they tend to fly off too quickly for me to capture more than a blur on the glass. Sometimes—most of the time, if you want to know—not even that.'

She was rambling in an attempt to regain her composure. The way he had watched her finger tapping her bosom had made her feel featherheaded. But it was not her finger he had been looking at, was it? She had not meant to draw his attention there, why would she? As bosoms went, hers was not terribly impressive.

'But a dead insect could not scramble away,' she announced before the point she had meant to make could elude her again.

Something was wrong with her. Being around a man had never made her thoughts ramble. Certainly she had never lamented the size of her bosom before. It was a good, practical bosom, easily contained and never fussed over.

'You wish for me to hire you as a photographer?'

She gave herself a mental shake, bringing herself back to the conversation she had instigated.

'Yes…well, no.' She went to the doorway to peer at the sleeping children and regather her position. 'I do not wish for you to hire me in any capacity except as your governess. I only wish to be helpful with the book. Photographing your insects allows me to indulge in my passion at the same time as you indulge in yours.'

Oh, so subtly, his mouth lifted at one corner. Not so subtly, her heart flipped in her chest and her cheeks flamed.

Perhaps she should have used a different word than passion…interest would have been more appropriate.

Somehow, ever since she came into his chamber, it had been one inappropriate thing after another. And all on her part. She had never been a flirt and did not feel like one now. She ought to start calling him Mr Marston again. It would establish safe boundaries, put a social distance between them. Not that she was in any peril except in her own mind. Her employer had acted like a perfect gentleman.

'You wish to act as an associate on my book? I never considered such a thing. I am not convinced it is wise.'

He would if he understood just what an advantage her photos could give him over his competitors.

'Nothing as important as an associate, Clement.' She liked his name and decided to continue to using it. 'You are the one with the knowledge. Photos will only help to set your work apart from others, that is all.'

'I cannot say I have ever seen a photo of an insect in a book before. Is it even possible?'

Somehow Vivienne must convince him to allow her to photograph his subjects. A dead insect would be ever so much easier than a flitting bird.

'The world of books and photography is changing.' In her eagerness she grabbed his hand and squeezed it. 'Did you know that a couple of decades ago, a book was published with photos of algae?'

The best of it was, the algae had been photographed by a woman. Anna Atkins had probably not been required to wed nobility as Vivienne was, but still, the woman was her inspiration.

Did he realise that her hand was still in his? She would need to take it back, but for an instant she wanted to feel how firm and large his fingers were while they pressed her palm. And hadn't his thumb just skimmed her knuckles? If he was pressing and skimming, he would be aware that they still touched one another.

Aware, both of them, and yet neither of them making the first move to let go.

How confusing. How inappropriate.

How mesmerising. How impossible.

Clement must have come to the same conclusion in the same instant because his fingers uncurled from her hand, one by one.

With a quizzical glance and a hesitant smile, he said, 'I cannot agree, you understand. It is not something I have ever considered. At the same time I cannot disagree. The more thought I give it, the more intriguing the idea is.'

There must be bees buzzing in her mind, scrambling her good sense, because she was suddenly not certain he was speaking of photographs of insects. Sparks of gold flickering his eyes made his expression warm, curious. But he was a scientist and so he would by nature be curious about everything.

'Let's see where it goes, shall we?' he suggested, removing his spectacles, setting them on the desk with a soft clink. While not loud enough to wake the children, it brought Vivienne back to the here and now.

Here, being at this inn because she was governess to this man's children. Now, being for the summer only. Even if she allowed her heart to explore the path it was gazing down, it would be madness to follow. Vivienne Louise Curtis was not mad. She was sensible.

And, sensibly, all they had ever been speaking of was her photographing his insects.

'Once you see how it looks, you will want nothing else. Photo illustrations will be all the rage one day. Mark my words.'

Chapter Four

It had been two days before the rain stopped. Three before the waves subsided enough for safe exploration of the tideline.

This morning a breeze blew in off the sea, drying out the land.

At long last Clement was free to hunt whatever creeping treasures he might find. Today, his focus was on beetles.

He found them to be sturdy insects. More predictable in their movements than those which flitted about looking pretty in sunshine.

Things that looked pretty could be distracting. Vivienne's smile was an example of it. When he ought to be focused on practical matters he found his attention all too frequently drawn to her lips. They were pretty and expressive. Sometimes they were wide, showing humour. Other times they were pressed tight showing a firm attitude. Sometimes they were round, pursed in introspection.

Seeing them round and introspective was particularly troubling for him. It was then that his curiosity was highest, wondering what she was thinking about…but more, wondering what it would be like to kiss those lips.

Last night he had been completely distracted by her. Her lips had pursed for only an instant before she'd smiled widely and tried to convince him to include photographs in his research, but an instant was all it took to make him wobble inside.

Oddly, he'd never been a man to wobble.

She'd been so eager that he'd become caught up in her enthusiasm. Firelight had reflected on her cheeks and lent them a pink glow. Passion for one's calling, he knew, could make a person glow just like that.

In his wobbly state, he'd had a crazy thought. What if, in part, the glow had to do with him...with her reaction to him as a man?

It was incredibly forward of him to imagine such a thing. They had only just met. When she'd grabbed his hand it had been out of excitement for her idea. It was unlikely that she had meant anything else by the gesture.

What he must keep in mind was that simply because her lips were round and pouty, it did not mean it had anything to do with him. It was simply how they looked...in the moment.

Birds circling and calling overhead brought him back to the here and now, to the wonderful hours spread before him.

Life was good.

Walking over a grassy dune, he scanned the sand watching for whatever might scuttle across.

'Papa!'

He looked up, saw Alice waving her arm. What a relief to see her fully recovered.

Turning away from the path he'd meant to follow, he approached his daughters and Vivienne. They sat on a blanket several yards from the surf rolling tamely onshore. A pair of grey plovers dashed in and out with the tide, pecking holes in the sand.

Evidently Vivienne had taken the morning lesson outside. He approved of that.

The three of them made a pretty scene. Vivienne had a book open in her lap, her blue skirt spread out like a fan. Alice sat on one side of her and Jayne on the other. Their skirts spread across the sand in the same way but smaller, one green and one yellow. If he were not so eager to go exploring, he would sit with them and go along with them on whatever adventure was in the book.

Not that he would be paying much attention to it, he realised. Watching the sunshine glimmering in Vivienne's dark curls was far more interesting. Not properly contained, her hair blew about her shoulders, fingered by the breeze.

'What did you find, Papa?' Jayne asked.

'Nothing yet.'

He noted that the girls' braids were not as neatly plaited as when he did it.

Plaiting hair was clearly not one of Vivienne's skills. Who was this woman he'd hired? Accomplished in some ways and yet not in others. He wondered now if she might be a gently born lady who'd been forced to seek her own way in the world... If so, such a woman was only to be admired.

In the end, he felt it was better to have a governess who the girls seemed to nearly like than one they loathed who could fashion proper braids.

What did a neat hairstyle matter out here in the beautiful wilds, anyway? Who was nearby to judge them for it? Their host and hostess were the only other people nearby and they took life quite casually.

Vivienne tipped her head, presenting one cheek to the sunshine while she looked up at him, shielding her eyes from the brightness with her hand. It was her left hand.

The same one he had held. The same hand a wedding band would go on.

Now there was an odd thought which had come out of nowhere. He reckoned she would be stunned if she could hear his thought. He was stunned. Not horrified, though. Random thoughts came at men all the time. He would count this as one of them.

'Have a good lesson, my dears.' He bent to kiss Jayne's cheek, then Alice's.

In what might be one of those random thoughts, he saw himself kissing the governess. On the cheek, he amended in his mind. He was finished envisioning improper actions.

Which, he reminded himself, even a kiss on the cheek would be.

'I shall see you at tea,' he announced, his voice suddenly tight. Striding away with a brisk step, he did not allow himself to dwell on what it would have been like to kiss Vivienne. If he did, it would no longer be a random thought, but an invited one…which would not do at all.

It was too early to rise, Vivienne thought, snuggling deeper under her blankets while looking the window. Sadly, life as a governess began earlier than life as a lady did.

There were still lingering stars on the horizon when she heard Clement begin to move about in his chamber. Apparently, life for an entomologist began earlier, too. Hopefully he would not wake Alice and Jayne. With a bit of luck they would sleep for another two hours.

After what happened yesterday, Vivienne needed some time to herself in order to practise a skill which she was clearly lacking. She had seen the look on Clement's face when he had stopped by to greet his children while they read on the beach. He had been looking at their hair, his brow slightly furrowed. Obviously, he had been thinking their grooming was not up to standard.

Feathers, but he was not wrong. The only experience she had with styling hair was having it done to her. Her lady's maid had a gift when it came to containing her perverse strands.

Alice and Jane had far better-behaved hair than she did and yet she could do nothing with it. Suppressing a groan, she rose from the bed, crossed the room, then sat at the dressing table. She picked up her hairbrush and stared at the mirror.

'Practice makes perfect,' she mumbled, not really believing that in this case it was true.

She simply must conquer the skill if she wished to fulfil her tasks properly. And she did wish to. Accomplishing her goal of photography was all well and good. However, she was being paid a wage to care for Alice and Jayne.

Keeping their hair in order was all a part of it. Keeping her hair neat was, too, if she wished to play her part believably. A governess who was orderly in every way. By the time the girls woke up, she would be properly groomed.

First, she brushed her hair thoroughly. To show its gratitude, it made a curly puff all around her head. Dividing the mess into three equal sections was challenging. When they were somewhat even, she began the process of crossing the hanks, one, then two…and didn't neglect to do the third in proper order or the process must be begun again.

The problem, she decided, was with the mirror which made all her movements look backward. No wonder her fingers got tangled. Resigned to failure for the moment, she tied her hair in a blue ribbon instead and fashioned a bow at the back of her neck.

She frowned at her image but then noticed that the mirror reflected the sky growing lighter beyond the window. She turned on the bench to see clouds pulsing with pink and gold…in some places they were red, making it appear as if there was fire glowing within.

This sunrise gift would only last for a few moments. She hurried to the window and looked out. A figure strode across the beach towards the dunes, cast in the same pink hue which reflected off the sand and the water.

Clement. Who else would be setting off at this time of morning with a pack slung across his back? His posture was straight, but he leaned forward slightly, as if the angle would lengthen his long strides and somehow carry him more quickly to his goal.

Efficient, orderly…this was a man who would expect his children to have neat hair. Perhaps she would make a better job of it today than yesterday.

She watched him reach the crest of the dune. He paused. Long grass teased the knees of his trousers. He lifted his face as if he were sniffing the morning breeze, appreciating the scents of sand, sea, and dawn.

While she watched, the clouds faded from bright pink to golden.

Not as brilliant, but just as beautiful in its way. Rather like Clement, it occurred to her.

So many society gentleman were like peacocks, flashing their bright feathers, so handsome and refined. To Vivienne's way of thinking, not one of them was more interesting than Clement Marston was. Watching him disappear around a stony embankment, she wondered why some perceptive lady of London had not grabbed him up.

While he was not titled or as blatantly handsome as some men, she thought that he was, somehow, more than they were.

It came back to hair, she decided. When she had met Alice and Jane for the first time their braids had been neat and tight, no wild ends poking out at odd angles. There was only one person who could have done it. She could not imagine another father in London who would braid a little girl's hair and make certain she began her day properly.

How many fathers even looked at their daughters, let alone were responsible for their immediate care? She had known many fine gentlemen over the years. Now she was discovering what went into making a genuine man. Clement Marston was proving to be genuine in every way a man could be.

By now the sky was bright blue, the clouds fluffy white.

She squared her shoulders, firmed her resolve. It was time to begin her day. This morning she would not be beaten by unruly braids. Today she would be a better governess than she was yesterday.

She might never convince Clement to include photographs in his books. She might never be a professional photographer. But no matter what came of her life after this, she would succeed for this summer as an employed woman.

Other than herself, Grace and George would be the only ones to know she had done it, but she would feel pride in her accomplishment for ever.

That afternoon Jayne and Alice came to tea with blue checked ribbons holding their hair in place. For all her effort, Vivienne still failed at weaving braids. However, she did have a talent for fashioning a nice bow.

While their father might not be pleased with the freer look the girls wore, Vivienne had gained some favour in her charges' eyes.

Earlier this morning while she had brushed their hair

Jayne had wiggled, Alice had squirmed. Both had glared at her. All in an attempt to sabotage her efforts, she was quite certain.

While the girls tolerated her better than they had the governesses who preceded her…indeed, even seemed to like her at times…they had not finished testing her.

Matters changed a bit when she tied their hair in bows and openly admired how grown up they looked. They had preened before the mirror, run fingers through their hair and giggled.

It was in that moment she felt the tide turn in her favour. She could not be certain, but for the first time she had hope of being accepted by them.

But now, while waiting for their father to enter the cosy parlour for tea, she wondered if he would be accepting of the change in his girls.

She had not asked permission to make this alteration in their appearance so perhaps she had overstepped.

Alice and Jayne were happy with how they looked so Clement might have a struggle of it if he made them go back to neat plaits.

The fact that Mrs Prentis had gushed over how pretty the girls looked would not help his cause if he sided with braids. Especially after their landlady had run upstairs to the attic and brought down a dozen more bows which her own daughters had worn.

If there was a confrontation over their hair, Vivienne would be to blame. And so here she sat, watching steam curl from the spout of the teapot, waiting for Clement to arrive and give his verdict. There was more than a hairstyle at stake here. How much authority did she have as their governess?

For a normally self-assured lady, she was jittery. It might

be wise not to pick up a teacup and risk dribbling on her fingers. That would show a great lack of confidence. Governesses, as she recalled them to be, were ever self-possessed.

When she heard heavy footsteps in the hallway, she pasted on a smile.

Passing though the doorway, Clement was smiling. He nearly always entered a room smiling, she was learning.

His hair looked damp. The lingering scent of shaving soap hovered about him.

As he saw his daughters sitting beside Vivienne on the sofa, his eyes widened. Of course she had expected him to be surprised. What else was he, though? Other than that immediate widening of his eyes, he revealed nothing.

'Papa!' the girls exclaimed in chorus.

Jayne reached him first. Stepping on his shoes, she hugged him as she always did.

Alice stepped forward for her braids to be tugged but, of course, there were no braids.

Vivienne held her breath. She had forgotten about this special show of affection between Clement and Alice.

'Hello, my dears.' With a smile he tugged on each side of Alice's bow. 'I hope you have had a good day. Come, sit with me and tell me all about it.'

There was another sofa facing the one Vivienne sat on. Clement sat down, one little girl pressed to each side of him. Jayne twirled a lock of strawberry-blonde hair around her finger, grinning.

'Do we look grown up now?' Alice asked.

'And pretty?' followed Jayne.

'Well, let me see…' He turned Jayne's chin this way and that, slowly looking her over, but smiling when he did. 'Very pretty.'

He did the same with Alice and said, 'You do look grown

up. But you must not do it too quickly, for when you grow up and move away from me, I shall be sad.'

'We won't go away, Papa, we love you too much.'

'Good girls… Now, did you remember to thank Miss Curtis for arranging your hair so prettily?'

Alice slipped out from under her father's arm, dashed from one sofa to the other, then gave her a hug. Jayne followed close behind. Wrapped up in small arms, Vivienne felt her heart swell. She hadn't known how having their affection, which apparently she now had, would touch her to her soul.

She glanced across the rug at Clement. His smile seemed genuine, but it might be for the sake of not hurting his children's feelings.

Later, when the girls were sleeping, she would discover the truth.

Later that evening after his daughters were asleep, Clement left the door adjoining theirs open. He hoped that Vivienne would notice and take it as an invitation to join him.

Most of his nights were lonely ones after the girls went to bed. It had always been that way, but never really troubled him. He had not minded that his days went on, one after another in a familiar rhythm. With his mind attentive to his work, he had rarely noticed.

Being set apart was what he was accustomed to. He had never been kindred spirits with his brothers, him being a studious young father and them being society bachelors. Lately, he had noticed. The difference between then and now was Vivienne. The first evening they were here, when Alice had her stomach trouble, the governess had spent time in his chamber. He had enjoyed that.

He had his girls and it was wonderful…and yet, perhaps

no longer enough? He was a lonely man and could no longer deny it. What he needed right now was a way of getting her attention without rapping on her door and blatantly announcing he wanted company.

It would not do to appear needy. He decided to hum. It might draw her attention.

Sitting at his desk, he withdrew the scribbled notes he had made while exploring the tideline this morning. He began to copy them neatly in his journal. If the off-key tune did not attract her notice, nothing would.

His voice must be even worse than he thought for it took only a moment before he heard her door open. There was an unobstructed view from his desk, across the children's beds and to her doorway. He glanced up with a smile.

'Oh, good evening, Vivienne.'

'May I have a word?' she asked.

'Of course.' He stood, sweeping his hand towards the pair of chairs he had placed in front of the fireplace. 'Nice fire tonight.'

From the corner of his eye, he watched how her skirt swished around her hips when she walked around the children's beds. Paying attention to the way a woman walked was not what he was used to doing. So many things lately were not. But he did not mind in the least.

It occurred to him, not quite out of the blue given the way he had been thinking about her lately, that he was glad he was not the titled brother. An untitled man and a governess might make a match of it if—

But there was nothing like putting the cart ahead of the horse. They were employer and employee, nothing more than that. He did not know why the thought had even come to him.

'The girls were pleased with the way you did their hair.'

He sat down, then she took the chair beside him. 'What is it you wished to speak with me about?'

Relaxing, he stretched his feet towards the fire. Ah, the evening felt better already.

'Just that, their hair. I hope you do not mind the change. Braids and I have always been at odds. I do not have the patience for them the way you must.'

'Necessity, more than patience, I assure you. When Miss Logan, their nanny, resigned, there was no one to do it except me.'

'I have been wondering, Clement—why do Alice and Jayne dislike the women who care for them? They seem like sweet girls except when it comes to that.'

This was not a subject he liked to discuss. It cut him to the quick every time. She ought to know, though, since she was the one being bedevilled by those sweet girls.

'I told you they are not my children, but my nieces.' He paused while she nodded. 'An hour after my sister died I took them home with me. I also took the neighbour who had been caring for them during the week Alice Jayne lingered. She had just lost a child and so it was a good fit. Miss Logan loved them and they her. You might imagine how they felt when she left us to begin her own family.'

'As if they had lost their mother, I would think, not having known another.'

'They were only seven years old then. I could not explain that Miss Logan did not belong to us. They cried for her every night. I admit that I cried once or twice, too, once they were asleep. Seeing them suffer was not easy for me.'

'So, then…is it your belief that they rejected their governesses because they were not Miss Logan?'

'That is part of it, naturally. But more, I think they did

not wish to have another woman leave them. Better to reject them from the beginning.'

Vivienne bit her lip, looked away. Even though she hid her face, he knew she was frowning.

'What is it, Vivienne?'

She did not answer, but shook her head. He reached across, covered her hand on the arm of the chair.

When she turned her face to look at him, her brown eyes shimmered.

'Your daughters and I are growing close. They no longer see me as an intruder.'

'But that is wonderful!'

She jerked her hand out from under his. 'No, Clement, it is horrible. Have you forgotten that my employment is only until summer ends?'

Hardly. He would have reached for her hand again, but she folded her arms across her middle, making herself unapproachable.

'What if I offer to double your wage? Would that be enough to make you cancel your next service?'

Summer was such a fleeting season. It was true that his girls were bound to be heartbroken again.

'Please, Vivienne, stay on with us.'

All of sudden she stood, shaking her head. 'I cannot.'

And with that, she rushed from his chamber. Passing through the centre room, she paused to gaze down at Alice, then at Jayne. She pressed the back of her hand to her mouth, then fled to her own chamber and closed the door. Not walked, not strode, or even hurried...but fled.

Why had a simple question upset her so deeply? It was curious. She had not given any indication of anything being wrong, yet the mention of her service ending seemed to distress her.

There might be more to her turning him down than he was aware of. There was so much that he did not know about her…or her past, really. But it was not for him to pry or coax it out of her. When she was ready, she would confide in him…he hoped.

Chapter Five

It was Vivienne's day to herself. Her time was her own to do with it what she wished.

Standing on the inn's porch, she watched Clement and his girls walk along the path towards the sand.

What did she wish to do with her day? Read, walk, attempt to photograph a grey plover?

No, not the last. She would only have taken the cap from the lens before the bird flew away. Surprisingly, photography wasn't what she wanted to do today. There was still a great deal of summer left in which she could take her photos.

What she wanted to do was go with the Marston family on their exploration of a group of rocks and boulders Clement had discovered a distance down the beach.

'Don't be foolish,' she reminded herself.

It was important to keep her relationship with Alice and Jayne friendly, but not intimate. After speaking with Clement the other night, the last thing she wanted to do was break hearts, her own heart notwithstanding. Joining them when she was not being paid to do so would cross that line.

At the crest of the dune, Jayne spun about, waving her hand in invitation.

Cupping her hand to her mouth, Alice called, 'Come with us!'

Vivienne shook her head, a clear 'no'.

It was far too tempting to give in. She must remember what was at stake. Only sorrow would come of her becoming too involved with this family. She would not take their hearts with her when she left, nor would she leave her own here.

Alice tugged on her father's arm. Drawing him down, she whispered something in his ear. He straightened and nodded, then walked back across the sand towards the porch.

He stood at the bottom of the steps, wearing a big floppy hat which hid his eyes but not his smile. Wide and flat with brackets on each side of his lips, she saw the invitation in it.

'Will you come?' he asked.

'It would not be wise.'

'You are worried about becoming too close to them and then leaving them heartbroken. It might happen. I cannot stop that. But consider this—are they to live their lives not ever having a close connection with a motherly figure? You are the only one they have allowed in since they were seven years old. I fear that if you reject their affection it will be worse for them than losing it.'

What he said made sense. At some point there would be an emotional price to pay in one form or another. However, it would not be called due today.

He reached up. 'Come, Vivienne.'

She placed her fingers in his broad, long-fingered hand. A calloused palm and a bookish mind? What a fascinating contradiction he was. It was a lucky thing she could not fully see his eyes under the hat brim. If they were looking at her with glimmering gold flecks, well, she could not be blamed for becoming infatuated with him on the spot.

What woman with a smidgen of sense would not?

* * *

The walk towards the rocks was not long or difficult. It was why Clement had saved the excursion for a time when the girls were with him.

The place he had in mind was ideal because the rocky area he wished to inspect was near the shoreline. This meant he could explore with Jayne and at the same time keep an eye on Alice, who did not like peeking in dark places for creatures which scurried from the light.

Butterflies were more to her liking. And to Vivienne's. While she was not trying to get them to land on her finger as Alice was doing, she did smile and point out how pretty they were.

Having Vivienne come along hadn't been part of his plan for the day. His intention had been for her to have time away from the children to do whatever she wished.

He was glad she'd agreed to come. More and more he found he enjoyed being in her company more than being away from it.

'What will we find under here, do you think?' Jayne asked, kneeling beside a stone and reaching to lift it.

'Remember what I taught you? Turn the stone and have your specimen jar ready in case you find something. If it is a spider, put the rock back down and call me over.'

He repeated those instructions each time they went on a hunt. Not all insects were harmless.

He watched while Jayne carefully turned the stone. His attention was not completely on it, though. He could hear Vivienne laughing, Alice giggling.

While he watched for what might be under the stone, he imagined hands reaching for butterflies, sunshine on up-turned faces…bare feet in the sand.

He did not know that Vivienne had taken off her shoes,

but it was the practical thing to do so it was what he pictured. Stockings might have been removed, too, so his mind's eye saw bare ankles. If she was leaping for, say a damselfly, her skirt might fly up. It was why he pictured her smooth, bare calf.

What was amiss with him lately? His thoughts tended to roam too freely when it came to his children's governess. And why wouldn't they? Vivienne was becoming more than an employee. Friend was not the precise word. Was there a word for a person a man liked with equal parts admiration and longing? Longing for her company, naturally.

Although there was the other, too. Being a man he could not deny the physical attraction to her, the itchy longing to be closer to her than was acceptable in their situation. Her casual company, friendly companionship as it were, all he was free to indulge in.

When he glanced over his shoulder he did not see Vivienne leaping barefoot after a damselfly. What he saw rocked him more than his ridiculous imagination had: Vivienne sat in the sand with Alice on her lap, the pair of them studying a seashell.

He saw his child in the arms of a woman who cared for her. Vivienne might not wish to form a bond with his girls, but there was no denying the affection he saw when she bent her dark head to Alice's fair one. No mistaking the tenderness in her touch when she drew his child close while they studied the shell.

All at once, Jayne gasped. He had not noticed her wander to a fallen log several feet away.

She lifted one finger to her lips and pointed down at the rotting wood.

His quick but silent dash to the log must have caught Vivienne's attention. She and Alice crept forward.

What interesting find had his daughter made?

'Will he attack her?' Jayne whispered.

It looked rather as if he would, but, no, the impressively large stag beetle had something different in mind while he circled his lady with antlers raised.

'It might look as if he will, Jayne,' he whispered, 'but he will not injure her. Now had this been a case of two males they would battle one another fiercely.'

He waved for Vivienne and Alice to come and have a look at this rare sighting. How often did one see a mating ritual between two magnificent insects?

Alice came slowly forward. To all appearances, Vivienne meant to remain where she was, but then she hurried after Alice. The expression in her eyes, the set of her lips, indicated that she meant to conquer her dislike.

She peered over his shoulder, much as she had done when he drew the illustration of the butterfly. Her hair tickled his ear. Being so close, he sensed it when she shivered.

For all that she tried to put on a brave front, he knew that, for her, this was not a fascinating moment.

'Well, then,' he announced. 'Shall we give them a bit of privacy?'

'Why do insects need privacy, Papa?' Alice asked while clinging to Vivienne's hand.

'Because they… The natural way of things is… Well, you see—' There was no explaining the mating act to a ten-year-old girl.

'It is because they have a secret which is between the two of them only,' Vivienne explained. 'It is a dance which no one else may be privy to.'

'Oh, it is very good then that we do not watch,' Alice declared.

He'd heard of shoulders sagging in relief. It turned out

to be a true thing. This was one discussion he did not wish to have with his daughters. But with no woman to guide them, he feared he must one day.

In only a few years there would be certain things his girls would need to be made aware of. Physical changes that he could not bear to consider, let alone disclose.

Perhaps he ought to wed.

He had not considered marriage in the past but maybe he ought to have. The girls needed a woman's guidance. They needed it from a woman who cared for them. Since Miss Logan, no woman had. Not until Vivienne came into their lives. She would be perfect for the girls.

But he could hardly marry his children's governess... could he? No matter that he was attracted to her, it would not do.

'Shall we have lunch?'

Food was what was needed. A bit of sustenance for his body and a few moments to get his mind straight.

Vivienne had made it clear that she had another engagement at the end of summer. It would do him no good to indulge in thoughts of anything more intimate between them. Not for him. Nor for his daughters either.

When lunch was finished, the girls dashed down to the water to splash their feet in the waves.

'Thank you for coming up with that story about the secret dance,' he said. 'I was floundering trying to explain it. And you were right about it being a dance; it's all a part of the courtship, you see.'

'Insects courting?' Her quiet, disbelieving laughter snared him. 'I shall never view a ball in the same way again.'

'Have you seen one, then? It is what I think of whenever I must attend one, which is hardly ever.'

She nodded. The sweet biscuit she was holding crumbled, fell from her fingers and on to her lap. 'Whoops, that was clumsy of me.'

'The insect world is intriguing. Most people have no idea how fascinating it is. Would you like to know something truly astonishing?'

She tossed biscuit crumbs in the air. A seagull swooped down, snatching two before they hit the sand.

'More astonishing than that?' she asked, arching a brow at the bird and giving him a grin.

He gave her back the same look. 'Termites are monogamous.'

'Clement Marston, you are making that up!' She flicked a finger of sand at him.

'Oh, it's true. I promise.'

'You shall write that in your book, I hope.'

'I must. It would be irresponsible to leave it out.'

'Well…' She turned to more fully face him, her eyes bright, eager and pretty. 'How much better would it be if you had photos to go along with it?'

'I would never ask that of you, Vivienne. You would be miserable having to handle insects.'

'I would get over it.'

'The creatures will not become any more endearing. They are what they are.'

'I already look more kindly on termites.'

'A test, then. Are you willing to prove you can change your feelings on the matter?'

'Indeed. Test me.'

'Go back to the log and bring me back one of the stag beetles.'

'That is not a test. It is torture. Nor is it an indication of how well my photographs would improve your book.'

'Since I do not wish to torture you, I will get by with my drawn images.'

'Feathers,' she declared, then joined the children at the waterline.

Later in the afternoon, Vivienne decided there was only one way to prove her point and that was to show Mr Clement Marston she was correct.

Vivienne slung the case holding her camera and three glass plates across her shoulder, then took the children towards the kitchen to spend time with Mrs Prentis.

'But where are you going?' Jayne asked. 'We want to come along.'

'Not this time. I am only going to the cove to take a photo or two. I will not be gone long.'

After seeing them settled in the kitchen, she hurried outside.

With a bit of daylight remaining and the walk to the log containing the amorous beetles only taking fifteen minutes, there was plenty of time. With any luck the insects would still be smitten with one another and she could get a photo of them.

Surely that would convince Clement of the benefit of her photos. It would also prove that she was up to the task even if she did not care for her subject matter.

Walking along the shoreline, she went around the rocks which created the alcove where the log was. To her relief the insects were there. If they were still courting or done with it she did not know. The main thing was, they were quite still. If she hurried she might get her shot.

The surf sounded louder than it had a few moments ago, but she did not take the time to look at it. Her attention was on putting the camera in the exact spot she needed it to be before she lost the daylight.

She had not noticed before, but there was a third beetle there and it was dead.

Lifting the cap from the lens, she allowed what she estimated to be the right amount of light. Just…right…there. She replaced the cap.

Something about the sound of surf rolling onshore seemed different than it had before…closer .Glancing over her shoulder, she gasped. Those waves really were closer. Larger, too. Only a narrow strip of sand remained when moments ago there had been a wide swathe.

She would need to work quickly. It was important to take two more photos. One could never count on only one. Especially when what she was going to present to Clement had to be outstanding.

Being caught up in capturing their image, she forgot how repulsive beetles were. She bit her lip, closed her eyes and then nudged the dead one with her fingernail in order to scoot it closer to the others.

With her attention focused, everything else faded. The world narrowed to two satisfied beetles and one expired suitor.

And then her feet got wet. Startled, she glanced down. Water rushed around her shoes, dragged at the hem of her skirt. Another wave splashed on the log, sending up a tall spray of saltwater.

She screeched, then snatched up her camera and the bag containing her glass plates an instant before a wave would have carried it off. Lifting her treasure high above her head, she turned to wade back to safer ground.

Too late! She had left it for too long and now there was no safer ground. The sand had completely disappeared.

While she watched, the water grew ever deeper. What to do? If she tried to walk back through the water, she might get jostled and drop her equipment.

Scrambling on top of the log, she gazed about. There really was no place to go except up and she was as high up as she could get. Behind her there was only a rocky cliff.

How long did high tide last, anyway? How high did it get? She had been out here longer than she'd expected to be and the sun was beginning to set.

Naturally she was frightened. Who would not be, facing the prospect of being swept away in the dark and not knowing how to swim?

Oh, dear, the log was beginning to rock with the force of the water rushing over and beneath it. She lifted her equipment over her head. No matter what, she was not going to let go of it until the waves ripped it from her hands.

Where was Vivienne?

Clement checked one room after the other without finding her. He needed to apologise for taunting her with that challenge of bringing him a beetle.

The moment had been light-hearted and so he had teased her. He'd hoped to see that charming expression she had… the one where her brown eyes grew warm while she gave him a reprimanding glance. The opposing expressions given at once were charming.

It had not turned out that way. She'd gone to splash in the surf with the children. Between then and now he had not found a private moment in which to beg her pardon.

Going into the kitchen, he found Mrs Prentis stirring something in a pot, his daughters looking on.

'Do you know where Miss Curtis is?' Whatever was in that pot made him anxious for dinner.

'She went to the cove to take a picture, Papa,' Jayne said.

He glanced out the window. Wind stirred leafy branches of shrubbery in the garden, casting long shadows in the dusky light.

It would be approaching high tide in the cove.

'Are you certain she has not returned?'

'She hasn't,' Alice said. 'I've been waiting for her.'

Hurrying outside, he scanned the path to the beach. Vivienne was not on it.

The surf was loud, crashing hard as it rushed onshore. In the cove there would be no shore at all.

He ran, hating the drag of sand slowing his steps. While the water in the cove would be no more than hip high, it would be swirling fiercely. A woman with water weighing down her skirts would have little chance of wading out of the cove.

By the time he came within sight of the cove wall, water soaked the soles of his shoes. The closer he got, the deeper it became. Waves swirled around the rock wall, cutting the cove off from the rest of the beach. Up and over was the only way to reach it. He started climbing, but it was slow going with the rocks being slick with sea spray.

Once on top, he had a view of the cove. Peering hard through the dim light, he spotted her. She was standing on something. It must be the log where they'd discovered the stag beetles. It did not appear steady. Vivienne rocked and swayed, trying to keep her balance.

'Vivienne!' he shouted.

She looked up sharply.

'Hold on! I'm coming!'

With that, he scrambled down the rocks, then jumped into the water. The tide swirled around his hips. It tugged him backwards when it went out, then gave him a push forward when it came in. Rough going, but he made it across without slipping.

When he reached Vivienne, he lifted his arms. 'I will carry you,' he called over the noise of the water.

She looked at the swirling tide, then shook her head. He could not blame her for hesitating.

'Wet skirts will drag you down.'

She had been gripping her camera to her heart. With a nod, she opened the case she had slung around her shoulder, put it inside, then snapped the lid closed. Placing one hand on his shoulder, she bent her knees. She hesitated, clearly uncertain about which was safer, the log or his arms.

'I won't let go of you. Come down now.'

All at once the log shifted.

She tumbled. Her legs flailed awkwardly and yet she managed to lift her case away from the water. Only good fortune landed her smack in his arms.

In spite of his best efforts to keep them dry, Vivienne's skirts got soaked. The extra weight made it tough going. His thighs pressed hard with each step. His arms ached with the effort not to let her go.

Getting back to the cove wall seemed to take a very long time, but he made it without losing Vivienne or her camera. He set her on her feet, but kept her pinned between his body and the rocks.

'We need to climb over.' He had to speak loudly because the water was noisy, crashing all around.

She nodded as if she understood, but she still kept the case lifted over her head. How did she think she would manage to climb without using her hands?

There was no time to argue the point. The water was

cold and they would soon be growing weak with exertion. They needed strength for the climb.

He lifted the case off her and slung it around his neck.

'Go up, Vivie. It's steep and wet, but I'm behind you. I won't let you fall.'

She started up, slipped, but he caught her with a hand under her thigh. He boosted her higher, one hand pressing her ever upwards and the other finding purchase in rock crevices.

Making the top, he took a moment to catch his breath. The hardest part was over. Only the descent remained and gravity was with them this time.

By the time they reached the safety of dry sand, night had settled. It would be dark if not for the huge moon on the horizon casting its bright, bluish glow.

He sat down, bringing Vivienne with him. They sat silently for a few moments while their ragged breathing eased.

'I am sorry,' he managed to say at last. 'This is my fault. I should not have teased you about bringing me the beetle. I should have made certain you knew about high tide. I should have—'

'You are hardly to blame. Going to the cove was my choice.'

'Because I said—'

'No, Clement. I take full responsibility for what I did and now, because of you, I am not drowned. And my equipment is safe.' She touched his cheek with cold fingers. 'You are my hero.'

Then she leaned towards him as if she meant to kiss him. Yes, she did mean to. Why else would he feel her breath on his face? Her eyes would not look like melted brown sugar if she meant to do something else. Then all at once she dropped her fingers, sighed and then leaned away.

'Vivie…' He cupped her cheek in his hand, drawing her back towards him. He would have that kiss.

And so he did.

Nothing felt more perfect in this moment. She must have felt the same for she leaned into him once again and wrapped both arms around his neck. It was not proper. Logically he knew that. But his longing didn't know it and that was what was speaking in the moment.

When the kiss ended, logic slowly regained control, pointing out that he had not behaved like a gentleman. He could blame it on moonlight, or a reaction to the danger they had faced. It would be a lie, though. It was his overwhelming attraction to her and his inability to control his desire at fault.

'And now I must apologise for this, too.'

'Apologise? I think not, Clement. You saved my life and I kissed you in thanks.'

In thanks? He'd been on the other end of that kiss and knew better. There was much more to it than she was willing to say. It was, however, a graceful way out of what they had so impulsively done.

'I'll admit, I've never been thanked in a nicer manner.' He stood, reaching a hand down to help her up. And then, because he would likely never have the chance to do so again, he dipped his head and gave her one more kiss. 'Now I thank you, too…for forgiving me when I challenged you to fetch the beetle.'

'Did I say that I did?' She gave him that soft-eyed look, her lips still glistening from the kiss while they walked towards the lamps glowing in the inn's front windows.

'You did. It was when you nearly kissed me first.'

'Oh, then,' she said and then did not speak again until they reached the porch steps.

She looked up at him with moonlight on her face, with her hair dampened by sea water.

'I liked it when you called me Vivie. But, Clement, you must not do so again.'

He liked it, too, but she was correct. The endearment was far too intimate.

The end of the summer would come. She'd go away.

The less she took of his heart with her, the better. Unless he was very careful indeed, she would take more than a little.

Chapter Six

Vivienne was a liar. This was the third, or maybe fourth time she had accused herself of being one while she worked in the dark room which Mrs Prentis had allowed her to set up in the corner of the cellar.

That moment she'd shared with Clement had nothing to do with gratitude. Except that she had been grateful she was kissing him. Grateful indeed. Once she wed Everett she would never have a kiss like it again.

How was it that Clement's lips could bring her blood to a simmer, yet at the same time make her nerves shiver? Deliciously hot and cold all at once. What a confusing state to be in…wondrous in the oddest way, too.

It was unthinkable to even imagine giving Everett Parker the kind of kiss which made her go blurry and fuzzy. Just because he was a good man and a match society would approve of, he had never made her heart go wild. He was her father's friend, not her heart's desire.

Mr and Mrs Stag Beetle probably had more passion in their union than she would ever have with the Marquess of Winterfeld. She was about to begin worrying about how there could ever be an heir to Winterfeld, but just then the image on the glass plate came into focus.

It was amazing! Far better than she could have dreamed

it would be. The live insects were as sharply focused as the dead one was. She found it a stunning revelation, but insects were clearly co-operative creatures when it came to holding a pose.

All of a sudden she did not dislike them quite so much.

It was late when she rushed up to her bedroom with all three images in hand. Too bad. She was itching to show them to Clement, but after this evening's misadventure he was probably exhausted. It would be better to show him the photos and then press her cause once he was refreshed.

Oh, feathers! How was she to sleep? She was far too excited to close her eyes. Once Clement saw the images of the stag beetles preserved for ever, once he imagined them in his book, he would surely relent and allow her to help with his project.

Vivienne opened the door between the rooms to check on Alice and Jayne. Since they would never know she did it, she gave each girl a goodnight kiss on their forehead.

She had always expected she would have children one day, truly wanted them. Now that she had kissed Clement, now that she understood more about the nature of what led to conceiving them, she could not imagine how it would happen.

Not with the man she was promised to.

Going to the window, she stared out at the full moon, thinking about her sister and her husband. For the first time, she envied Grace having her love match.

Having spent so much effort avoiding marriage in favour of independence, Vivienne had not given proper thought to the benefits of it. Marriage meant you had a friend for ever. A lover for a lifetime. Everett was pleasant and considerate. She supposed she would at least have a friend once she married him.

Now, though, she was not convinced friendship on its own was enough. Now that Clement had kissed her and shown her what it could be like between a man and a woman, how intimate moments were a bond which set a couple apart from anyone else, the independence she'd believed so essential seemed less than fulfilling.

Kisses were fulfilling; indeed, one could get quite addicted to them!

Feathers, but she was confused. She was not sure of anything anymore except that her future was not with an entomologist.

'I am certain there is no one like him, but you must know that,' she murmured to the moon even though she understood that it had no answer for her.

Was there a way out of her promise to Everett? In society, once one gave one's word on such a thing as marriage it was often binding. Alliances were made, family lineages ensured and social status fortified.

She tapped her lips with one finger, deep in thought. The engagement had not yet been announced. Not that it mattered greatly. If she did not go through with it, she would let down the people she loved most. And even if she did refuse to go through with the engagement, what then? She must still marry some noble fellow of the right rank.

All at once she noticed her reflection on the glass, her finger touching the very lips Clement had kissed.

She sighed, turned away from the silent, unhelpful moon and stared at his closed bedroom door.

In that very instant, it clicked open.

'Can't sleep, Vivienne?'

If only she had not been forced to tell him not to call her Vivie. It had sounded so nice when he did.

'I did not mean to wake you, Clement.' The only noise she had made was to whisper and sigh. He could not have heard her unless he was awake and listening.

Was it their kiss leaving him restless? Unlike her, he probably had many to compare it with. What to her was unforgettable might be ordinary to him.

That moment, while constantly on her mind, was not the reason she was awake. She had only just run upstairs from the darkroom, all aglow and frustrated that she must wait on showing him the photos until morning. What a bit of luck that she might not need to wait after all. Once he saw the three images, he would understand how extraordinary…how unforgettable they were.

'You did not. I wasn't sleeping,' he said.

'Good, then.' She turned to rush for her chamber, but then spun back. It was late and… 'Do you mind having company? There is something I wish to show you.'

Did he mind? Not at all, because more than ever he craved her company. And, yes, he did mind, because more than ever he craved her company…her kisses. This had certainly not been his first kiss, but it had shaken him as if it was. Somehow, after Vivienne, he could not even recall the others.

What he must do was learn to enjoy her companionship while he could and yet understand that his time with her was not for ever. Summer would end and she would take up her new position.

For all that he wished to, the one thing he must not do was kiss her again. He must guard his heart or it would be far too easy to fall in love with her. He must have a care for his daughters' feelings as well. No one was better off with a saddened heart.

Vivienne returned from her chamber, smiling when she passed through his doorway. She smelled odd. Like chemicals of some sort. 'Wait until you see, Clement!'

She set a folder on his desk, then whirled to look at him with a smile glowing in her eyes…sparkling on her lips. 'Come and look. Here is proof that I will not be tortured by helping you in your work. And you, my friend, will be greatly helped.'

He opened the folder and saw three photos of the stag beetles. The images were sharp, clear in every detail. He could not speak for a moment. While the living creatures had sadly been washed away in the tide, wonder of wonders, here they were preserved for ever.

'You see? I brought you not one, but three beetles. As I recall you asked me to bring one, not touch them. I did touch the dead one with my fingernail, though, so it would be in the frame of the picture.'

'Clever and brave,' he said. How was he to resist her? 'It means a great deal to you to be a part of my work, doesn't it?'

'You cannot imagine how much. And not only for my own sake. As you can see, my photos will give your book a great advantage over your competition.'

'Hmmm.' He snatched his reading glasses from the corner of the desk, then leaned down to peer more closely at the photographs. 'Excellent work, Vivienne.' He straightened, took off the glasses and set them back in their corner. 'I think you are correct. And what you said before about being able to validate any find I made, a photograph would do that. No one could dispute it then.'

'You never know what sorts of unscrupulous people are out there.'

'Indeed, even in the scientific world.'

'Will you let me be a part of this project, then?'

It would be a risk. They would be working shoulder to shoulder on it. Which would mean their lips would not be so far apart.

Maybe he was already safe and she never wished to kiss him again? How was he to know what she truly felt about what had happened earlier tonight?

The photos fanned out on his desk had to do with research, not romance...so perhaps they might manage to work together...

'Tell me, why is this so important to you?'

'As you can see...' she waved her hand before her face, before making a sweeping gesture from hair to hem '... I am a woman.'

Indeed, he knew that all too well. It was the only thing keeping him from giving her an enthusiastic yes.

'As a woman I am not free to pursue a career the same as a man is. I have an obligation to wed, to produce an... to have children. I am speaking in general, of course. I do have a career as you well know, but I will never be free to open a little shop and sell my work.'

'Some women do...hat shops and the like.'

'I do not wish to sell hats. Trust me, Clement, working with you is the only way I will ever see my photographs for sale.'

No doubt she was correct about that. The odds of her having the career she wished for were rather slim. Easier for a woman of her station than a lady of high society, but difficult none the less.

'Join me, then. Let's see what we can do about getting

ourselves a successful, published work.' He extended his hand, a gesture of agreement.

Rather than take it, she threw herself against him, giving him a quick, tight hug. Then, as if remembering herself, she backed away. 'I apologise; that was not professional.' Then she shook his hand. 'I will be far more circumspect in the future.'

No doubt she would.

No doubt he would be sorry for it.

Clement stood at the shoreline watching his helper, her photo equipment slung across her back, while she rattled the branches of a bush. When she bent over, her skirt swayed and shimmied with her search. No entomologist had a more appealing helper, he would wager.

Or a more dedicated one. To his surprise, she became bolder by the day in their quest for specimens. She no longer backed away in revulsion when she spotted a creepy crawler. Only an hour ago she had called him over with a grin, pointing to a dung fly. Just this moment she was in pursuit of a cricket.

Now that Vivienne was involved, excursions were far more entertaining. Everything was more entertaining. No longer were his late-night studies lonely.

Each evening after the children were asleep, Vivienne came up from her darkroom to show him the photos she had taken during the day. No more yawning over tedious illustrations for him. There was nothing routine about her leaning over his shoulder and admiring his drawings. They were still necessary to illustrate the finer points of the insects' bodies…and make notations on size and colour.

More and more Vivienne began to ask questions regarding the insects he wrote about. He did not think her interest was feigned. Especially when it came to butterflies. She often admired the Creator's artistry in the beauty of their wings.

Last night when Clement had explained how the creatures looked delicate but were, in fact, not, her eyes had grown wide, sparkling with incredulity. Her lips had parted in amazement.

Which had meant he'd had to fight the urge to kiss her again. He'd managed by explaining how a butterfly could carry forty times its own weight.

'If only a photograph could capture colour,' she had said with a sigh. 'Wouldn't it be a wonder?'

And so the nights went. All this time—his whole life, in fact—he had not noticed how lonely he had been. Study had filled his hours and seemed satisfactory. Now that he knew the difference, how would he get by when he was alone again?

Although he was not really alone, he knew, while he watched Jayne and Alice building a sandcastle at the water's edge. His heart was fulfilled for the most part.

Not all, though.

'Found it!' Vivienne called.

He hurried over, but the cricket jumped away before he could capture it in a jar.

'Ah, well. We have other crickets to put in our book and tomorrow we will search inland, see what is to be discovered there.'

Interesting that after only a week's time he no longer considered it his book, but their book.

'The girls will miss their afternoons at the beach.' Vivienne inclined her head towards Alice and Jayne. 'That is an impressive castle.'

'How are their studies advancing this week? Are they giving proper attention to them? And behaving?'

'You would be proud of your daughters, such quick learners. Both of them are studious when they put their minds to it.'

'I hope they have stopped testing you. From what I can see, they have.'

He recalled the seashell, how Alice had snuggled close to Vivienne while they studied it.

'We have found our peace. Not that they do not enjoy a good prank now and again. It is all in good fun, though, not like before.'

'They are like their mother. I've always thought so.'

'I imagine it is a special moment whenever you see their resemblance to her.'

'Quite. She would have liked you, Vivienne. I think she would be pleased if she could see you with them.'

She nodded, but looked away. It might have been better if he had not said that. He knew she feared growing too close to them.

'Mrs Prentis is going to town tomorrow,' she said after a moment. 'I thought the girls might like a morning off from their studies. It will be good for them to explore the shops and have a bit of girlish fun.'

'Girlish fun…that is something I have not been able to give them.' Honestly, he knew far more about insect anatomy than he did about girlish fun. 'Thank you, Vivienne.'

'No need for thanks. I will enjoy the outing as much as they will. In my opinion there is a great deal that goes into making a well-rounded young woman. A balance of studies and outdoor playtime…and shopping, naturally.' She gazed at the girls, smiling with her hand over her heart.

It was impossible to look away from the soft, affectionate light in Vivienne's eyes.

He was ever grateful to have found a governess who
truly cared for them. Loved them a little even, he believed.

'You have given them a brilliant start, Clement. They
will become modern independent ladies. You should be
proud.'

Modern? Independent? For all that these were enlightened times, he was not certain an independent attitude
would be in their best interest.

As Baron Granville's nieces they would need to take
their place in society. Perhaps Vivienne did not understand
that. Not existing within the stricter requirements of the
upper class, she had a bit more freedom.

Not that he knew for certain her station since she kept
that part of her past to herself. A vicar's daughter or perhaps a genteel lady from the fringes of society fallen on
hard times was his best guess.

Still though, Alice and Jayne were only ten years old.
There were several years before they would need to settle
down and behave by society's rules.

Let them have their fun, he decided. For as long as Vivienne remained their governess, let them have it.

Vivienne walked across the children's bedroom, watching them sleep and thinking about what a splendid sandcastle they had made. It had been the four of them at the
end, building towers and a grand moat.

They had screeched when the tide rushed in and filled
the moat, then moaned when a wave knocked the castle
over. With shrieks of feigned outrage, they'd dashed about,
stamping and splashing in the water which had carried off
their creation.

It had all been great fun but now, hours later, the best part of Vivienne's day was just beginning. This was the fulfilment of her dream. The reason she had become a travelling governess. What did it matter that she was taking photos of insects instead of birds?

What she had never imagined when she'd set out on this adventure was how much she would enjoy working with Clement. His enthusiasm for his subject matter was contagious. Tonight, she might try to impress him by picking up an ugly insect. Ugly to her, at least. Her partner considered them all to be wondrous creations, each with a purpose for being in the world.

As was her custom, Vivienne stopped beside Alice's bed, bending to kiss her forehead. Perhaps she should not. It would only make it more difficult to leave them. But that was still weeks away. This was now and she would indulge in the moment.

Turning to Jayne's bed, she stroked the hair from her brow, then gave the child a goodnight kiss as well. But wait…something was wrong. Her skin was too hot.

Vivienne turned back to Alice's bed, touching her skin in order to compare. Humm…cool, moist. She swiped her fingers over Jayne's cheek. Hot, dry. Rushing for Clement's door, she knocked.

Clement smiled when he opened to her. His grin fell at once. Her expression must look quite worried.

'Jayne is ill.'

Clement walked towards the girls' doorway, not looking terribly alarmed. 'Children get sick. It is not unusual.'

'It is for me.'

He touched Jayne's forehead with the backs of his fingers, then bent to kiss her cheek. 'You have never had one of your charges fall ill?'

Never, not one single time. How could she? She was an imposter.

Now Jayne would pay the price because Vivienne had absolutely no idea how to deal with this situation. How irresponsible of her to have taken this job. What she had believed was that she would simply keep the girls entertained for the summer. She ought to have anticipated that one of them might become ill.

Please do not let it be something horrible, she silently prayed.

'I wonder if Mrs Prentis is still up,' she said. 'She did raise six children and will have dealt with fevers many times.'

'Of course she has. Try not to worry. If Mrs Prentis is alarmed, we will send for a doctor in the morning.'

And between now and then, she would sit by Jayne's bed and watch her breathe. It was what her mother used to do, she recalled now, watch at her bedside until the physician arrived.

Chapter Seven

Before dawn Jayne developed spots on her back.

Mrs Prentis diagnosed them as chickenpox. Each and every one of her children had had them, so she knew the signs.

'I shall go for the doctor at once.' Clement rose from his daughter's bedside.

'Surely not.' Mrs Prentis bent lower to look at the red welts on Jayne's back. 'The poor man will not be pleased to be called away because of a common childhood ailment.'

'It isn't dangerous?' Clement asked.

'It can be, but usually it is merely uncomfortable for a week or so. I suggest we wait and see. If it seems more serious, we will call for the doctor then.' Mrs Prentis tugged the blanket over Jayne. 'There now, my dearie, how are you feeling?'

'Bad in my head.'

'No need to fret. It will soon pass and then your father and Miss Curtis will do all they can to keep you entertained.'

Jayne smiled, closed her eyes and went back to sleep.

'Alice, lift your gown, will you?' Vivienne asked. 'Spots tend to jump from one child to the next in a blink.'

This did not sound at all good, but Clement kept the thought to himself. No need to add to the anxiety.

It was somewhat reassuring that Vivienne did not seem worried when moments before, she had.

'Ah, there one is. It is to bed with you, too, then.' Vivienne eased Alice down, covered her up, then kissed her cheek.

'Not to worry, Mr Marston.' Mrs Prentis patted his arm. 'Having them get it at the same time is for the best. Why, when one of mine came down with it, I put them all together to make sure they all got it at once. Better to get it over and done, I say. And it is far safer to have it when they are young. Once they recover they will never get it again.'

'I never had chickenpox,' he said. 'Will I catch it from them?' He might since he would not avoid them, especially when they were ill.

'Why, of course you did. That little scar near your eye is from it. You are quite safe to be around your children,' their landlady reassured him.

He must have been very young when it happened. He did not even recall the event.

'Vivienne, have you had chickenpox?' he asked. If she had not, she must leave the room at once. He would not allow her to risk her health to care for Alice and Jayne. She had already taken a risk by kissing Alice's cheek.

'I have—both my sister and I caught it when I was nine years old.'

'All is well, then,' Mrs Prentis declared. 'I shall go to the kitchen and make a good nutritious broth.' With a smile and a nod, she bustled from the bedroom.

'And I suppose that leaves us to find a way of entertaining them until they recover.'

'I will do it. If you will stay with them for a few hours, I will go with Mrs Prentis when she goes into town. I'll purchase a few things Jayne and Alice will enjoy.'

'Thank you, Vivienne. I cannot imagine how I would get along without you.'

She bit her lip, glanced away.

Dash it, he'd done it again. Reminded her that the time would come when she must leave them. Growing closer to the girls was not something she could prevent. No wonder it grieved her to think about it.

He would be careful not to say such a thing again. Not that he could keep from thinking about it, though…and wishing circumstances were not what they were.

It was the oddest thing, but looking back, Vivienne recalled those two weeks of her childhood when she was sick with chickenpox to have been a good time.

Once she and Grace had got over the fever, they'd had a great deal of fun playing games with their mother. Great-Aunt Anne had been visiting at the time and had spent hours each day telling them stories.

The trip to town today had been a great success. She had brought back paper dolls, coloured chalk and chalk boards, as well as too many books to be carried upstairs at one time.

Coming into the girls' bedroom, she found Clement sitting on a chair placed between his daughters' beds. The girls were asleep and so was he. A large book with paintings of butterflies lay open across his lap. His head lolled back on the chair and his lips were parted ever so slightly in sleep.

She set the armload of books she had carried upstairs on the desk. Crossing to Clement, she meant to wake him before his neck grew stiff.

Instead, she stood over him, looking at the scar Miss Prentis had pointed out. She had not noticed it before, but there was no reason she would have, never having had the opportunity to watch his face in repose before.

What a good face it was. Bold, humorous, studious and, most of all, loving. What sort of man, and barely a man at the time, put his dreams on hold to raise his infant nieces?

Indeed, this was a very good face. Not refined, not swoon worthy, but by far the most handsome she had ever seen. Here was a man who gave love without hesitation no matter the sacrifice to himself.

And he had wonderful lips, so warm and expressive. She did not mean only when they were smiling, either. No, just now she was thinking of how they had felt when he'd kissed her. How those lips had spoken in emotion rather than words.

Slowly, his eyes opened, he blinked once and then smiled. 'You're back from town,' he murmured.

Yes, clearly she was. What he probably meant was why was she standing over him?

'I just arrived. I was about to wake you. You fell asleep with your neck at an angle. I thought it might be getting stiff.'

He turned his head this way and then that, up and down as if testing for soreness. 'You rescued me in time, but thank you for your concern.'

It was a fortunate thing he could not be inside her mind right then. If he could, he would find that concern was only a small part of what she had been feeling.

At that point Alice woke up. 'I'm itchy,' she complained.

'Let me see, then.' Vivienne went to the bed and lifted the back of her gown. 'You are coming along nicely.'

'It doesn't feel nice.'

'It will once you begin to recover and are able to play with the toys I brought from town.'

'Toys!' Her eyes brightened a bit at the news.

'They are the very type my mother gave me when I had chickenpox. Now, the most important thing you must remember is not to scratch. If you do, it will leave a scar.'

'But it feels so itchy. I might.'

'I will dab some calamine lotion on your spots. It should help.'

'You are lucky girls to have such a splendid governess.' Clement smiled at her, his eyes soft and his grin wide.

And all at once, for the first time, she did not feel like an imposter. She was a governess.

Clement sat at his desk, Vivienne shoulder to shoulder beside him. He stared at the insect he was drawing without really seeing it. His mind wandered, he needed sleep. Photographs might have kept him focused but there were not any tonight. His assistant had been caring for sick children all day, insects forgotten.

Even though she sat here beside him, she must be far wearier than he was. She was the one who cooled their fevers with damp cloths, who dabbed their blisters with soothing lotion and fed them broth.

He had tried to help, but she'd shooed him off with a wave of her fingers. This was her job, she'd insisted. The reason he had hired her was to care for the girls and she meant to do it. Even so, he was exhausted. There was nothing like worry to drain a soul.

Just because Vivienne and his landlady's children had come through chickenpox unscathed, and just because he apparently had as well, did not mean that all children did. In spite of the ladies' sunny attitudes in the face of this illness, he well knew that some children did not survive it.

Until the fevers passed his nerves would be on edge.

'Clement…' Vivienne wriggled the pencil out of his grip '…you just drew a line across the paper.'

Had he nodded off for an instant? For the first time that he could recall, his research was unfocused.

Seeing Vivienne's bemused expression, he frowned. 'I will need to start the drawing again.' He reached for a blank sheet, but she put her hand on the stack, preventing him.

'The damselfly will not mind waiting for her portrait until you have rested. We are finished here for the night.'

'I cannot do her justice in this state, anyway.'

'Go to bed, Clement. I will watch the children sleep.'

Would she? Her lids drooped with weariness. There were dark circles under her eyes and her shoulders sagged.

'No, Vivie, you sleep while I watch.'

It took a moment for him to realise his mistake in calling her by the endearment. The fact that she did not mention it only went to prove how exhausted she was.

'I will earn my wage.'

It's what she always said, but he knew that her motivation in caring for the girls was not financial. In fact, she seemed remarkably unconcerned with money. Everything she had purchased in town had been with her own funds. Naturally, he had tried to reimburse her but, oddly, she had refused. How puzzling that a young lady fallen on hard times would have any funds to spare. Since he did not wish to pry, he kept the thought to himself.

'We will sit together,' he decided. 'Take turns watching them breathe.'

'Listening so they do not unknowingly scratch.'

Vivienne got up from the desk and then went into the girls' bedroom. She sat on a chair, a hard wooden chair with no cushion. He'd spent enough hours in it to know it was not an ideal place to pass the night.

There was a small sofa in his chamber. He looked it over to see if it would slide through the doorway. Good, it would clear with half an inch on each side.

He made a space for it along the wall under a window where they had a clear view of his fitfully sleeping daughters. Funny how he had long since stopped thinking of them as his nieces. That was the relationship they had with his brothers. As far as uncles went, though, they were not terribly doting.

The distance between London and Whisper Glen was further than the miles accounted for. If they wished to, his brothers could easily take the train and visit. But they had only done so a handful of times.

Clement could have taken the girls to London, but Miss Logan had not liked travelling and the thought of taking them by himself was daunting. Better to keep them at home where life seemed safer and healthier.

'Where have you wandered, Clement?'

What? Having become lost in his thoughts he discovered he had been standing beside the sofa, gazing out the window. Below in the garden, he saw bushes being lashed in a stiff wind. One pane of glass vibrated, apparently loose in the frame.

'Ah, I'm just thinking about my brothers.' He indicated the sofa with a sweep of his hand. 'I imagine you are as done with that chair as I am. Sit here with me instead.'

'Quite done,' she said, then eased down and snuggled into the cushions. 'This is heavenly.'

It was, but in a way she would probably not guess. The sofa was not as wide as most and so it put them close enough that he caught a whiff of rose water in her hair.

'Tell me about your brothers.'

'Duncan is the older one, Eldon the younger. Both of them live in London.'

'Alice and Jayne must enjoy having uncles.'

'The truth is, they barely know their uncles. Duncan used to spend all his time entertaining himself in various ways. He wed six months ago and now his bride keeps him fully occupied. Eldon is now sniffing about the marriage mart. Busy fellows.' He yawned, stretched. Since there was little room on the sofa, he rested his arm along the back behind Vivienne. 'You mentioned a sister. Any brothers?'

'A brother-in-law only. He is a wonderful man and I am happy for my sister…did you hear scratching?'

He shook his head. 'Are you and your sister are close, then?'

She nodded, 'Oh, yes. Grace and George are on holiday on the Continent. They must be in Paris now.'

All of a sudden she blinked, frowning. 'Not on holiday so much as business. George has ties in industry.'

'Did you hear Jayne miss a breath?'

She shook her head, then rested it on his shoulder. 'No.'

Under normal circumstances she would not do something so familiar. Surely even now she meant nothing by it except that she was hours beyond weary.

Because he was in the same condition, he let his arm slip off the back of the sofa and settle around her shoulders.

'I'm sad for your brothers,' she murmured. 'They have no idea what they are missing by not being good uncles.'

'Distant uncles. There is a difference.'

'I have a great-aunt. I see her several times a year even though my family lives in…oh, in a distant city from her. But families are all different. Mine are not like yours… yours are not like mine…'

Her conversation seemed unfocused, but it hardly mattered since his own attention was wavering.

'Clement, did Alice just miss a breath?'

'No, I would have noticed if she had.'

She closed her eyes. He closed his, resting his head on top of hers. Rose-scented curls tickled his nose and made him smile.

'Vivie, did you just hear scratching?'

Vivienne felt warm…and so comfortable snuggled against her pillow. She nuzzled her cheek into it. Sighed.

'Jayne, are Papa and Miss Curtis allowed to curl up all over each other?'

'I think not. You must be married to do that.'

'Perhaps they wed in the night.'

What?

What!!

Vivienne exploded off the sofa. So did Clement. They banged their heads together…then stared at one another in horror. She smoothed her skirts while he rubbed the sore spot on his chin.

'Papa, did you get married in the night?' Jayne asked. 'Is Miss Curtis our new mother?'

Clement cleared his throat, 'No, we did not wed.'

'Then why were you sleeping all over each other?'

'We were not sleeping, exactly, we were merely resting our eyes while we watched over you.'

A change of subject was called for and in a hurry.

'But look at you! You both seem much improved,' Vivienne declared.

She pressed her cheek to Jayne's and then to Alice's. Glancing up at Clement, she said, 'Nice and cool, no more fever.'

She saw it when a prayer of thanks crossed their father's eyes. And for good reason. It was wonderful to see the sparkle return to the children's expressions.

'We wish you did wed in the night, Papa,' Alice declared.

'We need a mother, after all.' Jayne smiled at Vivienne when she said so.

'Perhaps one day I will,' Clement stated. 'But for now you have very fine and dedicated governess. Wait until you see the gifts she's brought you.'

At the same time the girls leapt out of bed.

'Ouch!' Alice pressed the top of her head.

'That hurt!' Jayne sat back down on her mattress.

'And no wonder. You cannot leap about so suddenly. You need to rest so that you can fully recover. After breakfast, if you are still feeling better, I will show you what I have for you.'

'Maybe we won't mind being sick, Jayne,' Alice suggested.

'Not if there are new toys and we have Miss Curtis to play with us. We will have a merry time.'

The sooner Alice and Jayne recovered, the better, in Vivienne's opinion. An opinion which was not all to do with their health. Quite clearly she and Clement could not spend another night keeping watch together.

Their intentions had been well founded. Sick children needed attention. Two people guarding them was safer. One could not be too careful. They had not meant to doze off. Certainly had not intended to wake up entwined and have the children believe they had got married.

Caution was called for when it came to her employer. The last thing she should do was put herself in a position where she would be forced to marry Clement Marston.

Why, the very thought was— Not intriguing...no, never that. Unacceptable was what it was. Her father had made an agreement with the Marquess of Winterfeld. Everett and her parents had been generous in allowing her this time to go on holiday…with her sister. How thankless was she to have let the thought of wedding Clement cross the corner of her mind.

Well, she would not allow it to happen again. If Clement decided to give his children a mother, it would not be their governess. Even though he was not a baron, at this point in time he was next in line to be. Therefore he would feel he owed it to his family and children to marry to the best advantage.

Clement kissed each of his girls, then said, 'I will go to the kitchen, bring us all some breakfast. Mrs Prentis will be happy to know you two are on the mend.'

Once the door closed behind him, Alice and Jayne bent their heads together, whispering and smiling…casting Vivienne sidelong glances.

Perhaps it should not be, but it was reassuring to see them plotting a prank, for clearly it was what they were doing.

Vivienne would overlook a dozen mischievous plans if it meant seeing the fevers gone and the worst over. There would still be the blisters to deal with, but there would be games and books to get them through.

Soon they would be back to their studies and looking for specimens for their father's book…her book, too, now. While her name would not appear on the cover, her photos were on every page. Her heart was on every page. Afternoon excursions with Clement and the girls, evenings spent assisting him…oh, yes, her heart was in all of it.

Clement leaned against his doorway, looking into the children's bedroom. Vivienne and the girls sat on the rug. They looked like a flower bouquet, the way their skirts swirled about them in a blend of red, yellow and green.

The three of them were caught up in cutting out paper dolls so he did not think they noticed him. Good. Watching them in unguarded moments was one of his favourite things to do. Now that Vivienne was added to the mix, it was all the better.

They were laughing while they snipped paper dresses. It seemed a dull way to spend time to him, but Alice and Jayne were enjoying it and Vivienne, too, by the looks of it.

They attached elegant gown after elegant gown to their dolls. Apparently they were preparing for the most important ball of the year and deciding whose dress would best win the attention of the gentlemen.

Their fevers had been gone for a week and a day. The blisters were healing so well that the girls wanted to go outside. Vivienne would not allow it, telling them that they must not risk their trip to town by venturing out too soon.

Alice and Jayne did not give her more than a second's argument since they were quite anxious for the trip that chicken pox had thwarted.

Jayne glanced up.

'Look, Alice, Papa is here.' A smile passed between them…but not an ordinary one. Intuition and experience warned him something was brewing.

But then they hopped up from the floor and ran to him. Jayne stood on his shoes and gave him a hug. Nothing out of line in that.

Alice came up to him, chin pointed up while she smiled and waited for him to tug the bow in her hair.

Perhaps he'd imagined the look he had seen a moment ago, mistaken it for something else.

'Would you like to join us?' Vivienne smiled up from her spot on the floor. 'Each and every gown you see here is the height of fashion. All straight from Paris. Every woman will be wearing them this Season.'

'Our governess knows all about elegant gowns and shoes and hats and...everything,' Alice declared.

'Every single thing about jewels,' Jayne added.

'You must have attended many balls, Vivienne.' He gave her a teasing wink. He had been asked to join, after all. 'How else does one know how to dress a debutante in her finest?'

She gave him back a wink, a laugh. 'It says how to do it, right here on the illustration pages.'

Jayne whispered in Alice's ear. There went that secret look, putting all his senses on alert again.

'Papa, we would like for you to read us a story,' Jayne said.

That seemed innocent enough, on the surface.

'Of course, it would be my pleasure. Which book would you like?'

'One of our new ones. It is up high in the cupboard,' Alice told him. 'We cannot reach it.'

'What is it called?'

'"The Tail of Lost Dog".'

He went into the built-in cupboard. It was dim inside. Without his reading glasses he could not tell one book from the next. 'Which side is it on?'

Alice sat down on the wooden chair that had no cushion. 'On the left, up high.'

He reached up, felt a stack of books. Any one of them could be the one they wanted.

'What if I read the top one?'

'We have our hearts set on hearing that one. Maybe Miss Curtis can help you find it.'

There was little room for two people, but Vivienne squeezed in, going up on her toes to better see the book titles.

Fine hairs on his neck came to attention. Too late he realised this was a trap.

In the instant the door shut, he heard Jayne giggle.

He reached for the knob, but too late. A chair scraped on the floor, the knob jerked under his hand when one of the girls jammed the chair under it, making it impossible to open.

They were trapped. In the dark. With barely enough room to turn around without touching.

'Open this door immediately or there will be consequences!'

Skipping feet sounded across the floor.

'Alice! Jayne! You must let us out. I am terrified of the dark,' Vivienne called.

'Papa will keep you safe, just like he does us.' Alice's voice came from the hallway now.

'Come back here this minute, girls.' He gave the order in his deepest, most commanding voice.

'After we get cake from Mrs Prentis, Papa.'

'And after you fall in love.'

He heard the bedroom door close. After that, silence.

Nearly silence. Inside the cupboard he heard Vivienne's breath coming quick.

'You are afraid of the dark?'

'No, I was merely appealing to their tender mercies.'

'Apparently they do not have any. I apologise for their behaviour. This is unacceptable.'

She turned, something soft brushing his arm. He did not allow himself to dwell on what it was, but it wasn't an elbow, nor a shoulder.

'Please do not be too hard on them. Every little girl longs for a mother.'

'Longing is one thing. I know they do. But causing trouble in order to get their way will not do.'

'I wonder how long they think it will take for us to fall in love,' she mused.

The small space filled with the delicate fragrance of a rose. It would be coming from her hair he thought, but it might also come from the tender spot behind her ear where ladies liked to dab their scents.

'They must think we will emerge from here magically engaged. I have brought up monsters, I fear.'

She laughed, which he felt as much as he heard.

He pressed his back against the door, hoping to put some distance between them. Or, rather between him and temptation. It did no good. She was still so close that he felt it when the fabric of her skirt wrapped around his trousers. Even with no part of him touching her, he felt things he should not be feeling. He could so easily kiss her again, tenderly call her Vivie.

The one and only thing keeping him from doing both those things was that she was helpless to step away from him if she wished to. And yet, in the dark, both of them breathing hard, feeling one another's heat, the sensation was already as intimate as a kiss.

'How long does it take them to eat cake?' he grumbled.

'Not long enough, I fear.' Her whisper was soft and he thought he must have misheard.

'I beg your pardon?'

'Long enough, I fear,' she said.

He frowned. 'You have nothing to fear from me, I promise. I will protect you in the dark, just as my daughters said I would.'

She nodded, then said nothing else for what seemed a long time.

'I know.' Her whisper was once again under her breath. If he thought he heard regret in her tone, he would be as mistaken as he had been a moment ago.

And so they stood, nearly touching, breathing and wondering...at least he was—what would happen if he gave in to temptation and did what he wanted to do? What if he kissed her long and hard? What if this time it was not disguised as a thank you? Only confirmed that he wanted her. Would she reconsider her next engagement?

Beset by questions, he continued to breathe, in and out, long and slow...fighting the realisation creeping into his brain. He did not want to acknowledge it...it could not be and yet it was.

He curled his hands into fists and accidently caught a bit of lace in his fingers. Lace was utterly feminine. He ought to let go of it. To let go of the fog obscuring his good sense. In the moment all he knew was that his children needed a mother. They loved Vivienne, they wanted her.

And he...dash it...he was not going to lean closer to her lips, hinting at a kiss. He had promised she was safe with him. Safe was what she would be.

Pressing harder against the door, he suddenly fell backwards into the bedroom.

'Oh, my gracious!' He looked up from the floor to see Mrs Prentis leaning over him, fingers pressed to her round, rosy cheeks. 'They did lock you in!'

'And they shall pay for it.' This prank had gone too far. He had nearly gone too far.

'Oh, yes, Sir, you must discipline them.' Mrs Prentis's shoulders heaved ever so slightly. The woman wasn't taking this as seriously as she ought to. 'Just as soon as they finish their cake.'

As soon as they finished their cake! What nonsense was this?

'Do you realise what they intended to do?' She must not or she would not be taking this so lightly.

'The poor dearies were hoping to get a mother, I would expect.'

'In the most inappropriate way possible.'

'No harm was really done,' Vivienne said calmly.

No harm? He'd come within seconds of losing control, of doing something which would compromise his children's governess…his assistant.

Looking at her now, seeing her expression cool and unconcerned, he wondered if the temptation had been only on his part. It had to have been. Vivienne's cheeks were not flushed. Clement was pretty dashed certain all of him was flushed.

While he reflected on it, Alice and Jayne came into the room. Alice held her cake, grinning though a smattering of crumbs on her mouth.

'Did you fall in love?' Alice asked.

'That is not quite how it is done, my dearies.' Mrs Prentis tried to frown, but it did not come across as severe as it ought to have.

A pair of bright spots bloomed in Vivienne's cheeks. She walked to the window and looked out, apparently trying to hide her reaction. How was it that being alone with him had not made her blush, but Alice's question had?

'I will have a moment alone with my children.'

'Come, Vivienne,' Mrs Prentis said. 'There is more cake in the kitchen.'

Vivienne cast him a sidelong frown while she walked out of the chamber, side by side with their hostess.

Did she, like Mrs Prentis, not believe discipline was called for here?

He understood his daughters' feelings. Naturally they wanted a woman to love them and be their mother.

It was not their need for such a woman he was chastising, it the way in which they'd attempted to get one…to capture one, more to the point.

'Sit down. Give me the rest of your cake.' He held out his hand.

Jayne swallowed hard. Alice dumped a few dozen crumbs in his palm.

He paced before them, his mind churning.

'Please tell me you understand what you did wrong.'

They glanced at one another…holding their silence.

'What you did was unacceptable.'

'We are sorry we locked you in the cupboard,' were the words which came from Jayne's mouth, but he doubted they were sincere.

'I hope you are sorry. And I expect you to think over what you did during your punishment. For the next week you will not play with paper dolls, nor will you read any book which is not a textbook. And no cake.'

'But we only meant for us all to be happy.'

'I do not believe your governess appreciated being locked up in such a small space.'

With him, where the only thing to do was breathe, sweat under the collar and resist fiery temptation.

'Do you understand why you must face consequences?'

For all that he understood them wanting a mother and that they wanted their governess to be that special lady, what they had done must be addressed.

'I understand this is hard for you, not having a mother. But you cannot lock people up together in order to get one.'

'But don't you love Miss Curtis?' Jayne gave him a wide-eyed glance of disbelief.

'You cannot simply force people into a small space and expect them to fall in love. It is not done.'

Having said all he could on the matter, he walked towards his chamber to give them time to think over their misbehaviour.

'Only you needed to,' Alice mumbled.

That brought him up him short. He turned slowly about.

'What was that?'

'Miss Curtis is already in love with you,' Jayne said with Alice nodding agreement. 'So only you need to fall in love now.'

'You are ten years old. You cannot know such a thing. No one is in love with anybody.'

'Yes, Father,' the two of them said at the same time.

They were little girls and did not know what they were speaking of. Vivienne would get a good laugh out of if he told her.

Perhaps, though, he would keep this to himself. He was not sure why, only that it felt the wisest thing to do.

Chapter Eight

Vivienne sat on the front seat beside Mrs Prentis while their hostess drove the carriage towards Sea Mist, the village nearest the inn.

She glanced around at Alice and Jayne sitting on the back seat. The children looked as healthy as if they had never been ill.

During the week of their punishment the children had behaved so well that at the end of it, their father consented to let them go to the village for the long-awaited outing.

They would visit shops, make some purchases and then admire them over tea and sandwiches at the bakery.

Vivienne was in high spirits over the excursion, as much as the girls were. In a sense, their punishment had been hers, too. Only textbooks for entertainment had been a great bore.

The nights had been better when, after the girls were asleep, she had her time with Clement.

Seeing the book come together was exciting. Clement's drawings and detailed descriptions, enhanced by her photographs, were going to make it a great success.

No doubt their work would stand above the others. Publishers would gather at their door… Clement's door, she meant.

While she watched birds sweeping over rolling stretches

of grass, her mind wandered to the time she and Clement had spent in the cupboard…because that was where her mind tended to wander when left free to ramble. Even when it was not rambling it cut into her thoughts.

It was not easy to ignore the delightful afterglow of being confined in the small space with him.

He had been so…so very…responsible. He'd wanted to kiss her. She could nearly smell the desire calling them to act on it. How noble he had been fighting the battle to remain respectful of her.

She admired him for it, of course. Admired him for a great many things. He was brave when the occasion called for it, unrestrained in vulnerable moments and restrained when it was prudent to be.

But feathers. Far better to keep her affection for him a special secret within her heart. Let it glimmer in private since that was the only place it could exist.

Arriving at the village, Mrs Prentis secured the carriage at the livery and then left them to go about her own business. They agreed to meet at the bakery in two hours.

One only had to look at their faces to see how excited Jayne and Alice were. Living with only their father, they had not experienced a shopping trip like this one.

Vivienne was as excited as they were. To be able to share this first-time experience with her girls—

Very well, not really her girls, but she was as happy to share this day with them as if they were.

They were of an age to learn the pleasures of browsing the shops, looking for pretty hats, and the nicest gloves in which to clutch sweet little reticules.

They would not need any of those things yet, not having been exposed to society. Which Vivienne considered to be a good thing. A child's early years were meant to be carefree…days packed with sunshine and outdoor adventure. Balanced with study, naturally, but, in all, childhood was a time of happy exploration.

The day would come when they would need to put society's pretty trappings to use as tools, but not today.

Today was for having fun. Seeing it all through their young eyes was a treat. Vivienne recalled the days when she and her sister had shopped for adventure, not necessity.

In her real life as a high-born lady, making purchases was expected. A lady must be seen spending her father's wealth to a certain degree. Also there was the obligation to keep the shop owners in business.

What a lady purchased was often noticed and copied. Not Vivienne since her tastes were on the plain side and no one copied her, but her sister—people did tend to notice what Grace bought and wore.

Sadly, when shopping became something of an occupation, it took away from the pleasure. Today, with Alice and Jayne, it would be pure enjoyment.

'What shop would you like to visit first?' she asked, hoping it would be the hat shop…or the book store would be lovely, too.

'Mrs Fortune's Feathers and Frocks,' Jayne declared, her gaze seeming spellbound by a hat having red plumage, which arched majestically from a satin brim.

'Very well. We shall visit Mrs Fortune's. Now tell me again… What are the rules of polite behaviour?'

'One may speak and chatter, but not too loudly. It is rude to cause a distraction for other ladies who are shopping.'

'Excellent. What else?'

'Ask permission before you pick something up. Treat the merchandise with respect.'

'Excellent again. But what was that last bit we talked about?'

Matching grins lit their faces, ear to ear.

'If we see something we would like to purchase, tell you what it is and you will consider it.'

'Come then, we will have a grand time.'

With a happy screech, they hopped up and down, racing for the front door, eager to explore the feathers and frocks. It might not be all their fault that they forgot rule number one so quickly. There were flashy, pretty things wherever one looked.

Alice and Jayne made an effort to control their enthusiasm, but each item they asked to inspect shone brighter than the next. The volume of their admiration remained acceptable until they spotted a bird's nest, complete with eggs, nestled into the brim of a hat. It was a gaudy thing with a purple satin band and red streamers.

A woman standing in front of an oval mirror picked it up, placing it on her head. She gazed at her reflection, chin up, chin down, then side to side. She must have liked the look because she gave herself a pouty-lipped smile.

Undone, the girls' gasps of dismay were loud enough to be heard from the front door to the fitting rooms in the back.

The woman paused in her preening to give them a disapproving stare, or rather her reflection in the mirror did. She lifted one finger to her lips in a shushing gesture.

Jayne gave Alice a look. Oh, dear. Alice gave it back. They giggled which gained a harsher frown from the woman at the mirror.

Vivienne sided with the girls about the absurdity of wearing a bird's nest. No sensible woman should be seen in such a thing.

Not only did she not reprimand Alice and Jayne for their reaction, she was within a breath of pointing out that this was a business establishment and not a library.

'Pity the poor bird who lost her home and family in the name of fashion,' she told the girls, not as quietly as she might have.

'We should put it back where it came from so mama bird can hatch her eggs,' Jayne said, her gaze narrowed on the hat.

'It is too late for that,' she answered. 'Those will not be real eggs. Only paste.'

'The nest is real,' Alice declared, 'We should put it in a tree so mother bird can lay more eggs to hatch.'

'I am afraid we cannot, my dears. We do not even know where it came—'

'Miss!' The woman at the mirror spun about, pinning Vivienne with a glare, complete with narrowed eyes and a turned-up nose. 'You must control your charges.'

Vivienne began to simmer. Who was this person treating complete strangers, children no less, with such a haughty attitude?

'Do you intend to purchase that outrageous hat?' she asked, her voice crisp with indignation for Alice and Jayne's sake. It was all she could do to behave like a lady and not reveal her real identity.

The woman turned to the young lady standing behind the counter who had been watching the exchange in wide-eyed interest.

'I will not patronise your shop unless you remove this disruptive person and those children.'

The girl glanced back and forth between Vivienne and the woman, clearly not sure of what to do.

'I will pay you three times what you are asking for the hat,' Vivienne said.

'Of all the impertinent nonsense,' the woman declared, tying the purple ribbon under her chin.

The assistant grinned. 'The hat has been sold, Miss. I must ask you to remove it.'

And so in the end, Vivienne and the girls walked out of the shop only moments behind the offended patron, being the proud owners of an overpriced, ridiculous-looking hat.

Alice and Jayne carried it between them, gazing sorrowfully at the nest.

'No need to fret, my dears. When we get back to the inn we will find a tree to place it in. Perhaps a mother bird who's lost her nest will discover this one and then use it to hatch her eggs.'

'How brilliant!' Jayne grabbed her in a hug from one side. Alice hugged her around the middle on the other side.

'We love you, Miss Curtis,' they said, their sweet voices coming one on top of the other.

It was terribly difficult not to say the same back to them. But proprieties must be observed. A governess might express passing affection for her charges, but nothing more.

Vivienne bit her lip, blinked back a tear.

'May we take turns wearing the hat?' Jayne asked.

'Oh, please let us!' Alice hopped about on her toes. 'We may never get to wear something so horrid again.'

It was the truth and so Vivienne laughed when she wanted to sniffle.

'You may, but only if you share it with me.'

'And Papa, Miss Curtis paid three times the price of the hat so that we could put the nest in a tree for another bird to have,' Jayne told him while they stood a distance from said tree, watching Alice scramble out on a limb.

Vivienne stood underneath, her arms spread, apparently thinking to catch her if she fell. The branch was low so he resisted the urge to run to the tree and add his support.

'Three times?' Clement asked in case he had not heard correctly.

'Yes, Papa.'

Humph…how had she managed that? It must have cost her a month's salary.

'We still think you should fall in love with her.'

He was saved from having to argue the point by a carriage turning on to the drive. Perhaps Mrs Prentis had let out another room. But, no, as soon as the carriage stopped in front of the inn, he recognised it. How surprising to get a visit from Baron Granville here on the island. He hoped it was not to deliver some sort of bad news.

'Run along and help your sister and Miss Curtis place the nest, my dear.' Jayne stood on his toes, gave him a hug and then dashed away.

He walked to the carriage to greet his older brother. There were no trunks on the roof so they must not intend to stay.

The driver climbed down, opened the door. Duncan stepped down.

'It is good to see you, Brother,' Clement said, thinking that surprising would have been a better word.

They pounded one another on the back while the driver helped his sister-in-law down.

As always, Mildred dressed above the occasion. As far as Clement knew, there was no ball being hosted in the vicinity tonight.

'Clement! It is so wonderful to see you.' Mildred came

forward as if to embrace him, but then stopped short. She twirled about in her gown then waited, he thought, for it to be admired.

'You look quite fetching this afternoon, Mildred. What a surprise to see you and my brother here.'

'It happens that we are here on holiday. When Duncan mentioned you were here as well, I insisted that we must pay you a visit. You know, I have never met my nieces. I have been anxious to, ever since I married your brother.'

'It is true,' Duncan said with an indulgent smile at his bride.

'They will take their place in society one day and I must guide them, see them settled into advantageous marriages,' Mildred declared. 'After all, the higher they wed the better it will be for my own children when they come along.'

'While I appreciate your interest, that day is a long way off. They are only ten years old.' Naturally, his new sister-in-law would put position over childhood.

'I know that, of course. But as their only female relative, it is my duty to launch them into society. Such an undertaking cannot be begun too early.' Mildred touched her hat, fluffing a mound of silk flowers. 'I know all about them and how they came to live with you. It was kind of you to take them in.'

Kind?

Something about this conversation was beginning to set him on edge. Mildred set him on edge. She had ever since he'd met her.

In his estimation, she was a social climber. Being the youngest of four daughters, her prospects had been limited. When Duncan had shown a small interest in her, she'd reeled him straight in. A fish on a hook was the image he'd always had.

However, she was family now and so he did his best to treat her with courtesy.

'Please do not make us wait a moment longer, Clement. Where are our little darlings?' his brother asked.

Our little darlings? This from the uncle who had made so little effort to see them over the years.

There was more going on here than a family gathering.

'Over there, by the tree,' he said.

His gut rolled, uneasy. He had a feeling he was going to regret this visit in some way.

Vivienne noticed the coach as soon as it turned on to the drive, but did not pay a great deal of attention to it. Alice was wriggling about on a tree limb. A responsible governess would not let her attention wander.

'Why is Papa hugging that man?' Jayne asked.

'We will know soon enough, I expect. Give me the nest, will you, so I can hand it up to your sister.'

After a few moments, Vivienne was aware of Clement coming towards them across the grass, a man on one side of him and a woman on the other.

'Jayne, Alice!' Clement called. 'Come and greet your uncle and aunt.'

Uncle? The newlywed baron who had not visited his nieces in far too long? Interesting.

She helped Alice down from the tree, took the bird nest from Jayne and then set it in the grass to be attended to later. Alice and Jayne held hands, walking towards the visitors. They seemed uncommonly shy. She followed behind them, doing her best to appear a retiring, blending-into-the-background governess. With her eyes to the ground, she did not really look at them.

Not until Jayne blurted, 'It's her!'

Her, who?

'She's come to take our hat.'

Vivienne looked up sharply, stunned to see her adversary from yesterday.

'You!' Oh, there went that pert, superior nose, lifting in the air as if she were a queen instead of the wife of a baron. 'I cannot believe it!'

'She has come to take our hat, Papa.' Jayne crossed her arms over her chest.

'Tell her she may not have it,' Alice pleaded, then clamped her lips in a pout.

Clement looked at Vivienne, eyes narrowed in question, but the corners of his mouth twitching up ever so slightly.

'Three times the amount?' he asked. 'That hat?'

'Your governess stole it from me. I had it on my head yesterday and she robbed me of it. I cannot believe this woman is in charge of Jayne and Alice. It will not do.'

'No, she didn't steal it, Papa,' Jayne said.

'Our aunt is telling a fib.' Alice's mouth fell open in apparent shock at hearing such a blatant lie.

'Miss Curtis, would you mind taking the girls inside?' Clement asked. 'And if you will, please let Mrs Prentis know she has unexpected guests for tea.'

'Come along, girls,' Vivienne called on an inner well of composure, reminding herself that she was a lady. Well-bred ladies never flouted their social position. A lesson the new baroness had clearly yet to learn. 'Perhaps Mrs Prentis will have a treat for you.'

Vivienne would need one, too, along with a few moments to gather herself. She would never have dreamed that abandoning her position in society for the summer would be so difficult. Until this moment she had not fully appreciated having it.

* * *

'Well,' Mildred stated, rising from the couch in the parlour. 'Since there is no one to serve tea, I suppose I shall do it myself. But where is that Mrs Prentis? One would expect her to do it.'

'I rent rooms at her inn. I do not pay for her social services.'

'I am only glad that Duncan and I are staying in Ventnor and not this uncultivated…' She waved her hand towards the window which had a beautiful view of the beach and dunes.

'Seaside?' he suggested. 'I find it as close to paradise as an entomologist can get.'

Mildred answered with a dismissive sniff.

'How have you been, Brother?' Duncan asked. 'You look well.'

'I am well. You would not believe what a boon this place is for my research.'

'It is all so silly, if you ask me. No one really cares about insects.'

'Mildred.' Duncan smiled at his wife in the doting way he had developed since his marriage. Seeing him like this made Clement miss the brother who had been a carefree bachelor. 'Clement is happy in his pursuit. We are happy for him.'

'But of course. Please do forgive me. We have not come to criticise. What we wish to do is discuss our nieces' futures.'

His gut clenched harder. Surely Mildred was not suggesting she and Duncan were equally accountable for his children. Until this moment neither of his brothers had been involved in any decision regarding them.

'I have their futures well in hand. You need not be concerned.'

'I am, of course. How are they to become proper young women without a woman's guidance? That woman you hired to be their governess will not do at all. I assure you, she is not a proper influence on them. Really, Clement, she was allowing Jayne to climb a tree!'

'It was Alice in the tree,' he pointed out.

'I do not doubt the governess is qualified or you would not have hired her,' his brother put in, taking a long sip of tea and smiling as if he enjoyed it. He'd always disliked tea. 'But I wonder if—'

'She must be terminated, naturally. Especially after the way she behaved towards me.' Mildred had an unattractive way of lifting her nose and sniffing to emphasise a point.

Clement set his teacup down too hard. Hopefully he had not cracked Mrs Prentis's china.

'I appreciate that you wish to help, Mildred.' He did not appreciate it. Her meddling was beyond annoying. 'But I will handle my daughters' affairs.'

'Your daughters?' There went Mildred's nose again, but this time her eyebrows shot up, too. 'They are our nieces. Ours as much as yours.'

Clement stood, agitation making it impossible to sit. When he found his voice, he addressed his brother in firm tones.

'What part did you play in raising them, Duncan? What gives you the right to claim any part of them?'

'My husband is the Baron and you are not. Really, it is not as if we wish them any harm.'

'Mildred!' For the first time Duncan looked perturbed by his wife's attitude. 'You must not use my position in the family against my brother. He has done an admirable thing in raising Alice and Jayne when Eldon and I were…

when we were finding our way. Clement always was the responsible one.'

'And I respect that, of course,' Mildred said. 'However, now that we see how things are with the children, we shall proceed with what we discussed.'

What they'd discussed?

'If you have had a private discussion regarding my family,' Clement said more coolly than he felt, 'I insist on being informed of it.'

'Tell him, Duncan.'

'Indeed, please do that, Brother.' Before his temper got the better of him and he said something he could never unsay.

'We all know the girls will need to take their place in society eventually,' his brother explained awkwardly. 'Make matches to enhance the family name and position. What we propose is, when the summer is over and we have finished our travels, that you bring the children to London. We will engage a highly qualified governess and they will be strictly trained by her to fulfil their roles.'

Nothing in his life had made him angrier than hearing someone else make plans for his children. To direct their lives as if they had a right to!

'My daughters will not do well in that environment.'

'They need to have their manners refined,' Mildred said, looking at Duncan. 'Many of the finest ladies have flourished under a strict governess, as I myself did.'

If there was ever an argument against such a course of action, Mildred had just presented it.

'My wife is correct, Clement. Rest assured we shall find the very best governess for them.'

Clement yanked the door open, needing to go out before he punched his brother. They were no longer children and fighting was not acceptable to settle a disagreement.

To his surprise, there was Vivienne. Had she been eavesdropping? No matter. He had never been so happy to see anyone in his life. Calmed somewhat, he uncurled his fists.

'I am sorry to interrupt, Mr Marston. Mrs Prentis is asking for you.'

'Tell her we are not finished with tea.' Mildred insisted, looking lofty in spite of the fact that she was seated.

Vivienne looked at him, brow lifted. She would stay if he wished her to was what the gesture indicated.

'You are dismissed.' Mildred nodded at Vivienne, who ignored her.

'Stay if you do not mind, Miss Curtis. The matter we are discussing involves the children, which in turn involves you.'

'Of, course.' It was good to have an ally who was willing to spy behind a door on his behalf. He was certain that she had been doing so. 'What about the children?'

'They are not thriving under your care, Miss, and so Baron Granville and I will find them a proper governess.' Mildred did not address herself to Vivienne, but to him. 'I fear that your governess will need to find another position.'

'Miss Curtis's position is secure. Now, we would like to get on with our day. Alice and Jayne have a bird's nest to place in a tree.'

'I will take the nest and my hat with me.'

'But it is not for sale, Mrs Marston,' Vivienne announced pointedly.

'Duncan, tell her to address me as Baroness Granville.'

'Finish your tea, Mildred.' At last Duncan sounded put out with his wife. Possibly regretting he'd married her. 'We must be on our way.'

'Very well, as long as we have an agreement on our

nieces' education.' Mildred set her tea cup on the tray and stood.

'We do not have an agreement. You are mistaken if you think you have any authority when it comes to my family,' Clement declared.

'Alice and Jayne are misbehaved hellions who need a much stricter hand.' Mildred reached for her reticule. 'Since they do not have a mother to do it, an older, more authoritarian governess it must be. They will be set straight within the first few months, I am sure.'

While he scoured his mind for a scathing defence of his children, a perfect rebuttal, Vivienne spoke.

'You are greatly mistaken, Baroness.' There was a quality to her voice when she pronounced the title that made it sound dismissive instead of respectful. 'They are sweet children who naturally took offence to a bird's nest being used for a decoration instead of a home for hatchlings as the Good Lord intended it to be.'

'I insist on having that hat. It ought to have been mine all along.'

'You may have it, and with my blessing. However, the nest will remain with Alice and Jayne.' Vivienne delivered the verdict with a genteel smile.

'This matter has gone awry,' Duncan said with a resigned sigh. 'Please do keep the bird's nest and the hat if it makes the girls happy. Now, to the matter of their futures. We all wish for what is best for them. Since they do not have a mother, I believe they need a lady of standing to guide them in society. My wife is willing to take on this responsibility. I am sure we are all grateful, my love.'

His sister-in-law responded with a preening smile.

'I would suggest that we wait on the decision about hiring a new governess until the autumn. We shall see then what you have done to make sure the children have had proper guidance as young ladies.' Duncan glanced between him and Mildred. 'Will you agree to that, Clement?'

'I agree that they should learn what they need to. I do not agree that they have to learn it from some stifling, old-fashioned tartar of a governess.'

'Put your foot down, Duncan. You are the Baron and the decision will be yours. Apparently your brother believes they can learn what they must under the guidance of a common governess with hardly any experience.'

'Baroness…' Again Vivienne's voice dripped with dismissiveness, as if, somehow, the position of governess was higher than that of a baroness. 'We have met only once before and so I do not expect you to understand what I am capable of teaching my charges. I assure you, Mr Marston does not need to have you engage a martinet to teach his children in order for them to learn how to act in society.'

Once Mildred found her voice she said, 'You, Miss Curtis, have a very superior attitude.'

'Indeed? It is something I was born with.'

Mildred opened her mouth, but closed it again without speaking.

Who was this woman? Holding her own, no…surpassing his sister-in-law, in 'superior attitude'. It left him dizzy.

Clement and his brother said their goodbyes, but rather awkwardly. Still, awkward was better than angry. If he let his true emotions rule, words would have been spoken which could not be recanted. Contrary words would only divide the family. Nothing would be accomplished by creating such a rift.

Alice and Jayne were his children and he did not mean to lose them to anyone.

Once the front door closed, Clement turned to Vivienne.

'Who are you?'

She looked down and then back up. She blinked. 'I am myself, of course. Your friend and partner.'

'It is good having a friend and partner. I admit that I have rarely faced a more challenging moment.'

Late in the afternoon, Vivienne took the girls back to the tree so that they might set the nest in place.

She wore the gaudy bonnet. Long purple ribbons fluttered behind her in the breeze. Flags of victory was what they were.

It had taken her last thread of self-restraint not to admit who she was and put Mildred Marston in her place. If she had, there would be no question of her ability to teach the girls what they needed to know about becoming society ladies. Her hands were rather tied about it, though, unless she wished to admit her grand deception to the Marston family. Unless she wished to face the scandal that would be sure to follow.

And it would not be only her it followed. There was Clement's reputation to be thought of. This would surely be the very excuse his brother and his wife needed to snatch the girls away to London. She must teach Alice and Jayne what they needed to know and do it as their governess. The thought of them being taken from their father and sentenced to a strict, unloving governess was too outrageous to even consider.

Also, she had a book to finish, a dream to fulfil.

More, she was not ready to give up her friendship with Clement. The last thing she wished was for him to know she was a deceiver. He would never look at her the same way again.

She very much liked the way he'd looked at her lately.

The interest in his gold-flecked gaze was not like anything she had ever seen before. Many gentlemen of her acquaintance considered her to be awkward, not interested in feminine matters. She was interested of course, only not in the things which usually appealed to society ladies, such as balls and fashionable gowns.

There was no reason whatsoever a lady could not be a proper woman while at the same time following her own pursuits.

Herein lay her dilemma when it came to the girls. She must teach them what society required of them and yet show them that they had worth of their own. That what they wanted for themselves mattered as much as what others wanted of them.

And she must do it in a very short amount of time. When summer ended, who knew what the attitude of the woman caring for them after her would be?

'Is that a good place?' Alice asked from up in the tree. 'Will it fall down?'

'It looks splendid,' she answered. 'Come down, now. We are going to play a game.'

'Will there be a prize?'

'Every proper game must have one. But it will not be easy to earn. Let's visit the shoreline where we can play the game before the sun goes down.'

'What sort of game?'

'I will teach you how to curtsy. Whichever of you performs it best will win.'

'But who will judge?'

'Your father, of course.'

Clement felt too unsettled go to his study and make notes regarding an interesting moth he had seen towards sunset last night.

It was unusual for him to be so worried about a matter that studying did not offer relief.

From the hallway window he saw the sun getting ready to set. It was pretty tonight, with clouds drifting slowly across. In a few moments the sky would turn pink and orange.

With the girls being entertained by Mrs Prentis, he decided to go outside, walk the sandy path over the dunes towards the beach. Blowing grass made whispering sounds in the breeze which tended to come up each evening. Nature's lullaby, it seemed to him.

Ah, good, he would not be alone on the beach. Vivienne sat in the sand, very likely seeking solace the same as he was. After the way Mildred had treated her, she was probably feeling belittled, although, she had not seemed belittled or even particularly offended.

'It's uncommonly pretty tonight,' he said. 'May I sit with you?'

She smiled and nodded, patting the sand beside her. A cool, moist breeze lifted a strand of her dark hair, blowing it across her face. She swiped it away with the back of her hand.

Maybe he should not sit here with her. The temptation to kiss her was pressing. If he indulged, she might very well feel she had to resign her position.

What would he do then? He needed her to care for his children for as long as she was willing to do so.

This afternoon she had taught them to make pretty curtsies. As nice as it was, they would need to learn far more than that in order to avoid Mildred's plan for them.

Settling in the spot beside Vivienne, he let go of his troubles in favour of the glory of the sunset.

He breathed…beauty in…worries out.

'That was a difficult position you put me in, earlier,' he remarked, but smiled so she would understand he was only teasing.

'Appointing you as judge of the curtsies, do you mean?' Brilliant clouds over the sea turned her cheeks pinker than they normally were. 'You made a wise decision, though. Jayne being the champion for grace, then Alice for precise execution. Everyone was happy.'

'I hope you have a few more skills to teach them. Not that I expect you to know as much as...'

He hesitated, then thought better of hinting that her skills might not be refined enough to please his sister-in-law. It would be unfair to expect her to know all that a lady born and bred would know...all the ins and outs of what it took to be presented to society.

Then again, his governess was rather a mystery... Who had she been before she came to him? A shop girl? A merchant's daughter or a seamstress? No, definitely not. He'd wondered before if she might possibly be a gently bred lady, maybe from the lower echelons of society, who'd fallen from grace. But that didn't seem likely now as Mildred would probably have recognised her.

A well-educated vicar's daughter, then. It was the most likely explanation...or at least as good a guess as any.

'Do you think I should wed?' he asked after a moment, remembering that his lack of a wife had been mentioned in the recent argument with his brother and Mildred.

She caught a strand of hair whipping about her face, twirling it around her finger while she watched nature's show. It was as if the sky had caught fire.

'Well, it depends upon why you would be doing it, Clement. If it is because your children need a mother, perhaps... but be very careful who you choose. Do not sacrifice your own happiness. It will only make for an unhappy family in the end. If it is only to appease your family… I urge you not to wed for that reason only.' She was quiet for a moment, sifting sand through her fingers. 'But if you are in love… then by all means you should marry.'

'It all sounds so wise presented that way. Why then am I so confused?'

'Probably because there is so much at stake. Alice and Jayne's futures depend upon you making the right choices. I imagine there is no more difficult job than being a parent.'

'There is not.' But at the same time, none more rewarding.

'I admire you…choosing to become a father when you were barely grown yourself.'

'Ah, well. I will admit I did not fully know what I was getting into. In some ways I was as much a babe as they were. I don't know what would have become of us except for Miss Logan.'

'I have learned a great deal about her from the girls. I understand why they acted up when she left. In their eyes, she was their mother and so naturally they did not want anyone taking her place.'

'They don't want anyone taking your place, either.'

He ought to have left that unsaid. She had made it clear she was leaving at the end of summer. The problem was, he could not imagine his girls blossoming under another woman's care the way there were doing with Vivienne.

For a moment he got lost in thought. When, one day, he did get married, would there be any more of a sense of family than they already shared with this woman?

'I will confess, I have allowed myself to get more attached to them than is strictly professional. It is difficult not to when it comes to children.'

'Has it happened to you before? It must be hard on you, always leaving them behind to take another position.'

She did not answer with words, but gazed across the water, slowly shaking her head. He was far from a mind reader, but clearly she was dispirited over the prospect.

He caught her hand, gave it a squeeze. It seemed natural, not awkward. But then he brought her hand to his lips, kissed her fingers…and got sand in his mouth for his pains.

'Vivie…'

He should not push. She had her plans and was not willing to change them. And yet for his daughters' sake, he must ask again. But, no, that was not honest. It was for his sake, too.

Now that she had told him how fond she was of them, perhaps she would reconsider.

How to find the perfect words…

While he rummaged his mind for them, liked one and rejected another, she drew her fingers out of his, then she used one finger to brush the sand off his lips.

Her gaze was soft…could she be wondering, like he was, what a sand-dusted kiss would feel like? They were not stranded in a cupboard this time. Unlike before, she could resist his advances if she wished to.

For a moment life would be titillating, sublimely delicious. Then the kiss would be over. And if he saw regret in her eyes afterwards, it would be miserable.

Not only that, but what he needed to ask her was of more importance than a moment's elation…of knowing what a kiss with sand-chafed lips would feel like.

'Vivienne,' he said again. 'About your next engagement… would you not reconsider leaving? It would mean a great deal to us.'

Once again she sifted sand through her fingers. 'It is impossible, Clement.' Her expression transformed from soft to stricken. 'I cannot change my plans.'

'Surely you know how badly we need you, especially now.'

She closed her eyes, nodded. When she opened them, they were glistening.

'Ah, I'm sorry Vivie, I should not have pressed you. Please forgive me.'

'Yes, of course. If I could stay and help you, I would. But I simply cannot.'

It was nearly dark now so he almost missed seeing the single tear slipping down her cheek. He swiped it from her chin, stroked the shape of her jaw. It would be all too easy to swoop in for a kiss. Easy to do and hard to get over.

He dropped his hand. 'I will be grateful for whatever help you can give us before we must say goodbye.'

Dash it, why had he used those words. 'Goodbye' caught his gut and squeezed. Life was better since Vivienne had come rushing up his path seeking employment.

Imagining going back to life before her hit him hard. He feared he might not be the same man. What if his studies and explorations were no longer enough to satisfy him? Having shared them with her, they might not be.

'I suppose we should go inside. Mrs Prentis will have dinner waiting,' he said heavily.

He stood, reaching a hand down to her. She took it. Fine sand grated between their palms. Not a kiss, but nearly one in his mind.

Chapter Nine

Two days had passed since Vivienne had watched the sunset with Clement. Those stunning clouds had brought rain which went on and on.

Earlier in the day he had gone out in his raincoat and rubber boots, hoping to spot water-loving insects, he said.

Vivienne thought this was an excuse to get out of the house. Being used to the outdoors, he probably felt confined after two days of being inside.

Vivienne and the girls had kept themselves busy in the kitchen, helping Mrs Prentis prepare meals.

They had studied arithmetic and read books. Their lesson in etiquette had covered how to properly and elegantly hold eating utensils. But at ten years old, how vital was that?

In real life not terribly useful, but to keep from being consigned to a dragon of a governess, it was vital. Vivienne preferred real life where little girls were meant to have fun, not become small replicas of debutantes.

This was especially true for Alice and Jayne, being accustomed to living freely out of doors.

By the end of two days they were as restive as their father had seemed.

For all that they begged and pleaded to go out with him,

he would not allow them out in the elements. Chickenpox had been one illness too many for the summer. No matter how Alice pouted and Jayne scowled, he insisted they remain safely inside.

Which had made for an endless day for Vivienne.

But now here her charges were, tucked under their blankets looking as content as slumbering kittens.

She kissed Jayne, then turned and kissed Alice. She should not allow herself to indulge in this nighttime habit. She had also begun the ritual of stroking the hair back from their brows before she kissed them. There was something about stroking hair…it was such a tender gesture of affection. Indulging in it was only going to make it that much harder to say goodbye to them when the time came.

But that time was not now and so she would stroke those soft strands, kiss those smooth brows.

Rain pelted the window. She tucked the blankets around their shoulders and then looked through Clement's open doorway.

At last she was free to join him at his desk. She wondered if his outing had resulted in anything other than release from the indoors. Perhaps it had. He was bent over something on the blotter. He had a magnifying glass lifted to his eye even though he wore his glasses.

To her surprise, she was interested to see what the creature was. Incredible as it seemed, over the course of the summer, she'd lost some of her distaste for crawling creatures. Some of them were even pretty.

This one, for instance. It was such a pure white, it did not seem real.

'What have you found? Something for me to photograph?' she asked, peering over his shoulder. She liked looking at his treasures this way. It gave her an excuse to breathe in his scent, for one thing. He smelled like fresh sea air. It clung to him at all hours of the day, but only in this position could she fully appreciate it.

Also, this vantage point gave her a better look at the insect so that she could see how to best position it for a photo. It was acceptable to be this close to him in the name of research, of absorbing knowledge. And yet it was more than knowledge she was absorbing. It was memories. Each night brought her closer to the time she would be forced to leave him.

So she memorised the scent of his skin, the raspy feel of his wool coat…his breath which tended to come quicker when he was fascinated by a particular aspect of a many-legged creature.

Summer's end was creeping closer and she meant to hoard the things she loved about him for a day when she missed him.

'It looks delicate. What is it?' she asked.

'A White Plume moth.' He turned to smile at her. One more reason she liked standing over his shoulder. It always brought his smile so close that she could feel his delight. 'It must not have taken shelter in time. I found it in a puddle of water.'

'What a shame. It's beautiful. Those wings are so bright and reaching. Makes me think of a small dragon who has moonlight shining out of it.'

'Or an angel with her wings spread.' He glanced quickly away.

Not quickly enough that she did not feel a jolt of awareness zip through her. He meant the comment about her and not the insect.

He would look at her far differently if he knew the truth about her. That she was a deceiver, who had used his family to achieve her own goal. It would crush her heart to see him look at her with reproach. She must be very careful to make certain he did not discover who she really was.

The time was coming when all he would have of her was a memory. She needed it to be a good one. He must remember her with the same affection that she would remember him.

She sat beside him, watched him sketch.

'I think our book will be a great success,' she said. 'Your drawings and descriptions make it seem as if the moth will flutter off the page.'

'Your flattery will give me an inflated head. I have colleagues who are as talented. All of us wish to have our work published.' He set down his pencil, gave her a conspiratorial glance. 'But they will not have photographs.'

'Photographs will make the book unique, but your talent and your knowledge are what will sell it in the end.'

'I do hope so.' His gaze was soft, it nearly felt as though he touched her…as if his eyes were fingers stroking her hair, her cheeks and her lips.

'Teach me to draw the moth,' she said to cover the fact that she had reacted so intensely to a simple glance.

It would not do for either of them to look too closely at this friendship of a special nature thrumming between them. While they could not look directly at it, neither could they deny seeing it. The only thing to do was ignore it… to find ways of becoming distracted in moments of temptation.

Which was why she had asked to be taught to draw the moth, quite grateful it was something pretty and not a spider.

He handed her the pencil. 'Give it a try.'

She did. While his lines were precise and created an

image which was accurate in each fine detail, her line meandered, looking more like a worm than a moth.

'Here, hold the pencil just so...' He arranged it in her fingers, then drew her hand along under his. 'It isn't so hard. It only takes practice...and patience.'

He pressed her fingers so that they made strokes on the paper which gradually took the shape of a wing.

'At times you may not recognise what's coming into shape.' The line she drew under his guidance looked like a heart. One, two, three of them. To her eyes it was romantic. 'Then, all at once, what it's meant to be is revealed.'

The hearts became the slender body of the moth.

Slowly, he let go of her hand. 'You see?'

She did, more than he probably realised. Any tracing could have been used to form the moth's body.

'And now you must show me how to take a photo,' he stated. 'It is only fair to exchange lessons.'

Fair, yes, and fun. But now, with the household asleep and the cellar dark, it was also too risky. Temptation would far outweigh distraction.

At least for her it would.

'Yes, then. Tomorrow. It will be a thrill for Alice and Jayne to watch the magic happen.'

He nodded, holding her gaze for a second too long. What she read in his smile was only two of the words she had spoken.

Thrill and magic.

She was not overly experienced with flirtation nor, did she think, was he. Which could only mean, what they were seeing in the moment was truth. To be romantic with Clement would be a thrill, more magic than she had ever experienced.

She glanced away. So did he.

If she allowed him to look too deeply within her, he might see deep regret and sorrow. He might see the lies.

Feathers, there was no way he could do that. Still, even if she kept her secrets as tight as a miser kept his funds, one day the truth might be revealed.

Not today or tomorrow, though. She would probably make it through the summer keeping her secret.

Oh, but one day when the girls were older, Clement might return to society.

What if she and Clement saw one another at a social event…would he recognise her? The Marchioness of Winterfeld would look very different from his governess. She'd act differently, too.

But if they happened to meet and their gazes collided, he would surely know her. Know her to be a liar who'd taken advantage of him and his children and all for her own gain…for a summer free to follow her own dream.

Her dream, his nightmare.

'What is wrong, Vivienne?'

'Wrong? What could be?' Except that she was a wretch, deceiving everyone she cared for. 'I am only missing the sunshine. Perhaps tomorrow will be a brighter day.'

'Perhaps it will.'

Sunshine did return the next morning. So did his governess's normally cheerful attitude.

Her troubles of the night before must have run their course. While he was curious to know what had been bothering her, he would not press. Everyone had private matters which they wished to keep to themselves.

He certainly did, as much as anyone. Especially when it came to Vivienne.

While he had asked her to stay on more than one occa-

sion, he had claimed it was for the sake of the children…
mostly that was true. Far from the complete truth, though.
What would happen if he told her the rest of it? If he admitted that his affection for her was growing quite deep.

Would it make a difference if he confessed it? If he told
her that he believed they would work well as a family…
mother, father…

Husband, wife. Especially that.

Would she trade her next assignment for his heart?

He no longer questioned that she affected it in a way no
woman ever had. If things went very well, perhaps they
might one day find themselves in a love match.

Ah, but it was better not to look at that possibility too
closely. For now, surely it was enough to feel exceptionally fond of her?

Working together had shown him how well they got on.
If only she would open her mind to the idea, he was certain they'd be content. However, it was not her mind which
needed to be opened. It was her heart. How was he to know
which key to use to unlock it?

This afternoon, the four of them were to go to the meadow
and discover whatever interesting specimens the rain might
have unearthed.

Alice and Jayne would be happy for the outing since this
morning they would be spending their time in an etiquette
lesson. His suggestion to Vivienne had been that it should
be how to properly greet a gentleman.

She had laughed, reminding him that the way a ten-year-
old would greet a gentleman, if she even did, was far different than how a debutante would. In her opinion it was
inappropriate for them to be learning manners beyond their
age. Indeed, he agreed with her in that. He greatly feared

that other young girls in London were learning such things from their strict governesses.

If Mildred had her way, his girls would, too. Proper little society marionettes was what they would be. He only hoped that Vivienne had the skills to teach them enough to appease his sister-in-law.

If it came to it, he would fight his brother, but he'd probably lose. After all, a baron would always have his way over a younger son.

It did not bear thinking of how miserable his girls would be. They would rebel. Jayne might add moths to the governess's soup. Alice might put something crawly in her bed.

His brother might feel shamed if there was any gossip about how badly behaved his nieces were.

His sister's memory would not be honoured. Everything he had done in raising the girls had been out of love for Alice Jayne. He wanted to her look down from eternity and be reassured that her children were being well cared for.

Quite clearly, the girls must be raised at home with him, under the watchful eye of someone who loved and understood them.

Vivienne loved them, he was certain she did. He only hoped that she could teach them manners in the short time they had left with her.

Just now, he could see the three of them a short distance from the house where a swing was hanging from the branch of a tree. Alice was getting off the swing. Jayne took her place and laughed while she reached her toes for the sky, then swung back towards the ground and then up again.

The swing had not been there before the rain. It looked a great deal of fun which did not keep him from wishing it had not been installed. The time spent playing might be used in practising social greetings. Not only that, but children had been known to become injured on swings. Just like he had.

One day while trying to prove to his brothers that he was better at it than they were, he'd gone too high, then launched from the swing as if he were not subject to the law of gravity. It took a long time and a great deal of discomfort until his sprained ankle had healed. That was not the worst of it. His mother had the swing removed and ever after his brothers had blamed the lack of it on him.

Marching towards the laughter, he decided to follow his mother's example and take the swing down. Better to prevent an injury before it happened.

'Papa, look!' Jayne cried, flapping one arm. 'I can fly! I'm a butterfly!'

'Hold on to the ropes!'

'But she cannot flutter if she does,' Alice pointed out.

He tried not to be influenced by the joy both his children were experiencing. Joy they would not have in London if they were forced to live there.

'Vivienne, may I have a private word?'

She grinned, clearly enjoying the morning's play as much as the children were.

They stepped several feet away, but his eyes remained fixed on the swing. Perhaps he was too worried because of what had happened to him. Then again, danger was danger no matter how much fun it was.

'Where did that come from?'

'That? The swing, you mean? Mr Prentis brought it down from the attic. He remembered how his children used to enjoy it, so he set it up for Jayne and Alice.'

He might have grunted because Vivienne frowned at him. 'It was thoughtful of him, you must agree.'

Since he could not condemn their host's motives, he did not. 'Of course. I only worry about accidents.'

'We take a risk rising from our beds every day, Clement. We cannot control everything when it comes to our children.'

He blinked. Our children? She did not mean it quite that way, he was certain. Our children did not mean their children. More likely she used 'our' in the general sense.

'I suppose I feel more protective of them since Duncan and Mildred made their threat. If anything happens to Alice or Jayne, they might use it to say they would be better off living in London where they can keep a closer eye on them. Funny, but I never worried about them playing in the woods at home. Didn't have a swing, though.'

'You had a bridge with water running underneath instead.' She touched his arm, smiled. 'Do not worry. Alice and Jayne will not go to London. We shall make sure they do not.'

Then they ought to spend their time practising something, he nearly pointed out. Swinging would gain them nothing. Except fun...a childhood they could look back upon with smiles.

'I see what you are thinking.'

He shook his head. 'I don't know how you can. My thoughts are in my head...private.'

'Perhaps I cannot know them, then. But it doesn't change the fact that children need playtime as much as learning, otherwise they will not know how to play as adults.'

'Very well, that was something of my thoughts. You made a lucky guess. What am I thinking now?'

She studied his face, looking at him this way and that. He hadn't really had a thought in his mind when he'd offered the challenge. He did now. When her gazed settled on his mouth...he had something in particular on his mind.

'You are right. I cannot read your thoughts.'

Since she was blushing, he figured she might have read them perfectly well after all.

'Jayne, get off the swing. It is time to study manners,' he said.

'But I have not had my turn,' Alice complained.

'I saw you having a turn before I came over.'

'I have not had my third turn. It isn't fair if Jayne gets three and I only get two.'

It wasn't fair that they might have to act like small replicas of polished ladies, either. Not fair that the uncle who was baron would have more say in their upbringing than the one who was actually raising them.

Duncan and Mildred ought to be thinking of a family of their own and leave his family in peace.

'Come now, girls. Listen to your father,' Vivienne called. Then quietly to him, she said, 'You need to let Alice have another short turn.'

This wasn't something a hired governess would say to her employer. It was what a wife would say. Someone who was as equally invested in the children's well-being.

'I suppose you are right. Fair is fair. Alice, you may take your third turn.'

Vivienne's smile spoke of satisfaction in victory, but not without good humour. She gave him a playful elbow in the side. 'You are a wonderful father.'

And one day she would be a wonderful mother, only not, it seemed, for his children.

His chest felt heavy, knowing it was not ever to be.

'It just came up out of nowhere,' Mrs Prentis commented about the wind whipping around the corners of the house and huffing at the windows.

Black clouds, heavy with threat rolled in across the sea. A wicked-looking storm was aiming for the coast.

'It happens this way, every good while,' Mr Prentis announced. 'I wish our young ladies had picked a different day to go to the village.'

Clement, done with staring at the road and seeing no one on it, announced, 'I'm going to get them. Do you have a tarpaulin?'

'Oh, no, Mr Marston, you must not do that.' Mrs Prentis shook her head firmly. 'It is not safe to be out. And more likely than not, they have taken shelter at an inn in the village.'

More likely than not? That was no reassurance.

'I understand it is not safe. It is all the more reason to go out and fetch them.'

'I will get a tarpaulin from the attic right away. But my wife is right. While we stare out of the window wringing our hands, they are probably sitting beside a nice fire sipping cocoa.'

'And I shall make us a nice spot of tea.' His hostess bustled from the room.

Clement raced up the stairs to get his raincoat and rubber boots.

For all of their reassurance, Mr and Mrs Prentis had not successfully raised six children by drinking tea while their offspring were in peril.

Clement shrugged into his heaviest coat, dragged his boots out from under the bed and stepped into them. Snatching the blankets from his bed, he wrapped them up in his raincoat.

He glanced out of the window while rushing for the door. Dash it, but there was not much chance of getting to them before the downpour did.

In whatever condition he found his family, the blankets ought to be welcome.

The best outcome would be that he did find them waiting out the storm at an inn. In that case, they would have dry blankets to offer him.

Considering how the weather had been bright and pleasant one moment and then a freakish wind sweeping a storm onshore the next, reason would indicate that Vivienne and the girls had been caught unawares.

He knew what time they'd meant to leave the village for home. According to his calculations, they would be halfway between there and here.

Running down the stairs, then across the hallway, he caught the scent of tea.

'You really mustn't go,' Mr Prentis advised, but he handed him the tarpaulin anyway.

'Keep the tea warm for our return, my friend.' That said, Clement closed the door.

Gusts of wind fought his progress down the steps. It whipped left, then right. Once on the drive he had to lean into it in order to fight his way forward to the road.

Luckily, he was still ahead of the rain. Not by much, he figured. Glancing back towards the shore, he saw a wall of rain dumping from clouds which looked an odd shade of green. The downpour could not be more than a quarter of a mile away.

Acres of grass pressed flat to the ground. Wind hissed around his ears. Even this far from the shore he heard waves pounding on the beach. They had to be huge.

He pushed harder. No normal storm, this, it was working up to be a beast—a beast which would not consume his family.

* * *

He was about halfway to the village when the first splatter of rain slapped the back of his neck.

A moment later he spotted the Prentis wagon. The horse stood with his head bent to the wind, his mane whipping madly about. The good beast was making a valiant effort to hold his stance against the wind.

But where were Vivienne and the girls? Not in the wagon.

He glanced about, but did not see them. His stomach churned at how dim the afternoon light was becoming.

It was only when he was close enough to pat the horse's flank and praise his courage that he spotted them.

They had taken cover underneath the buggy. Vivienne must have decided it was a safer place to be than on top. There was some shelter there, but not much.

The worst of the rain was nearly upon them. He could see a line of water advancing across the land. The air had an unnerving tint to it. It was the same murky green shade as the clouds.

The horse was beginning to look nervous. Poor beast. There was nothing to be done for him until the storm blew over.

Clement checked the wagon brake, relieved to see that Vivienne had thought to set it. If the horse panicked and ran, the result might be disastrous. With the wind rocking the wagon and a sense of violence in the air, it was not out of the question.

Peering under the wagon, he only saw Vivienne. In the instant that fear crushed his belly, he spotted the tops of his daughters' heads. Vivienne had them wrapped up in her skirt. A hen protecting her chicks. Vivienne's face was hidden by a shawl she had drawn over her head so she was not aware of his approach.

Ducking under the wagon, he touched her shoulder. She jerked, startled. And then she wrapped her arms around him, squeezing tight. Next, his daughters were hugging him, too.

Rain dumped from the sky all at once. It seemed as though they sat within a waterfall. So far it was dry underneath the wagon, but it would not be for long. He hadn't much time to fashion the shelter he had been planning while he looked for them.

On his knees, he scrambled to unwrap the blankets.

He spread the raincoat on the ground, indicating the girls and Vivienne should sit on it. His hope was that it would keep them dry from beneath while the tarpaulin would do the job from above.

He draped blankets over Vivienne and the girls.

Next, he snapped the tarp open. It seemed a good thick one so his plan might work.

Vivienne moved under the blanket, settling the children on each side of her. He draped the tarp over their heads, tucking the ends under the raincoat.

As makeshift tents went, he thought this one might just hold.

Then he crawled under, tucking the loose ends beneath himself.

The wagon creaked, the horse snorted. For now they were dry and safe. He had done what he could. All that was left to do was pray that the wind did not upset the wagon and the horse did not panic.

'We knew you would come to get us, Papa,' Alice said.

'I am your father. I will always come.'

'That is what Miss Curtis told us. Those very words.'

Had she? It touched him, knowing that.

'It's not scary any more,' Jayne said, snuggling closer against Vivienne.

He was sitting next to Alice and he reached out and gave her shoulders a squeeze. It was warm under the tarp, too, with all four of them to ease the chill.

'What shall we do to pass the time?' Vivienne asked, her voice whispery under the canvas.

'Practise sums,' he suggested, smiling at the moan he knew would follow.

'It is Miss Curtis's day off from teaching us things. It is our day for fun.'

'Ah, then we shall tell stories,' he suggested brightly, even though bright was the last thing he felt.

The truth was, he was worried. The wagon rocked harder. The tarp snapped around their heads…wind blew more fiercely.

'I'm a little bit scared.' Jayne pressed closer to her governess.

'I'm not scared.' Alice announced. It might be because she was wedged between him and Vivienne and therefore had an illusion of safety.

'Tell us a story about someone brave, Jayne,' he suggested.

Jayne told a tale of the bravery of the horse standing stout-heartedly against the storm.

'Your turn, Alice,' he said.

Alice told of how brave Mr Prentis was when he'd climbed the tree to put up the swing.

While they talked, he began to think the tent would hold. He relaxed somewhat and the others seemed to also.

Alice's story went on for a while and Jayne fell asleep during it.

'How long will this last, Papa? It's dull with nothing to do. Then having said so, Alice fell asleep, too.

How content they looked with their heads resting on

Vivienne's bosom. Oddly enough, there was nowhere he would rather be than here, in this moment. Again, he had a sense of them being a family. It was nearly impossible not to wonder what could be if Vivienne was not set on leaving them.

'We've lost them, it seems,' he said quietly to Vivienne. 'Tell me your story of someone brave.'

Perhaps he would discover something about her father, perhaps? A former love? He really knew very little about her other than that she had a married sister. There was nothing he would like more than to know about her life away from here. But, no…he would be patient and in time she might confide in him.

'I have a daring tale of bravery to tell, Clement.' She snuggled closer to him, whether by choice or necessity, it was hard to know. 'I met a man once, the bravest I have ever met. He carried me through swirling water to take me and my camera to safety when I was stuck on a rock.'

'That was brave…your heart must have been aflutter over his courage,' he added in the light-hearted spirit of her story.

'Oh, it was. But he did something even braver than that.'

Now wasn't this a pleasant way to pass the time, hearing his praises being sung by a desirable woman. Even though he still heard fierce rain pelting the tarp, he did not mind so much.

'Braver than rescuing you from an incoming tide?'

'Oh, much braver. You see, this hero took orphaned children to his heart. He loves them as if they were born to him. He has as kind and loving a heart as any man I ever met.'

The story was getting better by the moment. He waggled his brows. 'And I suppose he is a handsome fellow, to go with all that gallantry.'

She could not properly turn, being pressed on all sides by his children. Nor could she reach her hand from under the blanket without disturbing their fragile shelter.

What she did do was slide her fingers over, press them on his chest where his heart was going through some odd manoeuvres.

'His eyes are an interesting colour, green and brown mixed with nice gold flecks in them. And his mouth…' She looked at his lips for a moment as if she were waiting for them to move, to say something. Not that he would know what to say even if he could speak in the moment.

'His lips are funny…at times they do not know whether to smile or frown.'

'It's because this brave fellow does not know what to do with them in certain circumstances. Laugh…or kiss.'

'Kiss, Clement. I would say this moment calls for one… but only one.'

'Two would not be prudent, I agree.'

She nodded and touched the button on his shirt. She rubbed it with her thumb.

So, before the moment passed, before real life invaded the intimacy of their canvas shelter, he kissed her once. And then again, despite everything, because it seemed that once was never enough when it came to Vivie.

A thousand or a million might not be either. Not for a woman—this woman—that he was in love with… Denying that he loved her, as he had been doing, was useless. The truth was the truth…and it broke him a bit.

What was he to do, fight for her? Let her go away as she intended to do? Watching her eyes, her lids still closed in pleasure, he nearly wept because the conclusion he came to was no conclusion at all. The reality was, there was very little he could do.

When she opened her eyes and gazed up through the dim light cast by the canvas, he gulped down a welling pressure in his throat. He was as certain that he loved her as if he had researched the matter all his life.

There was no going back from it.

Chapter Ten

What? My word… Vivienne could not believe she had fallen asleep. But here she was waking up, so apparently she had.

Well, then…show her a lady who would not lay her head on her hero's shoulder and drift away to sweet dreams?

He had a strong shoulder, a manly one. She'd shifted position so that her head now lay in the pillow-like area between his collarbone and his throat.

It was dark now and she could not see who was awake and who was asleep. But judging by the sound of their even breathing, everyone was asleep.

It was no longer raining, nor was wind flapping the canvas as it had done for the past few hours.

The storm had passed.

At least the storm outside the tarpaulin had. There was another one still doing considerable mischief and it was inside her. This storm was not so easily waited out. It tossed her emotions every which way, leaving her confused…and at the same time content.

What a mess she had found herself in after allowing him to kiss her again. Feathers…not allowing, but encouraging. She had all but demanded a kiss…and then received two. If she was to make it to the end of the summer without breaking hearts, she would need to do better than this.

She wriggled, sat up straighter. While it would be ever so nice to continue sleeping entwined like a litter of puppies, it was quite wrong to let the horse shiver in the dark.

'Clement.' She poked him in the chest. He stirred, sat up straighter. 'The rain has passed. We should go.'

She jostled Alice, then Jayne.

'Mama?' Alice blinked her eyes.

For a second, Clement's expression looked stricken. He must have thought of his sister, perhaps reminded of all she had missed by dying.

'No, dear. It is me, Miss Curtis.'

'She had a dream again,' Jayne explained. 'She always dreams you are our mama.'

'Come now.' Clement lifted the tarp off them. The air was suddenly cooler. 'We should get home. Mr and Mrs Prentis will be worried.'

Emerging from under the wagon, they found the ground to be a mass of puddles.

Clement unhitched the horse. Pulling the wagon through deep mud would burden the beast who had already stood out in the storm for too long.

They walked towards the inn, Clement leading the horse and Vivienne holding the children's hands.

The sky was black but spangled with stars. They walked for a very long time with no one speaking.

'I wonder what time it is?' Vivienne said, at last. There was no way of knowing for certain how long they had been sheltering under the wagon.

'The stars indicate it is about....' He was silent for a moment, glancing up, pointing his finger at this group of stars and then moving his finger left and up. 'Eight-seventeen.'

'About that? Eight-seventeen seems fairly precise.' Walking in the dark with a scientific man had its advantages.

'Give or take a few minutes. No, I'm just jesting with you. I've got a watch. I wonder if Mrs Prentis has held dinner for us. I hope so.'

Such an interesting man…completely heroic…she had meant every word of her story. At the same time he was practical…thinking first thing of his appetite once the danger passed.

If only she had not agreed to marry Everett. The more she got to know Clement, the more of her heart he took. Day by day she regretted giving her word to become engaged.

Not that she, a prime conquest in the marriage mart, would be allowed to wed an untitled man. Feathers…she was of an age to wed whomever she wished to in the eyes of the law. But she knew well that marrying a man who had no title of his own would severely disappoint her father, who'd always had his sights set very high for his daughters.

More than that, her marriage was supposed to unite the families, fulfilling Great-Aunt's dearest wish.

Oh, but Alice had called her Mama. No title could be grander than that one. In a choice between Mama and Marchioness, she would pick Mama every time. She wasn't going to be allowed to pick, though. No more than she was allowed to pick a career.

What she ought to do was rebel. It was in her nature to do so.

Feathers. What a muddle since she'd been raised to be obedient to her father. Her father who, in turn, had been raised to be mindful of the dictates of society.

If only she had been born to a different family. But even then that might not have done her a bit of good when it came to wedding Clement…who, she reminded herself, had not even hinted at a proposal, only requesting that she remain in his employ.

She directed her mind back to her first thought. Even if she was from a well-established but untitled family, Clement might not wed her. Being the brother of a wealthy baron, he'd be unlikely to wed his children's governess. Not that such a thing had never been done. It happened rather frequently in romantic novels.

Feathers...feathers...a mattress full of feathers! What a mess she had got herself into. It was only by a thread in a tattered, old coat that she was not falling in love with Clement Marston. At any point the thread might break and then what would she do? Wed one man while in love with another?

It might work for some ladies of society, but not for her.

If only she could be more like Clement. How fine it would be to go through a storm and then have her first thought be of a warm dinner.

So much easier than—

'Papa, my feet hurt. Carry me,' Jayne complained.

'No!' Alice whined. 'Mine hurt more. Carry me.'

'You are too old for being carried. But here, give me your hands.'

They dashed to their father. He handed the reins off to Vivienne. She walked a few paces behind, thinking what a sweet sight they were.

'I don't like being too big to carry,' Alice muttered.

Clement picked up her hand, kissed it. Then he kissed Jayne's hand.

'But I do carry you. Right here in my heart. Always.'

And then he turned about, gazing through the dark at Vivienne.

She thought she saw sadness in his eyes...and longing.

She might be mistaken, though. It was dark after all. But she was not mistaken about the sadness and longing in the smile she gave him back. Right then, the thread in that old coat broke. She was irrevocably in love with Clement Marston.

What a fortunate thing Clement and his children walked ahead of her. The only one who knew she was silently weeping was the horse.

He whickered, nudged her in the arm.

'I do not suppose you have any advice for me?' she whispered.

He blinked his great brown eyes, but naturally had nothing to confide.

The situation she had got herself into, she must now get herself out of. And she had no idea how to do it. Grace, the one person she could confide in, was in Europe, mailing letters meant to deceive their parents.

By the time the inn came into sight with its welcoming lamps aglow in the windows, she had managed to stuff her heart back into its proper place. Her eyes were dry and she had gathered the fortitude to continue with what she must do for the remainder of the summer.

More, for what she must do when it ended.

The problem for her now was how to go away without breaking hearts. As far as her own went, it was too late… it would simply have to stay broken.

But the children's hearts? She nearly wept anew.

Alice had called her Mama. Mamas were not supposed to go away and yet the girls had lost two already. The one who'd given birth to them and their first nurse. Imagining how they would feel when they lost her, too, was nearly too much to bear.

And Clement? She believed she had seen something in that last glance of his, too.

What a mess she had made of everything. When summer ended, she would have caused such damage. And if she did not leave, what about her parents and Great-Aunt Anne? They were rejoicing at the prospect of her marriage to Everett. The only one who would not be affected was Everett. He was only fond of her. No one languished over losing fondness.

When they were several yards from the front door, Mr and Mrs Prentis rushed out, looking relieved to see them safely returned.

'I am so grateful to see you, my dearies.' The couple hurried down the steps. 'We were so worried. Come in to dinner now. I've kept it warm.'

Mrs Prentis bustled them inside, resembling a hen flapping after her chicks.

'We are relieved to have you home safe.' Mr Prentis clapped Clement on the back and then took the horse's reins from Vivienne.

Home. She could not say she had ever felt more at home anywhere than she did here. It had been said that home was where the heart was. But soon she and Clement would part ways. If the saying was true, her heart would remain here. This place, these people, would be a moment out of time for ever. Nothing was ever going to be the same again.

She gave herself a good shake. So much drama within one's heart could drive her to despair if she wasn't careful.

If this was all the time she had left with Clement, she did not intend to spend it morosely. Indeed, it had never been in her nature to be a gloomy puss.

She had a job to do. Teach the girls to be little ladies so that Clement would not be separated from them. That would simply not happen, not while she was in charge.

And as for the book, she had a job to do there, too.

Wasn't it wiser to live in the moment and take what joy one could from it? Of course it was. Why take misery from a future which had not even happened yet?

With her mind settled, she gathered her resolve and declared, 'I am so glad you were right about dinner waiting for us, Clement. I am quite hungry all of a sudden.'

'As am I,' he said with a look in his eyes which did not seem to relate to the prospect of a warm meal.

Joy in the moment, she reminded herself.

The look could go nowhere as far as a future went.

This, though, was not the future, it was now, so she allowed herself to fall into his gaze.

Clement was grateful for his family's safe delivery from the storm. Last night he had lain in bed counting his blessings, but fallen asleep before he came to the end of them.

Now that it was day, worries crept back. He stood on the porch, watching the grass on the dunes gently swaying.

Yesterday, while under the tarpaulin, two things had happened. One, Alice had dreamed of Vivienne being her mother. It seemed that, once again, his poor child was headed for heartbreak when it came to losing the women in her life. He hoped that when Vivienne left them, it would not be like when Miss Logan had.

He was not certain he could manage their tears again. And he pitied the woman who tried to fill their governess's shoes.

It did not make him feel good, realising that as his daughters grew, he might no longer be enough for them. Perhaps had they been boys, he would have been. But girls needed a mother.

He tapped his fingers on the porch railing, absorbed in

thought. He was in love and he didn't yet know if it was an affliction or a blessing.

Poets had written thousands of words on the wonder and the misery of falling in love. Until now he had thought them a bit dim-witted. Now here he stood, feeling as dim as a fellow could get. How was it possible to feel elated and deflated in the same breath?

What he really needed to do was speak with Vivienne. Find out what was so pressing about her next engagement. If he knew what it was, he might convince her to change her mind.

He wondered—would telling her he loved her make a difference?

It might not go in his favour if he did. It was a fact that she responded well to his kisses…indeed, she seemed as overcome by them as he was. And yet in every instance it had not served to draw them closer, but more distant.

Last night had been no exception. He had waited for her to come to his chamber so they could work on the book, but her bedroom door had remained shut.

It might be that the events of the day had worn her out. That was what he'd like to think, but had he not kissed her, he thought she would have come.

What had come over him? He had been determined not to kiss her again, yet he had done it without hesitation. He would like to put the blame on water and on being in danger, as both times he had kissed her, those elements had been present.

What, though, was more pointless than lying to oneself? For a researcher, factuality was everything. He must speak to Vivienne…now.

It might be difficult to get her alone since she was no doubt instructing the children in how to act in any given social situation. Each day that passed made him more concerned that Vivienne would not have time to teach them enough to satisfy Mildred.

He would like to believe that having acted as their father all their lives he would prevail in an argument with Duncan. Regrettably, his brother had two things which he did not. A title and a wife.

There was nothing he could do about the lack of a title.

But a wife? He could wed.

Vivienne had advised him not to do so unless he was in love. And here he found himself…in love with her. Her social position might not be acceptable to some, but for the most part, he doubted society would give whom he wed a thought.

More, he did not care if they did.

Clement looked for Vivienne and the girls in the study, but they were not there. Good, then, it was for the best if they spent their time learning to use a fork or make a curtsy. Reading and arithmetic could wait.

Walking back through the parlour, he paused to look out of the window. Maybe Vivienne had taken them outdoors for a lesson.

'Are you looking for Alice and Jayne?' he heard Mrs Prentis ask from behind him.

He turned, smiling. 'Indeed I am.'

'Miss Curtis has taken them down to her darkroom.'

'Ah, thank you.'

Darkroom? Was there really time to be time to be indulging in their governess's passion when it was etiquette they needed to learn?

As interesting as the process was, Mildred would not be impressed that the girls knew how to coax a photograph from a plate of glass.

Coming down the cellar steps, he heard Jayne's voice.

'I don't want to learn manners. They are dull.'

'You must learn them, though. One day you will take your places in society.'

'I want to be an entomologist like Papa.' Jayne's statement warmed his heart, but saddened it, too. His daughter might wish to follow in his footsteps, but her 'occupation' had been determined at her birth.

'I think that is wonderful. You must have something that is your own.' Vivienne stated. 'Something apart from what will be asked of you when you are grown ladies. You must never give up who you are.'

What? It sounded as if she was encouraging them to reject their future roles. Just because a governess was allowed such freedom, did not mean the nieces of a baron would be.

As much as he wished it was the case, it was not. The world they must live in was what it was.

'I don't want to be a lady,' Alice said.

'But you will be. And there are many rules to learn. It is important to pay careful attention to everything I have to teach you.'

Oh, good. He had misunderstood. The fist gripping his middle eased.

'I would rather learn to take photos like you do.' Alice said. 'It seems like magic.'

'Only chemicals. But it is fulfilling. Which is what I meant when I said you should find something of your own. Something that fulfils you while you are going about the rest.'

'Curtsies are not fulfilling.'

'But they can be. Performed just the right way…if you challenge yourself to make each one more perfect than the next.'

'Mine will be better than yours, Jayne. That will be fulfilling.' Although he could not see his daughter's expression from his shadowed hidey-hole on the stairs, he knew she would be making a face.

'No, it won't! Mine will be.'

'Here is what you must keep in mind. Your father has asked you to learn manners. He deserves for you to try your best. He loves you both very much.'

Alice and Jayne did not know what was at stake for them. How was one to tell a child such a thing?

'We shall both make perfect curtsies then.'

'For Papa. We love our papa…' Alice said.

'Do you love him, too?' Jayne asked.

Clement nearly choked on his breath even though it was not possible to do so. Clearly his little matchmakers were making another attempt to have Vivienne as their mother, bless their yearning little hearts.

'I admire your father. He is a good man.'

'But you should love him,' Alice said. 'He loves you.'

He should not stand here, breath lodged in his throat, eavesdropping. And yet…how was Vivienne going to answer that?

She did not, but instead swished a glass plate in chemicals.

'You could be our mother if you married our papa,' Alice said, her voice gone soft.

'One day you will have a mother and you will love her very much.'

'Not as much as you,' stated Jayne.

'Come now, girls, let's go up to the kitchen and see if Mrs Prentis has made anything we can have as a treat.'

Not wishing to be caught on the stairs, he quietly went back the way he had come.

Then, standing several feet from the cellar stairs, he made it appear that he was only just walking towards them.

'There you are!' he exclaimed. 'I have been searching for you.'

'We watched Miss Curtis make picture magic.'

'That sounds as if it was fun. Now, you may take an hour away from your lessons while I have a word with Miss Curtis.'

Whatever conversation Clement wished to have with her, he asked to have it while they walked along the shore.

With the storm having moved on, the weather was ideal. One of those days when the breeze brushed softly against one's face and waves sweetly lapped the beach. Not like yesterday when they'd pounded like a furious beast.

Not like yesterday when emotions had pounded her heart. She felt better about everything today. Or she had until Alice and Jayne said their father loved her.

Of course, they were children who wanted a mother. No doubt they were seeing what they wished to see.

The last thing she wanted was for him to love her. It was the first thing she wanted as well…but it simply could not be.

They walked for quite a distance without Clement coming to the point of this stroll.

'What is it you wished to speak with me about, Clement?' Someone must begin.

Her guess was that he wondered why she had not come to his room to help with the book last night. She had been simply too raw inside, not that she could admit it.

'Do you mind if we sit?' He gestured to a sandy mound several feet from where waves lapped at the shore.

'I do not mind.' Sitting in the sand was one of the things she had come to enjoy this summer.

He was quiet for so long that it became uncomfortable. Extended silence was rare between them. Most of the time, conversation came as easily as breathing.

'Look at that, Clement. There is an unusual butterfly. What is it?' Perhaps casual chit-chat was what he needed to warm up to what he wanted to speak with her about.

He did not look at the pretty creature fluttering about her skirt, but rather into her eyes.

Intently into her eyes, as if he were trying to see secrets which she meant to keep to herself. No one would be better off if he knew she loved him.

'I have asked before and now I am asking again. Vivienne, please stay beyond the summer. The girls…they need you. I—'

'But you know I cannot,' she said quickly to keep this from going any further. 'I am committed to…to my next assignment.'

Which was exactly what it felt like…an assignment. One which she would be fulfilling for the rest of her life.

'Whatever your next employer is willing to pay, I will triple it.'

'It is not the money. I have an obligation.'

'What can I say to change your mind?'

Or do, was the clear intention in his eyes. Gold flecks in the green glimmered with purpose.

But, feathers! Kissing would only lead to worse trouble.

'You know how deeply I care for Alice and Jayne. Surely you do. But I cannot stay. It is impossible. Nothing has changed.'

'Hasn't it?' He touched her hair, drew it back over her

ear. He stroked the curve of her cheek. 'How deeply do you care for me?'

'Deeply enough, Clement. You know I do.'

She looked away so that he could not read how deeply. Those few words confessed too much as it was. She must make an attempt to amend them.

'I have not had a better friend. I admire you as a father and as a colleague. I am grateful you have allowed me to help you with your book.'

'Our book now.' He turned her chin back towards him. Unable to look away, she glanced down.

Under no circumstances must he see her heart in her eyes.

'Yes, our book. I will always think fondly of our time working on it.'

'On our time…or on me?'

'Both, of course.' She made her voice sound crisp. If she used the tone coming from her soul, it would be too soft with affection, he would surely recognise love.

'My children need—'

'A mother? Yes, I heard Alice say so.'

'Vivie, what she said is that she wanted you.'

It would be so much easier to utter the words she must if he had not called her Vivie. The endearment never failed to make her want to hand over her heart…as if she had not already done so.

'I am certain they will have a devoted mother when the time is right.'

'Look at me, Vivie, and tell me the time is not now.'

He leaned forward as if he would kiss her…prove to her that it was, that they were—

No! She could not! Standing quickly, she shook the sand from her skirt.

The children had not been wrong when they claimed he loved her. She could not stand here, looking at him and not believe it. Even if she had not been looking, there was no denying the longing each felt, one towards the other.

'Now is not the time,' she said, tears swelling her throat.

'Now' would never be the time for her. Love was not in her future. Everett was. He would never care for her this way, no more than she would him.

If she walked away without letting Clement declare his love, she would never hear it from anyone else.

Then she fled, kicking up sand behind her. She could not hear one more word from him or everything would be ruined. Once he offered her his heart there would be no postponing what must be done. As it stood now she could pretend she did not know, carry on as before...work on the book, teach the children.

Stopping at the foot of the inn steps, she pressed one hand to her middle, caught her breath. What she must remember was that staying, especially in the way he hinted at, would only result in Clement knowing she had deceived him all this time.

There was no way possible for her to join this family without them knowing who she really was.

When they did, they would not want her...a woman who was deceiving not only them, but her own family as well. What, really, was the importance of pleasing herself for the summer in comparison to Alice's and Jayne's deep need for a mother?

She did not deserve their affection.

Chapter Eleven

Clement stood on the path to the shore, insect jar in hand.

His attention was not on insects. It was on watching through the large parlour window while Alice and Jane competed with one another to perform a perfect curtsy.

At least competing was what he assumed they were doing. The window was open to the warm afternoon air and he heard the three of them laughing.

Laughing…while he had been going through his days, a man in misery disguised as a cheerful one.

Three days had passed since Clement had nearly revealed his heart to Vivienne. In part it had been an attempt to convince her, once again, to stay with them. But also because he simply needed for her to know it. Needed to know if she returned his love.

For a moment he'd thought, yes, she must. But in the next she'd called them friends…colleagues…and had run for the house when he was on the verge of pressing his suit.

There was nothing for it but to smile through his confusion. He would not let on how perplexed the encounter had left him.

Insects. He reminded himself they were the reason he was standing on the beach with a jar in his hand. What he needed to do was delve into the quest for one more perfect specimen. Exploring ought to set him to rights.

One exquisite insect was all they needed in order to finish the book. Quite soon it ought to be ready to send to a publisher.

Before he decided which direction to go in search of the perfect insect, the front door opened, then closed. Jayne tiptoed down the porch steps and across the yard. She gave the parlour window furtive glances while she dashed for the tree where the swing swayed in the breeze.

He had his mouth open to call her to account when Vivienne lifted the window and peered out.

'Alice Marston!' she called. 'That is not the way to the water closet!'

Head down, his daughter walked back inside the house. The sight of her pout gave him the first chuckle he'd had in hours.

Turning towards the west side of the inn, he decided to see what he could find in the meadow.

Last week he'd thought it would be a fine thing to join Vivienne in her darkroom. He'd been curious to see how a small plate of glass could reveal the image of an insect.

No longer, though. Now, being alone in the dark with Vivie? His mind would not be on glass plates and that was a fact.

He forced his attention away from what it would be on. Focused it on what it should be on.

What he needed was an insect so fascinating, so absorbing, that he would not be aware of Vivie working closely beside him at the desk, would not feel the tickle of her hair or the scent of her skin while she peered over his shoulder.

'If you exist, make yourself known,' he announced to whatever creatures called the meadow home.

Not so much as a rustle of leaves.

He found himself watching a bird circling, dark against a bright blue sky.

Which meant he was not absorbed in the hunt.

How could he have guessed a time would come when his daughters and his research were not all he needed in order to be fulfilled?

Now he needed his daughters' governess.

To his everlasting regret she, quite clearly, did not need him.

Vivienne sat at her dressing table, drawing a brush quickly through the tangles she had acquired during the day. Over the summer she had not learned to style her hair properly, so she'd continued to wear it loose or fastened at the back of her neck with a bow. She found she liked it better this way than swept up in stiff curls.

When she went back to her old life, her maid would style a stiff pile of curls on her head. If she attempted to wear it free and swinging, there would be no end to the talk.

If only she did not have to go back. But moan and groan as she might, nothing would change.

Between now and when she left, she would put on a happy face. No one else needed to suffer because she was miserable. If she was caught in a web of lies, it was of her own making.

She rose, went to her chamber door. Before she opened it, she set her smile in place.

It took only a moment to walk across the children's bedroom to Clement's door, even stopping to kiss foreheads and wonder what they were dreaming about.

Night by night it took nearly more fortitude than Vivienne could muster to join him at his desk.

She did it, though. Living her dream was the reason she had become a governess and she would not leave her post before her time was up.

Even though Clement's door was open, she knocked.

He stood at his desk, bent at the waist while he peered at a specimen.

Adjusting his glasses, he waved her in without looking up.

It was just as well that he was standing since she did not think it wise to watch over his shoulder tonight.

'Here, have a look,' he said, standing to the side. 'I found this in the meadow today. I would have enjoyed seeing it flutter about, but it was dead when I came across it.'

'What is it?'

'Garden Tiger…a moth. I spread the wings so you can see the orange it displays when it is frightened.'

'How beautiful. I hate to think of it being frightened.'

'Do you?' She had to catch her heart when he gave her that flat, turned-up-at-the-corners smile. 'At the beginning of the summer, you would have squashed it. You've come a long way. I am proud of you, Vivie.'

Was he…truly?

At this point there was no use in asking him not to call her Vivie. Bringing it to his attention would only serve to emphasise the endearment. She was trying so hard not to look too closely at the affection they withheld from one another.

'No, I would not have squashed it!' she protested, but he was likely correct, she would have.

'Do you recall the Speckled Bush cricket when we first met? You would have done the poor girl in if you could.'

But he had stopped her from harming it and they'd ended up on the floor together. And she had become employed.

'Yes, well… I would not do it now.'

He arched a brow, looking playful. This felt right. Like who they were supposed to be. Neither of them was typically full of anxiety.

He was quiet for a second, watching her smile. His attention clearly focused on her lips. Then he blinked, the intensity in his gaze vanishing. The tingle on her mouth remained.

'This is the last one we needed to complete our book.' He tapped his finger next to the moth. 'Once you take your photograph all our information will be gathered. We only need to put it in a sensible order.'

'Here, then. I will take her photograph now. Would you like to come and watch it develop?'

'I'll wait here. But bring it up when you've finished. I'm anxious to see how she photographs. Her colours will not show, but still, she should be magnificent.'

'I wonder if moving images will ever be caught on glass. It would be magical to watch her fluttering about long after her short lifespan ends,' she said.

'Wondrous things are being invented every day. Who knows what a clever mind might come up with?'

They carried on talking about wondrous scientific things for a few moments in the easy way they had.

If only her memory could be like a moving photograph. She hated to think that once she went home and returned to her old life…began a new one…that her remembrance of this time would fade.

She would hold on to it for all she was worth, but it was the way of things for memories to fade.

For the two weeks remaining of their stay on the Isle of Wight, she meant to live each moment fully.

* * *

Clement stood up from his desk, stretched. He hated to step away from his work because as soon as he did, he would begin to worry.

With such a short time until his daughters must face the possibility of being taken to London by his brother, he feared they were not ready.

Dash it. Why should they be at ten years old? It was only a prideful baroness, wishing for it.

In his opinion his sister-in-law's motives were selfish. Presenting two accomplished players to the marriage mart would make her more respected and cause her own children to be looked at in a positive light.

Clement had reason to fear for their happiness. He had reason to fear for his own happiness. It was hard to imagine life without their bright spirits in his home.

The prospect preyed upon him.

What he needed was a visit to the classroom to reassure himself that their lessons in ladylike comportment were going well. He was not certain that Alice and Jayne were giving the matter the attention they ought to be.

He was certain that Vivie would teach them all she knew…but please let it be enough.

Coming to the bottom of the stairs, he turned right, then went down the hallway leading towards a room which he thought must have been used as a schoolroom when the Prentis children were young.

Before he went into the classroom, he heard Vivie's voice. It sounded as if she was reading.

Going inside, he found all three of them sitting atop pillows on the floor. Sunshine streamed through a lace window curtain and cast them in dappled light.

If only he could capture the image on one of Vivie's glass

plates. He could look at the memory whenever he wished to. Pull it out and cherish it…live the moment again and again.

Come this time next year, would he have any of them? Alice, Jayne, Vivie?

The thought was too grim to dwell on, which did not mean that the fear went away even when he tried to think of something else.

Dread was the shadow which followed him each day.

'Hello, Papa.' Alice scrambled up from the floor. She gave him a hug. He tugged the bow in her hair.

'What are you reading?'

'Alice's Adventures in Wonderland.'

Wonderland? He was aware of the book, it was famous. He had not read it, though, and was not certain his daughters should be doing so either.

The title alone sounded too fanciful. They ought to be reading something that would help them with proper decorum. They could read about Alice's adventures once they were allowed to be children again.

'It sounds interesting,' he said. 'But tell me, what have you learned today? Proper speech? Ladylike posture?'

Jayne came up, stood on his feet and gave him a hug. 'Nothing as dull as that, Papa. We learned that Alice fell down, down, down a hole where she encountered strange creatures. There was a talking caterpillar.'

'A word, Miss Curtis?'

After instructing the girls to read to one another, Vivie joined him in the hallway.

'You look troubled, Clement,' she said. 'Is there something you need?'

Something besides her? Well, yes, there was.

'We are nearly out of time until the girls must show off

their manners. Have you run out of what you are able to teach them?'

She frowned and he thought he caught affront flash in her expression, although he could not imagine why. It was a reasonable question.

'It is not as if I expect you to know every nuance of society,' he tried to explain. 'But have they learned enough to appear all they should?'

'I will continue to press the importance of impeccable comportment, but they are children and do not take it seriously.'

'They must, though.' He scrubbed his hand through his thatch of thick curls, frustrated.

'Unless you wish to advise them of the consequences, they will not. To your daughters, life is playful. At their age it is how it ought to be.'

'What ought to be and what is, are not always the same thing.' He spoke more sharply than he should have. 'Sorry, Vivie, I am on edge.'

'But who would not be? I think that when the time comes, Alice and Jayne will do well. I have approached this as a game for them so that they will—'

'A game!' He had to remind himself that none of this was her fault. She had been hired to keep them safe, entertained, and advancing in their studies. She had been doing exactly that when his brother and his wife had paid their visit.

'I know you are worried, Clement.' She touched his arm, softly, soothingly. 'But this must be presented to them as an amusement. If they are forced to perform, they will not do it. You of all people know this to be true. But they might play a game.'

'I apologise for being sharp, Vivie. But I cannot imagine

them not being in my life every day. Please…focus more time on teaching them their social graces.'

'Very well, as you wish.' She nodded, seeming distant all of a sudden. He did not like that she suddenly felt more like his employee than his friend. Perhaps it was for the best. One day he would have to live without her, too.

At one point, he had come close to telling Vivie he was in love with her. Now he wondered if he should have gone ahead and done it. Perhaps if he carried through with it, she would change her mind about leaving. A marriage proposal could change everything. If she no longer needed to earn a wage, wouldn't she be free to cancel her next commitment?

Marriage would be a boon to him as well. If the girls had a mother, Mildred might not see it as her place to guide their debut into society. His attitude brightened considerably at the thought.

There was no doubt about who their mother should be… who he wanted for his wife. When he proposed he would not be asking for a marriage of convenience. He would make it clear that it was coming from the depths of his heart.

Tonight, he would press his suit. If she argued, he would kiss her. Nothing proved they were intended to be together more than their kisses did. Surely she felt it in her soul the same as he did?

This time he would not let her run away from what was meant to be. They were meant to be. He might be the only one to realise it right now, but it was true none the less.

He grinned inside imagining how, later, he would take her for a walk on the beach. There, under the stars and with the blessing of the moon, he would convince her they were destined for one another.

It was a romantic plan for a man who had never been romantic.

He liked it.

After Clement left the classroom, Vivienne considered teaching the girls one of the more frustrating lessons about being a lady of society. Oh, how it chafed that there were matters which a lady must not discuss in the presence of gentlemen. Politics and money were not proper for a lady to talk about, no matter how strong an opinion she had on the subjects.

She considered the lesson and then rejected it. It was nonsense which she would have no part in perpetuating. If in the unlikely event she had a daughter, she would be raised to believe her opinions mattered.

Here she was, though, and Alice and Jayne were not her daughters.

'Well, my dears, I believe we are finished with Wonderland adventures for the day. Which game would you prefer to play? Manners or swinging?'

They laughed, as she knew they would, then dashed out of the classroom.

Jayne ran ahead of Alice. She hopped on the swing before Vivienne was halfway down the steps. Up she went and then down, laughing.

At the highest point of up, she let go of the ropes, lifting her arms high.

'I'm Alice falling down the hole!' she cried.

'Hold on with both hands!' Vivienne shouted, rushing towards the tree.

Jayne was at the bottom of the sweep when she slipped off. She caught her fall with one hand under her.

Vivienne knelt beside her. 'Have you been injured?'

Jayne's bottom lip quivered. She nodded, then lifted her hand. Then she screeched.

Her arm was not straight. It sagged a few inches from her wrist.

Somehow, Clement was kneeling beside them. Where had he come from? Oh, but she was so grateful that he was here.

'There now, little one,' he crooned. 'It is not so bad.'

It was bad…one of the worst things Vivienne had ever seen. Her stomach twisted just looking at the injury.

'Run to the classroom, get that book you were reading,' he told her.

Lifting the hem of her skirts high, she ran. Not so fast that she did not hear Jayne whimpering, and Clement comforting her.

Reaching the front door, she glanced back. Clement had his shirt off and was ripping one sleeve off the shoulder.

By the time she returned, he had the sleeve separated from the shirt. He snatched the book from her without giving her a glance.

She was glad he hadn't. The reproach she would see in his eyes would be unbearable.

'I'm going put your arm on the book to hold it straight, sweetheart, then I'll wrap it up to hold it secure. It will hurt but I need you to be brave. Do not jerk it away.'

Jayne nodded. 'I'm sorry, Papa.'

'Show me how brave you are, sweetheart.'

Still, he did not look at Vivienne. He did not need to for Vivienne to know what she would have seen if he had.

This was all her fault. Clement had been against having a swing in the tree from the beginning, yet she had allowed the girls to use it.

'In Wonderland, Alice did not break her arm when she fell down the hole.' Jayne sniffled.

Clement did look at her then. The resentment in his eyes cut her to the quick. She deserved it. She was not a governess, had never been qualified to act as one and now an innocent child was paying the price.

If only she could run away from this moment, back up time and change it. Now that was a foolish thought. Adding cowardice to negligence was the last thing she was going to do.

Since she did not dare approach Jayne and have the child look at her the way Clement had, she went to Alice who was sitting several feet from the swing. The child was weeping, but in all that was happening, her distress had gone unnoticed.

Alice latched on to her, sniffling into Vivienne's sleeve.

'Don't worry, my dear. You see Mr Prentis is already on his way to get the doctor.' She pointed to the road where the wagon bounced quickly over the road.

'He has made the trip before,' Mrs Prentis said, her voice reassuring.

So absorbed in her own guilt, Vivienne had not noticed her approach.

'I know you feel horrid, my dear,' she murmured, patting Vivienne's shoulder. 'I was standing right beside my Mary when she fell out of the swing. She was pretending to be a bird. It makes you feel to blame, but these things happen.'

They did not happen to Vivienne.

No one could be more to blame than a false governess.

Vivienne stood in the hallway outside the door of the room where the doctor was tending Jayne. Clement had not asked her to come inside and she did not blame him. No doubt he regretted hiring her. Regretted the time they had spent together, the friendship which had been deepening between them.

How selfish of her to have sought her own adventure when there were children involved. It was just as well she would not be a mother if this was an example of the care she gave them.

A yelp came from the other side of the door, sharp, painful, but quickly over. She heard the doctor's voice murmuring encouragement.

Moments later, Clement opened the door and came into the hallway. He took a deep breath, set his shoulders as if he was gathering the courage to go back into the room.

'Will she be all right?' Vivienne asked.

He slid his gaze towards her, then nodded. 'The doctor said it is a clean break and will heal with no lasting damage.'

'I'm sorry, Clement, I never meant for—'

'How could you have let this happen? If you had been teaching them what you ought to have been, she would not have been on the blasted swing in the first place.'

She opened her mouth in an attempt to explain, but what could she say?

'I apologise.' She blinked back tears and then ran away.

'Wait, I—' She heard him call out, but did not turn back.

She knew what she must do. As soon as she was assured Jayne would indeed, recover, she would go home.

Jayne and Alice deserved a governess who really was one. Not a dragon like the one Mildred wanted to hire, but a kind, caring lady who would not put them in danger because of her inexperience.

She dashed outside to the porch, sat in a chair and stared at the dunes between the house and the shore. Butterflies flitted in the sunshine but seeing their carefree rambling only made her feel worse.

'Oh, there you are, dearie.' Mrs Prentis crossed the porch, then sat in the chair beside her. She pressed a cup of tea into her hand.

'Drink it up, now. Nothing like it to set one right.'

'I am not certain this can be set right.' She had injured a child and there was no undoing it.

'Of course it can. I have been a mother for more years than you have been alive. I promise you, it will be all right. Give it time. Once Jayne is acting herself again, you will see matters in a proper light and feel better. Believe me, accidents and children go hand in hand. You are not to blame. Oh, I know it feels like it right now, but some things are simply not within our control. I cannot tell you how many times I have sat on this porch feeling the way you do now.'

'Clement blames me.'

'Well, he's a man. On occasion they lash out without considering their words. It was fear for his child speaking, not good sense. Ask Mr Prentis how many times he has been forced to beg my forgiveness over the years. I'm sure your young man will do the same.'

'Mr Marston is not my young man.'

Of all the things, Mrs Prentis smiled, winking at her. 'I see the way he looks at you. It is the very way Mr Prentis used to look at me.'

'He still does,' Vivienne said.

While this was wonderful for her hostess, it was horrible for Vivienne.

She did not want Clement to be in love with her. Nearly as much as she wanted him to be.

Clement was an ass. The second after he'd blamed Vivie for what happened he regretted it.

He had just watched Jayne go through a great deal of

pain. Lashing out had been a release and Vivie had been his innocent target.

His behaviour was unmanly…inexcusable.

In an attempt to make amends he had followed her, but then found her sitting on the porch with Mrs Prentis.

What he had to say to her must be spoken in private so he went back to sit with his daughters.

Now, hours later, with dinner finished, and Alice and Jayne sleeping peacefully, where was Vivie?

Probably somewhere hating him for what he'd said. It was no wonder she wished to avoid him.

What a first-rate dunce he was, meaning to declare his love, intending to ask for her hand…and then to insult her?

He had meant to go down on one knee tonight, but to propose, not beg her forgiveness.

It would be his fault if she packed her camera equipment and went to her next assignment early.

No one would blame her.

'Ah, there you are, Clement.' Mr Prentis nearly ran into him coming around the corner. 'I assume you are looking for your young lady.'

'You have spoken to your wife? You know what I did?'

He grimaced, nodding. 'I've been in your shoes too many times. Last I saw of Miss Vivienne she was walking towards the beach.'

'Wish me luck, then.'

Moments later Clement left the house in search of his future.

There was a good chance it would not be the one he hoped for. Still he strode across the sand determined to do what he could to win his lady as well as a mother for his children.

Chapter Twelve

Vivienne sat on the sand, watching moonlight sparkle on the crests of waves.

The hypnotic roll of water rushing onshore did not soothe her, nor did the song of a night bird.

Hopefully what Mrs Prentis told her was correct. That once she saw Jayne recovering she would have a better perspective on what had happened. Right now she did not. She was haunted by the sight of a misshapen arm, by a scream of pain when the bone was set.

Of the accusation in Clement's eyes.

All at once she needed to walk. There was too much emotion rumbling through her to sit still.

She unbuttoned her shoes, rolled off her stockings, then walked towards the lapping waves.

Bunching up her skirt, she tucked the hem into the waistband. She stepped into the water, watched while froth tickled her toes.

Her chest ached. Her throat cramped. Tears which had threatened all afternoon dribbled down her cheeks.

Now that she was alone, she would finally allow herself to weep. If she did not release the tension squeezing her soul, she would not be able to fulfil her duties tomorrow.

Although she was a false governess, Alice and Jayne

counted on her. Especially Jayne. She was bound to need a great deal of care. Care which a genuine governess would know how to give.

The imposter would be figuring it out as she went along. Why, oh, why had she believed she could step out of her station in life…outrun her destiny even for one short summer?

If she could go home now, she would do it. That, though, would make her a coward. Any suffering she was going through in this moment was of her own making.

She had only a short time left to try to make this up to Jayne.

And to Clement. It wasn't as if she would ever forget how stricken he'd looked coming out of the room after the doctor set Jayne's arm.

It was fair to say she had never met a braver man. All through the ordeal Clement had given his child reassuring smiles, as if to tell her this sort of thing happened on occasion, but there was nothing at all to be afraid of.

No doubt he was sitting at her bedside right now while Vivienne indulged in her weeping fit.

She was simply pathetic…and would be for a few more minutes. Then she would go back to the house and pretend she was a responsible person.

Sitting down with a plunk, she did not care that the waves lapped at her hips. So what if the water was cold and her skirt was getting soaked?

She would try to cry out her guilt. Not that it was likely to go away, but it must at least be released or she would explode. It only took a moment for her face to become as drenched as her skirt.

'Vivie!'

Oh, no!

Instead of turning her face to look, she buried her head in her arms.

'Go away,' she whispered even though Clement was still a distance away.

Clement was the last person she wished to see. Or worse, to be seen by.

Coming to the top of the dune, Clement could not believe what he was seeing.

Vivienne sitting at the waterline…with waves lapping her skirt. Luckily the surf was gentle tonight…but what was she doing?

Surely his unguarded and inappropriate comment could not have caused her this much distress? He'd been wrong to say what he had, but she seemed too overwrought for it to have been only that.

'Vivie!' he shouted and started to run.

It was rough going in the sand. By the time he reached her he was a little winded.

'What is it, Vivie? Is it what I said?'

Arms crossed over bent knees, she cradled her head in them. Without looking up, she nodded, then shook her head.

'Go away.' The quiver in her voice cut him to the quick.

But go away? No chance of him doing that. He knelt beside her. The water was awfully cold. 'How long have you been sitting here?'

'Not long enough.'

'Yes, long enough!'

'Can't…' she sniffled '…a person have a moment of privacy?'

'To weep?'

Although she was not doing so now, it was clear that she had been.

'Forgive me, Vivie. I should not have said what I did. I didn't mean it.'

'But of course you meant it. Words do not come out of

one's mouth with no thought…' she hiccupped '…behind them.'

Still she did not peek up from her folded arms. 'Jayne might have broken her neck and not her arm…did you think of that?'

Yes, he had. Unreasonable worry had assaulted him. Although the last thing he was going to do was admit it. Now, with the emergency over and the doctor's reassurance that Jayne would fully recover, he saw the event in a more sensible light.

'I was wrong to say it. Jayne's fall was more my fault than yours. I should have insisted on having the swing taken down on the first day.'

Again, she shook her head, then nodded.

'Won't you look at me, Vivie?'

She did. He wished all of sudden that she had not. Even in the dark he saw how puffy her eyes were.

He wrapped his arms around her shoulders. Each foamy wave gliding around them seemed colder.

'Neither of us ought to blame ourselves or each other. What do you say, Vivie? Shall we call a truce?'

She nodded.

'Now, tell me why you are really crying.'

'Perhaps I turned my ankle.'

'Perhaps you are turning the truth.'

'Really, Clement. A lady is permitted to have her secrets.'

'You are shivering. No secret in that.'

'Yes, I will go back to the house.'

He stood, reached a hand down and then helped her up.

She dropped his hand, then turned as if she would walk away, her bare feet crusted with sand.

Now that his apology had been offered and probably

accepted…one could only put so much faith in a nod…he had more to say.

Dash it, though. A true gentleman would not make a woman weep one moment and then profess his love in the next. It nearly seemed as if he should wait. Nearly, but no. Summer was almost over, after all. She meant to leave him. He meant to keep her.

'Wait. There is something I want to discuss.'

Discuss? That was a clumsy word.

Clearly he did not have the skill to sweep a woman off her feet with suave declarations.

Kisses though…that was a language neither of them misinterpreted. They might have denied it…but not mis-understood.

'May we discuss it inside?' she asked.

Fair enough. He did not wish for her to become ill from being cold and wet.

'This won't take long—' That was wrong. If this went the way he hoped, it would take a long, intimate time.

'Clement, if you wish to terminate my employment, do it quickly. The wind is rising. You must be as cold as I am.'

'Come with me.'

He caught her hand again. This time he did not let go, even when he bent to snatch up her shoes.

Here was a dilemma. Her feet were too wet and sandy to be put back into her shoes. At the same time she could not go barefoot. Splinters and thorns would prick her feet.

Stooping, he indicated for her to climb on his back.

She shook her head, her puffy eyes wide.

'Hold your shoes.' He handed them to her. 'I won't drop you.'

To his surprise, she took them and then did as he asked.

He settled her weight across his back, adjusted her legs in the crook of his arms.

Her arms went around his shoulders, holding tight. Her breath skimmed across his ear, warm and sweetly scented.

He had never carried a woman piggy-back before. One sensation led to another and left him wondering how this had come to be called piggy-back.

If there was one thing Vivienne Curtis did not feel like, it was a pig. Curvaceous-woman-back would be a better term for it. For his part, he felt like he could walk this way for ever.

Rather, he carried her towards the inn, but then walked past it and went to the carriage house.

Once inside, he let go of her legs. She slid off his back.

Interesting sensation, that.

Moonlight streaming inside illuminated a lantern hanging on a wall. He lit it and then closed the door.

Without the wind, it did not seem quite so cold. Cold enough, though, with no stove to light.

He spotted a pair of blankets hanging on the wall and plucked them off the hook.

There were two spots where romance might bloom. A wagon bed or that clean pile of straw in a vacant stall.

The choice was clear.

He spread one blanket on the straw, then punched and fluffed it. He stripped down to his small clothes which were damp, but not as soggy as his trousers. He sat down and covered himself with the blanket.

'Take off your skirt and sit with me.'

'I shouldn't.' She crossed her arms over her middle while shaking her head. 'No.'

'I will look away. Really, Vivie, you can be covered by

a wet skirt or a dry blanket. Either way you are covered and the blanket is far more sensible.'

Still she hesitated.

'It's nearly warm under here,' he commented, giving her an encouraging grin.

She glanced between him and the carriage-house door as if deciding what to do.

Stay, go?

Love him…leave him? She was probably not thinking that.

Leave her post now or at the end of summer was more likely the decision she was weighing up.

A great gust of wind blew, rattling the door on its iron hinges. Vivie glanced back at him, a delicate frown wrinkling her brow.

He lifted the corner of the blanket. Love me, Vivie, love me was what he meant by it.

'It will be easier to speak if we are not across the stable from one another. And it really is getting warmer under here.'

Not much warmer, but once she joined him it would be. He hoped. If he could only manage to kiss her once, it would become heated in no time at all.

'Come now, your toes look white to the bone.'

'Oh, very well. Turn your head.'

He heard wet fabric thump on the floor.

A second later she scrambled under the blanket, but not close enough for him to coax a kiss out of her. Which he needed to do since it was the best way he knew of to express his feelings.

'Pivot this way.' He motioned for her to turn her feet towards him.

It surprised him when she did.

Surprised him even more that she did not kick him when he took her foot, held it between his palms.

What she did was close her eyes…and sigh.

'Icy,' he murmured while brushing sand off her toes.

Once her foot was clean he held, pressed and caressed it in the name of warming it.

'Nice,' he murmured, feeling her smooth skin and her fine bones. Her soft sighs of pleasure nearly made him sigh, too.

Ah, just there, her frown relaxed. That was encouraging. He picked up her other foot, cleaned and warmed it, too. Being under the blanket, her foot was hidden from his gaze, but his fingers learned as much as his eyes would have. Moving his thumb from her heel up her ankle, he felt how slim it was and smooth…strong.

With her foot properly warm, he was about to let go, but then she gave a long, delighted moan. Probably her calf was cold, too. No doubt it was as fine and smooth as her ankle was.

Did he dare find out?

Touching her would be an act of seduction and no mistaking it for anything else. If she allowed it, he would press for a kiss. If she did not, he would— Not give up! He'd brought her here to profess his love and then ask for her hand in marriage. He would not accept defeat until he had her answer.

'It's nice here, just the two of us.' He waited, praying she would return the sentiment.

'You said you wished to speak about something.'

'Yes, I do…' All at once his heart did not feel right. It galloped so hard he thought it might bruise his ribs. But bruised ribs did not amount to much when compared to a bruised heart.

'First, there is something I must show you…' He shifted closer, all the while stroking the back of her calf with his thumb.

'What?' She leaned away from him, but her expression softened. Her brown eyes looked like simmering whisky… so intoxicating that he felt woozy and yet, at the same time, determined.

He slipped his hand from her calf to the small of her back, drew her slowly closer. 'This will make what I want to talk to you about make sense.'

'You are ever logical.' Wonder of wonders, she leaned back towards him.

Her breathing came so quick and fast he could see her chest rising…falling. She touched his undershirt with her fingertips, probably noticing how the fabric pulsed with his heartbeat. He would kiss her and make no excuse for it. He was going to act on what was in his heart and then…and then he was going to place that heart in her hands.

'Sweet Vivie,' he murmured the whisper on her lips.

And then she closed that last gap and kissed him. She wrapped her arms around his neck, drawing him in. Into her heart, into her soul and into the rest of her life. Surely he was not mistaken.

'Vivie…' he murmured again, as if somehow in saying her name he claimed her.

He lifted away, but only far enough so that he could gaze into her eyes…and see his love returned. Because how could it not be? The kiss held the promise of their future.

He rose to one knee, cupping her face in his palms. Felt cool air pebble his skin when the blanket slid off his thigh. Then he kissed her again. Being able to kiss this woman whenever he wished to for the rest of his life was going to be a sort of bliss he could have never imagined.

'I love you, Vivie.'

He waited a heartbeat, then two, and then he could not breathe. She ought to have said she loved him, too, by now. Dim lantern light revealed tears welling in her eyes.

'If you say you don't love me, I'm afraid I will not believe you.'

She pressed her mouth with pale fingertips. Wind rattled the door. Loose bits of straw blew across the stone floor.

Surely she couldn't deny what was happening between them. He would not let her! On one knee, he hugged her tightly to him, not willing to let her say anything to douse the hope flickering in his heart.

'If…' The word tickled his ear. Please let what she was about to whisper be of a forever love. 'If I say I do not love you, it will be a lie.'

Her words were what he longed to hear, but the tone… it was all wrong. He'd better finish before she said something to prevent his proposal. Already on bended knee, he took her hand, pressing it to his heart.

'Vivienne Curtis, I love you with my whole life. Will you—?'

'Don't say it, Clement. Please do not!' She pulled her hand from his grip. 'Do not break both our hearts.'

'Loving me breaks your heart?'

'Yes.' She swiped at tears with the back of her hands. 'I tried not to love you. But you…you are—'

She'd tried not to love him! Why?

His heart split open, cleaved right down the middle. Pain unlike any he had ever known bled out of the wound.

'What am I, Vivie? If you love me, why won't you have me?'

She touched his lips with her fingertips. He did not kiss

them because her eyes were filled with sorrow…sorrow for loving him.

'Because you are as forbidden to me as the moon is to the sun.'

As if that explained it, which it did not, she leapt up. With a yank she snatched the blanket, wrapped it around herself, then ran for the door. She did not close it. Dumbfounded, he watched darkness swallow her fleeing figure. The awful silence was cut only by wind banging the door against the wall.

While he stared after her, not quite believing what had just happened, he noticed her shoes on the floor. The pointed little toes facing him gave him the oddest sensation. It felt as if the woman he loved, the one who had only just said she loved him, had simply vanished.

Well, she had, he decided. She was as lost to him as if she did not exist. What did exist was the ache in his soul and the confusion making him dark inside.

He sat down on the pile of straw, drew the other blanket around his legs while he struggled to make sense of what had just happened.

The reality was, Vivienne was not gone. He would see her tomorrow in her role as governess. Dash it, he would see her and, every time he did, his heart would break all over again.

Vivienne raced up the stairs, red plaid blanket tucked under her chin and dragging on the floor behind. It smelled a little bit like a horse, but also a great deal like Clement.

The wonder was that she could smell anything given how stuffy her nose was. She should never have allowed herself to share such an intimate moment with him. Should not have…and yet, it had been too beautiful to resist. The man too enticing to refuse. The temptation to reveal her heart to him had been overwhelming and in the end she'd been helpless to resist his draw.

Now she must pay the price…worse, Clement must, too.

Reaching her bedroom, she went inside, closing the door without a sound. Pure providence kept her from being spotted while she'd dashed through the house.

Who had she become, believing it was acceptable to remove her skirt in the presence of a man…to let him caress her bare feet…her ankle and her calf…? She was not a woman who was mindful that she was promised to someone else!

'Clement,' she whispered, leaning her head back against the door. 'I would marry you if I could.'

He had not asked, but only because she'd prevented him. An incredible man had offered her his heart, his whole future and she had all but slapped it away. What a heartless wretch she was.

Walking over to the window, she looked out at blowing grass and sand. From here she could see the corner of the house and the big tree where the swing went up and down as if it entertained an invisible passenger.

There in the distance was Clement trudging along the path leading from the carriage house to the inn. He was bent forward against a strong gust of wind, carrying her skirt under one arm and her shoes under the other.

And her heart. He carried that, too.

She actually kissed the window, pretending nothing blocked the distance between them. How wickedly sorrowful it was that this was the last kiss she would ever give him. The glass was cold, like her future was sure to be.

Choking back a sob of self-pity, she went to the wardrobe and withdrew a gown. She did not even notice which one, but put it on unseeing. The time had come for her to tell him the truth. Clement had confessed his love to a woman he did not even know. Going on as they had been was out of the question now.

Crossing to the desk, she opened the drawer and withdrew a sheet of paper and a pencil. Writing her confession was the only way to tell him what she must. How else was she to make sense of things which made no sense?

Speaking with him face to face would surely end with her stumbling over her words. Her mind would be preoccupied with kissing him. She did not dare to indulge in it again. The temptation to take a different path than her family wanted was too great. With only a little push she would be a mother to the children she adored…a wife to the man she loved.

And it would be the shame of her family. Clement and his daughters were not the only people she loved. She loved her parents. They were the dearest people in the world and had indulged her desire for independence longer than most parents would have.

There was also Great-Aunt Anne to be considered. Vivienne had it within her power to make her aunt's last years contented ones, with everyone she loved united in one family.

She set the tip of the pencil on the paper, stared at it while listening to the wind racing under the eaves and grains of sand pinging the window.

'Dear Clement,' she wrote, mouthing the words while she wrote. 'I am not who you believe I am…'

Well, she was…but she was not. She pressed the pencil tip to her lips at a loss as how to proceed.

'Clement, I regret to inform you of who I really am… who I am not…'

She wadded the paper, tossed it on the floor then took another.

'My friend, I have something I must tell you... You cannot ask me to marry you. I am promised to another.' She gripped the pencil hard, causing her usually smooth writing to be jerky. 'I regret that... I sincerely regret that...but perhaps you are acquainted with him.'

The letter sounded so cold. It would seem to Clement as if a stranger had written it. But it must be so. She, the real Vivienne was a stranger...she was not his Vivie any more.

'I hope that you will find a woman who will give you the love you are worthy of, but she cannot be me. With greatest affection, Lady Vivienne Curtis, daughter of the Marquess of Helmond...a lady shackled by expectation and yet bound by love. Doomed to sorrow.' Harsh, but the truth.

This time she did not wad the letter and toss it away. No, indeed, she ripped it into dozens of pieces, opened the window and let the wind take the scraps. A letter was a coward's weapon. Clement deserved to hear the truth from her own lips.

When she thought about it, there really was no danger of him trying to win her back with a kiss or a proposal. After the first few words of her confession, he was bound to hate her and be glad to see the last of her.

Leaning out the window, she let wind blow on her face while taking several fortifying breaths. She must be strong for what she needed to do, or at least look as if she were. What she must not look was pale and lovelorn. She patted her cheeks to give them colour and then closed the window, crossing the room to the mirror.

There was nothing to be done about her swollen eyes, but her hair could do with being put into some kind of order.

That done, she stared at her image. Interesting how she looked calm and not desperate with grief.

Why wouldn't she, though, when all her life she had been trained to disguise her emotions? How horrible that Alice and Jayne would be forced to learn the same. Thinking of the girls nearly made her weep, but she caught her heart in time.

Not for long, though.

After leaving her bedroom, she stopped at Jayne's bed. For having endured a broken arm she did not look so bad. Rather, she seemed peaceful. Just there, she smiled briefly, then relaxed back into her dream.

Vivienne did not touch her hair tonight, but she did bend to kiss her brow. 'I wish you could be my daughter,' she whispered.

Then she turned to Alice. Bent and kissed her, too. 'I would be your mother if I could.'

Vivienne paused for a moment, placing one hand on each child's head. She lifted her face, prayed that they would find a mother who loved them. Also for courage to get through the next few moments.

It was selfish, she knew, but she could not bring herself to pray that Clement would find a wife to love him. It hurt too much to think about.

She wished she had never admitted she loved him. Very soon he would know that, in spite of the fact that he had her heart, she would give herself to another. It wasn't as if she could take back her confession of love. All she could do was not repeat the mistake.

She lifted her hand to his door.

Let guilt be her guiding light. Shame would keep her aloof when all she wanted to do was wrap her arms around Clement's neck and feel him fold her close to his heart. A heart that would turn brittle and break within the next few moments. One day he would give his love to someone, only it would not be her.

Breathe in, she reminded herself, breathe out. Stand tall and do not weep. Although she went through her mental list of admonitions, she could not manage to rap her fingers on the wood.

How would she begin? She had not been able to write the words, so what made her think she could speak them?

Taking a steadying breath, she knocked, but softly so she would not wake Alice and Jayne.

Hopefully something inspired would come to her before the door opened.

Nothing did.

Seeing Clement's face was nearly too much. His lips were drawn tight and turned slightly down at the corners and his eyes held no spark of humour in them.

She could not bear it. Her brain went utterly blank.

He looked down at her with one brow arched in question. 'What is it, Vivienne?'

Not Vivie…and it hurt dreadfully knowing she would never hear the endearment again. She had made a mistake in allowing it to soften her heart in the first place. One mistake among many and all of them her fault. Here was her chance to begin her confession and all she could say was…nothing.

'I suppose you have come for your clothing.'

'Yes, of course.'

He did not invite her inside, but came back a moment later and placed her skirt and her shoes in her arms. They were damp, scented with the sea. Grains of sand rubbed her palms.

Giving her a dispirited glance, he started to close the door.

'Wait! I need to speak with you.'

'Tomorrow, perhaps.'

He continued to close the door. She wedged herself between the door and the frame, then wriggled past him. Once inside his room she walked to the desk which she had come to think of as her spot.

There were no jars containing insects, no crisp white pages waiting to be drawn on...no pencils sharpened and ready.

'You should not be here,' he said bluntly.

No, she should not. She never should have been. Her place was in London announcing her engagement.

'There is something I must tell you, Clement.'

Chapter Thirteen

In spite of her red-rimmed eyes, Vivienne looked composed. Clement believed it was a false front. She could not possibly be unruffled after what had happened between them only an hour ago.

It was as if she was drawing a mask over her feelings, closing herself off in a way she had not done before.

No surprise since he was doing the same. In the name of protecting his heart he was making it appear as if he did not have one...that it was not aching to hold her and love her.

The blame for what had happened was all on him. Had he not suggested Jayne's fall was due to Vivienne's neglect, matters would be much different between them.

He had seen how she'd been consumed with guilt over the accident and what had he done? Bungled things and pressed her for a commitment. A commitment she had refused in the past. It had been the worst sort of judgement to try to hold her with a proposal.

What he had mistakenly believed was that, if she knew he loved her, it would make a difference. The frustration of it all was that she returned his love and yet had stopped him from proposing. Surely she understood it was what he had been doing?

'I find that I must apologise, once again,' he said.

A moment ago he'd wanted her to leave him alone, but now, with a flick of his hand, he indicated that she should sit on one of the chairs beside the window.

The gesture came off harsher than he meant it to, revealing how confused he was.

The tall curtain over the window stirred. It must be cracked open and the wind seeping inside. He would deal with it tomorrow. Now he needed to rectify the division separating him from Vivienne.

How, though…when the puzzle pieces would not knit together in his mind? There was her next engagement and something to do with the moon and the sun being forbidden to one another. Which made no sense.

Now that they had admitted their love for one another, nothing was the same. Life's expectations had changed. Surely she must recognise the fact that they should remain together…that they were meant to be a family?

'Won't you sit down so we can discuss this?'

It would be best to let her begin, given that he had no idea how to. Clearly, telling her he loved her and beginning to propose marriage had been all wrong.

Perhaps her hesitation, refusal to be honest, had to do with him belonging to a ranking family and her being a governess.

If it was as simple as that, he could put her concern to rest.

Some in society might expect him to wed higher, but he had brothers to do that. It was unlikely that anyone would care who he married.

'No. I have something I must say to you. It will not take long.'

It would if she continued to stare silently at him, wringing her fingers.

'May I ask you something?' He would speak first after all since she seemed unable to.

'Very well.' Why the blazes was she staring at the floor instead of looking at him?

'I do not care about social rank, if that is the reason you turned me down.'

'It has something to do with it.' She looked up sharply, her face pale. Her pulse tapped hard in the tender spot under her jaw.

Only by the greatest restraint did he keep from reaching across and soothing it with his thumb…or a kiss.

'Let my brothers have their heiresses, Vivie. I desire a love match.'

'And I hope you have it one day. But it cannot be with me.'

He tamped down the urge to make a sharp retort because why on earth could it not be with her?

'You must give me a reason why not,' he said, using the most sensible tone he could muster. The facts all pointed to one conclusion. 'I have told you I love you and you have admitted the same. That confirms we already have our love match.'

She had not confessed her love with joy, he had to admit. But she had spoken the words.

'There are things you do not know about me, Clement.'

'No one can know everything about another person, but I do know you…your heart. What I do not know cannot matter so much in comparison.'

She blinked and he thought that she might weep. But, no, she shook her head, bit her bottom lip. She did not cry in the end.

'It matters. The engagement I mentioned I was going

to…it is exactly that. It is a betrothal. My betrothal. The formal announcement is to be made in a few weeks.'

What was this? No…it could not be true. And yet he had not misunderstood the words. Her lips had moved, his ears had heard. Now his heart lay at her feet, cleaved in half, gutted…slain.

'But you will not go through with it?' How could she? Not after what they had confessed to one another. 'Not now?'

'I am to wed the Marquess of Winterfeld.'

A governess marrying a marquess? It did not happen.

'Who are you really, Miss Curtis?'

No longer was she his Vivie for certain. Or perhaps she never had been.

More fool was he for not pressing her about her past. The secrets she kept did affect him and his children, after all. What a foolish thing to give his heart to her, not even knowing who she was.

'I am Lady Vivienne Louise Curtis. My father is Thomas Curtis, Marquess of Helmond.'

If a chrysalis had hatched a frog, he could not be more stunned. His governess, this woman he loved, was not just any stranger, but a lady of high rank!

Stunned, he felt like plunging headlong into misery. Instead, he set his shoulders, stood straight-backed…stiff.

'I deserve an explanation. Why have you have done this to us? How do you expect me to explain who you are to Jayne and Alice?'

'I never meant for this to happen. Please believe that I had every intention of doing my duty towards them. Surely you know I love your girls no matter what position I was born to.'

'Something occurs to me,' he said, wishing it had not.

'As the daughter of a marquess, and soon to be a marchioness, you far outrank my sister-in-law. I wonder—why is it that you did not admit who you were when Mildred threatened a more highly qualified governess? You are far more qualified to teach them than she is. If you had spoken up—'

But, no, she could not have. The scandal of having a lady of such high rank working for him...living with him...would have been ruinous to them all. A fact which did not keep him from feeling bitter, betrayed to his soul.

'What a fool you must think me, Lady Vivienne.' He knew his voice had a bite to it. The emotion was too raw to disguise.

She looked down. When she spoke, he barely heard the words. 'No, Clement, I would never think that.'

'A moment ago I thought you might not want me because my rank was above yours, that you might worry about feeling socially inferior, in society's eyes. And all the while—'

He had to breathe long and slow in order to not shout, or growl, or stamp out of his own chamber.

'All the while you were so far above me, that there was never any hope for us. You must have thought my proposal rather pitiful.'

'It's not true! That was the most touching moment of my life. I will never have another like it.' She blinked rapidly. He wondered if there was any truth to what she said. 'You must understand, my engagement is an arrangement of convenience. From the day I was born I was...but you know how it works. I have little control over whom I wed.'

Well, dash it all, he did know that. What he also knew, vowed in this moment, was that his daughters would never be forced to marry against their wishes.

If he had one thing to thank the governess for, it was pointing out the need for a woman to have a choice in the direction her life would take. He would never see Alice or Jayne forced to choose duty over love.

If that was all there was to what had happened, he might feel more charitable towards Lady Vivienne Curtis. To a great degree she was a victim of her birth.

There was more, though.

What she had failed to explain was why she was here acting the part of a governess when she ought to be at home planning her grand society wedding. What could she want from him and his family?

She must have a reason for what she'd done. Something that seemed reasonable in her eyes. But surely it was not worth the cost of breaking his daughters' hearts? He might eventually learn to live with his own misery, but not theirs, not again.

'May I offer you my congratulations?' he stated formally, his heart as far from the sentiment as it could be.

'I would rather that you did not. I will fulfil my duty. There is nothing to be congratulated or celebrated.'

Indeed. Only mourned.

'Goodnight, Clement.' She turned towards the door and so did not see him reach for her. He had not meant to, was not even certain why he had done it. Wishing, perhaps, that life would turn back to what it was yesterday.

'Why?' he asked, watching her fingers grip the doorknob and turn it. 'What was worth the cost of this deception?'

To save a life, perhaps, or for the betterment of…of something…anything. He might understand it, if it was.

The knowledge would not help when he was alone in the night and missing her…imagining her married to someone who was not him. But understanding might ease the ache. Or make it worse. Whichever it was, he needed to know.

She opened the door and stepped into the dim light of

the girls' bedroom. It seemed as if she would not answer, but then she stopped between the beds, turned.

'I wanted one last adventure before I wed.'

'And I was it? I was your adventure?'

'No, you were my love.'

With that, she spun about, went to her bedroom and closed the door. The quiet click sounded like an explosion in his heart. She was not gone and yet she was. He had never felt so bereft.

He left his door open in case Jayne awoke and needed him. It wasn't as if he could expect Lady Vivienne to rise in the night and do it.

It was fair to say he ached for the governess...perhaps for the lady, too. He could not say for certain since he did not know who she was.

Only that he ached.

Sitting at his desk, he stared at the stacked pages of his book, their book. Without Vivienne he would have been only one among dozens of authors hoping for publication. Now he had great hopes his work would be seen.

If they had nothing else between them, they at least had this.

And memories. He did at any rate. Vivienne would go on to make memories with another man...have his children, be the love of his life.

One thing was for certain—he would never attend another society ball. Not that, in the past, he had attended all that many of them. If he had, he might have encountered the Marquess's daughter and recognised her that first day on the drive.

Now his visits to London would be even fewer than before. If he happened to encounter the new Marchioness

Winterfeld at some elegant event, he was not certain he would recover.

Getting through the next several days until her time was up would be a trial of its own kind.

An adventure was all this had been to her? All he had been to her? No, not all…she'd also said he was her love. It would be better not to have heard her say that. Knowing she loved him, but would marry another anyway…how was he to get over that?

He picked up a page, the one with the illustration of the White Plume moth. He clenched his fist around it, remembering Vivienne's interest in it. He let go, watching the illustration flutter, crumpled, to the desk.

Clement did not expect to sleep, but he had and so deeply it felt as if he had been knocked out.

His limbs were heavy, his eyelids seemed glued together. This was the sleep of grief; he recognised it, having felt this way when his parents had left this earth. At least this time no one had died. Only a beautiful hope for his future.

Sun shone brightly through his window. He was late rising.

But what was that on the floor? An envelope. It appeared to have been slipped under his door. Although there was no name on it, he could only assume it was meant for him. Drawing a note from the envelope, he frowned.

'Dear Clement, if you wish, I will sponsor Alice and Jayne into society when the time is appropriate. Do not allow them to be sent to London.'

'It is not my intention,' he grumbled, but his intentions seemed to have mattered very little lately. However, he would accept what help she was willing to give. If her rank would keep them with him, he would accept it.

Rank, what a fickle thing it was. While Vivienne's might benefit him, allowing him to keep his girls, it would also separate him from her.

As a member of society he knew the rules. He understood that the higher the rank, the less a woman had to say about her own future. He could accept that, could forgive her in so far as that went. But to use him in her quest for adventure…worse, to use Alice and Jayne…

He ought to let her be the one to explain to them why she must leave…that, although they wished for her to be their mother, she would not be staying. True love would not win the day.

Dressing, he went downstairs. He would be late for breakfast, but he might beg something from the kitchen.

At this hour, the lady governess would be in the classroom with the children, which was just as well. He was not ready to face her, to paste on a smile for Alice's and Jayne's sake.

He was in luck in the kitchen. After a bite to eat, he felt somewhat revived, able to rise to the challenges this day was bound to present.

As much as he did not wish to, he would speak with Vivienne about her offer. Whatever the cost to himself, he must see his girls protected from Mildred's visions for their future.

If she got her way, they would have no choice in who they wed. Recent heartbreaking events had taught him just how important it was for them to have one.

Lady Vivienne was someone he did not know, but he did know the governess. Vivie would do her best for Alice and Jayne and do it out of affection for them, not because it would enhance her social standing…which needed no enhancing, being already so elevated.

Clement knew of her father, but hadn't ever met him. The man had a sterling reputation…and a daughter who had stolen his heart. The future Marchioness was a thief. In spite of it, he did trust her with his children.

What he needed right now was a breath of late summer air, something fresh to help set him right before he spoke with Vivienne about her offer.

Going on to the porch he found Mrs Prentis standing at the porch rail, looking towards the shore. He joined her.

'Good morning,' he said.

'Good morning, my dear.' She patted his hand, gave him a consoling look. That was odd since there was no reason for her to. She would not be aware of all that had happened between him and Vivienne.

Before he could give the matter more thought, he heard laughter coming from the direction of the shore.

'Miss Curtis must have taken their lessons outside this morning,' he said.

'Morning? It's just shy of noon by now.' This time she squeezed his hand. 'Mr Prentis has taken the girls on a walk.'

'Has he? Is their governess ill?' Worry gave his insides a tumble. Perhaps the drama of last night had got the best of her.

'I do not believe so. She was terribly distressed last time I saw her. Not ill though.'

'When was that?' Regardless of Vivienne's emotional state, he did need to speak with her. No matter what misgivings were between the two of them, his daughters' well-being must come first.

'But perhaps you would like to sit?'

'Mrs Prentis, you are giving me odd looks. Is there something you need to tell me that you think I will need to sit down for?'

She sighed, considered him up and down. She nodded. 'I believe you will do standing.'

Clearly the children were safe and enjoying their break from study, so what could be so dire?

'Miss Curtis has gone home…to London.'

Chapter Fourteen

The ferry crossing was not as turbulent as the first time Vivienne had made the trip, which did not keep her from gripping the rail and feeling ill.

She watched the Isle of Wight growing ever distant. Felt her heart grow tight and her soul…grey. Indeed, that was the very word. Grey like storm clouds, or perhaps it was grey like depressing fog.

How ever one described it, she disliked it. Disliked herself. She was miserable for more reasons than she could keep track of. The latest was leaving without a word.

She ought to have given Alice and Jayne some sort of reason as to why she had to go. Only, she could not look into their sweet grinning faces and tell them she could not be their mother because she must marry someone who was not their father.

How was she to say that, while she wished for nothing more than to become a part of their family, she was obligated elsewhere?

She would not be able to say anything of the sort without weeping because, unless Clement managed to prevent it, Alice and Jayne would one day stand in her shoes. At their tender ages, those sweet girls had no idea what was in store for them.

Vivienne squeezed her fingers around the rail. Please, oh, please let Clement accept her offer to take the girls under her wing. She would do her best to ensure they were not forced into a marriage not of their choosing.

As a marchioness, she would be supremely qualified to present them to society. Mildred would be agreeable to the arrangement since a close association with Lady Winterfeld would greatly advance her in society, too.

It was all a heap of nonsense, of course. Vivienne was the same person, governess or lady.

All of a sudden wind swirled over the deck. A wave rocked the ferry. She drew the hood of the cloak over her head.

Heavy wool covered half of her face. She could weep if she wished to and no one would know. Except for herself. She would know.

Over the past few days she had done far too much weeping. Her eyes ached. At the end of the day, life was what it was and she must accept it.

Now that she had admitted the truth to Clement, she must also admit it to her parents. Although she would keep the condition of her heart to herself. They would question why she had arrived home without her sister. While she could invent another lie, she would not.

One thing she had learned was that a great deal of harm came from twisting the truth. It did not matter how justified one felt.

What, she wondered, would her parents think of her being a governess and receiving a wage? Distressed, no doubt.

Yet she was going to miss the sense of worth it gave her. Doing a job and being recompensed for it had been fulfilling. All things considered, she knew she would have been happy as a governess had she been born to it.

The deck rolled and hitched. She had to adjust her weight, leaning left, then listing right in order to keep her balance. Funny, but the movement was a reflection of her life right now. Up, down, tossed this way and that.

Clearly, it was time to go below deck. When she turned she spotted a young couple at the rail. The man held his lady close. Cheek to cheek they gazed out at the water. She thought they were laughing at some small thing.

She and Clement used to do that. Not with the intimacy that the couple at the rail had, of course.

Oh, but there had been moments when she'd known how strong and lean his form was…how wonderful he smelled. How it felt to be pressed against him while under the spell of his kiss. Those moments had been intimate. But no more of that. She would gather her composure and move on.

Moving on proved to be more challenging than she would have wished. No more than a dozen paces along the way she encountered another couple, an elderly pair. The same as the younger couple, they held one another. Like them, they, too, were chuckling over something. No doubt their lives were bursting with memories to reminisce over. It would be best not to look too closely at them or her heart would break anew.

Vivienne's stomach turned. It was hard to know if it was from the turbulent crossing or her upside-down emotions.

When she looked back over the rail at the sea, the Isle of Wight was no longer visible. With an awful sense of loneliness, she continued on her way across the deck. A movement caught her eye. Something dashed in front of her hem. A tiny many-legged creature scuttled this way and that.

She stooped to peer more closely at it. My word, it was a Speckled Bush cricket.

'And how did you manage to get aboard, my little friend?' Who had she become, speaking to an insect as if it were a confidant? 'Clearly you are as lost as I am.'

It had been three weeks since Vivienne went away, each one longer than the next.

Clement sat at his desk, still at the inn, looking at book pages and photographs. He shuffled them top to bottom, bottom to top. He could not even feign an interest in the project. Insects used to be exciting, but now? A fifteen-legged beetle might crawl across the toe of his foot and he would barely give it a glance.

Who was he these days? Barely a researcher. No longer an employer. Not an engaged man. A miserable, grumbling pillbug all rolled up in misery was who he was.

On the first day after Vivienne went home to London he had walked about angry, probably with steam coming out of his ears. He could scarcely believe that on top of everything else, Vivienne had simply left. Bad enough she had come into their lives under false pretences, but to have run away like she had…

It was unforgivable. Until it wasn't.

Under the guidance of Mrs Prentis, he came to see matters in a truer light. It took more than a week of her reminding him that Vivienne had never deceived him and that she had been upfront from the beginning about not being able to stay.

She had, in fact, stated plainly that she had another engagement. He had been the one not to recognise the nature of the commitment. He had assumed it was another governess position which, Mrs Prentis had informed him, was assuming too much.

The good lady had pointed out another truth regarding Alice and Jayne. It was hardly Vivienne's fault that they had become so attached to her. She was a doting governess who adored her charges. And isn't that what he'd wished for when he hired her?

During the second week he'd tried convincing himself that life could go on as it always had. He could get past this.

What had changed, really? He had his daughters and his studies. It had been an interesting summer of exploration, just as he had planned it to be. If one did not count chickenpox and a broken arm. Or a shattered heart.

Yes, life would go on as it had. Perhaps it would. Although Mildred's plan for his girls was still a cloud on his horizon.

Now, here he found himself in the middle of the third week and missing Vivienne more than he had in the beginning.

Very clearly, life was never going to be as it was. The governess, or Lady Vivienne rather, had left her mark.

It did not matter how much he loved his Vivie. She had chosen someone else. There was no undoing it, so he must find a way of living with a burdened heart.

'Here you are, my dear,' Mrs Prentis slid a cup of tea across the desk, jarring him from his indulgent misery. 'Drink it up.'

'Ah, thank you. You always show up with aid when I need it most.' Also when she had something to discuss.

Mrs Prentis sat down in Vivie's chair. She patted his hand in the motherly way she had.

'Do you know where my girls are?' They must be finished with the reading he had given them to do by now.

'Keeping Mr Prentis out of trouble, I imagine.' She smiled kindly. 'If you were my boy, I would tell you to go after your young lady.'

'My young lady is about to become engaged to someone else.'

'As far as we know, she has not done it yet. I imagine we would hear the news even here on the Isle. Newspapers delight in society engagements. If you hurry, you might stop it in time.'

'Stop it?'

'You know you must try.'

'She has rejected me at every turn. I do not know why she would change her mind.' Or why he would hand his heart over to her to be crushed again.

How foolish could a man be?

'Vivienne loves you. I doubt she has changed her mind about that.'

'And yet she is in London, not here with me.'

'She did not reject you, you do understand that? All she did was accept her duty. In a sense, I find it admirable... yet also incredibly sad.'

'So, you are suggesting that I, the brother of a baron, present myself as a competing suitor to a marquess?'

'Not quite that. You will present yourself as a man who loves her, as opposed to one who does not.'

He did not drink the tea, which was not the point of her bringing it. The point was to listen to her advice. To hear what a woman with many years of experience in marriage and raising a family had to say...that was the point.

'It is a risk, my dear. I will not pretend it isn't. But if you don't try you will always wonder. Do not give up on Vivienne without a fight. For her sake if not for your own.'

Mrs Prentis might be wrong. Logically, there was a very

slim chance of winning Vivie away from a respected marquess.

And yet, slim was not none.

Energy buzzed through him at the prospect of battling for Vivienne's hand. He had not felt such a rush of hope since she went away.

'Love is a risk, but it is also life's great reward.' Mrs Prentis rose, collecting her cup and his, although he had yet to take a sip. 'Give it some thought, but don't take long. Once the formal announcement is made, there will be a scandal getting out of it.'

Mrs Prentis had not made it to the doorway before he sprang from his chair.

'I will take the evening ferry if Mr Prentis is willing to give us a ride to the village.'

'He will be relieved to know you have come to your senses. After all these years he still has not recovered from me nearly wedding a neighbouring farmer, don't you know?'

'I did not know.'

'The farmer was already on one knee, it was that close. Now, go and tell Mr Prentis to hitch the horse while I pack your family's belongings.'

He dashed towards the stairway, then paused, looking back. 'My children and I will miss you. This has been the best summer of our lives.'

Mrs Prentis smiled, then made a shooing motion with her fingers.

'Go on with you now, you will be back next year or the one after…you and your bride.'

Tomorrow night Vivienne's engagement would be announced. Mother had a dinner party planned for the event.

She had not seen her future betrothed since her return, although she understood he was also in London. He had sent her some lovely yellow roses, though, as a token of his esteem.

Friendship was what the pretty buds represented. Lovely in their way, yet she found herself lost in a fantasy that Clement had sent them. If he had, they would be deep crimson, the colour of love.

She had not meant to sigh, but after tomorrow she would no longer be able to fantasise about Clement, not without being unfaithful to her fiancé. Right and wrong were what they were, no matter how her heart perceived the situation.

'What is it? Don't you like them?' her mother asked. 'They are a lovely gesture.'

'Yes, quite a lovely gesture.'

'Come, sweetheart, walk with me in the garden. Everything is such a bustle in here getting ready for tomorrow. It is difficult to have a proper conversation.'

The garden was at its best with hints of autumn in the air. This time of year used to be her favourite. Now, she thought she did not have one.

There was only one thing she liked best. The man and his children she'd left behind on the Isle of Wight. Being separated from them had not helped her move on and accept her future. She only longed to see them more acutely. Everything reminded her of them.

'Look, Mother.' Vivienne pointed to a bush they walked past. 'It's a Painted Lady butterfly.'

'You learned this from the young man you spent the summer with?'

'He was my employer, an entomologist, you know that.'

'Indeed, yes, but I wonder…was he perhaps a bit more than that? I get the feeling he may have been.'

'It does not matter. Summer is over and here I am, ready to accept Everett's proposal. It will make Great-Aunt Anne madly happy, I suppose.'

'Madly happy. She is a great one for matchmaking. You do know that your great-aunt wed for love, though?'

'I have heard her speak of how much she adored Everett's father.'

'It is understandable after her first marriage. She was extremely unhappy in it.' Mother brushed a lock of hair from Vivienne's cheek that the breeze had stuck there. 'She did not love her first husband a jot. To make it worse, there was another man she did love. But her father forbade it and she was given to a viscount who was as wealthy as a bank.'

'I am glad Great-Aunt Anne was happy in the end.'

'It is the most important thing. Give that some thought, won't you?'

'Did you love Father when you wed him?'

Funny how her mother never spoke of it and Vivienne had never asked. Perhaps because in the past, she'd spent so much time thinking of how to avoid marriage. In those days she considered vows a trap, not a blessing.

For all the good it had done her. Here she was only a day from being entrapped…rather, engaged.

'No, dear, I did not. It took a bit of time. I love your father now, though.'

A servant hurried across the garden. 'The flowers have arrived, my lady. Where shall I direct them to be put?'

'Thank you, Morgan. I will be along.' Mother kissed Vivienne's cheek. 'Do you understand what I am telling you?'

'Not to despair. Love can come from unlikely beginnings.'

'Yes, something of the sort. Now let me see your pretty

smile. Everett is coming for dinner. Grace and George will be here, too. I'm certain you will want to know all about their trip.'

And later, Grace would want to know all about hers, too.

Even speaking Clement's name was bound to make her tear up. She had not spoken it more than was necessary in order to explain where she had spent her summer. And then she had called him nothing more personal than Mr Marston.

Her mother had been wonderfully forgiving of her escapade, once she'd recovered from being stunned. Father had not been. It had taken a week for him to stop glowering at her. Another after that for him to smile. It took a while, but once she'd convinced him she was ready to fulfil her duty to the family, matters were easier between them.

There was no point in wasting a lovely late afternoon inside the house so she sat on a bench, resting her chin on her open palm.

She would think dreamily of Clement one more time and then put him away, assign him and his children to the past.

Until tomorrow night, when fantasising about a man who was not her fiancé would be unacceptable, she would indulge. She would give herself up to Clement's funny, flat smile.

Sighing aloud would not hurt, this once, while she pictured him sitting at his desk with his black glasses low on his nose. The dedication he gave his research was endearing.

She nearly giggled, recalling how sometimes the top half of him would vanish into a bush while he chased a fleeing insect. His backside would shift the branches, then he would shout out in victory once he had his trophy.

Oh, and just there, her imagination watched him drawing, then writing. This one last time, she let him appear to her in the moonlight while he kissed her on the beach. Her imagination was vivid. It was as if she could hear the surf, smell salt air…feel his hands pressing her ribs in an embrace.

It was only a breeze stirring the hair at her temple, but it felt as warm as Clement's breath.

It was not only Clement she had to tuck away in her heart…there was Alice and Jayne, too. How was she to forget being called Mama?

Rather than making her feel fulfilled, her fantasy left her aching. One thing was certain—Everett Parker would not be able to heal her heartache.

'What,' Mildred demanded, peering at Jayne with narrowed eyes, 'has happened to Alice?'

Alice shot Jayne a glance, Jayne shot it back.

The girls did not look alike. The fact that their aunt could not tell them apart showed how little she actually thought of them.

'I jumped through an enchanted hole,' Alice said.

'And,' Jayne added, 'she got attacked by a mad hare.'

Mildred turned her narrowed eye on Clement. 'This is not acceptable. You were to teach them proper behaviour and look at them! Making up outrageous stories.'

Indeed, look at them. In spite of everything that had happened, his daughters sparkled. Right now, it likely had to do with some mischief they were clearly brewing. But in part it had to do with him not being completely forthcoming about why their governess had left.

He had told them there was something Miss Curtis needed to do in London but they would see her again soon. Now that they were in London the girls were in high anticipation of a reunion.

'Papa, may we play in the garden?' Jayne asked.

He did not feel awkward giving permission since he had grown up in this house. It was still his family home even though Mildred was now its baroness.

'You may, but do not do anything I would disapprove of.'

'We won't,' Alice answered.

They would, he knew. It was the very reason they'd asked to go out.

Perhaps he ought to have taken rooms at an inn. It would have been wise to keep the girls away from Mildred.

However he meant to make his position of authority clear. He might be their uncle the same as Duncan was, but he was the man who'd raised Alice and Jayne. He was the one they considered their father.

Let Duncan and Mildred argue the point if they wished to. He was who he was, their father.

Hiding the children away would not serve any good purpose other than making him appear less than confident of his authority when it came to their futures.

'A word, Mildred,' he said when it looked as if she would leave the drawing room.

'I assume you have come to discuss which governess the girls should have. I will fetch Duncan. Clearly, they still need proper training.'

So far Alice and Jayne had done nothing to warrant that comment. There was nothing like criticism of one's children to make one cross. It was an effort to hold his temper, but he managed.

'You will not pass judgement on my daughters within my hearing or theirs. You will not malign them or denigrate them in any way to anyone.'

'But clearly they need guidance and I fear it will not come from you.'

'The reason for my visit is to tell you to forget your idea of the children living in London. They will remain with me until I decide otherwise.'

'Shall we see what Duncan has to say about that?'

'About what?' his brother asked striding into the drawing room at that very moment. 'Clement! Welcome home, Brother!'

Duncan clasped his shoulders in a hug.

He returned the greeting.

'Thank you. It's a short stay, only. After I tend to a matter here, we will return to my house in the country.'

'Not with your nieces, you will not! Wait until you see, Duncan, Clement has not improved their manners in the least.'

'I saw them when they dashed past me a moment ago. They did pause to offer very sweet curtsies. And then they hugged me! Imagine that.'

'Sweet curtsies will not see them placed in advantageous marriages. They must have intense training.'

'Which they will have,' Clement said. 'But it will not be from you or from a martinet of an old-fashioned governess you wish to foist on them.'

'Foist on them? Do you hear that, Husband?' Mildred pretended to pout.

His brother nodded, looking thoughtful. 'I wonder if perhaps you have something else in mind, Clement?'

'Lady Vivienne, the daughter of the Marquess of Helmond, has offered to guide them in society when the time is appropriate.'

Silence followed this pronouncement, but only for half a minute.

'Your brother has lost his mind, Duncan. As if he has ever even met the lady.'

In that moment, running footsteps were heard in the hallway.

Alice and Jayne rushed into the room. Alice had both hands clasped behind her back.

'Auntie Millie, we have a gift for you.' Jayne announced. 'Because we are sorry Miss Curtis kept your nest and put it in a tree.'

'So we found you another to take its place.' Alice withdrew a mass of feathers and sticks, dried grass and who knew what sorts of fluff. It looked well used.

What Clement wondered was, what sort of insect the girls had stashed inside.

There was a time for discipline and there was a time for pranks. This was a time for pranks.

'You will call me Aunt Mildred, Jayne.'

'Yes, Ma'am,' Alice answered.

'Do not play games with me. You are Jayne. I will not tolerate your nonsense.'

'How do you expect to be responsible for them when you cannot tell them, one from another?' he asked exasperatedly.

'I don't mind, Papa,' Jayne said. 'But here is your nest, Aunt Mildred.'

Alice placed it in her hand before Mildred could snatch her fingers away. The grin his sweet daughters exchanged had him peering hard at the nest.

The insect turned out to be a grasshopper which blended in with the shade of the twigs. The marvellous creature made a leap. It alighted in Mildred's hair.

Mildred screeched, dancing about and batting her hair.

Heroically, Duncan plucked the grasshopper, carried it to the window and tossed it out.

'I am certain they did not know it was there.' Duncan soothed his wife with a pat on the shoulder.

An apology was in order, from someone to someone. Mildred ought to apologise for threatening to take his children away from him. Alice and Jayne should apologise for the grasshopper.

Weighing the sins, he decided, 'It was all but invisible, after all.' He could hardly censure his daughters when privately he applauded them.

'I suppose, so,' Mildred muttered, but her frown expressed doubts. 'But back to what you just said…about the Marquess's daughter.'

'That she has offered to teach them?'

'Why would she? Truly, Duncan, do you think he has ever even met such a high-born lady? We certainly have not.'

'But you have met her,' he pointed out. 'There was a bit of a disagreement between the two of you over a hat?'

'You are mistaken. That was with your governess. I do not even recall the awful woman's name.'

'One and the same… Lady Vivienne Louise Curtis.' This conversation was taking up valuable moments. 'Duncan, will you watch these two for a while? I have a marriage proposal to make before the woman I love accepts one from someone else.'

Apparently dumbstruck, his brother managed one nod.

Mildred clasped her hand to her throat. 'Your brother's research has finally driven him out of his mind.'

Chapter Fifteen

Rather than wait for his brother's carriage to be brought around, Clement dashed down the steps and waved over the first hansom cab to come by.

Fearing he had no time to spare, he did not wait for the driver to come down but scrambled up beside him. It might be days before Vivie announced her engagement or it might be moments.

There was also a chance that he was already too late. While he had wasted time blaming her and feeling sorry for himself, Vivienne might have already become engaged.

Although clearly surprised to see Clement riding on the bench, the driver did not protest.

'I'm in a great hurry.' Clement told him where to go.

Even if the announcement was still some time off, he would act while his courage was high. He must reach Vivienne before he thought too closely about what he was doing.

Had it ever happened that the humble brother of a baron had charged in to unseat a marquess for a lady's hand?

Better not to give that too much thought. It was as Mrs Prentis pointed out, Clement was the one who loved her, the other man was the one who did not.

The banner he carried into battle was love. Now wasn't that a noble and romantic thought for a scientist?

'Something is happening at the Helmond mansion tonight. Can't help noticing the fancy carriages dropping off high society folks. Since you are going there in such a hurry, maybe you know what it is?'

'Did you see the conveyance of the Marquess of Winterfeld among them, by chance?'

'It's a hard one to miss, being even grander than the others. I did spot it, though, when I drove past with my last customer before you.'

'I might know what is happening. But how long ago was that?'

'Oh, an hour or more ago. So, what is happening, Sir?'

'I believe the Marquess of Helmond is about to announce the engagement of his daughter.'

'Why, that is grand news! Do you know who the gentleman is?'

'Me… I hope. If you can get me there fast enough.'

He was not dressed for the occasion and the driver's sceptical glance said as much. But then the fellow grinned. 'Very well, Sir. Hold on tight.'

The driver snapped his whip over the team's ears. The carriage jerked, then lurched. Clement leaned forward as if it would somehow make the conveyance go faster. He clamped his hat to his head to keep it from flying off.

Still, the wheels could not turn quickly enough. At this very moment the announcement might already be in progress. His future happiness and that of his daughters could be slipping away from him.

What, exactly, made him think Vivie would change her mind about him, he could not imagine. It was only that he felt something drawing him to her with great urgency. He had never had a feeling like it before. Her soul calling his… again, a romantic notion and far from scientific.

Love was not scientific, he was learning…it was far from logical. Yet it was the truest, most compelling thing he had ever known. And so, yes, he did feel Vivie calling to him, even if she might not be aware of it. Hopefully he would feel her presence strongly enough to lead him to wherever she was.

The estate was impressive, as vast and formal looking as any he had ever seen.

He tried not to dwell on what he was up against, what he was asking her to give up for love…of him.

He lifted his banner and raced through the streets of London.

Vivienne stood at the foot of the gallows, more commonly known as the grand hall steps. The room where her fate was to be announced was one floor up.

Rather than look that way, she plucked a chrysanthemum from an urn, taking what comfort she could from the tickle of the petals on her palm.

'Where is Everett?' Vivienne's father slid a pointed look at her mother, impatience evident in the tight lines creasing the edges of his mouth. 'Dinner will soon be announced.'

'He is here, my dear. I imagine he only wishes to have a bit of time to himself. After the announcement is made he will not have a moment's peace with all the congratulations he will receive.'

Nor would Vivienne. Oh, what wouldn't she give for a moment's peace, as well?

Given a choice, she would be walking on the beach with Clement. Since she did not have one she had spent the afternoon submitting to the ministrations of three maids who were set upon making her beautiful for a fiancé who did not even love her.

This was all a show for society. To demonstrate her father's wealth and position. It had little to do with her. Perhaps not so much to do with Everett either.

They were dancing to society's tune, no matter how either of them felt about it.

She had fought this moment for years and now that it was upon her, it was worse than she'd ever feared. Dread cramped her stomach.

'Let's go to the dining room and make certain everything is in order.' Father extended his arm to Mother.

'I will meet you there in a moment, my dear.'

Once he was gone her mother touched Vivienne's chin, peering into her face.

'You look exceptionally beautiful, though pale. Are you feeling well?'

'I feel as if I will burst out of my skin.'

'I remember feeling the same way. You will get through the night, I promise.' Mother patted her cheek. 'And now I must join your father.'

Vivienne pressed her stomach. She wanted so badly to see Clement. To feel his arms holding her securely, to get lost in his kiss.

She ought to have let him propose that night. She ought to have accepted and then written her father a letter telling him she could not wed the man of his choice because she was marrying the man of her choice.

Mother paused where the grand hall met the imposing staircase.

'Everett is a good man. It is possible that you will come to love him. It was my experience. But you will recall what I told you about your Great-Aunt Anne. She could not love her first husband because her heart was with another. It is only a shame that she did not speak to her father before her engagement was announced. He might have listened to her.'

With that her mother went on her way.

Was she giving her advice or telling a story? It had been too vague to know for certain. Would her father listen if she went to him? Probably not. Now that he had her nearly betrothed, he would carry on with it.

Even if Vivienne picked up her elegant skirts and ran away from all this, what then? Would Clement still want her after what she had done?

The cramp in her belly crept to her throat.

Footsteps came from the grand hallway. A stranger came around the corner, looking as miserable as Vivienne felt. The lady clasped her a hand over her mouth, as if she were startled to see her. Then she dashed down another hallway.

It was just as well the other woman had not said anything. If Vivienne had to speak to anyone, her throat would clog and choke her.

She fled to the garden to gather herself.

Outside the air was cool, crisp on the brink of autumn. What, she wondered, was it like this afternoon on the Isle of Wight? Were Alice and Jayne still romping after their father in search of insects, or had they gone home to Cheshire?

Or perhaps he was working on his book. Was he, maybe, thinking of her? Missing her? Probably not. After the way she had left him without a word, he could surely only resent her. But she'd had the oddest feeling all day. Even with the bustle going on around her, she had felt her heart reaching for him. Probably because she missed him so intensely.

Yesterday, she had meant to put memories of him to rest, delegate him to a place in her past. A precious episode of her life, lived and now gone. Clearly the attempt had not worked. It made no sense, but she had the oddest feeling that if she turned a corner, suddenly he would be there. He would open his arms and she would run into them. Once she was there, no one would prise her out of his embrace.

Father would not, society would not.

Guilt for what she had done to Clement and his children might keep her from him, though. Guilt held her to this pending engagement as much as anything else. Since she could not have her Clement, she might as well go through with marrying Everett. What did anything really matter without her entomologist?

But then…was that what Great-Aunt Anne had thought? How bitterly had she regretted not fighting for love?

'I love you, Clement Marston,' she said because there was no one nearby to hear.

And that was the last time she would ever speak those words.

Unless…

She stopped where she stood and closed her eyes, listening to birds chirruping, to leaves shifting in the breeze… to her heart swelling with emotion.

'Should I fight for you?' Did she dare?

'Do it, Vivie. Fight for me as I am fighting for you.'

She went utterly still. This voice was not in her mind… not a dream. It was behind her.

Before she completely turned, Clement's arm stole around her waist. He spun her about, drew her tight to his heart. He tipped her chin.

'Tell me you will. If you love me as I love you, please, Vivie, fight for us.'

'I do love you. But…do you forgive me?'

'I was wrong to blame you. Do you forgive me?'

Before she could nod, he kissed her. For the first time she kissed him back not as a governess, not as an imposter.

She, Lady Vivienne Curtis, gave herself completely and without regret to her love. There was one emotion behind this kiss and it was joy…celebration.

Clement had come to fight for her. And now she would fight for him.

Father was formidable, yes—but she was in love.

The last thing Clement was inclined to do was end this kiss. It was the first one that felt truly binding between them. The others had been taken, or surrendered, but this one promised for ever.

'How did you find me?'

By the guiding of Providence, he could only think.

'I crossed paths with a woman—your mother, it turned out to be. When I told her who I was she led me through the house and out to the garden.'

'Truly?'

'Yes, truly. She said something about not ending up like Great-Aunt Anne. I thanked her even though I have no idea what she meant by it. Then your mother shook her head and pointed to where you were.'

It was a lucky thing, too. He would never have found her on his own. The garden, like the house, was immense, with hedges, trees and paths leading in every direction.

'I will explain about Great-Aunt Anne later, but now… Clement, I have missed you so much. Come…'

Gripping his hand, she led him a short distance away to a secluded patio. A pair of doors opened to a room with bookshelves on every wall. It could only be a library.

Once inside, she leaned against the doors, drew him close. He felt her heart thumping, her chest rising and falling with her quick breathing.

'Is this truly real?' She touched his cheek as if to be certain. 'It seems like another dream.'

Hands around her waist, he held her hip to hip. He nipped her lips, kissed her deeply.

'Seems real enough to me.'

He kissed her for a long time, until his lungs ached for air. Partly because he wanted to and partly to be certain she wasn't right and this wasn't actually another dream. Since dreams did not require one to breathe, this was real.

'If this was a dream—mine, I mean—your hair would not look like that.' Seeing it piled in stiff curls on top of her head wasn't what he was used to. He'd only ever seen it wavy and loose.

'Once we have your father's blessing, I will free you from all this,' he said, meaning her rigid coif.

'You might not get it. But apparently you have my mother's.'

'I am glad for that, at least. But, Vivie, all I need is your blessing. All I need is you.' He did need her. Now, urgently, in every way a man needed a woman. But first things first. A formal commitment, a wedding, and then the pleasure of being her husband.

He went down on one knee. This time he would do it the right way. Last time, although he had also loved her then, his motive had been to keep her from leaving him. This time he was offering his heart and his life because he simply couldn't imagine life without her.

'My Vivie, I love you with everything that is in me. Will you marry me?' Ever-prepared fellow that he was, he'd come with a ring. He drew it from his pocket, where it caught the fading sunlight streaming through the window and gleamed.

He heard a sniffle. That was odd since Vivie was grinning and waggling her hand for him to place the ring on her finger.

'Yes, I will marry you.'

He slipped the ring past her knuckle. A perfect fit. Just as she was a perfect fit for him and his daughters.

'It is the most beautiful thing I have ever seen, Clement. The tiny butterflies take my breath away—oh, and the diamond!' She turned her hand this way and that, clearly admiring it. 'It suits us, don't you think?'

'Love suits us.'

He rose from the floor, kissed her while backing her towards the couch. He eased her down to the cushion, then back. Half-reclined, he kissed her yet again. Somehow he could not get enough of tasting her. This time he felt a hint of her curves under all the clothes she wore. Even if he had intended to get them off her before the vows, which he did not, he would not be able to figure out how.

He contented himself with kisses. She was kept busy giving them back.

'We will be deliriously happy, Clement.'

'I am already delirious.' Getting lightheaded and out of breath. His good intentions were fast losing ground. 'I must speak with your father immediately before I lose control.'

He sat up, drawing her with him. 'Did you hear a noise?' he asked.

She shook her head. 'We must speak to someone else before we speak to Father,' she said, patting her hair although not a strand was out of place. 'Do not forget Everett is involved in this, too.'

So caught up in being with Vivie, winning her hand, he had all but forgotten there was another man believing her hand would be his.

'We do have challenges facing us,' he admitted.

'This won't be easy,' Vivie said while pressing her engagement ring to her heart. 'I do not even know where he is right now.'

All at once a door between the bookcases squeaked open. A woman stepped out.

'I know where he is,' the lady said through her sniffles. She swiped tears from her face with trembling fingers. 'And it might not be as difficult as you imagine.'

Vivienne remembered this woman from earlier. She was the very lady she had encountered in the hall.

Her name was Clara, they discovered while hurrying with her through the garden. What she breathlessly disclosed along the way was stunning.

The stuff of fairytales was what it was turning out to be.

They came upon Everett sitting on a bench beside the south-reflecting pool, head in hand and looking as miserable as she had felt not an hour ago.

And no wonder. He had just bidden a heart-wrenching farewell to the woman he'd fallen in love with over the summer.

Wonder of wonders, while Vivienne had been falling in love with Clement, Everett had been falling in love with Clara.

If he was as devoted to Clara as he'd been to his first wife, she would be a lucky woman.

'Everett.' Clara rushed to him, knelt and spread his hands away from his face. 'There is someone who wishes to speak with you.'

The Marquess stood suddenly when he spotted Vivienne, bringing Clara to her feet along with him.

Casting Everett a tremulous smile, Clara went to stand beside Clement.

'You have met Mrs Newport, I see,' Everett said heavily.

Mrs Newport? A widow, then. No wonder she and Everett had bonded so deeply and so quickly.

'Oh, yes, and quite by surprise,' Vivienne said with a twinkle.

'Then you must surely guess that… At any rate, the lady and I have just said our goodbyes. I intend to honour the agreement I made with your father.'

'That is upstanding of you, Everett, and I appreciate it. But you see, I will not honour it.'

Lines creased the corners of his eyes, showing his strain when he glanced at Clara and then back at Vivienne.

His pensive gaze reminded her that there was a generation between them.

'You would go against your father's wishes? Are you certain? Walk with me for a moment, my dear. We must discuss this.'

They did not go far, only around a rosebush and an alder.

'There will be consequences to you refusing my suit. Your father will not take it well.'

'He will not die of his disappointment. I do not see why all four of us should suffer broken hearts just to spare his pride.'

'I suppose pride does have something to do with it. The aristocracy does tend to suffer that flaw at times.'

'It can certainly be a trial for their daughters. But, Everett, I am so pleased you found your lady. Please accept my congratulations. Mine and Clement's.'

'Ah, the young man with the broad grin on his face? I assume by the ring on your finger that he has proposed.'

'It took a while, but here we are.'

'I envy you, Vivienne. Being young and in love is a wonderful thing. My best wishes to you both.'

'Thank you. And now that we are not to become engaged, you are at liberty to propose to Clara.'

'I intend to, just as soon as I am able.' He started to lift his hand, but let it drop. She wondered if he'd meant to pat her on the head. 'I admit I did struggle with your youth as you must have struggled with my age. But we would have made an adequate match, I think.'

'Not a happy one, though. Not with me weeping for Clement and you pining for Clara.'

'Indeed, not a happy one. Since I did not expect to fall in love again, I agreed to marry you in order to secure the future of the title. And if I could please my stepmother at the same time, all the better. I suppose your reason was much the same.'

'Yes, I did wish to make Great-Aunt Anne happy. I hope she does not take this too badly.'

'She is resilient. And don't forget she has a soft spot for love matches.'

'No point in putting this off, is there? I shall find my father right away and give him the news.'

'No, my dear, it must come from me. If I back out of our arrangement there is nothing he can do about it. I am afraid it would not go as well for you.'

'You are a gallant man, Everett. I shall make certain Father understands I am completely in agreement with you.'

'Shall we get on with it, then? I have a lady to propose to.'

A lucky lady, Vivienne thought. She was happy to have the Marquess as a friend. And grateful for ever that he would not be her husband.

'I rather doubt that they have eloped, Thomas,' Vivienne heard her mother say as she and Everett approached the doorway leading to the grand hall. 'Take a breath and calm yourself.'

Clement and Clara followed a few steps behind.

'My boy would not do such a thing, you know that, or you would not have agreed to let him have our Vivienne,' said Great-Aunt Anne.

'Good, my stepmother is with them,' Everett whispered while they paused out of sight. 'Better to get this said with all of them together.'

Vivienne peered around the corner. 'It is only the three of them.'

'The guests will be in the dining room by now, waiting for us to make our grand appearance.'

Everyone would suspect the reason for the gathering. Anticipation would be running high. What high-ranking gentleman would finally win the hand of the reluctant Lady Vivienne? they would be wondering.

Vivienne glanced back at Clement who in her eyes was the highest ranking of them all. He did not notice since he was busy murmuring reassurances to Clara that all would be well.

Clement walked into the hall in step with Lord Winterfeld, even though it was the Marquess who would be delivering the news. Perhaps it was presumptuous to take this position when he had no rank other than the brother of a baron.

He might be the Honourable Clement Marston, but all he had to present himself as was a man in love. A stubborn one who would not leave this grand mansion without being granted the hand of the Marquess of Helmond's daughter.

One thing went in his favour. It was easier to capture an

insect when it was stunned and although Vivienne's father was not an insect, he would be stunned to his core.

The principle might hold.

He matched the Marquess of Winterfeld's strides, his shoulders set as firm as his determination.

'Ah!' Lord Helmond declared. 'There you are. We are ready to begin.'

'Before we do, Thomas, I would like a word.'

Clement knew the Marquess must notice him standing beside them, but Vivie's father's attention was focused on Everett.

'A quick word, I hope. Our guests are anticipating the announcement.'

Vivienne's mother took a spot on one side of her husband, then nodded for the lady who must be Great-Aunt Anne to take his arm on the other side. In his mind he saw them flanking the fellow in support of Vivienne. It might not be true, but it was comforting thinking they did.

Lady Helmond had pointed him toward her daughter in the garden so perhaps he already had her support.

While her endorsement would be welcome, if he did not have it he would still leave here being granted Vivie's hand...somehow.

'I see that you found her.' Vivienne's mother spoke to him, but it was her daughter she smiled at.

'My deep thanks, Marchioness. I would never have managed on my own.'

'Found her?' Vivienne's father arched a brow at his wife, then lowered it at Clement. 'What is this about?'

Great-Aunt Anne spotted Clara standing beside Vivie near a potted palm several paces back. She crossed the foyer, took both of Clara's hands and gave them a squeeze.

'My dear, I am so pleased to see you out of mourning.

You look…' She tipped her head this way and that. Then with a glance at her stepson, she smiled. 'Oh, I see.

'What does everyone in this room see that I do not?' the Marquess of Helmond asked.

'I'm afraid I must back out of our agreement, Thomas. Over the course of the summer, matters have changed.'

Lord Helmond's complexion went through a few shades, but settled on pulsing crimson.

'You would insult my daughter? Tonight, when we have guests anticipating a betrothal announcement? I would not have expected this of you, Everett.'

'But, Father, I am not at all insulted. Truly.' Vivienne hurried forward, standing next to Clement rather than either marquess.

'Yes, dear.' Vivie's mother patted her husband's arm. 'Our Vivienne is in love.'

'With this fellow?' Lord Helmond seemed a formidable man, but Clement had no intention of being cowed. 'I do not even know who he is. Why have I not met him before?'

'I believe he has obligations which keep him in the country most of the time,' Lady Helmond pointed out.

'I am an entomologist. And I am in love with your daughter.'

He could point out that his brother was Baron Granville, but the connection was unlikely to impress a marquess.

More, he was who he was and would stand on that.

'Love? What has love got to do with it?' Vivie's father looked like a storm ready to burst.

'Love has everything to do with it. Open your eyes, Thomas. You will see that my boy is completely smitten with our friend Clara.' Great-Aunt Anne beamed at them all.

'I am in love with her,' the Marquess of Winterfeld declared.

'You see, no one wishes for this engagement, Thomas, only you.' Great-Aunt Anne was smiling at Clara when she said so.

'Perhaps because I have houseful of guests and no announcement to make.'

Ah, Thomas Curtis was properly stunned. This was Clement's moment.

'May I have a private word, Lord Helmond?'

'Private does not seem to be the order of the hour. You may speak to me in company. And if it is not an inconvenience, may I have your name?'

'No inconvenience at all, my lord. I am Clement Marston. I have been eager to meet you.'

'Ah, Marston, my daughter's former employer.' Quite clearly, Vivienne's father did not look pleased to meet the man his daughter had spent the summer with.

'Mr Marston is the brother of Baron Granville,' Vivienne pointed out.

The name must not be one the Marquess recognised immediately for he pursed his mouth.

'I believe you have met the Baron once before, my dear,' Lady Helmond murmured. 'The family is well respected… and the baronetcy is a prosperous one, I believe.'

'Indeed? Perhaps I did then. I meet a great many people.'

Lord Helmond stared at him, the silence strained, but Clement did make the observation that the corner of the man's mouth twitched.

In humour or anger, he had no way of knowing. What he did know was that it made no difference to what he intended to do.

'I stand before you, my lord, to request the very great honour of your daughter's hand in marriage.'

The Marquess responded with an ungentlemanly grunt.

Understandable, given that the man was being asked to hand over his daughter to a complete stranger and an untitled one at that.

'Tell me, Mr Marston, why would I not seek a fellow of higher rank than you?'

'Because no man will be more devoted to your daughter than I will be.'

The man looked back and forth between him and Vivie, probably torn between what he wanted for his daughter and what she wanted for herself.

All of a sudden his heart softened and he understood Lord Helmond's dilemma. There was every chance that Clement would one day stand in the fellow's shoes…twice.

'I understand your hesitation, my lord. But I will not leave here without having your blessing.'

'And you love this man, Vivienne? You will not consider another?'

'No, Father. There is no other man in the world I would touch a beetle for,' she said firmly.

'Touch a beetle? You did that?' Vivie's father tipped his head, narrowed his gaze as if judging the truth of what she said. He shrugged, then looked back at Clement. 'I have been rescuing her from insects ever since she was two years old.'

'You will always be my hero, Father, but now…'

She displayed her hand to her mother, then her father. 'This is my engagement ring. You see the sweet little butterflies. I am no longer afraid.'

'Oh, my dear, it is lovely.' Lady Helmond hugged her daughter while Great-Aunt Anne hurried over to have a look at the unusual ring.

'Well, Mr Marston, clearly you have won my daughter's heart.' The Marquess's expression was too stern for Clement to believe he was overly pleased. Which in no way put him off his purpose. 'I'd have preferred that you had asked me for her hand before you gave her the ring.'

Then the oddest thing happened.

Lord Helmond grinned and slapped Clement on the back. 'You have my consent and my blessing. Welcome to the family, my boy. I was losing all hope that any man would catch Vivienne. You should be warned, though, my daughter is stubbornly independent.'

'It is only one of the qualities I admire about her, Sir.'

'We've done it, Eleanor.' Lord Helmond turned his triumphant grin on Lady Helmond. 'We've finally got her settled.'

'She gave us a good struggle over the years, didn't she?'

'We will announce your engagement as intended, young lady. Your guests are waiting.'

That said, the Marquess enfolded his child in a hug.

'Thomas,' Everett, who had been standing in the background through it all, said. 'Since this was to be an event to announce my engagement as well, would you mind carrying through with it? As long as Clara will have me.'

Everett went down on one knee, took her hand and kissed it tenderly.

Clara gasped and accepted his proposal.

'Two announcements! We shall be the talk of society.' Lady Helmond waved to the butler who had been standing near the door.

'Smith, please take Mr Marston to my husband's chamber and find him something appropriate to wear. They are of a size.'

'This is all so romantic.' Great-Aunt Anne hugged Clara. Then she hugged Vivienne. 'You are a far bolder girl than I was, my darling. I admire you for not making my mistake.'

No more than Clement did. After meeting the Marquess, one of society's loftiest men, he understood how hard this all must have been for Vivie.

'Can you imagine, Thomas?' Lady Helmond glowed in pure happiness. 'A son-in-law and a… Oh, well I do not quite know what Clara will be to us, but some sort of family relation, to be sure. Isn't it wonderful to see our family growing at last?'

Clement was halfway up the grand stairway when he heard Vivie say, 'More than you know. I am to be a mother.'

Everyone went still. Had an insect been creeping across the floor they would have heard its scratchy feet.

'Alice and Jayne,' she explained hastily. 'Clement's daughters. I told you about them, Mother. You have grand-daughters!'

'You did tell me, darling. From all you had to say about them, they remind me of you.'

'Heaven help us, then,' Vivie's father said with a smile.

Heaven had and that was a fact.

Clement grinned down at his intended. He would no longer need to schedule a trip to find adventure.

Simply waking each day with Lady Vivie Marston would be the adventure of his lifetime.

Vivienne's parents had spared no expense for her engagement announcement.

There was a feast for their hundred closest friends, an orchestra and dancing.

It was lovely. But the truth was she would have been just as happy celebrating on the beach with only breaking surf and moonlight to wish them well.

'We are engaged,' she murmured to her fiancé while he danced her out of the open ballroom doors and into the garden. 'Can you believe it?'

'It depends.'

'Depends on what?' He twirled her down the patio stairs and it felt as light as flying.

'If one looks at the facts, how often does a lady meant to be a marchioness end up the wife of an entomologist?' he asked. 'Statistically it is beyond unlikely. It may never have happened in the history of England.'

At the bottom of the steps he simply held her, swaying as if they were still dancing. How delightful to live in a musical embrace.

'But then there is love. If you base it on how much I love you... Vivie, it was destined to be.'

'Destined.' She slipped her arms about his neck, swaying ever closer to him.

Then he kissed her for a long time. She kissed him back even longer. During it, he tried to pluck a pin from her hair.

'It's no use,' she said against his lips. 'I think my maid used paste. I will not have to arrange my hair again until our wedding.'

'Please say it will be a short engagement.'

'I would say so, but I cannot. My parents have been so accepting of us. We must give them a proper engagement.'

'It will be a grand event, won't it?'

'The talk of London.'

'I suppose I shall survive the ordeal, but only out of love for you.' More kisses, closer swaying. 'The worst of it will be missing you.'

'But why will you miss me?'

'Because you live in London. I live in Cheshire.' He breathed on her ear, nipping the lobe which gave her a shiver.

Feathers, why did society engagements have to be so long?

'Have you dismissed me as your governess?'

'Now that we are engaged I do not see how you can work for me. We can no longer live in the same house until we are married.'

'One would think a researcher would be more logical. See the obvious answer to the challenge.'

'Right now, the researcher is being kissed and he is not thinking clearly.'

'Let me help you then.' She traced his lips with the tip of her finger, watching the torch glow glimmer on her engagement ring. Even now she could not believe the past several hours had happened.

Clement twirled her about, probably in an attempt to keep up the pretence of dancing in case anyone was out walking in the garden. Glancing about she did spot two couples. Everett and Clara vanished behind a curve in the garden path. Grace and George were coming around the same curve, but returning from one of the secluded alcoves.

Spotting her and Clement, Grace waved her hand. George nodded and grinned.

'We cannot be wed soon enough,' she said with a great deal of envy that her sister and her husband could...well, better to leave that a thought for another time. Dwelling on it would make her as unfocused as Clement was.

Until she explained the solution to their dilemma, she needed to keep her mind clear and not muddled with intimate imaginings.

'You know I will not let another governess take my place with Alice and Jayne.'

'I pity the woman who tries to.'

'Quite. And so I will be Alice's and Jayne's governess until I am their mother.'

'Hmmm,' he whispered into the stiff hair near her ear. 'Shall we move to London then?'

'I could not be a governess here. It would be a great scandal. What I shall do is live with Great-Aunt Anne in Cheshire. During the day I will be your governess and then each night I will return and dream of you as I lie alone in bed.'

'I don't know why I didn't think of that.'

'You were not thinking with your logical mind, that's what you said.'

'I wonder if researchers place too much importance on logic.'

'Oh, well, I suppose it depends upon what they are researching.'

Several kisses later they stopped to breathe.

'In some cases research is all one wants to do…a fellow could work all night long on it.'

'And his assistant along with him.'

A moth flapped around their heads.

'Ah, to see a moth on one's engagement night is good luck,' he declared.

Vivienne touched the grin she adored, tracing the flat line, then the upward curve.

'Even if you are making that up, I shall believe it's true.'

'Our love is true, that's all that needs to be believed.'

The moth circled their heads, then fluttered towards the stars where, she suspected, wonders and miracles came from.

London—one year later

Clement decided he was a saint. During the year between his engagement party and his wedding reception, he had been the soul of discretion when it came to his fiancée. Working side by side with her on their new project had been a daily temptation. It hadn't helped that the subject they were exploring was the mating rituals of insects.

Now, with their vows spoken and the wedding breakfast eaten, he was finished with being discreet. It was time to explore the mating rituals of Mr and Mrs Clement Marston.

'Come, Wife,' he said after a well-wisher moved on from the ornately decorated table where they had just finished a magnificent feast. 'I believe that is the last of them. I have something special for you…in our chamber.'

His bride touched the corner of his grin as she was fond of doing. 'Do you? What could it be?'

Their chamber was actually a suite of rooms reserved in the Helmond mansion for him, Vivie and the girls. His mother and father-in-law had made sure to design the suite with a room included as a nursery.

His bride slid her fingertip across his mouth. Ah, then, let the mating ritual begin.

'I like it when you touch me that way.'

'If you like that,' she said while rising from her chair, 'you will love it when I touch the special thing you have for me in our chamber.'

He bolted out of his chair, her hand tightly held in his.

Across the room, he saw Mrs Prentis laugh and nudge Mr Prentis in the side.

It would be proper to bid each of their guests an individual farewell, but it would take too much time. He had already waited a year as it was.

Alice and Jayne would not notice they were gone. That very moment they were romping in the garden with a few other children. When the breakfast ended and the guests went home, they were to be taken somewhere for the night by their new grandparents. Exactly where they were going escaped him right now.

The main thing was that they would be occupied so that he and his bride could also be...occupied.

Taking the stairs to their suite, arms entwined, he was completely focused on being alone with Vivienne. Alone in a way which had been forbidden to them until a couple of hours ago.

The past year had been a good one and he would not have traded a moment of it. However, he was relieved it was finally over and the waiting was done. At last Vivienne Marston was his to have and to hold...especially to hold.

'Give me a hint about my surprise,' she urged.

'It is large.'

'Oh, my...tell me more.' His bride had an inquisitive mind and a pretty blush to go with it.

'Ah, well, it is hard until it is unveiled. After that it is more bendable.'

'Bendable?' Vivie's eyes went wide. She blinked.

'Malleable, if you wish... Perhaps even pliant?'

Her jaw dropped.

Perhaps he should not tease her this way. Any more of it and he would laugh out loud, spoil everything before he got her alone.

Better to have rooms here than at the Granville town house. The Helmond mansion was huge, the grounds were lovely and, most importantly, Mildred lived miles away. While his sister-in-law no longer tried to interfere with his family, she was still an unpleasant relative.

Still, they would spend most of their time in Cheshire where life was fresh and healthy for the children...for the ones they already had and the ones still to come.

Coming to the doors of their suite, he did not open them at first, but pressed her between the wood and his body.

'You, Vivienne Marston, are the most beautiful woman I have ever seen. I cannot believe you are my bride. Are you ready for your surprise?'

'I am and I might have a surprise or two of my own for you.'

'You fascinate me, my bride. I can scarcely think a clear thought wondering what your surprise…or two might be.'

He kissed her while he turned the knob, slowly opening the door.

Without letting go of her mouth, he shut the door with his boot heel. He backed her across the small drawing room.

Afternoon light filtered inside, but heavy curtains blocked most of it. The room had a soft romantic aura that even firelight could not match for romance. Besides, there would be no firelight until later tonight. He had no patience to wait for it. To his delight, it did not seem that Vivie had the patience to wait either.

When he figured they were near the desk, he broke the kiss, but covered her eyes with his fingers. One finger slipped and he felt his bride give it a nip, a kiss.

He turned her about, then dropped his hand. 'There, you have your surprise.'

She stared for a moment, probably not believing what she was seeing. 'Our book!' She dashed forward, picked it up and hugged it to her chest. With a squeal of delight, she twirled. Her skirts flared around her as if they also expressed happiness.

'Fresh from the publisher. My wedding gift to you.'

She slid her fingers along the binding. 'Hard, just like you said.' The glance she gave him was long, simmering and slipping slowly down the front of him.

After a moment, she set the book down on the desk, opened it and turned the pages, sighing over each photograph and drawing. 'Bendable, just like you said...pliable... quite malleable.' Finished, she closed the book, set it back down. 'We ought to do something about that.'

'I think you already have.' He shifted his weight from one foot to the other.

She took him by the hand, drew him towards their bedchamber.

Crossing the rug, he plucked pins from her hair, tugged stiff loops, sifting them though with his fingers until they were silky again.

'Thank you,' he whispered, then went to work on dress buttons that were too small for his fingers to undo quickly. Luckily he was a diligent man.

'For what, Husband? I have barely begun act like a proper bride.'

'The thanks were going to the Good Lord for the turn our lives have taken. And now...' With the wicked buttons finally conquered, the dress fell away. 'And now I am only yards of lace away from being a proper groom.'

She gave a low, throaty laugh. 'We shall free me together. We have always done brilliant work while exploring shoulder to shoulder.'

If there was one thing he appreciated, it was the thrill of exploration.

'Let me see, now. Shoulder to shoulder.' He traced the curve of her shoulder, the bend of her elbow where her gown had fallen away. 'Hip to hip,' he murmured while drawing her close, his hands tugging the spot where the nip of her waist gave way to the curve of her hips. 'Let's see how brilliant we can be.'

As it turned out, they were brilliant all night. And all next morning, too.

Beyond a doubt, Mr and Mrs Marston would be brilliant together for the rest of their lives.

* * * * *

A NOTE TO ALL READERS

From October releases Mills & Boon will be making some changes to the series formats and pricing.

What will be different about the series books?

In response to recent reader feedback, we are increasing the size of our paperbacks to bigger books with better quality paper, making for a better reading experience.

What will be the new price of Mills & Boon?

Over the past four years we have seen significant increases in the cost of producing our books. As a result, in order to continue to provide customers with a quality reading experience, the price of our books will increase to RRP $10.99 for Modern singles and RRP $19.99 for 2-in-1s from Medical, Intrigue, Romantic Suspense, Historical and Western.

For futher information regarding format changes and pricing, please visit our website millsandboon.com.au.

MILLS & BOON
millsandboon.com.au

HISTORICAL

Your romantic escape to the past.

Available Next Month

A Marriage To Shock Society Joanna Johnson
The Scandalous Widow Elizabeth Rolls

....

The Viscount's Christmas Bride Bronwyn Scott
One Night With The Duchess Maggie Weston

Keep reading for an excerpt of a new title
from the Historical series,
THE LADY'S PROPOSAL FOR THE LARID
by Jeanine Englert

Prologue

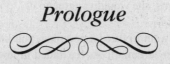

October 1745.
Loch's End, Glencoe, Scotland

'She must marry, brother. It is the best way to protect her.
In truth, it may be the *only* way to protect her.'

Susanna Cameron scoffed and halted her descent on the
stairs at the sound of her eldest brother's voice from the
cracked door of the study below. Her blood cooled as her
hand clutched the wooden finial of the railing, her slippered
foot hanging in mid-air, frozen by his words. Moonlight
streamed in through the stained-glass windows, casting
blotches of colour on the stone and on her dark gown, as
she stood on the landing and listened. Surely her brothers were not discussing *her*. She needed no husband, nor
any man's protection. She was a Cameron after all. She
frowned. But who else would they be desperate to marry
off for protection? Her youngest sister was already married with her first bairn due next year.

'She will not have it, as you well know. *Especially* if you
attempt to force it upon her.' Rolf answered with a chuckle
rounding out the end of his words.

Susanna smiled as her younger brother Rolf came to her
defence, and then frowned with the realisation and con-

firmation that it *was* she who was being discussed. She squared her shoulders, turned on her heel, and took a step onto the bottom set of stairs prepared to tell them exactly what she thought about their scheme to marry her off. In simplest terms, she wouldn't agree to it.

Ever.

'I do not want to force it upon her, you know that, especially after Jeremiah,' Royce added in low tones. 'But surely her safety trumps all. She must have another family to back her in case the worst happens—and we are no longer here to protect her.'

Susanna stilled. Her throat dried and her stomach dropped. She blanched. *No longer here to protect her?* She had never heard her brothers talk in such a way. The politics and unrest in the Highlands were precarious now to be sure, but Royce, her eldest brother and laird of the clan, feared nothing and no one. The Camerons were one of the most powerful clans in the Highlands, if not *the* most powerful. Who would dare attack or threaten them, especially now? And what reason could they possibly have to do so? They had alliances with almost every surrounding clan.

'You cannot even entertain such thoughts. You have a bairn on the way.'

'That is exactly *why* I must think such,' Royce countered. His boots echoed along the stone floor. 'And you must prepare yourself. Our sisters may become targets once all is revealed. So might Iona and our babe. If something happens to me, you must be ready to carry on. No matter what.'

'You know I will protect all of them with my life, but such talk is extreme. It may never come out, brother. All this worry and planning may be for naught.'

'While I hope you are right, Rolf, my gut tells me otherwise,' Royce replied. 'And once all is revealed, the Highlands may become the battleground we feared, and instead of the British being at odds with us, we will all be fighting one another.'

Chapter One

⁓⁓⁓⁓⁓⁓⁓

Two weeks later.
Argyll Castle, Glencoe, Scotland

Laird Rowan Campbell slammed the forging hammer down with force, the clash of metal against iron reverberated through his body. He relished the ache the repeated pounding created in his forearm. His nightly visits to the forge had become his place of peace, not unlike a religious man's house of worship. He set aside his hammer and turned the rough metal blade that would become a sword in his grip and frowned. The piece was becoming too cool to shape and would fracture if he wasn't careful. Setting it aside, he grabbed the shovel, scooped up a heaping pile of hot bright orange coals, and then added them to the forge before sliding the metal blade beneath them.

'This is the last place I thought to search for you, yet here you are.'

Rowan stilled at the sound of the familiar female voice behind him. It was a voice he had not heard for over two years. One he had not ever wished to hear again but wishes were fickle things prone to shatter much like hot metal when it cools too quickly and isn't properly tempered. And that was Susanna Cameron: fire and ice within the same breath and a woman quite prone to breaking things and relishing in her destruction.

'Susanna,' he replied, shifting the coals evenly over the flame in the forge, not eager to face her. He needed a moment to gain his bearings and counted to five as he ran his soiled hands down the leather apron protecting him as he worked. Then, he turned, and his body thrummed and heated at the sight of her like the first time he'd set eyes on her when he was fifteen years old with the beginnings of scruff on his cheeks. She stood framed by the doorway of the forge, covered in her signature dark hooded cloak, her glistening ice blue eyes gathering all the light in the room while her pearly skin and lush pink lips reflected the firelight and sent a surge of need straight through him.

Deuces.

His body didn't remember what his mind always did: her cruelty. He fisted his hands by his sides.

'You look far better than the last time I saw you,' she said, her gaze slowly assessed him head to toe as she pulled at the tips of her gloves one at a time to remove them from her hands.

She'd skilfully landed her first blow. He knew more was to come.

'What do you want, my lady? And how did you manage to get past my guards? And where are yours?' He wiped his forearm across his brow to keep the sweat from stinging his eyes as they swept the room. She was alone.

'Always to the point,' she replied, smiling at him as if she were about to steal from his pocket. Knowing Susanna Cameron, she already had, and he just didn't know it yet.

'Merely eager to get back to my work.' It had been over two years since his last bout with insanity, and he planned to keep it that way, despite her prodding. The forge brought him calm, salvation, and sanity, and his nightly visits were a necessary part of his recovery. Her presence was interrupting all of that.

She scoffed, her gaze flicking about the forge as if it were a dirty, forlorn place. 'You are laird. You have men to tend to these needs.'

'Perhaps it is *I* who need *it*.'

Her brow lifted for a moment, her interest evident, before she cast it aside. 'I need your assistance.'

'I doubt that. You have men to tend to your every need, and you have a way of bending them *to* your needs. Otherwise, you would not have been able to enter this forge.' He would deal with his men that allowed her entry later. Much later, after his temper had cooled.

She frowned. 'Perhaps, but not for this task. It requires discretion.'

'Then why come to me, a man who would relish in the idea of exploiting your clan's secrets for my own benefit.'

'Because I have no other options.'

She looked away and fidgeted with her hands, an odd display of weakness from a woman never prone to it. Her cool, calm, and icy demeanour slipped away to reveal a brief momentary glimmer of the young vulnerable lass he had known and thought he once loved many years ago before her mask fell back into place.

Curious. Now he *was* interested.

'A Cameron without options is an odd situation indeed,' he replied. 'Why would I be willing to help you? Perhaps you have forgotten our last exchange?'

Susanna's gaze met his, but she didn't answer. They both

knew well what that last exchange was, but she was loath to speak of it. So was he.

He set aside his tools and turned away to shovel a new scoop of coal into the forge and the blast of heat sent gooseflesh running along his wet skin. His tunic stuck to his flesh, soaked in sweat from his hour of labour. The sun had long gone down, and the nearby families in the village were tucked in preparing for bed, but not him. He had another hour in the forge, perhaps two, before his body and mind would be exhausted enough for sleep. This unexpected visit might well set him back another hour.

The barn door slid closed, and he lifted his brow in surprise as he stoked the coals and used the tongs to hoist a new strip of metal he needed to shape into the bright orange heap. There was a slight sizzle as sweat from his forehead dripped onto the hot embers.

'Do you not worry about your reputation? Being an unmarried woman alone with a laird in a forge, especially a man like me.' He faced her and was stilled by the desperation and agony in her gaze. He had only seen that expression once before.

'Instead of plaguing me with your barbs, I need you to listen,' she replied, her tone softening.

She had his attention now. He came closer, so close he could see the dark circles under her eyes and the tight agitated hold of her hands in front of her waist. She hadn't been sleeping and probably not eating either. He knew well the signs of prolonged desperation and worry.

'I am listening,' he said, crossing his arms against his chest.

'My brothers are keeping something important from me and my sister, and I need you to unearth what it is.'

He chuckled. 'You came all this way in the dead of night because you need me to find out a secret for you?'

Surely there was more to it. Susanna Cameron was not prone to care about such trivial matters, and nothing was ever as it seemed at first glance with a Cameron. Ever.

'Aye. It is undermining our family, and I don't know why. It consumes my brothers, especially Royce. I fear it will shatter us if I do not figure out what it is that plagues them so.'

'They are probably scheming as you lot are prone to do,' Rowan added.

'Nay. It is far more than that. I know it. They are even conspiring to marry me off to ensure I have the proper protection, whatever that may entail. Imagine me, a Cameron, in need of protection.' She shifted on her feet, another symptom of her growing agitation. He set aside his annoyance.

'And when did this change in their behaviour begin?' he asked.

'After they returned from Lismore a month ago, but it has grown worse in the last two weeks. They have been secretive and meet for hours at a time locked in Father's old study. They will not utter a word about it to me, and with Catriona no longer at Loch's End, I find I am shut out of my own family. I want to know why.'

'That merely sounds like Royce to me,' he replied with a frown.

Susanna's eldest brother was serious and rather unyielding like Rowan was. He had heard the rumours about Laird Cameron's disappearance over the summer. It was an odd recounting of Royce having suffered a head wound and memory loss before returning to his home at Loch's End with his brother Rolf after being missing on the mysterious isle of Lismore for over a month. No one knew why he'd travelled there in the first place.

'The old Royce perhaps, but when he returned from Lismore he was a changed man, and he still is. He is kinder, happy even except for this. He is married now with a bairn on the way. It is this one secret that I do not trust. I still do not even know why he was there. He will speak of it to only Rolf.'

'Why are you asking me to help you? Why not enlist a trusted warrior or guard within your ranks to assist you in this intrigue? Surely, they are better equipped to gain access to and information from your brothers.'

'Nay,' she shook her head. 'It is too great a risk. My gut tells me it is of a far more serious matter than what can be trusted to a soldier, even one within our clan.'

'And to ask my question again: why me, and why on earth would I help you?'

She lifted her chin and pulled back her shoulders like a bird splaying its feathers to make itself appear larger. It didn't really work for Susanna as she was far too petite, but her intention was clear: she would not be refused. 'Because I was promised a favour by your brother when he was laird years ago, any favour of my choosing when I need it, and I plan to collect on it. Tonight.'

'As you well know, my brother Brandon is not laird any more. I am.'

'But as *you* well know you are beholden to fulfil the promise he made to me two years ago as the new laird of Clan Campbell.'

He clenched his jaw. *Devil's blood.* He knew exactly what promise she was referring to. She had offered up her men to help rescue Brandon's son and the babe's mother

Fiona in exchange for an open favour that could be claimed for whatever purpose Susanna needed later. Without her men, Brandon's now wife and son would have been killed. Her assistance had saved their lives.

But that didn't mean it had not been a foolish and risky promise to make as a laird. The Camerons could not be trusted. Rowan had found that out when he had begun courting Susanna when they were teens. His opinion upon them had not wavered. If anything, it had grown more resolute.

He sighed, fisting his hand by his side. Brandon would want and expect Rowan to uphold their end of the agreement with her, no matter how much he wanted to deny Susanna. Honour was not something to be trifled with. She knew he could not balk at fulfilling such a request as it would put his lairdship and clan at risk.

One's word was almost all that mattered in the Highlands, especially now. And he still had much to prove as the reinstalled laird. Even though two years had passed since he had regained his title, the clan elders and villagers still scrutinised him and his decisions.

The woman had him finely wedged between duty and honour and she knew it. Exasperation didn't begin to describe his feelings. He felt trapped and his skin began to itch. He had to find some means of escaping her demands.

'And if I were to fulfil this promise, how do you plan for me to get your brothers, who generally despise me on a good day, to share their most pressing secret with me? I feel you have not thought all of this through, Susanna. Your brothers will see me upon their doorstep and slam the door in my face before I dare utter a syllable. I should know. I would do the same.'

Her gaze lifted to him, and her slow, seductive smile warned him of the danger that would fall next from her lips, but nothing could have prepared him for her words.

'You will offer for my hand, and we will be betrothed until I discover the truth.'

Subscribe and fall in love with a Mills & Boon series today!

You'll be among the first to read stories delivered to your door monthly and enjoy great savings.